THE FIGHTING TOMCATS

BOOK 4

SHOULD ENGLAND FALL

ROSE HILL PRESS, OLYMPIA, WASHINGTON

Should England Fall

Book Four of The Fighting Tomcat Series

First Edition

©2020 by Sofia R. Maki and Megan L. Maki

The views presented are those of the author and do not necessarily represent the views of the DoD.

Should England Fall is a work of historical fiction and speculation using well-known historical and public figures. All incidents and dialogue are products of the author's imagination and are not to be construed as real. Because of the speculative nature of this work, we have changed some present-day timelines, such as the fact that the aircraft carrier battlegroup depicted in this book has never existed. Also, we have changed the historical timeline in the present to suit the nature of the work. Any resemblance to persons living or dead who are not historical figures is entirely coincidental.

BOOKS BY M. L. MAKI

THE FIGHTING TOMCATS

Fighting Her Father's War

Divided We Stand

We So Few

HUNTER/KILLER SERIES

Shark Among the Minnows

CONTENTS

ACKNOWLEDGE-MENTS

We would like to thank everyone who contributed advice and help on this project. Without your kind help, it would never have happened. Our family cheering section kept up our spirits when it got tough. Unfortunately, 2019 was a challenging year for us. So, we also thank all of you for your patience. We especially want to thank our beta readers, Penny Sevedge and ETNC (SW) Scott M. Richardson.

THIS BOOK IS DEDICATED TO

To all our wonderful readers. You have given us so much help and have been so patience through this difficult year. Thank you.

Out of every one hundred men, ten shouldn't even be there, eighty are just targets, nine are the real fighters, and we are lucky to have them, for they make the battle. Ah, but the one, one is a warrior, and he will bring the others back.

HERACLITUS C.535-C.475 BCE

CHAPTER 1

GERMAN AIRFIELD, OCCUPIED FRANCE

0645, 23 September, 1942

General Lieutenant Ludwig Weber, commander of the 3rd Air Group, listens as Oberstleutnant Albrecht Meyer, a 1990 East German pilot, reports, "I think the Drachendame was shot down by Oberst Getz before he was lost. I saw her plane falling."

"How many Tomcat fighters are left?"

Meyer shrugs, "Three or four. No more than that. The British are fielding a jet fighter with fixed swept wings. At its best it is equal to our 163."

Weber smiles, then frowns, "So, they are behind us in development. That is good. But we must control the skies above our operation. Meyer, you and the 76th will cover the landings. I will send Jagdgeschwader 78th and 80th to hit the British fleet."

BRIDGE, GERMAN CARGO SHIP MARGERET, IN THE MOUTH OF THE TYNE RIVER

An aide approaches Field Marshal Erwin Rommel with a radio and salutes, "General Weber, Herr Field Marshal."

Rommel returns the salute and takes the radio, "Rommel."

"Herr Field Marshal, we have destroyed at least three of the cursed American fighters. Losses are high, but so is production."

"Does she still live?"

"She shot down Oberst Getz, but I'm told he hit her plane as well. It was seen falling toward the sea. Perhaps your men will find her corpse."

"Perhaps, or perhaps not. She is extremely hard to kill. We must assume she is alive, well, and still in command. Tell me Herr General, what would you focus on in her place?"

"Herr Field Marshal, it has always been the British Navy that protected the British Isles from invasion. It is the British, combined with the Americans, that may deny us resupply. She must protect the fleet. And, also, she is a naval officer. What would be more natural?"

"What kind of woman do you think she is, Herr General?"

"From news accounts, her people are devoted to her. She cares for them as a mother would, but she also sends them to fight. She has grappled with Baron Clausewitz and grown as an officer. I think she is aptly named. She is a hunter and a protector. She is singularly courageous, but more than that, she is an effective leader. Still, she does not revel in her victories. I think she is more the protector and less the killer."

"Good. Use her need to protect her fleet against her."

"Yes, Herr Field Marshal."

WINGNUT AND CUDDLES F-14, BEACH NORTH EAST OF NEWCASTLE ON THE TYNE, UK

0650, 23 September, 1942

Men dig frantically to free the two airmen. They can see the German invasion craft getting closer and hear sporadic rifle fire from the bluff above them. Finally, LT Tommy "Wingnut" Urland is pulled from the cockpit. The pain in his left arm and shoulder is so intense, he struggles to keep from passing out. He focuses on the man in front of him, "Do you have explosives?"

Uncle Tucker says, "No, friend. We have a farm."

"Fuck."

LT Gus "Cuddles" Grant is finally pulled from the backseat. He's barely conscious and his head and right arm are bleeding.

Wingnut looks around, then smells the JP-5, "Anyone have a lighter?"

Tucker smiles, "We'll get you boys clear, then the lads will light her up." Wingnut and Cuddles are helped up the steep embankment and away from the beach and their stricken plane. Wingnut turns when he hears a 'whumpf' and sees black smoke rising behind them.

BASE INFIRMARY, RAF ALCONBURY

0652, 23 September, 1942

Commodore Samantha 'Spike" Hunt, commander of Task Force Yankee and U.S. Naval Forces, UK, follows the gurney carrying her RIO, LT Eric 'Puck' Hawke, as an orderly and nurse wheel him into the surgery. His clothes are streaked with blood and his skin is pale. He makes eye contact with her and smiles, "I'm good."

She schools her expression, "Of course, you are." The 20mm round that hit their bird severely damaged his left leg and arm. That he is alive and conscious is a bloody miracle. She forces a smile, "You get better, Puck. I need you."

He smiles, "I know," and they push him into the surgery.

A nurse stops her, "Commodore, you have to wait out here."

She watches as the doors close, absently rubbing her right fist. She looks down at her hand and shakes her head, "It hurts, and it was worth it. But I just decked a Brigadier General. Damn."

She thinks back on the damage Brigadier General Altman did to the war effort and her people by hiding parts and ordinance from her unit to stockpile them for when the Army Air Corps took over in England. "My God, I don't care. I did the right thing. I guess, I'm not as afraid of the brass as I used to be. Oh, I am the brass. I am the man. God, help me."

She sees her reflection in a window. Her blonde hair is a mess and needs cutting. Her eyes are sunken. Her flight suit is covered in Puck's blood. She sees lines on her face that were not there before, "I'm 28 years old, going on fifty. That about sums it up." She sits down and puts her head in her hands, "God, please save him. Please. I need him. I'm sorry for all I've done. So sorry. Just don't let Puck be the one to pay for my sins."

She feels herself drifting into sleep and shakes herself awake. "Not now. Too much to think about. Too much to do." Her body stiff and sore, she forces herself to sit upright and to go over events in her mind, waiting to hear if the most important man in her life, her RIO, her flying partner, is going to live or die.

HOTPANTS AND GQ'S BIRD, RAF OUSTON, 8 MILES NW OF NEWCASTLE

LT Gloria "Hot Pants' Houlihan and LTJG Byron 'GQ' Standley are guiding an airport crane to lift their F-14 onto a trailer when a grey sedan races up. A Group Commander in flight uniform exits the car and runs up, "Say, I believe you should know we are evacuating southward to Duxford."

Gloria, still working, says, "We could use some help tying this thing down. We need to get it to Alconbury."

The Group Commander looks over the F-14. The left wing is crumpled upward and the left landing gear is broken. There are bullets holes all over the right side and the right tire is deflated from a bullet hit. "I understand how valuable these jets are, but yours looks a goner."

"If we can get it to Alconbury, the guys will have it in the air overnight. Can you help?"

"I came to tell you to abandon your efforts, but I see your point. I'll see what can be done." He does a crisp about face and gets back in the car.

FLIGHT LINE, RAF ALCONBURY

CDR Stephan 'Swede' Swedenborg, CO of the Black Knights, VF-154, and Commodore Hunt's Chief of Staff, walks to the lead A-10 and waits as the engines spool down.

Major Floyd B. Parks, USMC, commands VMA-324, the Devil Dogs, the first squadron of navalized A-10 Warthogs. He climbs down out of his bird, turns and salutes, "Good morning, Commander. Where can I find Commodore Hunt?"

"She's at the infirmary. I'm her Chief of Staff. When can you get back in the air?"

"We just flew across the Atlantic from the States. We need to recover and acclimatize."

"No time. England is being invaded. Pick your freshest pilots to launch as soon as you can load and fuel your birds. Put the rest to bed. You'll be flying around the clock until we stop them."

"You're serious."

Swede stares at him, his eyes hard and distant, then he shakes his head, "I'm sorry, but that's the way it is right now. I assume you'll want the first hop. I would. Come with me." He leads him into the HQ to brief him and go over the maps.

Swede sees LT Jerry 'Gandhi' Jacobs, his RIO, and motions him to walk with him. "When the other squadron leader lands, send him to me at HQ."

Gandhi salutes, "Yes, sir. I'll have our guys service these birds until their ground crew arrive."

3 ZUG, 2 KOMPANIE, 28TH RIFLE REGIMENT, BEACH NORTH

OF NEWCASTLE

Private Aldus Muller runs off the boat ramp and stumbles in the surf. The man next to him goes down and falls on him. He struggles to get his head out of the icy water and get free. He can barely hear Sergeant Zimmerman shouting, "Schnell! Schnell!"

Muller gets his head up enough to get a deep breath, and heaves up, pushing the body off. He wriggles out and manages to move forward out of the water. He stumbles and weaves, stiff from being confined in the boat for over a day. He sees more men fall, but the firing from the dunes ahead is lighter than he feared. Others are kissing the sand before the grassy dunes, but he keeps running. Muller pops over the dune in front of him and sees only three British behind it. They roll to bring their rifles to bear and he shoots them. Kids. Their young faces burned into his mind.

All the anger he had built inside for the fight flows out. He kicks the rifles away and asks, "Sprechen sie Deutsch?"

A blonde boy, hands pressed against his abdomen, blood spilling between his fingers, looks at him, "Why? Why?"

"Krieg. Ah, war." He shrugs and shakes out a cigarette for the kid, kneeling next to him. He looks at the others, one he shot in the head, the other is gasping, blood on his lips, a round through his lung.

The blonde takes the cigarette, "My mom…"

Muller realizes most of the firing has stopped. He looks down at the boy, "Wie alt vist du? Ah, how old?"

"14."

"Es tut mir leid. I'm sorry." He rises and continues inland, tears streaming down his face.

BRIDGE, HMS CUMBERLAND (57), 12 MILES NORTH OF THE INVASION FLEET

Captain Alexander Henry Maxwell-Hyslop stands still as a statue on the starboard wing as the forward mounts lay fire on a German cruiser. Three damaged German vessels, pouring smoke, are approaching at an angle. He shouts into the speaking tube, "Hard to port. New course, 160."

The reply is drowned out by shell fire, but the ship starts turning.

Rear Admiral Sir Philip Vian joins him as their heavy cruiser heels over in the turn. "Quite a hullabaloo, don't you think?"

"Yes, sir." Rounds form the German heavy cruiser Prinz Eugen fall short and the Cumberland's guns return fire.

A rating runs onto the bridge wing and salutes, "From Scapa, sir. Air raid warning. German jets."

Vian nods, "They will likely attack ashore."

Hyslop, still focused on the battle, says, "I agree, sir. Yet best to be cautious." To the rating, "Pass the word for possible air attack. Assign secondary batteries to air defense."

The rating salutes, "Yes, sir," and runs into the ship.

Then, the entire vessel shakes with a violent concussion and they see the light cruiser, USS Omaha, explode.

The Cumberland takes a hit aft of the third funnel, and the two men fight to keep their feet. The blast causes flame and smoke to billow up from their stern. Another round hits near aboard aft of the bridge and a wall of water soaks them. Hyslop picks up a microphone, "Damage control parties out."

Vian, pointing to dark specks getting larger as they dive toward them, "Are they ours, do you think?"

"I think not. Excuse me, sir."

Hyslop enters the bridge and Vian continues tracking the approaching German aircraft. He watches the planes changing course as they choose their targets. Three choose the Cumberland. As one, two objects detach from each aircraft. He smiles,

"Too soon. They dropped too soon."

But these are radar guided bombs, and they continue straight toward the ship as the AA batteries open up. The German jets pull up unharmed.

Three 1000-pound bombs fall short and one falls long, but two hit the British cruiser. One strikes amidships and the other just below A turret. The initial blast knocks the admiral off his feet. The second explosion from the 'A' turret magazine going up knocks him unconscious.

HARD SHELTER, RAF ALCONBURY

Two F-14's take off in a roar as LCDR Frank 'Thud' Jackson, XO of the Black Knights, walks up to the jet normally flown by LTJG Pauline 'Trollop' Cash. Speedy is already pre-flighting the bird as the ground crew hastily repair bullet holes.

Swede follows him in, "Thud, you're not cleared to fly. Your ankle."

Thud stops and goes still, then turns in a facing movement, "Swede, today it's all on the line. I have to fly."

Swede walks up and places a hand on each of Thud's shoulders, "You're right, Thud. I'll sort it out with medical and the boss later."

"Can we hold?"

A long silence, then Swede says, "We have to, Thud. We have to. If we lose Britain, we lose the war."

CHAPTER 2

U.S. ARMY, 1ST ARMORED DIVISION CAMP, BELFAST, NORTHERN IRELAND

81ST Armored Reconnaissance Battalion is in PT gear and running in formation when a jeep rushes by and skids to a stop in front of them. Lt. Colonel Charles J. Hoy yells, "Halt!" and steps forward. "What the hell?"

A captain stands in the jeep and salutes, "Sir, Division orders, sir. The whole division is shipping out today."

"Today? It can't be done. We have to reload our equipment and the transports are gone."

"New ships are pulling in, and sir, the orders are to draw track and personal ammo before loading."

"What the fuck is going on, Captain?"

"The Germans are invading England, sir." He salutes and peels out.

Hoy is silent for a moment, then, "Double time to the barracks boys. We got it to do."

'A' SABRE SQUADRON, 1ST BATT WELSH GUARDS, 32ND GUARDS BRG, GUARDS DIVISION, BOVINGTON CAMP, SOUTHERN ENGLAND

Sergeant Andrew Seymour is under his Churchill tank greasing fittings when he hears someone running into the maintenance bay. Sliding out, he sees his top sergeant. The sergeant shouts, "Button them up boys and get yer asses to the armory. We're moving out!"

Seymour asks, "What gives, Top?"

"The Hun is landing at Newcastle. You don't want to miss the war, do you?"

2ND PLATOON, 'A' CO, 1STOF THE 15TH REGIMENT, US 3RD INFANTRY DIVISION, NEAR PLYMOUTH UK

Private Andy McDonald lays prone on the grass and sights in his rifle. He fires off a shot then hears a ruckus behind him. The range operator waves a flag for his adjustments and he again adjusts his sights. He feels a kick to his foot. He sets down his rifle and rolls over, "Jesus Christ."

"Load up on ammo and get yer ass to the motor pool, Mick. We're moving out."

"Load up, Staff Sergeant?"

"Are ye hard of hearing? Get a fucking move on, Mick."

McDonald grabs his rifle and stands. As he walks to the arming station, the rest of his company is slowly joining him. He turns to the closest man, "Hey Josh, what's going on?"

Private Joshua Banner, shrugs, "Beats the hell out of me. Probably another exercise."

"For what?"

"Who knows."

They get to the arming station and the guy is issuing full loads of eighty-eight rounds for his Garand rifle. Andy asks, "Sarge, do you know what's up?"

"Shut up and move along."

As they leave the station, they see their lieutenant standing in a jeep, "2nd Platoon to me!"

Heading for their lieutenant, McDonald says, "In the Army, odd ain't good."

"Nope."

The SSGT starts counting heads, "Jesus Christ and Mary, where the fuck is Brown?"

"Coming Sergeant!" The smallest guy in the platoon is practically running with a Browning and four boxes of ammo. McDonald runs to help him. The lieutenant waits, then, "The Germans are landing at Newcastle on the north east coast. I've a truck to get you back to barracks. Load up and be ready to move out in a half hour."

LANCELOT 1, 40,000 FEET, APPROACHING THE INVASION FLEET

LT John 'Gunner' Harden asks his RIO, "Dude, where are they? Can you sort them out?"

LTJG Wally 'NOB' Nelson says, "Got 'em. Okay, left a bit." On radio, "Any British aircraft over the fleet identify yourself."

"Come on, man."

They hear, "Lancelot, Miami, five minutes out. The Krauts are attacking our cruisers."

NOB on radio, "Understood, Miami. Volley Fox 3." To Gunner, "It's a target rich environment."

Gunner fires all four AIM-1 missiles.

"Lance 1, Lance 2, raid four o'clock high."

NOB says, "Two, one, take them." Then, "Gunner, we got 20 plus at our front." "Splash three."

Some of the '262's turn toward them, but most continue on attacking the burning ships below.

Gunner says, "Focus on those attacking the ships. Get me lock."

"On it."

Gunner, "G's." and pulls and rolls violently, dodging a missile, then goes inverted, focusing back on the lower jets. He sees the bombs drop.

"Double Fox 1."

Gunner pickles off his two AIM-7 medium range missiles. One tracks on target and a '262 goes into the sea. He pulls up and hears the growl of the AIM-9. He triggers it off and it flies right up the tail pipe of another '262. The remaining enemy planes pull out and head east. Gunner pulls up and out, instead of going after them, and as he does, he sees tracer rounds where he was, "G's."

NOB shouts, "Fuck man, he came out of the sun!"

Gunner takes his '14 vertical and rolls until he can see the FU-279 pulling out of a dive. He sees its wingman rolling in on them and Gunner goes over the top meeting the German plane head to head. They cross and Gunner rolls and pulls expecting the vertical scissors, but the German crosses with his wingman, who is now on their six. "Fuck man. These mother-fuckers are getting better." He pushes his wings forward and engages his airbrake dropping speed and falling beneath the two planes, then dives, picking up airspeed in zone 5.

NOB, "They're coming around. Jedi is defensive about 10k up."

"Got it." Gunner goes vertical rolling to see his adversaries, pulls level as they also go vertical, and takes the shot. The lead '279 is stitched through the nose and cockpit. Gunner nudges his rudder, still inverted, and takes out the wingman.

As the two planes fall toward the sea, out of control, "Splash two. Two, one, how are you?"

LTJG Tyler 'Stinky' Lewis, RIO for LT Lorne 'Jedi' Luke, says, "Good to go. They bugged out. We put some holes in them, but no joy."

"That's okay, you kept them off us. Thank you."

"How many did you get?"

"Lost count. Fuel state?"

"Thirty minutes."

"Same." To Gunner, "Dude, the fleet got hammered."

Gunner does an aileron roll, "They still are. See the German ships?"

"Can we hit them?"

"No, we save our ammo for aircraft. The old British bombers can fuck them up."

BASE INFIRMARY, RAF ALCONBURY, UK

Samantha is waiting alone outside the surgery when a nurse approaches her, "Are you all right, Commodore?"

"Wha...what?"

"You're covered in blood. Come with me."

"It's his blood."

"Not all of it. You need to be checked for wounds and shock." The nurse takes her into an exam room, "No excuses. Now, sit down." The nurse helps her out of her flight gear and suit which are sticky with blood, and Sam starts shivering. Then she checks Sam's pulse and blood pressure, "Hmm, 122 over 78, that's good, but your heart rate is 195 and thready. You're in shock. It's mild as your skin is normal, but..." She checks her eyes, "Pupils dilate normally and are responsive."

The nurse cleans the blood off her skin. When the nurse gets to the back of her left shoulder above the shoulder blade, Sam starts, "What is that?"

"A small piece of glass, I think. I'll remove the glass and get this cleaned up. Do you desire anesthetic? I don't recommend it."

"I'm fine. It just surprised me."

An orderly barges in and the nurse goes ramrod stiff, "Mr. Davies, knock first, do you hear me?"

"My apologies. Commodore, your yeoman is here." He looks

over Sam who is down to her underwear.

YNC James 'Radar' Cooper follows the orderly in. When he sees where the looking, he grabs the guys shoulder and pulls him around. "Control your eyes or lose them, mister. Capiche?"

Startled, the orderly leaves.

Cooper shuts the door. "Spike, here are your clean clothes and stuff. Are you alright?"

The nurse glowers, "Out!"

Cooper smiles at the nurse, "Please, calm down." He hands the nurse a green duffle. "Is she okay?"

"Leave!"

"Ma'am, England is being invaded as we argue. Admiral Nelson expected everyone to do their duty. I'm doing mine, okay?"

Still glowering, but relaxing a bit, the nurse replies, "Very well. She has a mild case of shock and has a minor wound on her left shoulder."

Sam says, "I can fly, but someone needs to look after Puck."

Cooper smiles at her, "I know. I brought Hammond for that."

She smiles back, "Thank you, Radar. Give me a minute."

He turns and leaves.

The nurse says, "At least let me fix the damage before you go and hurt yourself again." She removes the glass from the cut and swabs it with alcohol, then dresses the wound. "I would rather stitch this up, but it's shallow enough that a dressing will do for now. After you've saved the world again, please get stitches, or it will likely scar. Now you may get dressed." She helps Sam get her clean flight suit on and leaves.

Once she's dressed, Sam calls in Cooper. "What's happening?"

"Swede has our birds being turned around and relaunched. Yours is shot to hell, again, but they're working on it. Thud and Lancelot are in the air. Oh, and we have two squadrons of A-10 Warthogs."

Sam smiles, "Yeah, good. That's good."

The nurse comes back with a doctor and he says, "Sit." Unceremoniously he pulls out a light and checks her eyes again. Then, he puts his fingers to her throat and looks at his watch, 96F. Still high. Commodore, I'm grounding you until your shock symptoms clear. You also need to eat."

Cooper says, "Let her out of here and I'll see that she eats, Doc."

The doctor turns and looks at Cooper as if he is an insect, then back to Sam, "I'll check on you in an hour." He turns on his heel to leave.

Sam says, "Halt!"

The doctor stops and turns, stiff.

"Doctor, I will not fly for an hour. But you are going to check me in the Control Room. England can't wait."

"She can wait an hour, Commodore."

"The German's are landing at Newcastle as we speak. No, she can't."

"I see. I'll see you in the Control Room in one hour, Commodore. Good day." He turns and marches out.

4TH PLATOON, EASY COMPANY, 2ND OF THE 509TH PARACHUTE REGIMENT, AIRFIELD SOUTH ENGLAND

0743, 23 September, 1942

PFC Johnny Rodriguez waddles across the tarmac to the transport plane. He's carrying 53 pounds of jump gear and 70 pounds of mission gear, all needed and necessary. He says to himself, "Generals ask, 'What does it do?' Congress asks, 'How much does it cost?' Soldiers ask, 'How much does it weigh?'" His M1919 Browning machine gun in its case just adds to the weight.

Once they're all aboard, they sit and the C-130 takes off. In the air the platoon forms up on both sides of the aisle and they do their gear check, each man checking the gear of the man in front of him. PFC Clyde Baker yells, "Hey, Johnny, you remember your timing tool?"

"I got two, Clyde. One for you to lose."

"Just checking. Don't want you to forget again. I got mine." He laughs as he finishes checking the guy in front of him.

"Fuck you, Clyde."

Staff Sergeant Sandusky walks the line, checking each soldier, "Relax, Rodriguez. Remember, collapse your chute before you break out the gun. Take your time and get it right. Right is more important than fast."

"Got it, Sarge."

"We're liable to be scattered to hell and back. The LT will be up wind. Don't move until you can fight."

"Yes, sir. Thank you."

"Just get that MG in action and pay attention to what you're shooting at."

"Roger, Sergeant."

"Good man." He pats Johnny's shoulder and moves on to the next man.

A few minutes later the jump master signals for everyone to hook up their static line to the cable running along the top of the fuselage. Fox platoon is hooked up behind them. The light turns green and they shuffle to the ramp. When it's his turn, Johnny jumps and curls his legs as he was taught.

In a moment, he feels the chute open and looks around. It's morning and the clouds are above them and below are fields and farm houses. It is an amazing pastoral setting. Then he sees tracer rounds reaching for them. "Tracers. Shit!"

The field below him seems to race toward him and he feels horribly exposed. Then he hits the ground and drops to his side, pulling down his canopy. Once it's bundled, he looks around and sees several German soldiers moving out of a hedge toward him. The Browning takes too long to set up, so he draws his 1911 and carefully aims. The Germans are firing at him. He squeezes the trigger and feels the pistol buck in his hand. The lead German looks startled and blood blossoms on his tunic. Johnny fires again, but the German have taken cover.

The rest of his platoon are laying covering fire, so he shifts his focus to his Browning. By now he can assemble it drunk and blindfolded. Still, his hands tremble as he fits the pieces together. PFC Danny Todd, takes a knee beside him and cracks off three rounds.

Johnny says, "Mount." Danny gives him the tripod for his gun. "Where is Clyde?" He loads the belt and lays behind his gun. He can still see the German he shot.

"He's dead, Johnny. Just dead."

"Get me his ammo." He sees a German helmet over the hedge and fires a quick burst. The helmet disappears in a cloud of red. A grenade flies over the hedge and they tuck their heads down as it goes off.

Johnny raises head and sees about fifteen Germans come over the hedge and run toward them. He opens up on them, falling them like hay from the central valley of California where he is from.

CONTROL CENTER, RAF ALCONBURY, UK

Spike walks in, "What do we have?"

Gunner replies, "Just got in. Swede and BUG are heading out. Thud is coming back. The Germans have shifted focus to the fleet. The Brit's have one battleship, four cruisers, and eight destroyers sunk. We have lost two cruisers and three destroyers. The Germans have lost two cruisers. The airborne unit just landed near the beach and everything army is scrambling. We have four A-10s working over the beach."

"Tell me about the A-10s?"

"We have a Marine and a Navy squadron on station. Twelve planes each, and they work for you, Commodore."

She sits, "Okay. I see. Without interfering with their flight schedule, I want to meet the commanders as soon as possible."

"Roger that, Commodore. Ma'am, are you okay?"

"A scratch. Where is Percival 1?"

"They're still at RAF Ouston loading their bird on a truck."

"Are they injured?"

"No, Spike."

"Send a helicopter with a couple of AD's to escort the bird and get them back here."

"Roger."

Under her breath, "Pappa, I need you."

She looks over the table below her. It shows the location of all friendly and enemy aircraft.

LT Shawn 'Lizard' Todd walks in, "Request to enter and speak." She smiles and motions him in. "Ma'am, how is Puck?"

"When I left, he was still in surgery."

"Then you need a RIO?"

"No, Lizard, I have you. What's the status of our bird?"

"It's pretty fucked up, ma'am. They've pulled the wings. A 20 mike was lodged in the mechanism. They've dropped the engines. It's coming along."

"Thank you, Lizard. Understand, I don't have time to take care of it. The bird falls to you."

"It was the same for Pappa."

She closes her eyes, remembering, then, "I know." Taking a deep breath, "We'll work it out, and Lizard, please don't call me ma'am."

"Yes, ma'am. Um. Sorry."

She smiles as he turns red then leaves. She looks back at the board and the smile disappears. "Tell Galahad to orbit 40 miles south west of point Bravo. At that location he can intercept aircraft attacking land or fleet."

CARGO QUAY, NORTH SHIELD, ENGLAND

The SS Ceuta slows as it comes to the quay. German soldiers are on the upper works with guns and sailors are scrambling from small boats to receive lines. "Engine stop."

"Engines stop, aye."

"Back slow."

Back slow, aye."

"Throw heaving lines."

The word is passed and his sailors heave over the messenger lines that will pass and haul in the mooring lines.

There is no one to be seen. No people on the streets or on the quay. Then the Captain hears a thrumming roar and looks up. The SS Thalia behind them in the river lights with sparks as a strange jet dives on it. Flames spews from the nose of the plane as it fires.

He orders, "Open the elevator hatches, turn on the cargo vents, and run out the landing ramps. We need to unload as fast as possible."

EAST RIDING OF YORKSHIRE YEOMANRY, CATTERICK CAMP, NORTH YORKSHIRE, UK

0802, 23 September, 1942

Trooper David Preacher is under his Covenanter tank with a grease gun lubricating the fittings when he hears his troop Sergeant shouting. He slides out from under the tank, forgetting the grease gun, "What, Sarge?"

"Preacher, get your arse in the driver's seat and get your tank to the armory, now!"

"Yes, Sergeant."

He runs and leaps into the tank and gets in the driver's seat. He goes through the start sequence, hearing the sergeant yelling at the others. "What the bloody hell?" He starts rolling and hears the grease gun clank as it falls from the top of the track. He stops and starts to climb out when the sergeant sees him. "Go Preacher!"

"But, Sergeant, there's a grease gun under my track."

"I don't give a fuck, Preacher. Go!"

He gets his tank rolling, "Fuck. Fuck. Fuck. This ain't no drill."

2ND BATT, 1ST REGIMENT, 2ND US AD, SOUTHERN ENGLAND

0805, 23 September, 1942

CPL Lance Nicholson is ramming a cleaning brush into the bore of 75mm gun on his Sherman M-4, when his tank commander, Sergeant Steve Gains runs up. "Pull it out! We got to go!"

Nicholson pulls the brush out and starts breaking it down, "You late for a date?"

"We've been ordered to deploy." The sergeant straps his bag onto the turret bustle as the rest of the crew arrive.

"I need my stuff."

Private Mead runs up carrying two bags. "I got it. I even remembered your porn."

Nicholson starts stowing tools and spare parts on the tank. His TC yells, "We got to go. Leave that shit."

"Ten miles down the road when we conk out, you're gonna want it."

"You're right. Guys, help him."

CHAPTER 3

WHITE HOUSE, WASHINGTON, DC

0312, 23 September, 1942 (0812 GMT)

President Franklin Delano Roosevelt sits at the head of a conference table with his military commanders. "What can be done?"

Admiral Ernest King, CNO, says, "She has first priority for new aircraft. We are training new pilots as fast as we can."

"Marshall?"

General George C. Marshall, US Army Chief of Staff, says, "We have sent deployment orders to all units based in the United Kingdom. We have four of the new amphibious ships pulling into Belfast to load the 1st Armored. We sent them to exercise with the unit. They can move the division to England one brigade at a time."

Roosevelt turns to Admiral Craig Klindt, Vice CNO for Special Projects, "Tell me about the new ships."

"Sir, they have a well deck to accommodate the new Landing Craft Air Cushion."

"What are these air things? Planes?"

"Sir, they are neither fish nor fowl. They use an air cushion to lift the weight off the water. They cannot fly like an aircraft, but they can stay out of the water and travel right up on the beach and drop off troops and their equipment dry. They do not set off magnetic, contact, or pressure mines. Also, if the sea state isn't terrible, they travel at about fifty miles an hour, giving the enemy less time to engage."

"Who came up with this thing?"

"As I recall, a Brit named Cockerell in the '50's."

"I mean now."

"A naval officer named Hughes, sir."

"I hope he's giving us a good deal."

"A shipbuilder he partnered with is handling the business end. It's a fair deal, sir. We ordered a thousand."

"How many ships?"

"Two hundred, sir."

"How many do we have right now?"

"The four in Bristol, eight others completed and undergoing training out of Norfolk, and eleven on the west coast."

Admiral King says, "Sir, if we move them all to the east coast, we can land a division behind the German lines."

Roosevelt, "I don't want the Germans to have lines to get behind. How long would it take?"

King replies, "If we issue the order now, about a month. Six weeks if we practice."

"I see. Issue the order. How do we keep Britain in the fight for six weeks?"

Admiral Leahy says, "Send everything we can. Keep Hunt's unit in the air and fighting."

CIC, USS COLUMBIA CLG-56, NORTH OF BOUGAINVILLE, SOLOMON ISLANDS

2110, 23 September, 1942 (0910 GMT)

LCDR Shawn Hughes stands in the CIC, his hands behind his back. The Carl Vinson is 100 miles to the south east and the Columbia is the northernmost radar picket. He has a two-dimensional Mark 49 air search radar on the main mast and two targeting radars on the stern superstructure. All the boilers are on line in case they need a surge of speed. He stands like a statue listening to reports.

A first class enters, "Request permission to enter and speak with the TAO."

"Enter."

BT1 Jim Williamson quietly says, "Sir, boiler two ABC's are still hunting, but it is better."

"Good. Give the Hagan reaction valve a slight turn in the shut direction. Turn it slowly and only an eighth of an inch or less."

"Yes, sir."

The Mark 49 operator shouts, "Raid warning north! Thirty plus at 200 miles and 500 knots!"

Hughes says, "General Quarters. Calm, please." To Williamson, "Hold off on changes until after the fight. Thank you."

They hear the familiar sound of General Quarters. Shawn picks up the phone and calls the captain, "Raid, sir. Thirty plus at 200 miles."

"Proceed."

Hughes says, "Come right to new course 075."

The Mark 49 operator, "They are continuing course and speed."

Hughes picks up a phone, "Radio, send a message to Group and confirm this is not friendly."

Phone talker, "Missile house manned and ready."

Another phone talker, "Condition Zebra set."

Hughes, "Very well. Load and prep missiles for a sustained barrage."

"Captain in combat."

Captain William A. Heard walks in, "Carry on." He stands beside Hughes.

"Sir, we are turning to 075 to unmask our battery."

"Good."

A phone talker, "Confirmed. Raid is hostile."

Hughes, "Very well. At 100 miles commence firing the Mark 10."

A minute later they can hear and feel two missiles leaving the rails. In moments, they see the outbound missiles on radar. On radio, "Columbia, Felix 277, we are inbound with four Foxtrot one fours. Six minutes out."

Hughes, "Roger, Felix. Make certain your IFF is on."

"Will do."

One of the missiles finds its target. The other misses and burns itself out, dropping into the sea.

LCDR Curt George, "Directors, don't chase the targets."

WASHI (EAGLE) JAPANESE BOMBER, 85 MILES NORTH OF COLUMBIA

Captain Hata watches the plane ahead of him burst into flame. A missile misses him by a hundred feet. On radio, "Missiles from below."

Colonel Okumara in the lead bomber, "Stay in formation."

CIC, USS COLUMBIA CLG-56, NORTH OF BOUGAINVILLE, SOLOMON ISLANDS

The second round of missiles hit two of the enemy aircraft. Six planes detach from the formation and dive on the Columbia. Hughes says, "Missile officer, keep the third volley on those staying on course. After that they will be out of range."

LCDR George says, "Yes, sir."

Captain heard nods, "Good call, Commander." The missiles fire and both hit.'

Radar operator, "Inbound planes are accelerating!" Despite the bombers accelerating to supersonic, the next round of missiles hit two bombers.

WASHI (EAGLE) JAPANESE BOMBER 50 MILES NORTH OF COLUMBIA

Captain Hata can't see the Columbia in the dark. He sees two of his formation blown up, but continues, keeping the bump on his radar oscilloscope centered and his engines firewalled. He flies a bomber too large for a carrier deck. It's a two-seater with a 55-degree swept leading edge and a 10-degree swept trailing edge on a delta wing. The vertical stabilizer is alone aft of the wing without elevators. It likes to fly fast and climb like a bird, but it does not like to land. Focusing on his radar screen, he releases both 1000-pound glide bombs at 15 miles. The radar guidance system was designed in Germany.

USS COLUMBIA

Hughes says, "Focus on incoming. Let the jets go." Two more missiles fire and hit the falling bombs. Six more bombs come at them. "Sparrows, engage when in range. CIWS on auto." The Sea Sparrow missiles in the box launcher behind Mount 2 start firing. They hit two and the CIWS hits one. The remaining bombs fall short, but the concussion shakes the entire ship.

The captain grabs the 1MC, "Investigators out."

LANCELOT 2, 25,000 FEET, NORTH BOUND OVER THE BIGHT, UK

0925, 23 September, 1942

LT Lorne 'Jedi' Luke asks his RIO, LTJG Tyler 'Stinky' Lewis, "What do you see?"

"It's a mess. There are aircraft attacking the fleet. I think there are some British birds defending. None of them have IFF."

"Okay, then, no AIM-1's. This is our first time flying without a lead, so let's not fuck this up."

"No prob's brother Jedi. Just keep your laser sword close at hand."

"If they get that close, I'll just use the mind trick."

Stinky laughs, "These are the missiles you are looking for."

"May the Schwartz be with you."

They hear, "Lancelot 2, Ghost Rider, Gawain 1 is ahead of you."

Stinky, "Ghost Rider, Lance 2, I have Gawain 1's IFF. Gawain 1, Lance 2, coming in from the south."

Speedy, "This raid is bugging out. Orbit 40 miles south west of point Bravo and wait for the next one."

"What have they been sending?"

"'262's. Thud calls them delta wing coffins. They have radar now and are carrying medium range missiles, so keep your eyes out."

"Will do." To Jedi, "I'm searching for the next raid. They have to be out there 'cause I have a hard on."

"I thought you had a girlfriend."

"Yeah, but shit man, she's awesome, but killing German's, that's a high. Thud will be passing to our left."

"Roger," as Thud's jet flashes by. "Do you want me to land so you can take care of your little problem?"

"Nah. I'm taking care of it fine."

Jedi rotates the jet inverted, "There, just what you need."

"Not cool, man."

RIDGE EAST OF HENDERSON FIELD, GUADALCANAL
2136, 23 September, 1942

SGT John Leigh Hunt lays under a wild pile of bushes carefully studying the valley below him. He can see the trail the Japanese use to move supplies forward. He and his squad silently wait. Bugs are crawling on him, and more than few are enjoying a meal at his expense. He waits, motionless.

The jungle is never silent. There are always small animals moving through the brush and birds calling. But he and his men are still, silent. Then, he hears a clink of metal on metal from down the hill. He hears it again. He touches the man on his left in warning. They see movement below. A line of Japanese is slowly working their way along the dim track.

The lead Japanese stops, looking and listening, but Hunt is watching them out of the corner of his eye, not straight on. After a long moment, the column moves forward. After the squad of Japanese soldiers are men carrying boxes tied to their backs. It is at least a company. Just as the lead element starts to disappear, he opens fire on them with his Garand. Six quick shots and the lead element falls. His men take out the rear security element, then shoot the box carrying soldiers in the center. Many run up the hill away from the Marines. Hunt yells, "Claymore."

Twenty mines detonate on the facing hill. In a few seconds it is done. Over a hundred Japanese lay dead in the valley. Two of his men turn and vomit. Hunt feels moisture forming in his eyes, but takes a deep breath, controlling himself. Corporal Steven Lewis says, "Jesus Christ, Sergeant, it was a fucking slaughter."

The two friends look at each other for a long moment, then Hunt, "Police up. Gather all the supplies. Our guys can use them."

RUNWAY 21, RAF ALCONBURY, UK

Spike winds up her engines feeling her aircraft shake. She's flying Gunner's bird for now. "Rolling," and trips the brakes. The '14 picks up speed and they hear, "Arthur 1, Yankee, climb to angels 44 and fly 042. Multiple bandits 200 miles at 225."

LT Shawn 'Lizard' Todd, Spike's RIO, says, "44 at 042, Arthur, aye."

As they disappear into the clouds, Spike asks, "Where is Galahad?"

Lizard relays the question, "Arthur 1, Galahad is engaging 8 bandits approaching London. Texas and Kansas are scrambling. You will arrive first."

Lizard, "Yankee, Arthur 1, roger."

Spike, to herself, "He isn't where he was told to be." She comes to course 042. "Lizard, I know it will take a bit to get the hang of me. Don't tell me what to do, tell me where they are. Let me fight the bird. If you need to call a break, that's fine."

"Yes, ma'am."

"Lizard, if you 'yes, ma'am' me one more time, I'm going to clock you. Spike, got it?"

"Yes, m....Spike."

"I'll call 'grunt' when I'm going to lay on the G's, okay?"

"Right, m...Spike."

She smiles, "Did you have this issue with Papa?" The memories flood in and her smile is gone.

"I called him boss, um, Spike."

"If you want, that would be fine, just not ma'am."

"Can I ask why?"

"Sure, ma'ams are 83 years old with too many cats."

"Got it. Bandits on radar, Boss. We have about 30 bandits inbound at angels 30 and 145 miles at 240."

"Okay, when we're in range, shoot all four."

"Roger, Boss. They're reacting to the radar. Eight turning our way."

"They're protecting the ones behind. Hit the planes that are continuing on. We'll blast through and focus on them."

"Yes, ma'...Boss. The ones...the bombers are accelerating to high mach. Come to 35." She adjusts her course, staying at full military power.

Lizard, "Quad Fox 3."

Spike pickles off the four AIM-1 Extended range missiles and follows them in. She hears the warning tone that they're being targeted by the closing fighters. "I'll try to keep us nose on, but I'm going to have to maneuver."

"No prob's, Boss. Double Fox 1."

Spike pickles off two AIM-7 medium range missiles and goes to zone 5 afterburner. They're each targeted to a different German fighter. The missiles race ahead, adjusting course as the enemy fighters close.

LT COLONEL KURT WELTER, YELLOW ONE, GERMAN FU-279, CLOSING SPIKE

Welter transitioned from the MiG-29 just days ago into the new FU-279. I knows it's based on the F-5 Tigers found at Brandenmeyer and it's all good. He loves his new aircraft. He's smiling when he hears the radar lock tone and pickles off two radar guided missiles. "Yes," he chuckles, "The Americans no longer dominate the skies."

His missiles cross the American missiles and he yanks the stick back, maneuvering to get clear, pickling off chaff and flares. The missile misses, passing below him. On radio he hears, "Four is hit."

ARTHUR 1

Spike says, "Grunt," and pickles off chaff and flares as she dives beneath the incoming missiles in a corkscrew that avoids breaking her radar lock on the German bombers. She sees the missiles and a tumbling fireball from the German fighter she hit.

As they close with the Germans in the merge, Lizard asks, "What the hell are those? They've got two close set in engines and look like oversized F-5's. They've got F-15 intakes."

"Watch them." She rolls left and continues to close the ME-262's and sees three of her long-range missiles hit home.

Lizard cranes his neck, "They're rolling right and coming around."

YELLOW 1

"He's focusing on the bombers. We've got him. Close from multiple directions at the same time. One of us will get the shot."

ARTHUR 1

"Tally ho." She finally has visual on the enemy bombers. As she closes, they scatter out of formation like doves attacked by a hawk. As she closes, she hears a Sidewinder growling in her ear and takes the shot. The Sidewinder zigzags to the nearest '262, hitting it in the right engine. The engine explodes and there is a puff of black smoke from the left engine. The German plane inverts, showing green bombs on the wing pylons. Then, it rolls upright, trailing fire. She sees puffs as the pilot pulls the extinguishers on both engines. The engines continue burning and the pilot ejects from his doomed bird.

Spike adjusts course looking for another target as the pilot's chute opens for the long drop to the North Sea. It's her sixth kill for the day.

They hear on radio, "Arthur, Texas in. Please zoom."

"Grunt." She pulls back on the stick, sending her jet rocketing vertical. With only one missile left on the rails, she's light enough to really climb. Some of the '262's attempt to mimic her maneuver, but they are too heavily laden with bombs, and the British missiles bore in, devastating the German aircraft.

Lizard, "Missile launch, seven high!"

"Grunt," and she pulls over the top inverted and applies rudder, hitting the chaff and flares. "Grunt." When she sees the missile, she rolls upright and goes vertical again, dropping more chaff and flares. The missile fails to track and passes beneath them and she meets the German head to head.

YELLOW 1

When he passes in the merge, only feet from Spike's plane, he sees all the flags on Gunner's bird. He calls on the radio, "It's an ace many times over. Be cautious. A bottle of Schnapps to anyone who downs the plane."

He hears subdued cheers and "Jawohl!"

ARTHUR 1

Lizard, "He's an ace. Saw his flags."

"Focus." She pulls into a hard climb, bleeding speed for altitude. The German passes just above them in the scissors. She rolls, continuing up, but this time, the German bugs out to the south east. "We let him go. Where are the bombers."

"Closing the coast at 270. He's circling back and we've another at 8 o'clock."

"Okay, grunt." She rolls inverted and dives. A '279 is on the six of a British Griffin. The Griffin jinxes left. The '279 follows, flying right into her cross hairs. A burst of 20mm and the '279 loses his vertical stabilizer and the left rear aileron. He noses down and rolls, parts falling off as he falls to the sea. The pilot ejects.

Then she pulls the stick back to regain altitude and tracer fire passes just below them. "Where is he?"

"Looking, Boss."

"Grunt," and she violently pulls past vertical in zone 5.

YELLOW 1

Welter cusses, he's out of missiles and low on fuel. "I fucking had him. Below and behind. It was the perfect set up. Fuck!"

On radio, "Yellow leader, Strike leader. We couldn't find the fleet. Dropped on backup targets. Withdrawing."

"Strike 1, Yellow 1, acknowledge. Yellow flight, disengage."

The dog fight is playing in his mind. "The American ace survives. I survive as well, and we will meet again."

ARTHUR 1

Spike and Lizard are supersonic closing another '262. The Germans dropped their bombs on the beach south of Newcastle and are turning for home. She's at full military, exchanging altitude for speed. With eight British fighters engaged, the fight has devolved into individual engagements. Five miles from her prey, a missile streaks in and destroys it. "Lizard, the Brit's can mop up. Let's get more fuel and missiles."

"Roger, Boss."

As she pulls out of her dive, a '262 flies into her cross hairs. She fires her last Sidewinder and it runs right up the left engine. Both engines grenade and the vertical stabilizer falls off. The pilot struggles to control the doomed plane, then ejects.

CHAPTER 4

GHOST RIDER, AN E-2C HAWKEYE, 35,000FEET OVER YORK, UK

LCDR Michelle 'Dolly' Parley flies a slow circle as the radar crew monitor the battle. LTJG Clive 'Parsec' Kessel, her Combat Information Center Officer (CICO), says, "Ma'am, we have two fast movers inbound on the deck."

"Call for help," and rolls to the left, diving west.

"Any unit, Ghost Rider is under attack. We are over York and diving west."

Lizard, "Ghost Rider, Arthur 1, roger. All Yankee units, close Ghost Rider's position. We are coming your way at five. Hang on."

They are near the do not exceed speed in the dive, when her co-pilot, LTJG Nancy 'Lady' Wilson, says, "They're targeting us. Missile launch."

Parley fires off chaff and flares and turns left. She sees the missile fly by and rolls back right, continuing west. She's at 6000 feet and descending. Lady says, "Another. Two heat seekers."

Parley breaks right and fires off more countermeasures. A missile hits the top of the left wing near the engine exhaust. They can hear and feel parts hitting the fuselage. Then the aircraft pulls hard left. They hear, "Fox 1, fox 1. Lancelot closing Ghost Rider. Splash one. They're bugging out."

Then, "Ghost Rider, Arthur 1. How are you doing?"

Lady, "She wants to turn left. One engine hit and we're losing hydraulic pressure."

Lizard, "Yeadon Aerodrome is two miles at your two o'clock."

Parley, "Tell them to make crash preps."

Lady, "Yeadon, Ghost Rider, declaring an emergency. Please clear the field and alert services." Then on intercom, "Secure your stations and lock your seats. It's going to be a rough landing."

Both pilots fight to maintain level flight. Lady, "I see the field. One o'clock."

Parley, "I see it."

"Ghost Rider, Yeadon, what runway do you want?"

Lady, "The east west one."

Parley, "They want to be picky and expect us to land on the runway, God. Um, no gear. They got the landing gear with engine. Damn."

"Roger."

"Hang on."

TOWER, YEADON AERODROME

The tower crew are all at the windows. The E-2C's left engine is twisted in its cowling creating incredible drag. They watch the plane belly land in grass south of the runway. For a few seconds the wings are level as the plane skids on the grass, then the left wing hooks the ground and the plane spins counterclockwise. The pilots get her level again, but then the right wing dips and digs in and the right wing buckles. The stresses cause the radome to break off and tumble away as the aircraft slides across a taxiway and into the corner of a hanger.

REAR OF GHOST RIDER

LTJG Clive Kessel unbuckles his harness in the sudden silence. He orients himself and stumbles toward the cockpit, yelling,

"Help me! Get the damn door open!" The left tilt of the plane hinders him and the strong smell of JP-5 fills the cabin. He can hear his men getting one of the overhead hatches open. "I'll get the pilots. Figure out how to get them out."

Kessel moves fallen gear and gets to the rear of the cockpit. The entire front of the plane is smashed in and the flight console is crushed against the legs of the pilots. Parley whispers, "Everyone okay back there?"

Parsec, "We're fine. Let me get you out."

Parley, "Get Lady first."

Parsec reaches in and feels Lady's legs. They're both broken at the femur. Lady says, "I smell smoke. Just go."

"No way," and he finds the seat adjustment and lowers it. Lady screams and passes out. He removes her harness and pull her out, dragging her aft. Grateful she's passed out. His men grab her and lift her to the waiting firefighters. The smoke from the burning fuel is coming into the cabin.

Parsec goes back for Parley. The damage is worse on her side and the hull is getting hot. Parley gasps, "You've done your duty. Go."

"No way," and searches for the seat controls with his fingers.

"Parsec, go. You're indispensable."

"Fuck you, ma'am."

He finds the controls and pulls it. The seat lowers a bit, but it sticks, and he can't pull her free. He heads aft for a tool kit, and armed with wrenches, goes back forward. His head close to her lap, he reaches around her with the wrench and starts unbolting the chair. The cockpit fills with more and more smoke. He can hear Parley gasping for air. He gets one bolt free and feels someone grab his legs. Two firefighters pull him from the wreck. "Damn it, I almost had it."

They barely get off the fuselage and away from the burning plane, when it explodes, the shock wave throwing them off their feet.

GRUMMAN AIRCRAFT, BETHPAGE, NEW YORK

0510, 23 September, 1942 (1010 GMT)

Vice Admiral Richard 'Dixie' Lee walks around a brand-new F/A-14B. It's not painted except for the orange on the wing tips, elevators and vertical stabilizer. He looks at the test pilot walking with him, "How many flights have you taken?"

"This will be my fourth and first in the back seat."

"What do you think?"

"It goes like a bullet, sir. We've had a few bugs, brackets and such. Also, it's real finicky to land."

"They've always been finicky to land. Have you tried ACM?"

"No, sir. I've just been establishing the envelope."

"Butch, what is different from our old birds?"

Commander Ronald 'Butch' Cassidy, the project officer at Grumman, and the only person to work the F-14 assembly line before going back in time, just smiles. "Not much, sir. The hydraulic seals in the swing mechanism are a little different. We're hoping they'll leak less. The instrument package is a bit different. The HUD is a little larger and doesn't auto-dim yet. The radar system has a slightly larger turning arc and has terrain following and ground attack function similar to the Hornet's. The bulb behind the day and night cameras is a laser designator that isn't finished yet. They're still working on that at Hanford. It's pretty close, sir."

"Laser? We'll be able to laser designate?"

"It should be out in a mod soon. Instead of carrying a targeting pod on a rail, all the rails will be free for ordinance. I understand, Captain Richardson and Commander Severn came up with that one."

"Do the terrain following and attack functions work?"

"The attack functions do. When you select air to ground with the target designate switch, it will switch the HUD and VDI to air to ground. You still have to designate stores for dropping bombs. Terrain following can be enabled in either mode using the switch on the autopilot panel. It hasn't been tested yet."

"I see."

"Also, the camera will be slaved to the laser, so the RIO can clearly see and record the target he is designating and the results of the strike, as long as the pilot keeps the bird flying within the sweep area of the camera."

Dixie nods, "I see. Well, let's do this." He climbs into the cockpit and sits still as Butch straps him in. Then the test pilot climbs into the rear seat. They carefully go through each check list, then start the engines. When the engines are run up, Dixie starts the taxi. "Call me Dixie. What's your call sign?"

"The commander calls me 'Einstein.' He hasn't said why."

"Okay, Einstein, take off checklist," then, "Ask for unlimited climb out."

"Roger, Dixie."

When they are cleared for take-off and unlimited climb, Dixie trips the brakes, and they accelerate down the runway. Airborne, Dixie continues down the runway, picking up speed, and cleaning up the bird. Then, "Grunt." He pulls back on the stick and they rocket vertical, still accelerating. At 26,000 feet, he pulls the fighter inverted, then rolls upright.

Einstein, "Holy shit! I'd no idea."

"Just getting started. Grunt." He rolls and puts the jet into a minimum turn, then rolls that into a loop, then a Cuban 8. Picking up speed, he climbs in a vertical scissors. Twenty-five minutes of intense air combat maneuvering later, he brings the'14B around into the landing pattern. Dixie has a huge grin on his face. Ten minutes later, they're on the ground and opening the canopy as they stop in front of the hanger. "God, that felt good."

"Sir, what we just did? Is this how Commodore Hunt flies?"

"She's a better pilot than me, but it does give you a taste."

"The Hun is fucked."

"Understand, Einstein, most of her people can do all of this as well. We have years of training to develop our skills. In time, the Germans will get much better. That's how combat works. The sloppy or lazy die. The best pilots survive to fight again and get even better. Well, until they burn out."

Cassidy helps them unhook and climb down. Dixie asks, "Butch, how many do we have?"

"Two for testing, sir."

"Who do you have who can ferry them to England?"

"Right now? Just Einstein here."

"Why do you call him that?"

"He's a test pilot without a death wish, sir."

"Okay, prep these two to fly to England tomorrow. Einstein and I will deliver them."

"Sir, we haven't even started weapon release testing."

Lee looks him in the eye, "Butch, she's down to three usable aircraft to stop an invasion. There isn't time. Prep them. Put a weight in the rear ejection seat and load us with ferry tanks, missiles, and 20 mm. Get us a tanker if you can. We fly out tomorrow at six. Oh, and paint them grey with Black Knight markings."

Leroy Grumman joins them, "Sir, I understand the urgency. But, can you please give us a little more time for testing? Getting them there is useless if it kills her."

They stare at each other, then Lee nods, "Shorten the test schedule and work it around the clock. When I leave here, I'll be flying to England. Am I clear?"

"Yes, sir. Thank you, sir."

"Then we ship aircraft to England until she has twelve new birds. Once she has twelve, we can supply everyone else and keep testing."

HARD SHELTER 1, RAF ALCONBURY

1048, 23 September, 1942

Spike is walking from the bathroom when Swede walks up and salutes, "Spike, tell me about the new German bird." They walk toward Control.

"Swede, why were you over London? I put you on intercept."

"Fighter Control redirected us while you were pre-flighting."

"Okay, I put you there because protecting the fleet and A-10's is pri one. We lost Ghost Rider. I'll talk to him."

"Roger, Spike. Can you tell me about the fighter?"

"It looks like a Super Tiger, but the intakes are more like ours or the '15's. It's a nine 'G' plane. I think they can turn with us at altitude, but I'm not sure of all of its capabilities yet."

"I'll brief the crews that the Germans have a generation four bird. The pilot any good?"

She nods, "He tried to snipe us from below. Had I not climbed when I did, he may have nailed us. Swede, make sure the crews are getting their rest, okay?"

"Roger, Spike." He stops and turns her to face him, "Are you okay, Spike?"

She avoids eye contact. "I have to be, don't I."

"How many?"

"Seven. God, I'm tired, Swede. When is it going to end?"

"Spike, you need to go straight to bed. Doc Swede is ordering no less than eight hours of shut eye."

"I can't."

"Bull shit. If you don't, I'll knock you out and dump you in your bed. If I knew how wasted you were, I would have left you to sleep with Puck...You know what I mean."

She rolls her shoulders back and stands straight, looking him in the eye. "Swede, do you have anyone else?"

He nods, "Trollop and Mouse. They've rested."

"Okay, have someone wake me if I'm needed." She turns on her heel and walks away, then stops and looks back, "Swede, we're only about two hundred miles from the invasion beach. The Germans could be here in a day. Find us a field south of London. If London falls, we're doomed anyway."

"You don't think the Brits can stop them?"

"With what? Most of their troops are in Africa or the south of England."

"Fuck, you're right. Okay. Fuck, you know they're probably gunning for this place."

"Yeah, and turn around all the trucks Thud is bringing up here."

"Will do, Sam. Now, get some rest."

"Going."

BRIDGE, HMS CUMBERLAND, NORTH OF INVASION FLEET

1051, 23 September, 1942

Captain Maxwell-Hyslop stands on the starboard bridge wing of his command. The beautiful canoe stern is awash. Black smoke boils up amidships and from Mount X. Looking aft, he can see the mangled aft superstructure. His crew is taking to the boats. The old girl's a goner and there is nothing left to do. A steam explosion mixes white steam with the black smoke.

Beyond his ship, not a thousand meters away, the Scharn-horst's guns pound away at the HMS Suffolk. Both ships are damaged, but still fighting. As he watches another salvo from the German ship find its target, he begins to shake. His hands on the rail whiten and he clenches his teeth, "You son of a bitch. You whelp of a whore. I will make you pay." He makes his way to the boat check, checking for survivors as he goes. Most of the boats are gone, and he finds a lieutenant organizing men into the last of the them. The LT and ratings stop and salute. "Carry on, gentlemen. Lieutenant, is this the last of them?"

"Chief Anders is doing a final sweep, sir."

Chief Anders walks out and salutes, "No remaining personnel in any accessible compartment."

The boat lurches beneath their feet.

"Very well, Lieutenant, get boat eleven underway."

"Aye sir."

The captain and Chief Anders climb into boat twelve and they help man the ropes lowering the boat into the water. Then they unhook, and using an oar, they push the boat clear of the stricken cruiser. They are about fifty meters away when the Cumberland lurches her bow up, rolls over, and slides beneath the waves.

QUAY, NORTH SHIELD, UK

1056, 23 September, 1942

Rommel paces back and forth as one by one his unit drive off the boat and onto the pier. A civilian ship's captain approaches, "Herr Field Marshal."

Rommel turns, "How many of my men did you kill?"

The captain lowers his head, speaking quietly, "Sixteen, Herr Field Marshal. They started the vehicles before they were ordered to. The exhaust exceeded what our ventilation was designed to handle. I, of course, take full responsibility."

"Very good, Captain. You are responsible. Make sure it does

not happen again, understood? We must take care to proceed and lose no more. Good day."

A staff lieutenant approaches, "Herr Field Marshal, I have General Weber on the radio."

Rommel strides to the command vehicle, steps in and picks up the mic, "What did you know of the attack jets the Americans are using?" He can hear the drone of propeller engines in the distance.

"They are new in theater, Field Marshal. We had no intelligence."

"I see. Transfer your focus to these new jets. Interview your pilots. I want to know everything there is to know about them." The drone is louder.

"Yes, Herr Field Marshal."

Water geysers up as bombs start falling on the waterfront. Rommel looks up and sees a formation of Lancaster's at about 15,000 feet. "We're being bombed by Lancaster's. Lancaster's! You must control the skies."

The light cruiser Koln fires two missiles and two bombers tumble out of the sky. "It will be addressed, Herr Field Marshal." Two more Lancaster's go down.

4TH PLATOON, EASY CO, 509TH PARACHUTE REGIMENT, NORTH OF NORTH SHIELD, UK

1508, 23 September, 1942

PFC Rodriguez lays behind his M-1919 machine gun. They've moved a few times to consolidate the battalion lines. It's quiet now, but his barrel is so hot it sizzles when any grass touches it. The guys are frantically digging in behind him.

SSGT Sandusky taps his foot and whispers, "Time to fall back into the trench, Johnny."

He nods his head as the guys lay down suppressing fire. PFC

Danny Todd jumps out and helps him haul the heavy gun back into the trench. They make it two steps and Danny stumbles, red blossoming on his chest. Danny drops his end, and Johnny gets hit in the head and goes down.

500 FEET ABOVE THE INVASION BEACH, NORTH OF NORTH SHIELD

LT Albert 'Okie' Henderson, USMC, rolls his A-10 on its side to take another pass at the beach. He can see burning trucks, tanks, and other German equipment. A shadow passes over him as he rolls in and he instinctively pulls up on the stick. He feels the thud of rounds hitting his new bird. "Okies hit. Still flying." He pushes the climb to meet his new adversary and sees a ME-163B ahead of him.

Captain Buck 'Poke' Hall, his element leader asks, "Were you hit by ground fire?"

Okie turns and inverts trying to get a shot at the high-speed jet, but the 163B is already circling to another area. "Negative, a German jet." He feels the plinks of ground fire, realizes he's too close to the ground, and pulls up, clearing a tree. He goes back down. Staying low is safer.

Okie hears LT Peter 'Loony' Thun, "Loony's hit, lost number 2 engine."

Poke, "Loony, what hit you?"

Looney, "A German jet. Jesus, it's fast."

Okie swivels his head trying to locate the German jet and avoid obstacles. A German soldier stands up with a tube launched weapon, so he adds right rudder and fires a burst. He barely sees the man go down, before he's past him.

When he turns to look back, he sees the German jet on his six approaching fast. Okie pulls up and rolls to the right causing the German to miss. As the German flashes by, Okie rolls left and adjusts for windage and fires a burst of 30mm. He stitches the plane in front of him in the wing root and cockpit. The aircraft continues on for a moment then rolls and augers in.

Okie yells, "Shit howdy, I got one!"

Captain 'Buck' Hall, "Radio discipline, Shit Howdy."

LT Larry 'Tip Toe' Timpkins, "How did you get him?"

"When they jump you, fly low and slow. They have to attack on your plane of flight. As they fly by, pull in on them."

"Thank you, Shit Howdy."

"But, I'm Okie."

Buck laughs, "You're Shit Howdy now."

MOUSE AND TROLLOP, 10,000 FEET ABOVE THE FLEET

ENS Julie 'Mouse' Mulligan, RIO for LT Pauline 'Trollop' Cash, says, "Another raid to the east. Ten aircraft."

Trollop, "Okay, Mouse. We have two AIM-1's left. Give me a steer."

"Five right. Lock."

Trollop, "Fox 3, Fox 3." The two missiles streak toward the inbound bogies.

On radio, "Gawain 2, Whiskey India 7, Dog flight 2 is under fighter attack. Come to 210 and engage."

Mouse, "Splash 2. There's another raid closing the fleet. What is your priority?"

WHISKEY INDIA 7, 36,000 FEET OVER CAMBRIDGE

Flight Lieutenant Thomas, "Understood. Disregard. Do we have any aircraft to cover the A-10'?"

They hear Shotgun in Yankee control, "All units, Yankee. Yankee actual has established the priorities. At this time, the fleet is priority one. The A-10's are priority two. The air bases are priority three and all other areas are priority four."

Thomas to his men, "We need more planes. Many more planes. Instead, we're losing what we have."

4TH PLATOON, EASY CO, 509TH PARACHUTE REGIMENT, NORTH OF NORTH SHIELD, UK

Johnny comes to, rain on his face. He's lying face up, in the mud, and looking at someone's legs. He hears his gun fire and sits up.

"Johnny!" The corpsman grabs him, "You okay?"

"My head hurts."

"Fucking 'A', your head hurts. Your one hard-headed mother fucker. A bullet bounced off your skull. Can you fight?"

"Fuck, yeah."

Their captain runs toward them and drops into their trench, "Boys, the major is talking to a local. He has a way for us to cross the Tyne and get south. Get ready to move out."

GAWAIN 2, EAST OF THE BRITISH FLEET

Trollop and Mouse are completely defensive against the six ME-262's circling them. Mouse squeaks, "We're outa missiles. What the fuck are we doing?"

Trollop, calm, "I still have 150 rounds."

Mouse, "Break left!"

Trollop yards the stick over in a left snap roll and puts on the afterburners. "G's." She pops the plane back level and pulls. A '262 overshoots and she turns after him, "G's." Tracer fire from his wingman passes behind them just as she squeezes the trigger. Her rounds hit right behind the cockpit of the lead plane and tracer rounds go into the fuel tank. She smiles when she sees flames.

Mouse, "Break! Break!"

Trollop rolls right, "G's," then snaps back left and inverts into a dive. With the afterburner still on, she accelerates like a bullet. The Germans pursue, but they're far behind.

Mouse, "They're falling back." On radio, "All units, Gawain 2 is exiting west at high mach. We are skosh."

WHISKEY INDIA 7, 36,000 FEET OVER CAMBRIDGE

Flight Lieutenant Thomas, "Understood, Gawain 2. Texas flight is inbound. Thank you, Gawain. I counted six kills."

To his radar operators, "I'll tell you this, these yank Shiela pilots can really fly."

One of his ratings says, "I would like to dive into the covers with her. I bet she shags like a rabbit."

Thomas, "Guiles, you will retract that remark right bloody now, or I will have you on the docket."

"Sir, they ain't here to hear me."

"I'm here, and those Valkyries are saving our country. I'll not have a cross word said about them. Am I understood?"

"Yes, sir. I'm…I'm sorry. It won't happen again."

"See that it don't."

GAWAIN 2 OVER THE BRITISH AND AMERICAN FLEETS

As Trollop flies over the fleet at 2000 feet, she rolls the plane to check the damage. "Oh my God! Mouse look. More are sinking than afloat, and they're still fighting."

Mouse, "We're all in, ya know? We're pushing in all our chips."

"So much death."

"All because of a handful of megalomaniacs."

"Are you up for another flight, Mouse?"

"A piss break and more missiles and bullets. That, and I'm good."

Trollop smiles, "All in."

4TH GERMAN ARMY CORPS, NORTH SHIELD, UK

1852, 23 September, 1942

Field Marshal Erwin Rommel walks from his Tiger HII tank to his command communications track, "Manfred, how many units do we have south of the river?" His armor fills the streets and are hard to see between the tall buildings.

"First Division has about half of their units south of the river. Only air attacks and light skirmishing thus far. Eighth Division is ashore. They are securing North Shield and Newcastle. They have been heavily engaged with parachute units. Those units have disengaged and slipped into the population."

An SS Oberfuhrer approaches and salutes Rommel, "Heil Hitler."

Rommel returns the salute, "Oberfuhrer Werner. Is your division unloaded?"

"It is Herr Field Marshal. We depart south now. You must halt the movement of the other units so we may pass."

"I will do no such thing. You're to travel west along the road to Corbridge and Hexham. Secure the bridges and hold."

"You don't understand, Herr Field Marshal, our orders are to race south and destroy Alconbury. When we destroy their base and capture their ground crews, the Luftwaffe will own the sky."

Rommel nods. It was not at all unusual for SS units to receive orders from Hitler himself. "Will you move as a division?"

"No. My units will race to Alconbury, while your forces plod behind. Glory will fall on the first unit there."

Rommel stares at the SS officer and shakes his head, "Very well, we'll make room. You will keep me informed so that I may coordinate with your, um, efforts?"

"Of course, Field Marshal. Though we may have victory before you even sort out your formation."

CHAPTER 5

SPIKE'S QUARTERS, RAF ALCONBURY

0418, 24 September, 1942

Sam wakes with a start, disoriented. Then it all comes back like a weight. She listens and hears nothing. Stiff, she climbs from her bed and goes to her wardrobe. There is one flight suit and some underclothes. Everything else is gone. "Radar!"

She has her underwear on and is pulling on her flight suit when YN1 Cooper walks in with a cup of coffee. "Thud and Jedi are up. Gunner just landed. Your bird is still down. Air Marshal Dowding has found us a new home. The field is RAF Kenley south of London. It has an eight thousand foot and a five-thousand-foot runway. Miami and Kansas fly out of there. He's moving them to Biggin Hill. Oh, and Dowding wants to talk to you soonest. I can turn on a helicopter when you want it."

"How long for us to move?"

"Spike, do you really think they will attack here?"

She meets his gaze, "Yes, I do. I know this disrupts our operation, but it's necessary."

"Oh, okay."

"Radar?"

"What about all the girlfriends. Are we going to leave them behind to get raped and killed?"

"No, Cooper. I'll see to it."

"Sorry."

"It's all right. Thank you for the coffee and the update." Now dressed, she hands him the cup and walks to the operations center. As she enters, "Report."

Major Louis 'Shotgun' Mossberg, USMC, repeats Cooper's report and adds, "Swede is on ready 5. We've dispatched Dim Bulb for dust off. Hot Pants and GQ are getting checked out at the infirmary. The Warthog ground crews have arrived. We are shifting them to Kenley and trying to keep pressure on the Germans. Ma'am, we've lost two '10 already. The German's have SAM's. I know they are pri 2, but they need high cover."

She shakes her head, "Murphy's laws of combat, when you are out of everything but enemies, you're in a combat zone. Is everyone, including ground crew getting sleep?"

Mossberg, "We don't have enough aircraft to keep the ground crews busy. Ma'am, three birds. One bad sortie and we're done."

"I'm aware of that, Major. We cannot have that sortie. We must survive more than we must win."

"Yes, ma'am."

"Spike, please." She takes a clearing breath, "I need to talk to the A'10 CO's. Set that up without disrupting their flight schedules. That and get me Dowding on the line."

Cooper comes in with a tray holding her breakfast, "Eat."

Mossberg, "Ma...Spike, it's 0430."

"I don't care and neither does he. I also need to know what the Germans are doing on the ground."

"Roger, Spike."

She studies the map below her, absently eating her breakfast. The Germans are returning from a raid on Portsmouth and Miami is battling four Germans over York. "Section Officer Lorrie."

The woman managing the control room looks up, "Yes, Commodore?"

"Would it be possible to mark the forward progress of the German land units on the map?"

"I'm not sure, Commodore. I will find out."

"Thank you."

Shotgun says, "Dowding on line, Spike."

On radio they hear Speedy, Thud's RIO, "Splash 1, no, splash 2."

She takes the receiver, "Hunt."

Air Chief Marshal Hugh Dowding, Commander of British Fighter Defense, says, "Commodore, how many aircraft have you?"

"I have three flyable and one or two I might get repaired. Thank you for finding us a home south of London."

"Of course, I do hope it's an unnecessary precaution, but you were quite right."

"How many Griffins do you have?"

"Sixteen flyable. We're building four a day, but the invasion will disrupt that."

Spike grimaces, "Do you think the Army can stop them on the beach?"

"No, I'm afraid not. We had quite discounted the likelihood of a northern invasion. Over half of our army is in the Middle East, and those are our most experienced."

"The new A-10 Warthogs will be a force multiplier, but we must protect them from air attack. They're powerful uncompromising ground attack planes, but they are slow and vulnerable to air attack."

They hear, "Yankee Control, Rusty 1. Can you please give us the forward edge of battle? It's chaos here."

Spike, "Excuse me." She picks up a microphone, "Rusty 1, Yankee actual. I'm sorry, no. We are trying to get that information."

"There are good guys engaged on the ground and I can't tell who is who."

"Understood."

"Chief Marshal, we need to know the forward edge of battle to help guide the Warthogs."

"I'll see what can be done, but right now, it's chaos."

On radio, "All units, Arthur 2. I'm with a British Home Guard unit south of Newcastle and engaged with German mechanized units. I can walk you on, Rusty."

Spike, "Arthur 2, Yankee actual. Authenticate."

"Roger, Yankee. I wasn't there, but I'm still wearing my pink ribbon."

"Roger, Wingnut. Rusty 1, take your steer from Wingnut. He is confirmed Arthur 2."

Dowding, "Pink ribbon?"

"I'll explain later. One of my downed air crew is acting as a forward air observer. That will help, but he can't be everywhere."

"So, you have set the priorities for the defense of Britain?"

"Sir, I have to. My assets are limited. The fleet is engaging the invasion fleet, making them pri 1. The A-10's are vital for destroying their armor and vehicles. They must be pri 2. The airfields are vital for air operations, but we have more than one, so they are pri 3. Everything else must be pri 4. As Admiral Halsey said, "I don't have to win every battle, but we absolutely must survive.""

"Your logic is impeccable, and I quite agree. Parliament will be quite disappointed, though, to know they are at the bottom."

"I understand, and I don't envy you your job. I should point out; a new politician is much easier to find then a new jet or pilot."

Dowding laughs, "Have you heard what the Germans are calling you?"

"No, but I'm sure it would be an unwelcome term in polite society."

"Quite, but not really. You are called the Dragon Lady. I'm told it's a phrase that connotes fear and respect."

"Oh, well, not so bad. Do you have a call sign, sir?"

"I do. I'm called Stuffy, Spike."

She smiles, "Thank you, sir."

"You're welcome. I'll let you get back to it."

SOUTH OF GATESHEAD, UK

LT Tommy 'Wingnut' Urland stands next to a Home Guard sergeant, Andrew Tully. North of them, they see a column of German armor in the early morning darkness. "Rusty 1, Wingnut, please turn your running lights on and off for identification."

"Roger."

They see the lights wink on and off to the east. "Got you. You're heading mostly north. Turn west and descend. I'll flash a light. Germans 400 yards north of our position in a field near houses."

He hears the engines change pitch as the pilot turns. He shields his light and flashes it at the A-10.

"I have you, Wingnut. Hunker down."

They hear the brrrt of the chain gun and a bright explosion silhouetting a tank turret launching into the sky. Another burst, and a second tank goes up. The concussion thumps them in the chest. "Rusty 1, Wingnut, good kills. Keep them coming."

"Rusty flight, Rusty 1, we have a hunting ground. Approach east west and roll in by the numbers. You'll find me by the burning tanks." After his unit acknowledges, he asks, "Wingnut, Rusty 1. Are those houses evacuated?"

"Stand by," and Tommy turns to Sergeant Tully, "Are they?"

"It can't be helped, Yank. Just keep it coming."

"Fucking bullshit. We don't kill our own." On radio, "Negative, Rusty 1. We have no status on the houses."

The sergeant grabs Wingnut by the lapels, pulling him in close, "We're at war, Yank. The Germans got to be hit!"

Tommy, a large man, pushes the sergeant away, "We are at war, SIR. Sergeant, I'm a fucking officer. Don't you fucking forget it. I will NOT kill innocent people."

"The Krauts will, sir."

"That's why we're fighting them. If they were good people, we could settle it over a pint."

"Yes, sir."

GENERAL WEBER'S HQ, OCCUPIED FRANCE

0542, 24 September, 1942

Weber stands studying a map of Britain. A staff sergeant approaches, "Field Marshal Rommel on the radio, sir."

He picks up the microphone, "Air Group West."

"General, what are you doing to destroy the Yankee cross, the American attack jet. It has a high capacity, large caliber gun that cuts up our armor. It needs to be your focus."

"Yes, Herr Field Marshal. I'm drawing the American fighters away and attacking those planes. I'm told it's very hard to kill."

"How many jets do they have?"

"Three, perhaps four."

"Soon, I wish that number to be zero."

"Yes, Herr Field Marshal."

"We do well, and I'm pleased with your accomplishments, but

the issue before us, it is still very much in doubt."

"I agree, sir. But their weakness is an advantage we may exploit."

CHEESEBURN GRANGE, NORTH OF RAF OUSTON

0502, 24 September, 1942

LT Gus 'Cuddles' Grant moves from concealment on the roof top and stops, looking east. The Home Guard and the base security are making a go of it in and around the buildings south of the field. Uncle Tucker and his nephew, a Home Guard radioman named Charles are with him. Tucker asks, "Maybe they're all going south?"

Cuddles replies, "The Germans aren't stupid. They'll want this field."

"You suppose we can stop them?"

"Doubt it, but it's why we're here." He sees an A-10 climb and turn for a pass. "See that?"

Tucker, "A German Jet?"

"No, that, my friend, is an A-10 Warthog. I heard we were making new ones. Charles, have you heard from the regular army unit north of us yet?"

Charles, "They're close. A few miles away."

In the distance Cuddles sees a Panzer 4 break through a hedge, followed by German infantry. He turns on his radio, "Any Warthog, Cuddles."

"Cuddles, Dog flight 3, authenticate."

"Dog flight, Cuddles. Tell Yankee actual I know her jeep was dark blue and she beat me three of four in training."

"Roger, Cuddles." A moment later, as Cuddles watches, more defenders get cut down, he hears, "Cuddles, Dog 3, standing by for tasking."

"We have three tanks on the tarmac at RAF Ouston in contact

with British troops."

WAR ROOM, SOMEWHERE UNDER LONDON

0542, 24 September, 1942

Churchill slumps in his chair at a table with Air Marshal Dowding, Field Marshal Brooke, and General Eisenhower watching the staff update a huge map. Aids come and go handing notes and taking replies. "Tell me, Air Chief Marshal, how many jets does she have left?"

Dowding, "Three, Prime Minister. Two others may be repaired. We also have 16 flyable Griffins and several under repair."

Churchill nods, "Do we have an estimate of the German strength?"

Dowding, "Only a rough estimate. They have at least sixty of the delta fighters, the ME-262. They have possibly forty of the ME-163. They've just brought a new fighter in and I'm told it's quite good, but the numbers must be small, perhaps ten or twenty. Overall, they have approximately one hundred jets."

Churchill, "Eisenhower, tell me you're building replacement F-14's."

"We are, Prime Minister, as fast as possible. But they must be tested before they can be brought over."

An aid reports, "Alconbury is requesting to be updated on the forward edge of battle."

Brooke, "Why?"

Eisenhower, "We have ground attack planes now, and we're trying to avoid fratricide."

Brooke shakes his head, "Minister, I would rather hold that tight."

Churchill frowns, "No. Give it to them. Give them whatever they need." He turns to Brooke, "You don't handicap your only hope."

"Sir, in truth, we aren't sure where the line is."

"I know that. Give them what we can."

Eisenhower, "Our paratroopers are heavily engaged and encircled. Their major is asking to fall back."

Churchill, "Of course, but where will they go?"

"They have a plan to head south."

Brooke, "But, that will pin them against the river."

Eisenhower, "They major said he has a way across."

Churchill, "Granted and God speed."

Brooke, "The 27th Armored Brigade is rolling north. We need to choose their first defensive position."

Churchill, "What do you think?"

Brooke, The Tee river, sir. We blow the bridges and make a stand there."

Dowding, "If we blow the bridges, we trap those people fleeing south from the Germans."

Brooke looks at Eisenhower, then back to Churchill, "We must. If we don't, we may lose the island entire."

Churchill, "Blow them."

BERGHOF, OBERSALBERG, NEAR BERCHTSGADEN, GERMANY

0700, 24 September, 1942

Hitler walks into the conference room and his officers stand, "Heil Hitler."

Hermann Goering, "Mein Fuhrer, the British are on the ropes. As promised, the 4th Corps has landed nearly intact. We have, with the navy's indispensable help, sunk most of the British fleet. Those units still surviving are limping north to lick their wounds. The North Sea is ours and the skies over Britain, though still contested, are ours as well."

"Yes. Admiral Raeder, how do you assess our position?"

Admiral Erich Raeder, commander of the Kreigsmarine, replies, "I cautiously agree. We have an opening and we should exploit it. I have no doubt the Americans and British are, as we speak, gathering every asset available to wrest control of the North Sea. Should the jet carrier make an appearance, that would be a complication."

Hitler, "That carrier has been seen in Australia. Even if it set out now, it would be too late to make a difference in what we do."

"Yes, mein Fuhrer."

"How many aircraft does she have?"

Goering, "Four at most. Likely less. She has been sending up aircraft without cover from a wingman. It indicates they have very few and need every plane."

"Good. Oberkommando Keitel, can Rommel take London?"

On paper, the man that commanded all the German armed forces, Oberkommando der Whermacht Wilhelm Keitel, Hitler's military chief of staff, replies, "He can, mein Fuhrer. He can and he must. When London falls, resistance in Britain will end."

Hitler, "London will fall. The King will come and bow before me, or lose his head. Our U-boats must prevent resupply or any escape form the island. This is critical."

Raeder, "Yes, mein Fuhrer."

"While the British fleet rests in harbor, sink them at their anchors. Destroy the dock yards and landing piers. Those merchant ships that escape our U-boats will have no place to land. And we will resupply at will. Their defense will grind to a halt and we will be victorious."

ARTHUR 1, 35,000 FEET OVER DOVER

0822, 24 September, 1942

The sun is well above the horizon at this altitude, it's brutally bright in Spike's face as they race to intercept a German flight approaching the channel, "Lizard, illuminate." She's happy to be back in her jet.

"Alright, Boss. We have ten bandits at 120 miles. They're at 30K and 500 knots."

"Remind Hot Pants to stay north. Make sure you have them good, then I'll ripple fire the lot." They're flying with the 'John Wayne' loadout; six AIM-1, Long Bow, long range missiles, and two AIM-9, Sidewinders.

"Roger, Boss, Steer 55."

"55."

On radio, Lizard, "Percival, Arthur, the boss wants you on our toes up there."

"Roger Arthur 1, standing by."

"You sleep well, Boss?"

"We're about to kill people, Lizard. No chit-chat."

"Roger, Boss. Okay, I'm ready."

"Volley Fox 3." She pushes and holds the fire trigger and all six missiles drop and light up.

HAUPTMANN (CAPTAIN) HEINRICH GUNTER'S ME-262B, 30,000 FEET, NORTHERN FRANCE

Gunter has only forty-five minutes of flying time in the new '262 and he already loves it. It's not as agile as the '163 he flew before, but it's blindingly fast. With his new promotion, he's leading his squadron on a bombing raid on Portsmouth. It matters not that he is a distraction to open an attack on the American air attack jets. He's in charge and he has a mission.

The first indication of a problem is the white exhaust from missiles eighty miles ahead of him. "Red flight, Red 1, incoming missiles."

The incoming missiles are fast, making the timing of his evasive action critical. He watches intently, then yanks back his stick, pickling the chaff dispensers. The missile passes beneath him and fails to detonate, but five of his aircraft are hit. "Half. Fuck. Fucking half of my force. Time to kill this son of a bitch!" On radio, "Drop ordinance and attack."

ARTHUR 1

Lizard, "They're '262's. They're dropping ordinance."

"Okay, Lizard, let's play with our food."

"Boss?"

"I want them to go to afterburner and try to fight. Run them out of fuel and they can't kill anyone."

"Roger, Boss. 25 miles."

Then, "Raid warning north. Designate Raid 8. Ten fast movers over the North Sea."

"Boss?"

"Hot Pants knows what to do. Lock them up on radar."

"Boss, we're out of long-range missiles."

"They don't know that. Lock them up."

"Roger, we have five closing."

"Call Fox 1 in the clear."

Lizard, "Fox 1, fox 1." The Germans take evasive action, engaging their afterburners. "They're scrambling!"

They hear GQ on radio, "Volley Fox 3."

HAUPTMANN GUNTER'S ME-262B, 28,000 FEET OVER THE CHANNEL

Gunter violently barrel rolls his '262B looking for an exhaust plume. "No incoming. Close and engage." He pulls into a climb and inverts to keep an eye on the American. His flight is scattered, with no semblance of a formation.

ARTHUR 1

Spike has the altitude advantage. She sees a lone jet climbing as the others scatter. She picks a '262 to her left and dives in, engaging afterburner. Her prey rolls right and she cuts the corner, closing rapidly. Lizard, "The climbing bird is rolling over the top."

"Where?"

"Four high, five miles."

"Okay," She hears the growl of the lock on the bird in front of her and pickles off a Sidewinder. It zigs twice and explodes right below the jet's engines causing it to pitch forward and dive. They see pieces fall off the bird as the pilot desperately tries to bring it back level, then an engine explodes and it turns and rolls inverted, diving for the sea. She turns off her burners.

Lizard, "Six high. Rolling over the top."

"Grunt." She pulls hard, climbing to meet the jet. As she does, another '262B crosses in front of her. She applies rudder and dissimilar thrust and fires a burst from her gun. The crossing plane catches on fire and rolls on its back.

Adjusting rudder and thrust, she closes the diving '262B. The German fires a missile, forcing her to break off and drop chaff and flares. Lizard, "He's pulling out below us." She rolls over and sees the jet 100 feet under, flying parallel.

The German hand salutes and she returns it, then snap rolls and pulls, "Grunt." As she completes the Immelman, she sees the German bugging out south.

HAUPTMANN GUNTER

Gunter is racing south as he continues to descend. On radio, "Form on me. Form on me. It's the Drachendame. Only she flies like that."

Lieutenant Jochim Vogel, "Are you certain it was the Dragon Lady?"

"I have fought her twice. I saw her close. It is she."

RAF ALCONBURY

Spike flares her bird to land. Lizard, "Ten, five." The main gear chirps and the nose comes down. As they taxi, "Six kills in one sortie, Boss. Is this a record for you?"

"God damn it, Lizard. I don't talk about the kills."

"Not even with your RIO?"

"No."

"Can I ask why?"

"Because I'm a fucking mass murderer. I'm good at it, but I fucking hate it, every time. I'm sure as fuck not going to brag about it just to make some ignorant fuck think it's cool." The cockpit is silent as she taxis to refuel and rearm.

"I'm sorry, Spike. I didn't know."

"I'm sorry, too. I shouldn't have yelled at you. I need to be better than that."

"You are, Spike. Everybody loves you. It's okay that you, umm...loose it once in a while. Everyone needs an outlet."

"Did you and Papa talk a lot in the cockpit?"

"Sure. We talked about all kinds of stuff."

"Did he talk about me?"

"Boss, I will never, ever, reveal what you and I discuss in this cockpit. I will never reveal what he said, either."

"Okay, then. I loved him as a friend, Shawn."

"I did, too."

She opens the cockpit as the ground crew begin refueling the bird. "I need to pee."

"Got it, Boss."

CHAPTER 6

SOUTH OF THE POW CAMP, CATTERICK, UK

1127, 24 September, 1942

Trooper David Preacher stands in the loaders hatch of his Covenanter tank. They are parked on the left side of the road, clearing the way for the vehicles streaming south. Behind the last civilian vehicle there's a line of military trucks filled with German POWs. A driver waves at him and he waves back, "Lucky sod, all the Germans you face are unarmed."

Then, he sees a German in Kriegsmarine uniform jump out of a truck and run into the field right in front of him. The driver of the next truck stops and jumps out with his rifle, shouting, "Shoot him!"

Preacher unlimbers his BESA machine gun and sites on the fleeing man. Just like in training, he sights over the barrel and squeezes the trigger. The gun jumps and the bullets find their target. The Germans arms fly out, as the rounds hit in the center of his back, and he falls.

Soldiers run from the trucks and pick up the dead POW. Sergeant West comes up out of his hatch, "What the fuck are you doing, Preacher?"

Preacher, bile rising, "I killed a German" He leans over the turret and vomits.

4TH PLATOON, EASY COMPANY, 2ND OF THE 509TH, NORTH BANK OF THE RIVER TYNE, NEWCASTLE, UK

1913, 24 September, 1942

Johnny Rodriguez lays in the shadows, searching north for any movement, his machine gun ready. There are Germans all over the place and tanks rolling over the bridge above him. He struggles to control his breathing. "Deep, slow breath. Remember, deep, slow breath." The cartridges in the ammo belt are rattling and he realizes it's him and takes his hand off the belt. The Germans are only twenty yards away. Taking deep breathes, he closes his eyes and calms his mind. Slowly, his shaking subsides and he puts his hand back on the action.

He feels a tap on his foot and gradually, slowly moves back. His sergeant guides him onto a metal support rib under the bridge, and they carefully make their way across. Their movement covered by the vibration caused by the tanks above them.

25,000 FEET, EAST OF LONG ISLAND, NY

1409, 24 September, 1942 (1909 GMT)

VADM Richard 'Dixie' Lee is at the controls of a F-14B loaded with test missiles and bombs. Flying to his right in the F-14B chase plane is Einstein. "Butch, are we ready?"

CDR Ronald 'Butch' Cassidy says, "Yes, sir. There are no radar contacts remotely in range. The radar is on and set to straight ahead."

Lee replies, "Okay, call it."

Butch, "Ready to start test one."

Einstein, "Roger. In position. Camera is rolling."

The control center at the Grumman factory says, "Range is clear. We are green."

Lee, "Roger. Fox 1," and fires and AIM-1 Long Bow. The missile drops and fires, shooting ahead of the '14. The missile sways a bit, then settles on the beam, continuing until the rocket motor runs out of fuel and it tumbles into the sea.

Lee, "Great. Perfect. Perfect. On to test two."

200 FEET, DURHAM, UK

1918, 24 September, 1942

LT Albert 'Shit Howdy' Henderson, USMC, puts his Warthog into a steep bank, turning onto a formation of the smaller German tanks racing for Durham. He hit the lead tank on his last run. Now, the darkening evening light is making it harder to see. They've pushed the burning tank out of the way and several of the tracks have rolled into a field in an attempt to bypass. The one using the stone fence to avoid getting stuck is his next target.

Then he sees the Germans pulling canvas off a half-track exposing a missile carrier. Fortunately, it's pointed in the wrong direction. "All units, Shit Howdy, they got missiles."

Captain 'Buck' Hall, "Avoid the missiles."

Shit Howdy fires at his target, lighting it up, then turns pulling out to go around. He sees a missile fire and turns, attempting to race away. "Sam launch. Evading."

Shit Howdy feels a kick in the ass and his warning alarm sounds, fire in the left engine. "Shit Howdy is hit. Shit Howdy is hit. Still flying. Just west of Durham." He rolls back to target the missile launcher.

Buck, "Bug out, Howdy. RTB."

"I'm gonna kill the mother fucker."

"Howdy, Buck, RTB."

Howdy pulls up just above the trees and sees another missile launch and track him. "SAM launch. SAM launch. Howdy evading. Chaff and flares," and pickles countermeasures. The missile is spoofed, but then, as it flies by, it picks up the heat of the hot engine and regains track. The second missile detonates behind the right engine.

"Howdy is hit. Howdy is hit. Double flame out at 300 feet."

"Punch out Howdy."

"Stretching south."

"You don't have the altitude to fuck around, damn it. Punch out!"

Howdy pats the dash of his A-10, "Sorry, baby. You've been good to me." He pulls the ejection handle and soars into the air, passing out.

VALKYRIE 1, 2000 FEET, OVER LEEDS

On radio, LCDR Sandra 'Cargo Britches' Douglas, "Dog units, Valkyrie 1 inbound for dust off. Where did you lose your bird?"

"Valkyrie 1, Dog 1. He went down west of Durham. There are Germans about a mile north. Be advised, the Germans have SAMs."

"Understood, Buck. Can you circle and cover him?"

"Affirmative. We are doing so."

FIELD NEAR BRANCEPETH, WEST OF DURHAM, UK

Howdy comes to just before he hits the ground. He has no time to brace and he feels stabbing pain in his left ankle and leg as he hits. He rolls onto his back, shakes off the rain on his face and gets onto his hands and knees. He gathers his chute, "Howdy, remind yourself to never, ever to do that again."

He sees his flaming wreck of an A-10 about 300 feet away, "Well, I suppose this is the better option."

To the north he hears the brrrt of an A-10 and smiles, "They're covering me. Give 'em hell, boys." He finishes pulling in his chute and gathers it into a messy bundle.

RAF ALCONBURY

Spike settles into the cockpit as the crew finishes winching up the last missiles into place. AE3 Washington climbs up and helps strap her in, "Spike, you got two AIM-7's, four AIM-1's, 2 AIM-9's, and your fuel and gun are topped off."

Spike smiles, "Thanks, Handy." He kisses his two fingers and touches the crown of her helmet.

Then Swede climbs up, "Thud is over Durham covering the A-10s. The Germans brought SAMs. We just lost another A-10. I'm asking Wizard to do his dance. I would like you to pair with Thud rather than work alone."

"Roger, Swede. Tell the A-10s to fly NOE to limit the target window for the SAMs. Do the A-10s have counter measures?"

"I'll find out."

"How goes the move?"

"We're getting there. It'll be a day or two before we're completely moved."

Spike, "Not fast enough. Focus on people first. Then the equipment we can't do without, then everything else. And Swede, the civilian workers, their families, and the guy's girlfriends are our people."

"How are we going to move them all?'

Swede, you know those folks are who our guys fight for. We can't afford to lose our families again."

"Roger, Spike."

"Swede, the easy stuff, they give to the Air Force."

They make eye contact and smile, "Roger that, Spike," and jumps down. The ground crew run clear waving the ordinance flags and a yellow shirt indicates she can start her engines.

FIELD NEAR BRANCEPETH, WEST OF DURHAM, UK

Howdy sits in the field waiting, then remembers his survival radio.

"Howdy, Buck. Howdy, Buck."

"Go for Howdy."

"You got German infantry in the trees to your west. If you can, run south."

"Roger." Drawing his 1911, he looks toward the trees and starts running south. He sees movement, "Damn, a pistol to a rifle fight." The stabbing pain in his ankle slowing him down, he hobbles past his burning A-10, and hears bullets zipping by him, and changes direction. Then he hears the brrrt of an A-10 laying down suppressing fire. He feels a swat in his ass and tumbles forward.

"Come on, Howdy. Come on." His ass on fire and his ankle throbbing, he gets up and runs, firing a shot at the Germans. He can hear the whop, whop of a helicopter approaching. He keeps running, trying to get into the trees, then sees the outline of a German tank. As he turns east, a man steps out of the shadows.

SS-Obersturmbannfurhrer Rolf Meier smiles at Howdy, and in English says, "You won't be harmed, American."

Howdy freezes, looking at the German, then "Go to hell," he fires and keeps running. He feels a burning pain as the he his hit, again and again.

VALKYRIE 1 APPROACHING HOWDY

Cargo Britches sees Howdy fall and swings the chopper around, "Yogi!"

AW1 Paul 'Yogi' Chatman opens up with his mini-gun, "They got a tank!"

The Germans scatter as Yogi calmly mows them down and Cargo Britches settles the chopper on the grass. "Keep shooting." On radio, "Dog 1, we got a tank in the trees."

"Dog 1. Roger."

He copilot, LT Jim 'Smooth' Lowndowski climbs out of the chopper and runs to Howdy. He picks him up and gets him to the helicopter as Yogi lays down a steady stream of 7.62 rounds. "Go, Boss." Yogi keeps firing as they climb and transition to forward flight.

TREES SOUTH OF THE FIELD

Meier runs for his tank, then hears the brrrt of one of the attack jets and watches his tank go up in flames, his men trying to scramble free. "Shit! Shit! Fucking American whores! Jung, give me your tank."

LCAC, DEPARTING USS DANIEL J. DALY, 35 MILES WEST OF CAMP PENDLETON, CA

1201, 24 September, 1942 (2001 GMT)

SGT Tom Thompson stands with his platoon behind the ramp of the LCAC they are riding. The noise is palpable. This is their third practice landing, and it's starting to get boring. Their three M-2A4 tanks are arranged behind them. The tank crews are required to stay out of the tanks until right before landing. His platoon officer, 2nd LT Ed Shay says, "These air cushion landing craft are killer diller."

Thompson nods, "It is nice to land dry, but I wonder how well they'll survive under fire." They get the signal to mount up and climb into their tanks. Another signal and they start engines.

A sailor signals to hold the brakes as another pulls the chains. Moments later, they feel the LCAC hit the beach. The boat decelerates and tips up at the front. Then the ramp goes down and they pull forward out of the LCAC. His and SGT Porter's tanks race up the beach. The LT's breaks down behind them.

He can see the other LCACs land. "Driver advance." They pull up to their first AP and stop, waiting for the LT.

Waiting, they see some brass approaching. They're in a battle simulation, so he does not salute, "Sirs."

Admiral Klindt says, "Come on down, Marine."

Thompson un-asses his track and realizes that Major General Charles D. Barrett, his division commander, is behind the admiral, "Sorry, sir's. We were simulating combat and..."

Klindt waves his hand, "You were correct, Marine. Can you show me your tank?"

"Yes, sir. The M2A4 is a 1920's design, sir, with a 37mm main gun."

The admiral climbs into the gunner's seat, "What's it like at speed in here?"

Thompson, "It jostles us around a good bit, but it's a tank, sir, not a Cadillac."

Klindt nods, "My Marines deserve a Cadillac."

"Sir?"

"Marine, if you had a stabilized gun, something over 100 millimeters, and a bit more consideration for ergonomics, I bet you could hit targets out to two miles."

"Does such a tank exist, sir?"

"Not yet, but it will."

"Can I ask why you are here, sir?"

"To evaluate the LCACs. My team is in charge of all the new technologies. We need to get you all decent tanks. Simple and relatively easy to maintain. It also ought to be water proof, with filtered air."

"That would be wonderful, sir, but what is an ergonomic?"

Klindt smiles, "It's the study of how people interact with technology. I want the tank to fit the man, not the other way around." He climbs out, "General, I want to borrow one of your tanks. Also, a couple of your most experienced sergeants."

"Admiral Klindt, while you were in the tank, we got orders to ship out to Virginia."

"That will take some time. Your people and armor can meet you there."

Yes, sir."

ARTHUR 1, 40,000 FEET, SW OF NEWCASTLE ON THE TYNE

2013, 24 September, 1942

Spike, "Okay, Lizard, find out if Howdy made it."

Lizard makes the call.

Cargo Britches, "Arthur 1, Valkyrie 1, he's breathing, but critical. We dropped him off at Guys. Three in the chest. It isn't hopeful."

Lizard, "Roger, Valkyrie 1."

Spike, "Fuck. Where's Thud?"

"18,000 feet, about 40 miles east of us. He just sent a couple of '262s home with their tails between their legs."

"Okay, we'll stay high. Let's head east and see who bites."

"Roger." On radio, "Speedy, Lizard, we'll stay on top. Let's trawl east for German bottom fish."

"Lizard, Speedy, great to hear you. High, low, time to go. We've two sevens and two nines and we're dark."

Lizard to Spike, "Does it feel good with Thud on your wing again?"

"It does. Please don't take this wrong, but I miss Puck."

"Sure you do, he was your left hand. Truth Spike, we all miss him. He was steady in an indispensable way."

"He...he's a good friend."

"Boss, twelve bandits at angels 30 and 250 miles."

"Roger. Change course?"

"Boss, if we fly straight, they won't know we see them."

"Good call."

"Spike, were you and Puck…?"

"Friends? Yes, very good friends. We were a good team in the air."

"I think he hated your friend, Hughes."

"I know, but I don't understand why."

"You don't?"

"No, Lizard. Do you?"

Lizard, "Umm…we're approaching time to play."

"Okay. Fire the four and guide Thud in."

"We got lock."

Spike, "Volley fox 3." She selects the AIM-1 and holds down the trigger. All four missiles leave the rails and streak toward their targets.

Lizard, "Duck your head, Speedy."

Speedy, "Si, Senor."

FU-279, 30,000 FEET, 100 MILES NORTH OF AMSTERDAM.

Hauptmann Kurt Welter sweeps his instruments with relaxed urgency. On radio, "Keep eyes out." Then he spots the exhaust of the missiles, "Incoming! Break! Break!"

He pulls up to meet the missiles, fires counter measures and climbs. As he passes vertical, he spins to see his flight. Three planes are tumbling into the sea. "The American will die. He will die. He is only one. He pulls onto his back and orients toward Spike.

GAWAIN 1, 24,000 FEET, CLIMBING TO MEET THE GERMANS

Thud, "Most jinxed up. Get me lock."

"On it. Tone two."

"Fox 1, Fox 1," Two AIM-7s scream toward the '279s. One hits between the engines as it pulls to break over the top, breaking the fighter in two. The second missile hits a second plane near the radome, the blast pushing into the cockpit. The jet goes out of control and into the sea. Speedy, "Splash two."

ARTHUR 1, 100 MILES SOUTH EAST OF NEWCASTLE

Spike, "Lock up two."

"Thud?"

"Now, Lizard."

"Fox 1, Fox 1. He knows what we're doing." Two Aim-7s streak towards the Germans.

Speedy, "Zooming, Spike."

As Spike fires at several FU-279s and rolls over the top, looking for Thud. She sees Thud racing vertical in full afterburner. He's above the carnage caused by her missiles. Lizard, "Splash 2." Then, "Oh my God!" He watches as the second stricken bird clips his wingman, taking out his vertical stabilizer, and sending them both to the sea. Lizard, "A twofer!"

"Grunt." Spike climbs violently, avoiding a missile. It explodes in her chaff, causing their '14 to shake. She drops her nose and dives, meeting a '279, head to head.

WELTER'S FU-279

Hauptmann Welter meets the F-14, head to head. The closure is a blur, but in his lights, he sees the flags. "It's the Drachendame. I've got her. She's mine." He pulls vertical, going to full afterburner.

On radio, he hears one of his men, "Who is the other?"

The American ace has matched his maneuver, "I don't care." He continues over the top and spins upright, yanking the stick back to bleed off speed in the climb. He realizes she is not there, and looking to his right he sees her five miles away, closing on one of his squadron. "Fuck!"

Then he feels the thud of rounds hitting his fuselage, and rolls his bird on its back again, maneuvering to get away. Alarms go off in his cockpit. His left engine is on fire and he's fighting to keep her straight. Then, he feels more rounds hitting his plane, and it tips up on its left side and slides down, out of controlled flight. The wingman sweeps past him. "Fuck, fuck. I'm in trouble." Out of airspeed, his aircraft spins straight down.

GAWAIN 1

Instead of following the wounded bird down, he rolls out, "Where is she?"

Speedy, "Looking."

Thud sees an explosion. He traces the missile to its source. "Found her. The Germans are bugging out."

Speedy asks, "How many?"

Thud, "We got three. I think that last guy might nurse it home."

"He's still down there somewhere if you want."

"Nah, let him go. He's no threat." Spike joins them on their right wing.

Speedy, "The boss got at least five."

They see Lizard use a flashlight to show six fingers."

Speedy, "That would be six."

Thud, "When we get back, tell Lizard not to do that. If Spike sees it, it'll piss her off."

"Thud, do you know her deal with that?"

"Yeah. Compadre, how many people did we just kill?"

"Three birds. I saw two chutes. One."

Thud, "No. We killed three. The other two will freeze to death or drown."

Speedy, "But, they would kill us."

"So, I hit Hans because Hans is going to hit me. Does that make it right?"

"In war it does."

"Speedy, think. When we are at war, should we give up our humanity?"

"Thud, we have to. It's the gig. We kill the enemy until they give up or die. The more we kill, the sooner that day will come."

"Then you would preemptively bomb Berlin with the gadget?"

"I'm not a monster, Thud."

"Speedy, who was the monster, Doctor Frankenstein, or the creature he made?"

"Fuck, dude. This is getting deep."

Thud, "How do you reconcile the killing, compadre?"

"I try not to think about it."

"For your mental health, for your sanity, you need to work through it."

On radio, "Gawain 1, Arthur 1, fuel check."

Speedy, "2 decimal 6, Arthur 1."

"Gawain 1, Arthur 1, come to 255. We'll RTB and load up."

Speedy, "255 and 28, Arthur 1, Gawain 1, aye," Intercom, "Thud, if I go down that hole, I'll be a mess. Combat non-effective. I'll take the hit when we're done."

"Okay, amigo, but don't go there alone. It's a dark and painful path."

"Who helped you?'

"My dad when I selected fighters. Swede and Spike when we were heading to Australia."

"Did your dad have kills?"

"Three in Vietnam. All three died."

Speedy, "He would be proud of you, Frank."

Thud, "Yeah, but worried, too."

"Thud, I don't get your question. The monster is the monster."

"No, my friend. The monster was a brand-new creature trying to survive in a world it did not understand. The doctor knew what he was doing and did it anyway. We have a job to do, but at the same time, we cannot lose our humanity."

"Is that why you let the wounded bird go?"

"Yeah, Speedy. I hope he makes it, too."

SURGERY, GUYS HOSPITAL, LONDON, UK

2116, 24 September, 1942

The on-shift surgeon walks to the sink and washes his hands. "Time of death, 9:16 pm, 24 September, 1942. Cause of death, severe trauma from multiple gunshot wounds to the chest and abdomen. We have a call to make."

The nurse says, "Yes, doctor."

CHAPTER 7

4TH PLATOON, EASY CO, 2ND OF THE 509TH, WEST OF SUNDERLAND, UK

2203, 24 September, 1942

Dead on his feet, PFC Johnny Rodriguez slides his back down a stone wall next to a barn to sit. What's left of the battalion is crashing as well. He pulls out his canteen for a drink, and it's dry, "Fuck." His sergeant motions for quiet.

Johnny gets to his knees, looks around, and sees a pump well in the barnyard. He gets up and walks to it, drops his pack and rummages for his gun oil. A little squirt and he tests the pump. It's quiet and he gets water on his first stroke. He fills his canteen, takes a long satisfying drink, and fills it again. The others have gathered with their canteens, so he steps away and looks over the barn.

It's an old, large stone barn. You could hide a tank platoon in it. He motions to his sergeant and walks up to it. A little more oil on the hinges of the man door and he gently opens it. He takes a couple of steps inside the dark interior and feels a knife against his ribs.

A voice, in British English, asks, "What unit are you?"

"509th Parachute Regiment. We're just getting water."

The knife is removed, "Sergeant Tully, Home Guard. Do you have a doctor?"

"We have a corpsman. It's the best we have."

"Good, we've a wounded Yank pilot."

Johnny says, "I'll get Doc."

CONTROL CENTER, RAF ALCONBURY

2221, 24 September, 1942

Spike walks in, "Report."

The watch officer says, "Lancelot 1 and 2 are over York. Trident is orbiting east of Scapa, processing a contact. The A-10s are at Kenley. Without forward air observers they can't see anything at night. Whiskey 4 and 7 are orbiting over London and Edinburgh. Texas has a flight with each radar plane. Valkyrie 1 is fishing a couple of British pilots out of the drink east of Newcastle. The last German raid on Portsmouth is heading home. Three air fields north of London have been hit hard. The refinery west of Portsmouth was also hit and is still burning. Fighter Command reports eleven Griffins flight worthy. And ma'am, Guys Hospital called. LT Albert Henderson didn't make it. Sorry, ma'am."

"Okay. Thank you. Does Major Parks know?"

"Yes, ma'am. He does."

"Where are the Germans."

"They are driving west from Newcastle and south past Durham. The southern push seems to be focusing to the east. They say that is a best guess."

"Okay, who is engaging them?"

"British Army out of Penrith are engaging units near Haltwhistle. That is all I know."

"Very good. As soon as it's light, send Dusty to support the units at Haltwhistle."

"Yes, Ma'am."

"Moving forward, units in contact take precedence for A-10 air support. I'll put in an urgent order for NOGs for our A-10 pilots."

"Yes, Commodore."

Two men in flight suits walk in, "Major Floyd Parks and Lieutenant Commander Leonard reporting."

Spike motions them over, "How many birds do you have that are flyable?"

Parks, "Ten. We just lost Shit Howdy. My apologies, LT Albert Henderson. He died of his wounds."

"I'm so sorry, Major."

"Ma'am, the Germans murdered him. They just shot him dead."

"How is your squadron taking it?"

Parks meets her gaze, "We want revenge."

Spike, "Winning is the best revenge. I'm going to try and get you NOGs. They're night observation goggles. If I can get them, we need to train your guys on how to use them. We also need to make the sure the cockpit is NOG compatible."

Leonard looks at her in wonder, "We could fly at night. Those NOGs would be so helpful. Right, I have eleven birds. Also, we're going through ammo and bombs at an insane rate."

Spike smiles, "When you're out of everything except enemies, you're in a combat zone. Have all your people moved to Kenley?"

Parks smiles back, "Yes, ma'am. We both got the word."

"Good. My orders are simple. If you lose a plane or person, I want my staff to know soonest. They know when to wake me up. We'll move heaven and earth to try to rescue a downed pilot. As a commander, take care of your people and they will take care of you. I can't have a tyrant. If you need something or someone, let my staff know. Right now, you are the difference between success or failure. We don't have to win every fight, but we must absolutely survive. Questions?"

Leonard asks, "Do you still fly?"

"I just landed a few minutes ago."

Leonard continues, "When do you sleep?"

"When I can."

Parks, "Why do your flights have knights of the round table call signs?"

"To confuse the Germans when they were listening to our communications. Our new radios have better encryption now, but we haven't changed the call signs."

Parks again, "Do you need us to change our call signs?"

"No, but I do need a list of your flight and personal call signs, so I can put them out to my pilots."

"Yes, ma'am."

Spike smiles, "Gentlemen, please call me Spike, or Hunt, or Commodore. I hate ma'am."

Leonard, "Can I ask why?"

"Ma'ams are old with too many cats."

The two men chuckle. Parks, "Roger that, Spike. I'll let my guys know, but they might slip up."

"No problem. What's your call sign."

"Sparks. Landed on a metal mat field in training and forgot my tail hook was down."

"Leonard, what's yours?"

"Book, Commodore. I kept threatening the guys that I would read them from the book and that's what I got."

Spike starts, then locks it down. Then, from an operator at the board, "Raid warning north. 10 plus, 100 miles east of Scapa Flow."

Spike, "Steer Lancelot. Launch the alert 5. Direct them to orbit over Dover in the dark."

She studies the map. "You can go if you wish, gentlemen.

Thank you."

Leonard, "May we watch?"

"Of course, this can be your watch time." The phone rings, "Yankee 1."

"Dowding, Commodore, could you launch a bird to orbit London?"

"Launching Percival now. I was going to put them over Dover. They're pounding our infrastructure down there. With the fleet withdrawing, port facilities need to move to pri 2."

"Yes, I agree and that would work fine. Are you getting ground forces locations yet?"

"It's spotty."

"We're scrambling everything to face the Hun. It's hard to know where they are until we face them."

"Could we at least know where the friendlies are?"

"That should be possible."

"The hardest part for our attack birds is knowing where our friendly forces are. We very much want to avoid blue on blue."

"I couldn't agree more. I'll get you what you need."

"Thank you, Air Marshal."

FIELD SOUTH OF DURHAM

2250, 24 September, 1942

The corpsman finishes cleaning and dressing Wingnut's wounds. "Sir, most of these wounds are superficial, but there's nothing I can do about your left shoulder. Some say immobilize it. I'm worried that will lock it up."

"It hurts like hell. What did I do to it?"

"It looks like you dislocated it, then it popped back in. You have torn muscles, at least two. It requires a surgeon."

"What happens if I wait?"

"The torn muscles atrophy and you may lose full range of motion and a lot of strength in that arm."

The company commander stands over Urland. "We need to medivac you out, sir."

Tommy looks up at him, "No. There's no time. You guys need a forward air observer who knows what pilots need. When they've trained guys in the field, I'll get fixed. If I can't fly. I can't fly."

The Captain says, "I've seen what the new planes can do. Point taken. You'll need a couple of squads to protect you."

SGT Tully stiffens, "We've done pretty well by him so far, sir."

"You have. I'm thinking your four men, with eight of mine. Sergeant Rodriguez, you've shown initiative and good sense. Swap your 1919 for a BAR and pick seven men."

"Sergeant, sir?"

"Yes, Sergeant Rodriguez, the war isn't giving us time for a party, so here," and hands Johnny his new stripes. "Make sure you get those on sooner rather than later."

"Yes, sir. Thank you, sir."

"Pick seven."

"Yes, sir," and Sergeant Johnny Rodriguez goes out to picks the best guys he knows.

The captain turns back to Wingnut, "Twelve should be enough to protect you and carry what you need. There is no way you can handle a pack."

Tully asks, "Captain, who's in charge?"

"Sorry, the Lieutenant's in charge."

GRUMMAN AIRCRAFT FACTORY, LONG ISLAND, NEW YORK
2348, 24 September, 1942 (0048, 25 September GMT)
Lee sits in a conference room listening to the engineers go

down the list. "Is the testing complete?"

Grumman frowns, "I'd like to sort out the hydraulic oil leaks."

Lee, "They all leak. If it isn't leaking, then don't fly it."

One of the engineers asks, "Why, sir?"

"Because a lack of leakage indicates a lack of fluid. Are we done?"

Grumman sighs, "Yes, sir."

"Paint them tonight, Black Knight markings. We fly out in the morning. A stop in Iceland, then on to England. We fly with full guns and two AIM-9s. Turn on a transport to fly us back."

ADMIRAL'S CONFERENCE ROOM, USS CARL VINSON, CVN-70

1705, 25 September, 1942

All squadron commanders are quietly listening as Admiral Halsey's staff goes over the intel picture. Halsey says, "We're going to San Diego to draw new planes. I'm told the Redcocks will be transitioning to the new Tomcats. The Knight Riders will also transition from the Intruder to the Tomcats."

Captain Van Zandt says, "Another thing to note. The Germans have invaded England. Our friends over there are having all they can handle."

CDR Norman 'Oyster' Osterman, commanding officer of the Tomcatters, raises his hand.

Halsey, "Yes?"

Oyster, 'To save time, we could start transitioning the two squadrons as we transit. When we get to San Diego, we'll be ready to go."

Halsey nods, smiling, "Good idea. Make it so."

HENDERSON FIELD, GUADALCANAL

1314, 25 September, 1942 (0514 GMT)

SGT John Hunt sits on the ground outside the mess tent eating a hot meal. His company commander walks up, but no one salutes. Even with the island mostly cleared, sniper checks are not allowed. Hunt says, "Sir," and starts to stand up.

Captain Neal Morris waves him down, "You heard we lost Captain Westland from Easy Company last night?"

"Yes, sir."

"They decided to move Lieutenant Portman to Easy, so I need a new Lieutenant for your platoon."

"Yes, sir."

Morris smiles, "We'll dispense with the formalities for now. I chose you and the old man agrees. Put on your second Louie bars." He hands Hunt a set of gold bars.

Hunt takes them, "Me, sir? I was a PFC not so long ago."

"You have a level head and are cool under fire. Will you do it?"

"Um…Yes, sir. I'll do my best."

"I know you will." He turns and addresses the platoon, "Listen up, jar heads. Hunt is your new platoon officer." They just nod their heads and keep eating. It's the first hot meal they've had in days.

"Who do you want for your platoon sergeant?"

"Lewis."

"Give him your old stripes."

"Yes, sir."

101 BATTALION, 1ST BRIGADE, 3RD SS PANZER DIVISION, MIDDLETON-IN TEESDALE, UK

0710, 25 September, 1942

SS-Obersturmbannfuhrer Rolf Meier looks over the bridge crossing the Tees. It's crowded with civilians trying to flee.

"Ah, what a lovely little town. Gentlemen, let us leave our mark on this place. Machine gun anyone on the bridge and continue."

The guns on three of his new Tiger HII tanks open up and soon the way is clear. They run over bodies and carts as they run up the road and cross the bridge. An old Ford truck on the bridge gets pushed over the side. When Meier's tank is halfway across the bridge, it explodes and his tank falls ten feet into the river below. On the radio he screams, "KILL THEM! KILL THEM ALL!"

Shots ricochet off his tank as he climbs out and falls into the cold river. He stands upright and walks to the north bank as bullet after bullet misses him. He pauses and studies the bank. Then, he climbs out, and walks to the column. "Baumann, get out of my tank."

"Yes, Obersturmbannfuhrer."

Once in the tank, he directs them into the river and across. He sees the sparkle of rifle fire from the bell tower of the church. "Gunner, church tower at ten O'clock. Fire." The 125mm main gun belches fire and the entire bell tower collapses. "Driver, continue."

GROUP COMMANDER HOLMES RESIDENCE, CUNDERDIN AIRFIELD, WEST AUSTRALIA

1633, 26 September, 1942 (0833 GMT)

Abigail Holmes is doing laundry in a bucket on her back porch when she hears a knock at her front door. She walks through the house and answers the door. A young copper-haired woman is standing there. Abigail, puzzled, asks, "May I help you?"

"I'm sorry to be a bother, ma'am, but could we speak? I don't know what else to do?"

Abigail steps back, "Please, come in. Would you like some

tea?" And offers the girl a seat in the front room.

"Actually, I think I should explain why I'm here."

Abigail sits, "Who are you?"

"My name is Betty Potts. I'm your husband's secretary. I've been having an affair with him for three months."

Abigail's feels a chill deep in her chest and her throat tightens. "I...I...I see. And the reason you are sharing this with me now?"

"I'm at least two months pregnant."

"You're certain."

"The curse didn't come, so went to the base clinic. It's confirmed."

"I take it, Howard is the father?"

"He's the only man I've ever known, um, like that."

"I see. Would you care for some tea, now?"

"Really?"

"Yes, dear. I'll not say I'm not angry. I am. However, the bulk of my anger is directed at my husband."

"Thank you, um... tea would be nice."

In the kitchen, Abigail picks up the phone and dials base operations. "Yes, this is Abigail Holmes. I need my husband home immediately. Thank you."

Once the water boils, she makes the tea and makes up a tray. She takes the tea into the front room and sets down the tray, "Here, dear. One lump or two?"

"One, please."

Abigail serves, then sits down, and they sip their tea. She asks, "Do you wish to marry him?"

"I honestly thought he was single. He said he was. I only found out about you a few days ago."

"Of course. Please, do you wish to marry him?"

"I'm so very sorry, but yes." Betty starts to cry.

At this point, Group Captain Howard Holmes walks into the house. "What is this?"

Abigail stands, "Well dear, I'm getting acquainted with your paramour. You have created quite a mess."

Howard turns to Betty, "Get the hell out of my house!"

Abigail raises her voice, "You will sit down and shut up, Group Captain. I'm certain Air Vice Marshal Bostock would love to learn that you're shagging your secretary."

Betty rises, shocked, and Abigail says, "Sit, Betty!"

Abigail continues, "You knocked her up and now you're going to divorce me and marry her. Your child deserves a good father. Instead, the poor thing is stuck with you. The least you could do is make it legitimate."

Howard goes white, "What child?"

"She's up the duff, and you're the father."

"I see. Why are you so calm?"

"Because killing you would not serve me or your child in the long run. You will see a barrister today. I am moving out. Today. I'm taking my things and I'm going home. I'll be reverting to my maiden name. You will pay for my trip and let me know when the divorce is final."

"I will."

Abigail smiles, "Good."

"So, you're going to run after your Yank flyer? I know you write him."

"I've been writing Lieutenant Houlihan. And Howard, what I do is no longer any of your concern. You've given up that right. So, go back to work and leave me be so I can pack. Betty, please leave as well."

In shock, the two walk out and Abigail closes the door behind them. She puts her fists to her head and finally lets her tears come.

CHAPTER 8

USS JAMES HOLTZ (DDG-1), FEDERAL SHIPBUILDING AND DRY DOCK CO, KEARNY, NEW JERSEY

0600, 25 September, 1942 (1100 GMT)

A destroyer sits on its slipway decked out in flags and bunting. It may have started as a Fletcher class, but now it's so much more. Unlike previous Fletchers, it has a three-post lattice mast to the rear of the bridge and a four-post mast just ahead of the aft funnel. She may look a bit like the old boats, but she has a new weapons suite. She's the very first guided missile destroyer built in 1942.

After the chaplain finishes the invocation, Admiral Ren walk up to the podium, "This ship, and her sisters to come, are the vanguard of a new era. She's the first destroyer built with guided missiles.

"But she can't begin her life without a crew. The men before me are the heart and soul of this vessel. Another man's soul resides in her as well. I knew Commodore James 'Papa' Holtz well. I knew him when he was a brash your aviator anxious to prove himself. I knew him when he was an assured commander at the top of his game. He died in a decisive battle thousands of miles from here, but I believe his courage, tenacity, and boldness will live on in you.

"Here today to christen this fine vessel is Commodore Holtz' widow, Lady, Audrey Holtz. Lady Holtz, thank you so much for being here."

Audrey, in an ankle length black dress and heavily pregnant, stands and waves, then sits down.

Ren says, "Commander Dallas?" CDR John Dallas, previously the XO on the Jarrett FFG-33, steps up to the microphone. "Thank you, Admiral Ren, Lady Holtz. Men of the USS James Holtz, we have a proud tradition to uphold of duty, sacrifice, and honor. We are the beginning of a new era in naval warfare, and we're going to show them how it's done. I know that you are the best of the best and together we'll make this the premier ship in the US Navy.

"This ship exemplifies a melding of two worlds, the future and the past. With her, we can carry out our mission and save our present. I know that this crew and this ship are the beginning of the end of our enemies. So, let's get it done. Thank you."

Audrey stands with the champagne bottle. Holding onto the railing, she swings the bottle against the stem of the ship. It breaks in a spray of foam and the James Holtz slides down the ways.

After the ceremony, Admiral Ren helps Audrey and Donna Bond into his car and gets in beside them. "Driver, please take us to the Navy Yard." He turns back to the women and sees Audrey leaning back, eyes closed, and Donna taking her hand. "Lady Holtz, Admiral Lee wanted nothing more than to be here. Unfortunately, he's on urgent business right now. Sorry."

"We're at war. I understand. Thank you for inviting me and Mrs. Bond."

He looks at her quizzically, "Of course, but you know, when we dedicate a ship to a lost hero, we try to have the family present at the christening. We needed you there." He smiles, "You seem tired. Are you all right?"

"I'm fine. Thank you, Admiral."

"So, given the circumstances in Britain right now, Admiral Lee has taken the liberty of arranging quarters for both you, and Mrs. Bond, at the Navy Yard in DC."

"We would be denying some other officer suitable quarters?"

"He and I have been batching it. They insist that admirals need a huge house. So, he's offered to look out after you. His girlfriend, Ashley Smith, will be there to get you settled. He wanted me to introduce you to her."

Audrey, "I think we should return to England and face the Hun like our neighbors."

Ren reaches for her hand, "Lady Holtz…"

"Please, call me Audrey."

"Audrey, there's nothing noble in war. It's hell, pure and simple. But something good must come of this to give meaning to all the rest. In you grows the future my friend will never know. Please stay here in America where you and your baby can be safe."

She nods, and looks at Donna, "Yes, and thank you."

PEENEMUNDE, GERMANY

1235, 25 September, 1942 (1335 GMT)

Hitler walks around the Vereltungswaffe 1 missile sitting on its launch rail. It's painted in alternating black and white for easy visibility. There's a large scoop intake on the top of the fuselage for the turbojet engine in the rear. Hitler touches the missile, "Why have you moved the engine from above the fuselage?"

Wernher von Braun says, "We have learned much more about the jet engine and it makes sense. A turbojet does not need perfectly uninterrupted air flow. Also, by placing the engine in the rear of the fuselage, we may store and transport the missiles in smaller containers."

"Doctor, explain the benefit of smaller transport?"

"Mein Fuhrer, first, a truck or train car may carry more missiles. Second, field storage may have more. Third, Mein Fuhrer, if we make the missile small enough, it can be launched from a submarine."

"Ah. I see. Very good, doctor. This one is to be fired, yes?"

"Of course, Mien Fuhrer. This is an early production model and not an experimental missile."

"Carry on, then."

GENERAL EISENHOWER'S OFFICE, ETOUSA, CAMP GRIF-FITH, BUSHY PARK, LONDON

1145, 25 September, 1942

'You know, General Altman, I expect initiative from my officers, and a certain amount of pride is to be expected. However, your pig-headed arrogance could have cost us everything. The war would be lost if not for the tenacious determination of a handful of Navy pilots and their superb commanders. I cannot have someone in my command who holds their own pride above the success of our entire endeavor. You sir, are dismissed from the service. Now, sign this letter of resignation."

"And, if I don't, sir?"

"Oh hell, Altman. If you don't, I'll clap you in irons and you will face your crimes."

"Crimes, sir. What crimes?"

"Dereliction of duty. Disobeying a direct order. That, and treason. Hell of an end to a career, Altman. Now, sign the fucking letter."

Altman takes the pen and writes his signature, his hands shaking.

Eisenhower looks at him sadly, "There's a transport leaving RAF Kenley in three hours. These gentlemen will escort you and make sure you're on it. Pack your bags and get on it."

GENERAL WEBER'S HQ, OCCUPIED FRANCE

1255, 25 September, 1942 (1155 GMT)

Weber studies a map of England. He can see the positions of the German armored units and what is known of the Allied forces. "I need to know what airfield the ant-tank jets far flying from."

"Yes, General."

"The British fleet are no longer in the North Sea. They appear to have retreated. They're not in Scapa, Portsmouth, or Plymouth. In the short term, they are no longer a factor."

"Yes, sir. The Fuhrer wants the port facilities destroyed."

"True. But the priority must be destroying the American jet fighters. When they are gone, we can destroy everything else at our leisure."

"What should we do?"

"We use the enemy's strength against them."

GENERAL MOTORS PLANT, DETROIT, MICHIGAN

0615, 25 September, 1942 (1215 GMT)

LTJG James Maki stands in the rain as a Marine tank comes to a stop. With him are Admiral Klindt, a Marine brigadier general and several civilian engineers, but they all look at him. SGT Thompson and his men climb out of the tank. Maki shakes his head, "Sorry, General, but it's a steaming pile of shit. It's too slow, too unstable, poorly armored, and the 37mm gun is pathetic."

The brigadier glares at him, "Lieutenant, you can do better?"

"Sir, I need guidelines. First, what kind of fuel. Gasoline is way more flammable than diesel Do you still want gas?"

"Yes, everything else we have runs on gasoline. The tank should, too."

"Yes, sir. What's the biggest gun made today that uses a single shell and powder charge?"

"The 75mm in the Sherman is one piece."

"Too small, sir. The German '88's would eat you up. The M-60 used a 105. Are we making a 105 today?"

"We're making a low velocity Howitzer near that size."

Maki sighs, "Sir, it needs to be high velocity if it's going to be accurate and penetrate armor."

Vice Admiral Klindt says, "I'll get you a gun with fixed ammunition, high velocity, and at least 100mm. What else do you need."

Maki is silent, then, "The undercarriage is critical. If it rides well, it shoots well. I'll work on it with the GM people. I'll start mocking up an interior right away so we know what shape it should be. I know the army was using composite armor in 1990, but I've no idea how it works. I'll start building sample armor so the Marines can test it, until we have something that works. We'll mock up the undercarriage to see how easy it is to work on. Sir, I need money, and the characteristics of the gun. Also, any intel we can get on the German tanks."

"Not worried about Japanese tanks?"

"It's a different kind of war in the Pacific. If the tank holds up to Hitler, it will hold up to Tojo."

Klindt smiles, "Okay, Maki, I'll assign someone to handle the bills. I'll have gun characteristics in no more than two weeks and a prototype gun in a month to five weeks. Give me a prototype in two months."

Maki, "Yes, sir."

A GM manager asks, "Admiral, how many do you want?"

Klindt turns to the brigadier, "How many for the Corps, and say, half the Army?"

The Brigadier says, "Gentlemen, we can give you a firm number in a week or so. For the Corps, we need at least two thousand tanks. The Army will need ten times that number. The order is contingent on testing." He turns, "Maki, that means it's contingent on you."

Maki salutes, "Yes, sir."

The flag officers walk to their waiting car. The brigadier asks Klindt, "Do you think a lieutenant can actually build a tank?"

"He's smart. He figured out how to shoe horn two turrets into the space for one on the Long Beach. He can do this, and his dad served in the army."

"If he messes this up?"

"Then, you'll still have the piece of shit you've already bought. Send a smart marine to help him, but don't forget, I put him in charge."

CONTROL, RAF ALCONBURY

1230, 25 September, 1942

Spike is reading reports as she listens to the radio and the plotters below her in the pit. Swede and Trollop are fighting FU-279s east of Newcastle and Hot Pants has scramble to meet a raid coming in from the south. She's reviewing the status of ordered materials when she hears, "Yankee control, Navy 120 requests to land on runway 24."

She looks up, "What's Navy 120?"

"A transport flight, Commodore. They're on the list."

She picks up the mic, "Navy 120, Yankee actual, if you have fuel available advise you land at RAF Kenley."

"Understood. I would very much prefer Yankee."

"Acknowledged. You are cleared. Switch to 170 decimal 4 for the tower."

"170 decimal 4, Yankee, Navy. Good day."

She goes back to her papers, then stops, sets them down, and walks outside. She walks through a soft rain and sees the ceiling is at about 3000 feet. She goes through a hard shelter and out onto the flight line. Fluffy walks out to join her, "Spike, do we have VIPs coming?"

Looking off to the west, she answers, "I don't know, Fluffy. The call sign is Navy 120."

"Only an unassigned aircraft takes 'Navy' as a call sign."

"I know." She watches two aircraft, in formation, break out of the clouds. Her heart rate elevates and she tells herself they can't be German. As they grow larger, she realizes the profiles of the F-14.

Admiral Lee sees her standing in the rain, "Einstein, make it crisp. Downwind, now. Break, now."

Spike starts to smile. Watching the break, her smile grows larger, "New birds, Fluffy. Dixie is bringing us new birds. Look, their even painted with the Black Knight tail insignia." The aircraft land together and roll down the runway in formation, then turn and roll onto the taxiway. As they come to stop, "Fluffy, get the guys out here to turn these birds around. We have a third flight."

"Roger that, Spike. I'm on it." For such a large man, Fluffy can really run.

Spike is soaked through and grinning like a fool, and she doesn't care. Dixie finishes shutting it down and pops the canopy. "Darlin, didn't your momma teach you to stay out of the rain?"

"Dad, you just made my day." The ground crew runs by her and take over the new planes. They help the pilots down, and Dixie walks into her arms for a hug. "I've missed you, darlin."

"I've missed you, too."

Around them is chaos: the ground crews are checking the planes over after their long flight, the ordinance crew wheel out missiles and gun ammo, and a fuel truck pulls up. The crew pause just long enough to salute and get back to work. Thud, Speedy, Shotgun, and Packs walk out in their flight gear. Thud salutes, "Anything we need to know about the new birds, sir?"

Dixie laughs, "My God, it's like you knew we were coming. You're all ready to go. Okay, you have to dim the HUD manually, but at least you have one. The wings transition a smidge faster. These birds have air to ground and terrain following that you'll need to be trained on. If you select ground on the target designation switch, it selects the HUD and VID to air or ground. Bomb release is available whenever the master arm is selected, but in air to ground it's more accurate. The RIO can select ordinance as before. The cameras work the same, and on screen, he can designate and laze targets for laser guided bombs. We don't have the laser yet, but it's coming. Oh, you can still fire the gun in air to ground, but the setting assumes you're strafing."

Thud says, "Thank you, sir." He salutes and the four men man up the birds.

Dixie shakes his head and smiles at Spike, "That's done. I need the head and is there coffee in our future." He motions Einstein forward. "This is Einstein, Grumman's test pilot and my ferry wingman. Einstein, Spike. I'm sorry, Commodore Hunt."

Please to meet you, ma'am. The Admiral is right, though. Head?"

Spike laughs, "Absolutely. Back through here." And guides the two men inside the hard shelter.

Later, in the officer's mess hall with plates of bread, roast beef, beans, and carrots, and mugs of coffee, Lee asks, "How are you doing?"

"We're preparing to evacuate, Dad. The army has no real idea where the Germans are and I'm concerned they're heading south quickly."

"The Warthogs helping?"

"God, yes. They've already shifted operations to Kenley. We're moving people and equipment as fast as we can. Soon, we'll be there as well."

"You're dodging the question, Sam."

Cooper walks in, "Spike, Cargo Britches wants permission to drop supplies to Cuddles in Scotland and Wingnut south of Durham."

"Approved. Give her a SAM update before she leaves."

Cooper leaves and Chief Robert 'Bobby' Gellar walks up, "Spike, Swede is in the air and we need to know what to do with Thud's and Hot Pants' birds."

"Is Thud's flyable?"

"Sort of. We have the engines and controls replaced. The cockpit and seats are good. The thing is, the wing swing motors went south with the actuators. The landing gear won't even retract. We could lock everything in place for a subsonic, non-combat flight, but if they get jumped the crew is toast."

"Set it up and arrange a flight back by chopper. I'll fly it in a minute."

"No, ma'am. No. I know you can fly it, but we can't be without you."

Einstein looks up from his food, "I'll fly it. I can't do combat, making me the most expendable pilot here."

Sam makes eye contact with the test pilot and nods her head, "Approved. What about Houlihan's bird?"

"It's on a truck somewhere between Darlington and RAF Dishforth. I'm worried the Germans will capture it."

"Are we in communication with the people moving it?"

"Through the RAF, yes."

"Order it destroyed."

"That leaves us with four, maybe five birds, ma'am."

"Admiral Lee just flew in two new birds. Blow it, Bobby."

"Yes, ma'am," and Bobby leaves.

Lee watching, "You don't catch a break, do you?"

"Of all people, you know what it means to be in charge."

"I asked if you are okay?"

She meets his gaze, "Dad, I don't know that I'll ever be all right."

"I see that. Your eyes have that million-mile exhaustion to them. When was the last time you slept?"

"I get sleep. Swede, Thud, and Radar see to that. I'm worried, Dad."

"The Germans?"

"Failure, Dad. It's on the line. No one is getting enough rest. Our equipment is running down, and people are beginning to make mistakes. It's inevitable. The German are building fighters faster than we can destroy them, and their pilots are getting better. Their new fighter is damn near parity with ours."

"What plane is that?"

"The guys are calling it the Tiger because it looks like an F-5, but it's larger and the engines have more thrust. It can turn with us and out climb us. We have a better roll rate, better acceleration, and better missiles. Lord knows how long that will last."

"I've ordered the first twelve '14s to be shipped to you. If you need more, I'll send more. We're training pilots, but they're flying F-1 War Eagles right now. I want them checked out on the Tomcat before I send them to you."

She nods, "Dad, I know you're doing all you can. I just hope it's enough. Up until the invasion, we prevented a single bomb from landing on British soil. Now, we've lost most of the home fleet and several cities and ports have been hit. They really nailed Portsmouth and Plymouth. The London docks have been hit a few times, too. They're all depending on me and I don't know what else to do."

"You're doing fine. You haven't left anything undone. I've no doubt the folks here are grateful."

"Do you know about the fuck up with the device?"

"Yes, I do. Is there a place for it in Kenley?"

"Yes, it's being dealt with. I'll fly it down when we shift. Should we have just dropped the damn thing? Would that end the war faster?"

"Maybe, but it isn't your decision. It's a good thing that it isn't."

MI-5 HQ, LONDON, ENGLAND

1341, 25 September, 1942

Sir David Petrie sits facing Undersecretary Malcolm Cox, assistant to Deputy Prime Minister Atlee. "So, please describe to me your actions on the morning of 23, September, 1942.

Cox, squirms in his chair, then sits upright, "I was reviewing dispatches for PM Attlee, as is my assignment."

"Is it your assignment to send dispatches?"

"No."

"Could you please describe for me a misfiled dispatch regarding an operation called Rosebud?"

"I read so many."

"Yes, of course you do, but...you sent only one."

"Um...I said I wasn't authorized..."

"Of course, you aren't, and for a damn good reason. Now quit lying to me. Out with it. We already know exactly what you did."

Cox deflates, slumping, "I was told to look for dirt on the Tory party to use after the war. The memo was a mission to bomb Berlin. Why wouldn't we bomb Berlin? We're at war."

"So, you took it on yourself to forge the Prime Minister's signature and order an American attack unit to risk itself in an attack on Berlin. The very unit that has kept us alive and in the war. Without the Yanks where would we be?"

"They survived."

"Several did not. So, you admit your complicity in this matter?"

Cox nods his head.

Petrie slides over paper and pen, "Very well. I need it in writing, and this time sign your own signature."

Cox looks up, "What will become of me?"

"You will stand trial in a secret court and likely spend what is left of your life in prison. That, sir, is too good an end for you, if you ask me."

FIELD SOUTH OF DURHAM

1406, 25 September, 1942

A helicopter hovers and LT 'Wingnut' Urland, his arm in a sling, climbs in. "Cargo Britches, can you move me and a squad south?"

"Where?"

"Ahead of the Germans. I've been calling in the Warthogs."

"I know. I brought you a new radio and supplies."

"The German push is south of us and we need to get ahead."

"Okay. Yogi off-load the supplies for the rest of the airborne and get Wingnut's squad aboard." Moments later, they lift off, barely clearing the ground, and Cargo Britches transitions to forward flight at speed. She only climbs to avoid trees and buildings.

Wingnut puts on a crew helmet. "The Germans passed us about eight hours ago. Do you know where the Brits plan to meet them?"

"Yeah, at the river Tees. We'll be there in a bit. How bad are you hurt?"

"Fucked up my shoulder and arm. I can't fly, but I can do this."

"Yeah, the Warthog boys swear by you and Cuddles."

"We got split up. Where is he?"

"Near a place called Bardon Mill. They're facing a mix of Panzers and motorized infantry."

NORTH OF BARDON MILL, NORTHUMBERLAND, UK

1410, 25 September, 1942

LT Gus 'Cuddles' Grant stands on a hill watching the battle in front of him unfold. They've been facing the Panzer 4, a damn fine tank. Down below, the Churchill tanks of the 51st Leeds Rifles, Royal Tank Regiment have just positioned themselves on the road south. Brigadier James Noel Tetley walks up beside him, "Well, Lieutenant, you've seen the Hun in action. Are there any suggestions you might share?"

"Sir, the training units using the Covenanter tanks out of Penrith have been mauled. Their rounds bounce off the German tanks."

"The Covenanter is an older tank operated by trainee crews. Our Churchills are brand new. I should hope we fare much better."

"Sir, why did your army name a tank after the Prime Minister?"

"Oh heavens, no, good boy. It's named after his ancestor, John Churchill, 1st Duke of Marlborough. He was quite an able leader as well."

Cuddles nods, "I see. Well, if your tankers hold off until the Germans are close, you might be able to hit their vulnerable points."

"And where might those be?"

"The driver and gunner's view ports."

"Hit a two-inch by twelve-inch spot on a moving tank? You think highly of our marksmanship."

Cuddles looks at him, "I'll do my best with the Warthogs, sir, but if your boys can't precisely hit the Germans, then they're going to die. Hitler seems to have sent his best to Britain. They are not going to miss."

The radio operator, "Reconnaissance reports they have contact, sir."

Tetley puts his binoculars to his eyes and looks east. "Very well."

Cuddles turns on his new radio, "Any hog flight, Cuddles."

"Cuddles, Dog flight 3, over." They see a Churchill tank explode. "Dog 3, Cuddles, troops in contact. We are taking effective fire north of Bardon Mill. Grid coordinates to follow."

CHAPTER 9

VALKYRIE 1, NEAR DARLINGTON, COUNTY DURHAM, UK

1428, 25 September, 1942

Cargo Britches keeps her SH-3 close to the deck as she flies south. As they race across a large field, small arms fire sparkles from a partly obscured vehicle. Cargo Britches, "Action, left."

Yogi mans the 7.62mm Gatlin gun and opens up. In a buzzing roar, the vehicle explodes. Moments later they fly over a line of German tanks and Yogi takes a swipe at them, hitting a commander standing in his hatch. A minute later, they drop Wingnut and his re-supplied squad off at a farm house just north of Hurworth on Tees.

The farm yard is full of tanks and other vehicles. Wingnut walks up to the house and is stopped by a British private, "Name, unit, and ID, sir."

"Lieutenant Urland, Black Knights," and presents his ID. The private salutes. Wingnut grabs him by the collar with his good hand, "Are you trying to get us killed? You don't salute on a battlefield."

"Sir, we're in England."

"Yep, and the Germans are entering Darlington right now." He lets the soldier go and walks through the door.

Inside, LT. Colonel Middleton, says, "Captain, you do not man-handle the men."

"Lieutenant Urland, VF-154 squadron, sir. Tell your men not to salute in a combat zone, sir. If I get shot, I get shot. I just don't want to die a stupid death when we have so much on the line."

You're one of those Yank fliers, then. The Hun is nowhere near. Right now, the thing is to evacuate the citizens and prepare a proper reception."

"Sir, we took small arms fire outside of Darlington. Unless you have a defensive line there, they'll be here inside of an hour."

"You're certain?"

"Yes, absolutely, incontrovertibly, beyond doubt, certain. They're coming. The only question is whether you'll hold or get crushed. I'll do what I can, but you need to get ready."

"It'll be several hours before the civilians are withdrawn. We must hold."

"Yes, sir. Find yourself a defensive line, and dig like mad."

The Colonel turns to a map, "Captain Smith, put all units out to form a circle that covers the town and both bridges. Tell the men to dig in."

"Yes, sir."

Wingnut, "Sir, I need a church steeple or other high vantage point. I have to see to guide in the A-10s and other aircraft."

"I'll see what can be done."

FLIGHTLINE, RAF ALCONBURY

1520, 25 September, 1942

Spike and Lee walk out to their '14s in their flight gear. Lee, "I promise. Just one mission."

"Okay. Stay on my wing. I get it, Dad." Lizard and Packs are pre-flighting the birds. A few minutes later, they're taking off in formation into the setting sun. Then they curve north, flying in uncharacteristic clear skies.

Then Einstein lifts off in Thud's bird and slowly climbs to 5000 feet as Spike and Dixie orbit above him. Then, on radio,

"Arthur flight, Whiskey Bravo Bravo, raid warning south. Designate raid 27. Ten bandits climbing through angels 25 at 500 knots at your 175 and 200 miles."

Lizard on radio, "Roger, Whiskey Bravo Bravo. Arthur is inbound. Packs, dark." On intercom, "You want a dark approach, right?"

"Yes, Lizard. Good call."

"Boss, is Admiral Lee your father?"

"He's sort of adopted me."

"Cool. He's an awesome guy. You know he and Papa were close."

"Yeah, Lizard, I know."

"Did Dixie, like, just ask to be your Dad?"

"Lizard, I've known Dixie since my first deployment in Hawkeyes. We're legitimately close."

"I know you are. Now, I kinda know why. Sorry for prying."

Spike smiles, "It's okay, Lizard. You know Audrey is in the States?"

"I didn't. Where? If she needs, I can set her up at my grandparents place in Milwaukee."

"She flew over to launch a new destroyer. Now, she's staying at Dixie's with Donna Bond.

"What destroyer?"

"The USS James Holtz, DDG-1. Dixie just told me."

"Oh my God! Papa is getting a boat. Cool."

On radio, "Arthur 1, raid 27 is 100 miles out at your front."

Lizard, "Roger, Whiskey. Packs, illuminate." On intercom, "Boss, ten at 32. I have lock."

"Volley." She fires off all four AIM-1s. One fails to track and tumbles ahead of them and she pulls up to avoid it, "Grunt."

The other three find their targets and one '262 goes up in a fire ball and other is hit in the tail and pitches nose down and spins into the sea. Lizard, "Splash 2."

Packs, "Splash 3."

Lizard, "They're boring in."

Spike, "Okay. Vertical thatch weave."

Lizard on radio, "Thatch, go down."

"Grunt." And Spike climbs and Dixie inverts in a dive. They both roll so they can see the enemy. Four are diving and one is climbing to meet her. Air brakes out, wings forward, she inverts and pulls her nose over. As her nose crosses the enemy jet, she fires her gun. She misses and the German rolls away. She puts on her afterburners and dives after him.

HAUPTMANN (CAPTAIN) HEINRICH GUNTER'S ME-262B

He has to roll out of position to avoid the gun fire and the big navy jet passes before he can regain his line. They pass so close he sees her flags, "It's the Drachendame!"

Arthur 1

Spike maneuvers in the dive, trying to get lead on another jet. Dixie passes her, "Sidewinder. Tone. Fox 2." The missiles twists toward the German.

GUNTER'S '262

Gunter, "Red 6, flares, break, break!" The sidewinder changes lock to a flare and misses. "Stay on your game." He dodges machine gun fire from the Lee's '14. He quickly pulls back in and the two nearly collide. "Fuck." He rolls away and pulls back toward the Drachendame, watching as another of his precious planes spirals into the sea.

ARTHUR 1

Her second AIM-9 finds a target. Lizard, "Dixie is playing with the leader. One V One, five up."

"He's got it." She rolls into a tight turn, "Grunt." And she's in a one circle fight with a '262. There is no way the German jet can win this. The issue is the other jets, "Where are they?"

"We've got one on our six!"

Packs on radio, "Spike, break left!"

She snap rolls left and climbs, "Grunt." She sees Dixie diving on the bird behind her and switches to the leader. He's trying to get onto Dixie's six. She lines up and takes the shot, the rounds hit the fuselage and the German breaks off.

They hear, "Splash 1."

The three remaining jets break off and bug out south. She climbs back to 35,000 feet, "Lizard, when he's back on my wing, let's do a damage check."

"Roger that, Boss." That last one, did we get it?"

"I don't know."

Lizard on radio, "Arthur 2, Arthur 1, damage check."

They circle each other and find no damage.

AUCKLAND CASTLE, BISHOP AUCKLAND, DURHAM, UK

1526, 25 September, 1942

The Rommel's Headquarters unit pulls to a stop in front of the 12th century castle. Troops run from the vehicles and run in to secure the castle. An Anglican priest in a black suit and clerical collar steps from the main door and finds the muzzle of a rifle in his face. The soldier butt strokes him to the ground and runs into the building.

Field Marshal Rommel climbs from his tank and walks to

the four-wheeled reconnaissance vehicle that is his communications track. He can hear General Weber shouting on the radio, "Tell command it is imperative that the American attack planes be given priority. If we lose our armor it's all for naught!"

The reply from Germany is faint. "We understand. The Fuhrer wants the Drachendame and her fighters destroyed."

Rommel picks up the microphone, "This is 4th Corp speaking. The attack planes disrupt and delay our operations. When you kill them, the navy fighters must come and also be destroyed."

There is a pause, then, "The 4th Corps will be supported."

Rommel says, "Good. We hold RAF Ouston, near Newcastle. If you fly out of there, less fuel is needed and the Americans must defend in two directions. Would Herr Goering be acceptable with this?"

He hears Weber, "Yes, Herr Field Marshal. I'm told he suggested much the same."

"Make the arrangements."

"Yes, Herr Field Marshal."

"Thank you, General Weber."

"Heil Hitler."

CUDDLES NEAR BARDON MILL

1541, 25 September, 1942

The British are being pushed back by the closing German tanks. The air is saturated with the smell of burning metal and gasoline and human flesh. The British leave over a dozen destroyed tanks on the field and fall back, hemmed in by the river to their south and rugged terrain to their north. The real enemy is the precise fire of the German artillery. Out gunned and under-manned, the Brits fight on, managing to take out a few more German Panzers, but unable to destroy their artillery.

Cuddles hears on radio, "Cuddles, Dog flight, 1 is inbound your location."

Cuddles, "Dog flight 1, best approach from the southwest. No observable surface to air. Battle line is north to south just east of the town."

"Roger, Cuddles. Three mikes out."

Cuddles, "Sir, the Warthogs are three minutes out."

"Good, very good." They watch another Churchill tank blow up. Then another. Brigadier Tetley says, "What the bloody hell? The Hun tanks are falling back?"

Another Churchill explodes. Cuddles picks up his binoculars. Scanning the area, he spots movement in the distance. Then he sees the flash of a gun and another Churchill is gone. "Sir, they're bringing in a new tank." He points out their position. On radio, "Dog 1, Cuddles, there's a group of tanks on the rise east of town. They are your target."

"Wilco, Cuddles. Have you identified their type?"

"Negative, but they're chewing us up."

FINAL APPROACH, RAF KENLEY, SOUTH OF LONDON, UK

1722, 25 September, 1942

Spike breaks through the overcast and into the rain on the brief flight from Alconbury. She flies over suburbs and villages on the approach to RAF Kenley, passes over a road and is over the base. Her tires chirp on the tarmac and she lays on the brakes. Following directions to a small taxiway, she comes to a stop as armed Marines surround her bird and ammo handlers push out a cart. "Okay, Lizard, sorry, time to get wet." She opens the canopy and climbs down.

LCDR Chatman salutes, "Commodore, do you want to see the new digs?"

"Please." The weapons shelter was hastily put together. Inside are exposed brick walls and steel columns and beams. She looks around, "Does it leak?"

"So far, no. They sealed the outside with concrete." They watch the device being wheeled in.

"Okay, if there's a problem let me know soonest."

"Will do. Are you doing all right, Commodore?"

"Yes, thank you for asking, Chatman."

"No problem. By the way, after your dog fight carrying the gadget we gave it a full inspection and tested all the circuits. No damage."

"Good, thank you. By the way, when is your engineers board?"

"I don't know yet."

Spike smiles, "We have the fight of our lives ahead of us, but we can't forget, there will be a tomorrow."

CUDDLES NEAR BARDON MILL

Cuddles and Tetley watch as the A-10s take out tank after tank on the eastern ridge, but it's not enough. The A-10s, out of fuel and ammo, have to leave, and still the Germans advance.

Cuddles, "I've got Spitfires, Hurricanes, and Mosquitoes coming in, but I don't know what they can do against these tanks. We have to try."

"Agreed. We have to plan our retreat. I've just received word that the Germans are redeploying their artillery."

SPIKE'S F-14, IN FRONT OF HER NEW HANGER, RAF KENLEY

The ground crew pushes her jet into a large wooden hanger where Admiral Lee is waiting with his flight bag. Seeing him, Spike smiles, and she and Lizard complete the shutdown. She climbs down and grins, "Are they letting you fly the transport?"

"Nope, it seems I'm to be a passenger. In fact, me and Einstein are the only passengers."

"How many people can that thing hold?"

"With seats, over a hundred."

"Could you talk them into a couple of flights out of Alconbury to get the civilians out? I need to evacuate the families who our people have grown attached to. These guys fight for the people they love. It would kill them to lose girlfriends and wives, again. Fluffy and Hamm are setting up the evacuation."

"Will do, darlin. Three stars ought to get it done."

"Thanks, Dad," and hugs him. "Fly careful."

"Always, darlin. I'll be back tomorrow with two more. I'm the gift that just keeps on giving," he laughs. "I love you, Sam. Be careful." He turns and walks to the waiting C-56.

She watches him until he's inside the plane. As she turns, Cooper appears at her elbow, "Shower or Control Center?"

"Control Center."

He walks her out the back door of the hanger and along a cobble path. They climb into a jeep, "Where are we going?"

"Under the tower."

"What tower?"

"See the water tower over there? That's the field tower. It's British camouflaging. You'll see."

"Okay, Does the barracks look like a stack of hay?"

"Nope, it's too late in the season for that. It looks like a grove of trees."

"I'm in Oz." The water tower appears to be on a hill, but the hill is really camouflage netting and canvas hiding a building and a car park. They go under the netting and Radar parks the jeep in a spot marked 'Commodore.' "And I have my own parking spot. Wait, Radar, where did you get the jeep?"

"I requisitioned it from Eisenhower's staff. They said I could have what I wanted, so I got twenty jeeps, five trucks, and I'm waiting on a bus."

"A bus?"

"This field is more spread out than Alconbury. We need the transport."

"Okay, Cooper. So, you got the transport. The jeeps are for getting pilots from the quarters to the field?"

"Yes, and the bus is for getting them from the ready room to the field in one go. Also, I thought a base bus would help the enlisted guys get around the place. We're spread out."

"Is there a gym?"

"Yes, and a ball field that can double as a parade ground. The Brits have an 'O' club and an 'E' club right on the base. Whyteleafe is just off base and it has several pubs. Are we going to be here long enough to do construction projects?"

"I don't know. It depends on the Germans. Get the base commander and we'll plan what we want."

"Spike, you are the base commander."

"What? How did that happen?"

"You're the senior officer. This was a Spitfire and Hurricane field. Most of those squadrons are refitting to the Griffin west of here. We have the A-10s and one squadron of Griffins that are now under your command. I haven't met the CO yet because he's in the air. I'll introduce him when he gets back."

"Okay, I need to meet the base operations officer. We need hard shelters."

The walk into the Control Center, a one-story wood building with the tower rising from one end. As she walks into the control room, a watch officer from Alconbury stands up, "Lancelot 1 and 2 are engaged with a raid twenty miles south of Newcastle. Galahad 1 and 2 are returning from an engagement east of London sans ordinance. We are cycling your flight around to launch. Texas flight 2 is engaging a raid of 16 east of Scapa. Miami flight 1, 2, and 3 are supporting a bombing raid against Bremerhaven. Chicago flight 2..."

"Wait. What are we doing bombing Bremerhaven?"

"I don't know, Commodore. The orders came from 8th Air Force and British Bomber Command."

"Who's covering the A-10s?

"No one, Commodore, except, we can redirect our flights if we need to."

"Continue."

"A-10s are supporting troops near Brandon Mill, just west of Newcastle. The British Army there is falling back to the west and north. We just got word that troops are in contact at Hurworth-On-Tees. It's west of Middlesbrough. We dispatched Dog flight 2."

"Do we know how big the invasion is yet?"

"Intel has it at five divisions. We know of the 1st, 8th, and 10th Panzer divisions. The other two are unknown."

"How many tanks in a Panzer division?"

"I don't know, Commodore."

Thud, from the door, "Three to five hundred tanks, depending on their configuration. Because of the focus of the invasion, I would assume the higher number."

Spike nods, "Thud, how many tanks per sortie can an A-10 kill?"

"About five or six. They've a lot of ammo, but the gun fires insanely fast."

"Okay, five divisions of five hundred tanks. That's twenty-five hundred tanks. We have twenty-one aircraft. Even in ideal conditions, it would take five days to reduce the invasion by air power alone. In five days, London will be gone if the army can't stop them. We need a strategy that will work. I need a helicopter and an appointment to see Eisenhower."

The Asst. Section Officer says, "Commodore, the headquarters is only twelve miles away."

"Oh," she turns to one of the communications sergeants, "Please patch me through to Eisenhower's office."

"Yes, Commodore."

A moment later, she picks up the phone, "Commodore Hunt."

"Commodore, this is General Smith. How may I help you?"

"I need to talk numbers with General Eisenhower and his staff. Thus far, we've been scrambling, protecting units as they call for it. If we don't create a more focused and effective air campaign, we are likely lose."

"Eisenhower has a meeting with the British Army and Airforce in 25 minutes. I'll set up a meeting afterwards for a few minutes."

"Can I attend that meeting?"

"I assumed you couldn't get here. You certainly can."

"I'll be there. Thank you." She hangs up, "Cooper, jeep, now. Thud, you got it," and starts for the door.

Cooper, running after her, "Shouldn't you change?"

"No time. Can you find Eisenhower's HQ?"

"Only been there once, but I've someone who can." He pokes his head back through the door, "Sergeant Valentine, we need you to drive us to Bushy Park." A pretty young brunette in the British WAAF uniform leaves her station and follows them out.

BRIEFING ROOM, NAS PENSECOLA, FLORIDA

1148, 25 September, 1942 (1648 GMT)

LCDR Truman 'Johnny' Walker stands in front of a chalk board, his cane leaning against the podium, his starched khaki uniform looking like it could stand by itself. "Pokryshkin, you chose to reverse in front of your adversary. Why?"

"I knew his timing would have to be perfect to hit me and by starting a yoyo in that direction, I could maintain my energy and pull onto his six."

"Did it work?"

"No. As I rolled over, he went vertical. It resulted in vertical scissors."

"Ensign Nix, why did you choose to go vertical."

"I needed more energy to stay with him. I knew he could yoyo, so I engaged afterburner and pull vertical, rolling to keep him in sight. When he spotted my move, he reciprocated, but now our energy was more closely matched, so I pulled back on the throttle a bit to get on him."

Walker, "Pokryshkin?"

"As he said, we were matched. I pulled so we could cross and elected to disengage, looking for distance to set up another attack. Equal is not good odds. He saw my maneuver and attempted to follow."

"Nix?"

"I did, but I wasn't on top of my airspeed. I needed a less violent maneuver. Instead, I tumbled. By the time I recovered, he had me."

Walker smiles, "Lessons learned? Pokryshkin?"

"At the beginning, I guessed his maneuver, rather than observed it. It could have cost me the fight. My decision to disengage was a good one."

"Nix?"

"I was right to deny him the fight, but I was too aggressive afterward and not attentive to my energy."

"Good. Popova and Boyington, your next."

CHAPTER 10

CAMP GRIFFITH, BUSHY PARK, LONDON

1715, 25 September, 1942

Spike, still in her flight suit and gear, including her pistol, walks into Eisenhower's headquarters. She hasn't taken three steps before Brigadier General Walter Smith sees her and clears his throat, "In a flight suit, Commodore? You couldn't be bothered with a uniform change?"

"I just landed a few minutes ago, Brigadier. My apologies, but the Germans seem to be impatient. Where is the meeting?"

"In the future, it would be good of you to dress appropriately."

"In the future, I shall keep that in mind. The meeting, sir?"

Smith frowns, "If you wish to see Eisenhower, you go through me. Do not be flippant with me."

"Jesus Christ! Are you even paying attention to what's going on? There isn't fucking time! I have a war to fight. Show me where the meeting is and go fix a fucking memo. Do not presume to deny me access to Eisenhower, the war may turn on this meeting."

He stares at her, silent, then, "It's the second door on the left."

Eisenhower opens the door and looks out, "There you are. We're just getting started."

Spike joins him in the room with Air Chief Marshal Dowding, Major General George Patton, Major General Ira Eaker of the US 8th Bomber Command, and Lieutenant General Kenneth Anderson in command of the British I Corps. Eisenhower says, "I apologize for not inviting you. I recognize how busy you are."

"Thank you, sir."

Eisenhower asks, "Can we beat the Germans in the air?"

"They're making an all-out effort, sir. We've shot down at least forty German jets in the last two days, and they keep sending more. Sir, we just received two brand new Tomcats. Tomorrow, we get two more. In two more days, we'll be at full strength for aircraft, but we only have eight air crew, and they have to sleep sometime. Right now, I can keep two to four aircraft in the air indefinitely. That leaves us outnumbered five to one in most engagements.

"We are holding, but we're going to lose aircraft and crews. More are coming, but they'll only have basic flying skills. Right now, we seem to have managed a degree of parity. If we can keep our aircrews alive long enough to exceed their aircraft production rate, we have a chance. I'm sorry if this doesn't answer your question."

Eisenhower turns to Dowding, "Air Marshal?"

"She's right. While we defend, we have few assets available to attack France or Germany. They grow stronger as we grow weaker."

Hunt asks, "Speaking of that, why was there an air raid on Bremerhaven?"

Eaker answers, "Commodore, we cannot win the war with defense alone. We take the war to the enemy."

Spike looks him in the eyes, "By supporting the raid with jet fighters, you pulled the air cover off our A-10's. We desperately need the A-10. They're the only weapon we have that can destroy a tank, besides artillery, and the artillery has not been able to get into a good position yet."

"Were they attacked?"

"Yes, General. By changing the assignments of those fighters without notifying me, we had a gap in coverage that the Germans exploited."

Eisenhower says, "General Eaker will keep you informed of his operations."

Eaker turns to Eisenhower, "Sir, I cannot be kow-towing to an upstart navy split tail."

Eisenhower's face hardens, "General, you will do what you are told. The defense of this nation comes before all other considerations. Instead of bombing Bremerhaven, why didn't you bomb the invading fleet or the German airfields in France or the Lowlands?

"You will not disrespect the Commodore. I have zero tolerance for such inappropriate behavior." He takes a breath, "Let's get back on topic."

Dowding says, "The exchange rate is about thirty to one. How long can the Germans keep coming?"

Eisenhower asks, "How can the Germans build aircraft so fast?"

Spike replies, "Sir, a Brit named Whittle invented the jet engine. It's the Germans, though, who saw the potential. Even if we had not come back in time, the Germans would have fielded jets during the war. What slowed them down was Hitler's indecisiveness and access to materials. They're managing their materials better this time, and Hitler must have been briefed on the value of jet technology.

"The reason the exchange rate is so good is because their training is too short. Most of the pilots we face barely know how to fly their jets. The survivors get better. In time, pilot training will approach something like parity."

Anderson asks, "What do you need in order to beat them?"

"Sir, we need to keep our supplies coming in, especially fuel and missiles. We also need to figure out how to beat them on the ground. All the aerial victories in the world are irrelevant if the island is lost."

Patton says, "Exactly. We need a hammer and anvil. It's what I've been saying, General."

Spike lays out the math on how many tanks per sortie the A-10s can kill, best case. "As I recall, the German tanks were pretty good. Are the British and American tanks doing okay against them?"

Anderson shakes his head, "In truth, no. We're facing two types of tanks. One is the Panzer 4. We fought them in north Africa and struggled to beat them there. Effective tactics, artillery, and numerical superiority can beat them. This new tank, though, has twice to three times our range and its shells can penetrate anything we have. The gun must be bigger than 100mm. Also, even if we hit them, our shells just bounce off."

Eisenhower, "Have we hit them with artillery?"

Anderson, "We've placed artillery behind the lines at the Tees. We should know soon."

Patton, "Commodore, how big were the tank guns in 1990?"

"I've a guy, Frank Jackson, who's an encyclopedia of military information. The state-of-the-art tank in 1990 was the M-1 Abram and it used a German 120mm main gun. I think even the British tanks used it."

Patton, "And armor to match?"

"Yes, the Abrams used what was called composite armor. The info on how the armor was made and its thickness was top secret. I'm sorry, I don't know."

Eisenhower, "We have what we have. Can you're A-10s penetrate the new tanks armor?"

"I'll find out, sir."

Anderson, "But the A-10 only has a 30mm gun. How could it

punch through if our 37mm guns can't?"

Spike, "They can hit in the top and the back. I think most tanks have thinner armor there. Also, velocity has a power of its own. The A-10 gun is extremely fast. It's why they go through ammo so fast."

Anderson, "Very true. Dowding, is there any chance you could bang together an anti-tank plane?"

Dowding, "We've started building Hurricane fighters with two Vickers 40mm cannon. They were for the African campaign, but I'm tasking them here. I'm also modifying Mosquitos to carry four cannon, as we speak. It's hoped they may be a stop gap until sufficient A-10 production is developed."

Spike, "I understand the need, but those aircrews are taking a huge risk. The Germans have SAM's and effective anti-aircraft guns. The wooden fuselage on either aircraft would be cut to swiss cheese."

Dowding looks at Eisenhower, then back to Spike, "You don't understand. The first Battle of Britain was a prelude. We are now fighting for our very existence."

Spike nods, "You're right. I'm sorry..." She stops, lost in thought.

Eisenhower, "Commodore?"

"Sir, we have Goony Birds, um, C-47 Dakotas. We have C-130 Hercules. In Vietnam the Air Force mounted six Gatlin guns out the left side and a sight on the pilots left window in the C-47. It was used for light-skinned vehicles and troop concentrations. One circle would put a bullet in every square inch of a football field. Later, C-130s were built with two 20mm Gatlin guns, two 40mm cannon, and a 105mm howitzer. The bigger calibers allowed accurate fire from higher altitudes. The 105 could practically lay accurate fire from outer space. A pylon turn makes accurate fire possible. It doesn't solve the anti-aircraft problem, but it puts a hell of a lot of firepower in the air."

Eisenhower looks at Dowding, then at Eaker, "How long would it take?"

"I can have a few airborne in a day or two. Learning how to use them will take longer."

Eisenhower, "Anderson, how long can you hold them at the Tees?"

"We want to stop them dead right there, but we've only about a division right now and the Germans are moving fast. That bloody blitzkrieg thing. The Hun seemed focused on the south rather than the north and the bulk of our army is in the south."

"Where's the next line?"

Patton, "Sir, we need to punch through their lines and mess up their rear."

Eisenhower, "Gentlemen, London must not fall. At the right time, we counter attack. Right now, we bleed them and fall back. Marshall and King are mobilizing everything we have. We're loading transports in Ireland. Canada is sending us everything available. What we need, and don't have, is time. We must blunt this attack. Slow them. Bleed them. Then we counterattack and destroy them. Where is the next line?"

Anderson, "We could draw a line north of York where the highlands act as a funnel. It's still a huge front, but it's something." He points to the wall map, "I can get one division there today and prepare defenses."

Spike studies the wall map, thinking.

Eisenhower, "General Patton, that is your line. Move the 3rd and 9th Infantry Divisions into the highlands on each side. Put the 2nd armored Division with the Brits in the center. Move them up as fast as you can."

Spike, "I'll have the A-10s take out the first vehicle in line and force them off the roads. It's the rainy season. If they get bogged down in the wet fields, they should be easier to kill."

Eisenhower looks at her, "Sound tactics. It focuses on the most important thing. Slowing their advance."

Anderson, "I'm told we have irregular forces removing and modifying traffic signs, blowing bridges, and blowing dikes. Hopefully, that will slow them as well."

Spike, "I need to create a class for forward air observers. I have downed pilots doing it right now, but it's not enough."

Eaker, "Why haven't you picked them up? You need the air-crew."

Spike, "They were injured badly enough they can't fly. They're more effective where they are."

Patton smiles, "Good idea, Hunt. I will send you students."

Anderson, "Is it open to my soldiers?"

Spike, "Absolutely. In fact, General Eakers, we could use a few of your men for the job. They're pilots, they would know what information was needed." She smiles at Eakers, "Each group large enough to work independently should have a forward air observer. Would that be a brigade or a battalion?"

Eisenhower, "Battalion. But it will take several classes to cycle enough students." He looks at Eakers, "General, can we count on you?"

Eakers gives a sour look, "Yes, General, but, it's a waste of my people and planes."

Eisenhower, "General, I understand, but that isn't the point right now. England must survive. Do you understand?"

Eakers glowers, "Yes, sir."

Spike, "Our A-10 units will support the training."

Eisenhower, "Okay, then, the next line; from the Humber to the Mersey."

Patton, "When the 1st Armored Division arrives from North

Ireland, where do you want them?"

"Plymouth, I suppose."

Patton, "It's a shorter trip to drop the 1st AD at Lancaster or Black Pool."

Anderson, "The next line should be the Severn to the Wash. General Patton, Lancaster lacks the port facilities to land armor."

Patton, "They'll be landing by landing craft direct to the beach."

Eisenhower, "LCACs. Good idea, George. Do it. Later we may need to circle them around. Our final line is a refused line around London. Hopefully, by then, we'll have sufficient reserves to push back. The Navy is scrambling some amphibious units from the east coast to give us Marines. If they arrive in time, I want them to land behind German lines. As their lines adjust, we counter attack. We now have plan. Adjust your individual plans to align."

He receives a chorus of, "Yes, sir."

Patton, "Are we getting the royal family out?"

Eisenhower, "If you were the King, would you run and leave your subjects behind?"

Anderson, "The King and his family will stay. London must not fall."

Spike, "Our focus with the Black Knights will continue to protect the A-10s, port areas, air fields, then everything else. Functionally, we tend to engage the Germans before we know what they are attacking. I will orient the A-10s to the Tees line and start hitting the Germans on the move. Once you have gunships, Air Marshal, we'll train aircrews and coordinate their use. I'll also request that some be built stateside."

Dowding, "Yes, indeed."

Patton stands, "With your leave, sir, I will get my forces reoriented. They're already moving."

Eisenhower says, "Go, George."

Anderson, "It's a good plan. In fact, it's close to the one I came in here with. Commodore, I'll have my first batch of students to you first thing tomorrow."

Spike smiles, "We'll be ready for them."

Eisenhower, "It's logical. How do you think the Germans will react?"

Anderson, "With maneuver. They'll seek the weak points to strike and blow through. My boys at the Tees will need to be ready to fall back."

Eisenhower, "We save who we can. If they stay ahead of the Germans, have them head to the coast and we'll pick them up. Thank you, gentlemen. Commodore, may I have a word?"

The others leave, but Eakers and Spike stay seated.

Eisenhower, "General, was there something else?"

"General, we're here to bomb German targets, not play, what was it? Forward Air Observer? We need to stop their re-supply and that means bombing into France and Germany."

Eisenhower, "The only bombing you will be doing will be on enemy ships in the channel, and airfields in France and Lowlands. That is the priority. And, General, send pilots and navigators to be trained. We need them right now."

Eakers stands, "General, Commodore." He walks, back stiff, from the room.

Eisenhower turns back to Spike, shaking his head, "I heard you having words with my chief of staff. What was it about?"

"He wanted me in dress uniform at headquarters, sir, and I agree, formal attire is appropriate in most circumstances, but today, there just wasn't time. I only found out about the meeting with twenty-five minutes to get here."

"Understood. Another matter," and he slides a paper across the table.

From: Commander in Chief

To: Commander, Naval Forces United Kingdom, Task Force Yankee

Regarding: Rosebud

Prime Minister's office has determined cause of erroneous order and will brief you soon. At soonest convenience brief SACEUR, General Eisenhower, on the events of 23 September, 1942 regarding Rosebud. Brief General Eisenhower on the general capabilities of the device. Operational control procedures have not changed.

President Franklin D. Roosevelt

Spike looks at the time and date stamp, it arrived while she was on the road. "May I borrow a phone?"

He points, "Of course."

She calls the operations center at Kenley, "This is Commodore Hunt. Is Commanders Jackson or Swedenborg in?"

In a moment, she hears, "Swedenborg."

"Swede, Spike. Did we receive a message numbered...?" and reads off the number code.

"Affirmative. We received it after you left."

"Thank you." She hangs up and turns back to Eisenhower, "I'm sorry, General. On the 23rd, we nearly destroyed Berlin with an atomic bomb. At Kenley, we have a weapon that can destroy a city with one bomb. It uses atomic fusion to release an enormous amount of energy. The only person authorized to order its use is the president, because these weapons are more political than military."

"These? There is more than one?"

"Yes. I don't know how many we have, but I do know Germany is working on a similar project. They could have the bomb at any time. Only our having it, and not using it, can deter other combatant nations from using theirs. It's called mutually assured destruction, or MAD."

"One bomb can level a city? Can you be more precise?"

"Yes. Basically, from ground zero, the spot immediately below the detonation, a radius of five to fifteen miles will be completely destroyed. Almost total destruction and nearly every person dead. Only strongly built concrete structures and only those people underground have a chance of survival.

"A further radius of five to twenty-five miles will have more people survive, in the short term. Many of these will die of radiation sickness. Also, a cloud of radioactive debris will spread downwind, causing more deaths. If it were detonated over Berlin, eighty to ninety-five percent of the population would be killed. How many millions of people that would be depends more on the population density than the device. The ranges vary because the yield, meaning explosive power, is adjustable."

"How...How can one weapon cause such destruction?"

"It is the power of the atom. I'm not the best person to explain it, but basically a helium atom weighs less than two hydrogen atoms. The difference in weight becomes energy using Einstein's equation: E equals MC squared."

"Do you understand what the equation means?"

"Again, I'm not the best, but the speed of light is 186,000 miles per second. That means a very small change in mass, the 'M' is multiplied by the speed of light times itself. It's a function of very big numbers. A couple of pounds of matter could lift an aircraft carrier into orbit."

"Who invented this bomb?"

"Your generation. There are a group of scientists in New Mexico right now designing it. One was dropped on Hiroshima in Japan, and another one on Nagasaki. Hundreds of thousands were killed. It ended the war with Japan."

"You have control of this weapon?"

"The president has control. If we receive an order from him, or Churchill, to launch the mission, we will man up, and go. Only the President can authorize dropping it."

"What happened on the 23rd?"

"We received the order from Churchill to launch the mission. We manned up and took off. In the air, the mission was aborted. That was when we discovered the invasion fleet."

"Who ordered the launch?"

"Churchill."

"May I see this thing?"

"If the President approves it. We keep it surrounded with armed guards who are authorized to use deadly force. Altman tried to force his way in."

"Altman was an ass. He's been removed from military service. Could you get me permission to see it?"

"I'll ask. Also, we have the materials we used to brief Churchill."

"Thank you, Commodore. The battle in front of us takes priority, of course. Another question?"

"Yes, sir?"

"What would prevent you from dropping it without authorization?"

"First, I and two other officers have to decode the authorization code for the mission to be legitimate. Also, the technicians loading it need to know it's a legitimate order in order to arm the device and set the yield. Most importantly, I don't want to have to live with the murder of millions of people."

"So, in the end, it rests on yours and your people's integrity."

"Sir, have you ever killed someone?"

"I'm ordering young men to death right now, Commodore."

"That is different. Your ordering people to chance their lives and some will die. I mean, personally kill another person."

"I haven't."

"I have. I've killed hundreds. I don't want to kill even one more person than I must to end this fucking war. If I'm ordered, I will drop that terrifying weapon. But I hope and pray I never receive that order."

A moment of silence, then, "Thank you, Commodore, I believe we are in agreement. You may go."

CHAPTER 11

USS COLUMBIA CLG-56, WEST OF GUADALCANAL

0430, 26 September, 1942 (1830, 25 September GMT)

The Columbia, her advanced radar and missile suite the best available, leads a battle line of gunships into the Slot. LCDR Shawn Hughes studies the night sky with binoculars, hoping to catch a glint, just in case the radar fails. He's also scanning for breaking waves on the island beaches to port and starboard. Behind them sail the battleships Washington and North Carolina, and behind them are the heavy cruisers Astoria, Minneapolis, and the Australian heavy cruiser, Canberra. Four destroyers are steaming in line on their port side.

The conning officer, LT Weston says, "I miss the Carl Vinson, sir."

"We all do. We got what we got. We have to cover until the Blue Diamonds can night fly. Focus on what you can do and get it right."

The XO, Commander Allister French walks onto the bridge, "A word, Commander."

"Yes, sir?"

"Word from the Commodore, there are no allied vessels or aircraft ahead. Any target, sea or air is hostile."

"Yes, sir."

The Captain wants us to maneuver to give the battle wagons room to fire. Because of our missiles, we are not to engage unless ordered, or we come under fire."

"I understand, sir."

"You said our missiles can be used against ships?"

"Yes, sir, they can. The missile will follow the beam wherever it points. The warhead is small, and I doubt it would do much damage to a battleship, but it would mess up a destroyer."

"How are you adjusting to the deck department?"

"Actually, better than I thought. We've a good bunch in the forecastle. I know I needed the First Lieutenant rotation and I'm thankful to have a good team. Snipes love to pick on boatswains mates; but this snipe is learning otherwise." During the conversation, he watches the sea and shore, "Conn, left standard rudder, come to new course 345."

"Left standard rudder, new course 345. Rudder is left standard."

Shawn says, "Very well."

The XO asks, "Did you see something?"

"Not yet. I just want to keep us in the shore clutter, if they're out there."

On the squawk box they hear the Captain, "Bridge, Combat, enemy spotted 34 miles at 310. Come to new course 025. Make speed 30 knots."

Shawn pushes the button, "025 at 30 knots. Surface contact to port, aye." He releases the button, "Helm, right standard rudder, new course 030. Lee helm make turns for 30 knots."

He receives verbatim repeat backs, and the ship begins to pick up speed. Shawn, "Boatswain of the watch, sound General Quarters, surface action port."

"General Quarters, surface action port, aye." The GQ horn sounds and the announcement is made on the 1MC ship wide circuit.

The motion changes as the light cruiser cuts through the

waves. The XO says, "It feels wrong running from the fight. I understand why, but it just feels wrong."

BRIDGE, IJN NAGATO, ESCORTING SUPPLIES IN THE SLOT NORTH WEST OF GUADALCANAL

Captain Hideo Yano studies the waters ahead of his battleship. To his starboard steams the light cruiser Nachi, in front of four destroyers. Behind him is the battleship Mutsu and heavy cruiser Ashigara. Approaching from the north is the heavy cruiser Kinugasa, light cruiser Naka, and four more destroyers. Behind his group, six transports follow with supplies and troops for Guadalcanal. He smiles. It's an opportunity to hammer the Americans on Guadalcanal and destroy any American ships he finds.

A rating approaches, "Captain, radar has picked up a group of ships approaching from the east."

"Perhaps it's our North Group. Send the blinker signal."

BRIDGE, COLUMBIA

Hughes studies the waters ahead, "Boatswain, remind lookouts there are shoal waters ahead at approximately 350 relative." He walks over to the chart, updated by the quartermaster, and studies it. Then goes out to the port bridge wing with his binoculars. The XO joins him, looking aft toward the battle. Shawn is looking forward. Then minutes later, they hear the firecracker booms of a battleship salvo.

The XO, "We got off the first salvo. Damn, we missed."

Shawn sees a sliver of white in the distance and pushes the squawk box button, "Combat, bridge, what do you have at 005 relative?"

They hear the Captain on the 1MC, "Action forward. Engage with all mounts that can bear. Take evasive."

Shawn looks astern. The gun fire from the Allied and Japanese ships is lighting up the horizon. He steps into the bridge, "Helm, right full rudder."

"Right full rudder, no course given. Rudder is right full."

"Very well." Shawn picks up a phone, "Captain, we're silhouetted by the action astern."

The ship shakes with a near miss. "Good call. High speed zig zag."

Mount 1 and 2 fire their guns, shaking the ship. "Yes, sir." The 6-inch guns on Mount 1 and 2 fire every six seconds, vibrating the whole ship.

The helm, over the roar of the guns firing, "Passing 030, no course given."

Shawn, "Steady as she goes."

Helm, "Steady as she goes. She goes 036."

As it comes to bear, Mount 3 adds to the din. Shawn, "Left full rudder."

"Left full rudder. Rudder is left full, nor course…"

"Right full rudder."

"Right full rudder. Rudder is right full, no course, um given."

Shawn looks at the helm, the man is visibly sweating and growing pale, "Boatswain, relieve the helm!"

Shawn studies the fall of shot raining all around them. He sees two SM-1 missiles launch from the Mark 10 launcher and race toward the distant Japanese war ships. Both hit. "Rudder amidships."

The Boatswain of the watch on the helm, "Rudder amidships, aye."

The relieved helm grabs Shawn's arm, "Sir, I was okay."

Without looking at the man, "Right full rudder. Petty Officer

Balls take the Boatswain's watch."

The young man is motionless, holding onto Shawn's arm. Shawn looks at him, "Now, Balls. Take the watch. Left full rudder." He picks up the phone, "Captain, we're coming about."

Balls releases Shawn's arm and goes to his watch station. They make it three quarters into the turn when they're hit in the aft superstructure. The ship staggers, but keep moving. He dares a glance at the fight and sees three Japanese ships burning, but more are still firing. Two are closing at high speed, "Right full rudder. Boatswain, announce torpedoes in the water."

As the ship straightens and begins to turn back to the right, he says, "Steady as she goes. Counter steer quickly." Two torpedoes pass to port and three to starboard. When the torpedoes pass, the secondary battery opens up on the destroyers. The three main gun mounts continue their withering rate of fire and because of the digital fire control, most shots have been hitting their targets. The Japanese are silhouetted by their own flames.

Shawn on the phone, "Combat, bridge, forward target is an Aoba-class heavy cruiser." Hanging up the phone, "Left full rudder, back full on one and two main engines."

He studies the sea away from the fight, "We're getting close to Buena Vista Island. Boatswain, remind the lookout to focus on navigation, not the battle."

The ship shakes in the turn. The burning Japanese cruiser fires a broad side from its two remaining turrets. A shell hits, and the deck jumps, throwing Shawn into the air.

His eyes snap open as he comes to, and he pushes off the floor. The bridge is illuminated by battle lanterns and the reflection from the flames forward. The helmsman is struggling to the wheel and most of the watch standers are getting to their feet. "Mind the helm!" The Quartermaster of the watch lays, a crumpled heap, his head nearly severed.

Shawn picks up a phone, "Combat, bridge." He smells the rusty, hot odor of steam and bile rises in his throat. He fights it down. The guns continue to fire, but the noise is muted and sounds remote. "Combat, bridge."

He faintly hears, "Bridge, Captain, it's time for us to retire."

"Retire, aye sir. One fatality on the bridge, sir." The wind whips his shirt as the ship turns. He looks out the bridge windows, then it dawns on him, most of the bridge windows are blown out.

BRIDGE, IJN NAGATO

Captain Hideo Yano stands on his starboard bridge wing. The guns are silent and his ship is down at the bow, listing heavily to port. The light cruiser Nachi is done, only its stern rising out of the water. The heavy cruiser Ashigara is burning stem to stern only a mile ahead of his own ship. A destroyer comes alongside his own ship, spraying water on the flames. The fire-fighting water just sinks his battleship deeper into the sea.

His engineer approaches and bows, "Captain, the flooding in 1 boiler room, 1 engine room, and 1 generator room is uncontrollable. I'm afraid our ship is lost."

"Very well, direct the crew to abandon ship. I must speak to the Admiral."

Admiral Gato stands on his flag bridge calmly observing the remnants of the battle. A rating announces the captain as he enters. Then, they hear "All hands abandon ship. All hands abandon ship."

Captain Hideo Yano bows, "My apologies, Admiral. The engineer has informed me that we cannot save the ship."

The Admiral turns, "And, what will you do, Captain?"

"My duty, sir. For you, sir, there is a destroyer alongside."

"I shall do my duty, as well. We faced two battleships and they fought well. I've directed the transports to flee with the remainder of our fleet. You see the damage we inflicted on the Americans. At worst, it is a draw."

BRIDGE, USS COLUMBIA

The XO calmly steps onto the bridge. His khaki uniform is torn and smoke damaged. Blood covers half of his face from a head wound. "First Lieutenant, you're bleeding."

"As are you, sir. One casualty, sir," and motions to the quartermaster.

XO, "We're lucky."

They smile grimly and nod, then look out the bridge windows. Shawn, "Helm, steady as she goes."

"Steady as she goes. She goes 132."

A medical team enters, assess the situation, and head for the quartermaster. Shawn, "Very well. Lee helm, what is our best speed?"

"We're down to 19 knots on two shafts, sir."

"Very well." He steps out on the port bridge wing and looks back. He sees the Japanese heavy cruiser and two of their destroyers settling in the water, flame and smoke rising into the tropical skies. Suddenly, there's an explosion on the heavy cruiser. The shock wave hits him hard in the chest, causing him to step back. He steps forward and surveys the Columbia. There is little left of the RIM-7 launcher ahead of the bridge. The shell impacted just ahead of the launcher creating a smoking crater. The shell's impact caused the missiles in the launcher to detonate, blowing out the bridge.

The XO comes to his side, "You've done well, Hughes. We all have."

"Thank you, sir. Do you know just how bad it is?"

"They hit forward, Mount 54, the aft superstructure and fantail, and 1 boiler room. We're fighting fires."

"Damn."

"I need to report back to the Captain on the status of the bridge."

"Roger that, sir." Shawn salutes and the XO walks down the bridge wing and heads aft. Shawn goes back into the bridge.

The starboard lookout shouts, "Sail, ho!"

Hughes answers in the age-old tradition, "Where away?"

"Five points abaft the starboard beam, sir."

Hughes picks up a phone, "Combat, Bridge. Surface contact five points aft the starboard beam."

"Bridge, Combat. Contact is American. We can't raise them on radio. Using blinker."

Hughes directs his binoculars to the contact and reads it reply. The code is for the USS Waller, the flagship of Captain Arleigh Burke. On phone, "Combat, Bridge. It's the Waller. They're asking for assistance. The rest of the fleet was hammered by the Japanese." The signal station relays the message to the bridge and combat.

"Bridge, Combat. Con us alongside the North Carolina. According to the Commodore, it's the worst off."

Hughes, "Combat, Bridge. Aye." He consults the chart. It hasn't been updated, but he works out their approximate position, "Helm, right standard rudder. Come to new course 320."

The ship heels a bit as they come about, and the acrid smell of steam, burning fuel, and burning flesh wafts through the bridge. BM2 Balls vomits in a waste can, but stays at his post. Another quartermaster enters the bridge and mans the watch.

HURWORTH ON THE TEES, UK

2045, 25 September, 1942

LT Urland runs down Strait Lane with his platoon. Another explosion hits behind them. The rat-a-tat of machine gun fire echoes between the buildings. Urland spots an old man loading a bundle into a Model T truck and stops, "Can we help you, sir?"

"I'm thinking, young man, it's the army that needs help."

"This fight is lost, sir, but if we could ride with you, we'll help you get south."

"I've my daughter and grandson to load. This way."

SGT Rodriguez asks, "What are you doing? There's no time."

Wingnut shakes him off and enters the house. The bottom floor looks like a locksmith's shop. A pretty red-haired woman hands Wingnut a baby and turns back up the stairs. He walks outside, fascinated by the tiny, calm baby looking up at him. The baby's mother runs up behind him, tosses a bag in the bed of the truck, and climbs into the passenger seat. "Thank you, please give William to me."

Tommy hands her the baby, "Here Willy. Here's your mama."

They all climb into the bed of the truck and Johnny slaps the roof and the old truck starts toward the bridge. As they approach the one lane bridge, they see a squad of German soldiers running toward it from the east. Rodriguez opens up with his BAR and Germans fall like mown grass. They start onto the narrow metal bridge and Wingnut spots a large German tank behind them and to the east. It's one of the new ones. He unlimbers his radio, "Any Alpha 10 over Hurworth, this is Wingnut."

"Dog 7. Go, Wingnut."

"We are crossing south on the one lane bridge and are taking fire from Tiger tank north east of our position." The tank turret rotates toward them.

"Roger, Wingnut. Confirm, you're in the truck?"

"Affirmative."

They hear a loud 'Brrrrrt.' The Tiger's turret explodes off the tank, landing on the road in front of it.

"Dog 7, Wingnut, good kill. It's time for the bridge to go." They're barely across when a unit of German infantry run onto the bridge and Johnny and the guys take them under fire. "

"Roger, Wingnut, taking the bridge."

As they hurry down the country lane south of the river, the A-10 drops a cluster of 500-pound retarded bombs on the bridge.

SOUTHWEST OF GUADALCANAL

0710, 26 September, 1942 (2110, 25 September GMT)

As the Columbia closes the fleet, LCDR Shawn Hughes sees the North Carolina listing 20 degrees to port and low in the water. The Washington is burning and floating on its lines. The Canberra is on the port side of the North Carolina, so he maneuvers into position onto the Carolina's starboard side. The Captain calls for the rescue and assistance detail.

Hughes says, "Boatswain, call for the line handling detail to muster, port side."

He jockeys the engines to bring her smoothly and slowly alongside. Already the crew of the North Carolina is dewatering. The damage is clear in the bright morning light. Nearly every ship visible is damaged. In the distance, he sees a bow rising out of the sea. Below on the port quarter deck, he can see the XO mustering the detail.

Captain William A. Heard walks onto the bridge. BM2 Balls says, "Captain on the bridge." Heard looks around, assessing the damage as he approaches Hughes. "What happened to QM2 Knox?"

"A chunk of the RIM launcher decapitated him, sir."

"Are you all right?"

Hughes meets his captain gaze, communicating more that words, "I'll make do, sir."

"I need to reassign you. The CHENG was in 1 boiler room when it was hit."

"How many people have we lost, sir?"

"It's preliminary, but about 40. Everyone in 1 boiler is dead. That will make you shorthanded."

"Understood, sir."

"I have Lieutenant Smith coming up to relieve you."

"Which ship sank?"

"The Minneapolis. The Astoria took a pounding, as well. We've lost the Minneapolis and the destroyer, Philip. The North Carolina is still questionable."

"Sir, do we know what the Japanese lost?"

"We sank the heavy cruiser and a couple of destroyers. The rest of the group sank at least one battle wagon, a couple of cruisers, and three or four destroyers. Most importantly, we prevented their landing."

"Sir, while we're alongside rendering aid, aren't we leaving the battlegroup exposed to aerial attack? The RIM is destroyed and we can't maneuver to unmask the Mark 10."

"It can't be avoided. They need our help. The Blue Diamonds out of Guadalcanal will have to cover us."

"Yes, sir."

GERMAN OCCUPIED RAF OUSTON

2156, 25 September, 1942

General Weber's plane circles the field, studying it. Most of the buildings are intact and he sees the anti-aircraft units he ordered setting up. "Land us east to west." The runway is in remarkably good shape. Once they're down, a truck approaches and Hauptmann Kerr steps out and salutes, "Sir, the fuel tanks were not destroyed. All but one contains motor fuel, not jet fuel."

"Understood. Send the fuel to the Field Marshal. He can use it. We'll depend on the one and seek another source. Are the facilities clean?"

"Yes, Herr General."

"Good. Now, we must plan a greeting for any enemy aircraft that ventures close."

NUMBER 1 BOILER ROOM, USS COLUMBIA

0821, 26 September, 1942 (2221, 25 September GMT)

LCDR Shawn Hughes climbs down the ladder into Boiler Room 1. The fires are out and the compartment is de-smoked, but the lingering smell is a horrid combination of burned fuel oil, burned insulation, steam, and burned bodies. When he sees the CHENG being scrapped off the deck by the medics, he nearly vomits. To himself, "Focus, Hughes."

Number 1 boiler is destroyed. The armor piercing round had to have exploded against it. Number 2 is damaged by debris. The canning is blown off and refractory scattered all over. "Great. It's no doubt asbestos." He looks at Number 3. It, thank God, is intact. The fires are out, but it's still lined up to fire. On the deck in front of him is BT1 Jim Williamson, dead where he dropped.

Hughes moves to Number 4. As he's inspecting it, BTC Jones from Number 2 boiler room, joins him. "What a mess, sir."

"It is. I need you to get a watch team down here and light off 3 and 4. Once the boilers are lit, we can deal with the cleaning up."

"What about the bodies?"

"Stretcher bearers are dealing with them. Chief, we need more than 19 knots."

"Are you the new CHENG, sir?"

"I am."

"Aye, sir."

COMMODORE'S QUARTERS, RAF KENLEY

0352, 26 September, 1942

Samantha wakes with a start. Her mind is muddled as she swings out of bed. She stumbles into the unfamiliar bathroom and flips on the light. She looks at her watch, 0352. "Why am I awake?" She looks at her reflection in the mirror and barely recognizes herself. Her eyes are sunken with dark rings. Her cheek bones are more prominent. "I look like a heroin addict." She does her business, washes her face, tames her hair, and pulls on a flight suit. Then it hits her. It's quiet.

Sam walk into the control room, "Report."

The watch officer says, "Lancelot 1 and 2 are orbiting east of York. Percival 1 and 2 are orbiting south east of London. Galahad 1 and 2 are returning. They will be on final in few minutes. Our new Griffin squadron has adopted the name 'Merry Men' and the call signs Robin 1 and 2, Little John 1 and 2, Tuck 1 and 2, Scarlet 1 and 2, Midge 1 and 2, and, finally, Maid Mary 1 and 2. Little John and Scarlet are engaging a raid near Portsmouth. We have two radar planes up. Dog flight 2 and 3 are covering the retreat from the Tees River line. There is a report that the Germans are not attacking into Scotland. Merlin is pre-flighting for a wild weasel mission. Texas lost four jets to the new German fighters. There are three new messages."

"Thank you." She picks up the messages.

FROM: COMBATDIV-5

TO: COMTFYAN

REG: Defense of Britain

Battleship Division 5 is en route to Britain and expect to make port at Scapa Flow on or near 0800 9/27/1942. We will join the home fleet in defense of Britain. We are accompanied by Cruiser Division 7 and a destroyer escort. Please advise on the availability of your unit to provide air defense of BATDIV-5.

Commodore Lewis James

She shakes her head and writes a reply.

FROM: COMTFYAN

TO: COMBATDIV-5

REG: Air cover for BADIV-5

Task Force Yankee will support the air cover mission where it does not interfere with the primary mission of defending the United Kingdom. Where BATDIV-5's movements are coordinated with the Home Fleet that is already part of TYFAN's mission. Current location of Home Fleet is Belfast, Northern Ireland, not Scapa. If BATDIV-5 is to work independently, please advise TFYAN of movements. Also, please advise how many and which vessels are in BATDIV-5.

Commodore Samantha Hunt

She picks up the next message. It's from Vice Admiral Klindt's office asking about storage and security of the nuclear weapon for which she is responsible. She writes a reply with the information requested. She picks up the third message.

FROM: CINC

TO: COMTFYAN

REG: Operational Authority

As the air defense of the British Isles is critical for the prosecution of war operations moving forward and the operations of Task Force Yankee are critical to the defense of the British Isles, it has been noted that other US and Allied commands may task TFYAN to missions not critical to the defense of the British Isles. Therefore, operational authority shall reside with COMTFYAN, except those missions requiring CINC authority. COMTFYAN will report to LTGEN Eisenhower, Commander, European Theater of Operations (ETOUSA), who shall maintain overall operational command of US operations in theater and report to Admiral Lee, NAVAIR, for all material and administrative matters. All Naval units in and around the British Isles shall report to COMTFYAN, unless specifically otherwise assigned. All USAAF units in the British Isles shall report to COMTFYAN for missions involving defense of the British Isles. These missions are priority 1. TFYAN is priority 1 for all war materials and supplies.

Commander in Chief, Franklin D. Roosevelt

She reads it twice more, then, "Swede is in the air. Get me Cooper and get me Thud."

Cooper materializes at her elbow and she hands him the President's message.

"Commodore, General Eisenhower is on line two."

Spike picks up the phone, "Hunt."

"I take it you've read the message?"

"I just got it and I'm still processing what it means."

Eisenhower asks, "What do you want to do with the 8th Air Force?"

"Can we shift them to anti-shipping? I want to prevent any re-supply from Germany or France."

"Done."

"If they can safely do it, I would like them to engage radar stations on the coast of France."

"Done."

Thud walks in and she hands him the message. "Sir, where are we going to move them?"

"We're shifting them south and north to keep clear of the Germans. We're also converting a couple of B-17s to gunships as you suggested. We don't have enough guns for more in theater, however."

Spike nods, "When they're ready, my guys will provide instruction and cover them."

"The Army Airforce is also tasking the first two squadrons of F-1 War Eagles when they've completed their training."

"The new jets? I've heard we had some in the pipeline."

Ike says, "Yes, we'll have them in a day or two."

"Where are they going to be stationed?"

"We were going to put them at Duxford, but now they're looking for a home."

"I can hold the first two squadrons here at Kenley so we can get used to working together. Jesus Christ, I'll have six or more squadrons working for me. I need a bigger staff."

Thud emphatically nods his agreement.

Eisenhower, "You do. Do you want Army or Navy?"

"I want knowledgeable and competent."

Ike laughs, "Is it okay if I put someone on it?"

"Yes, thank you. I have rather a full plate. I need good logistics, admin, and operations staff. In the Navy, we generally assign pilots to those duties, but our op tempo is too high for that to work. I also need a non-flight officer for a chief of staff. Someone who can handle what we do."

"I know just the person. I take it we're on track with the new aircraft?"

"Yes, we should get two more today."

"Good. Any status on pilots?"

"They need to check out on the '14 first, but they're coming."

"You'll have your new chief of staff there in about a day. You know you have my full cooperation."

"Thank you, sir."

"Take care, Commodore," and he's gone.

Thud, "You going to need me to train new air crews?"

"Soon, Thud. You, Gunner, Speedy, and NOB."

"Roger, Spike. I'll get to it." He leaves.

Cooper asks, "Are we getting more staff?"

"Yes, General Eisenhower is taking care of that problem."

"Fluffy can find them quarters. I need to get us more office space. Oh, and your breakfast is here. Eat." A young woman brings in a huge plate of food.

Spike takes a couple of bits and picks up a document, and starts reading. Cooper pulls the piece of paper out of her hand, "If you don't eat the doctor won't let you fly. Eat. I promised the doc, I would put five pounds on you."

She looks up at him and sighs, "Yes, Mama," and picks up her fork.

CHAPTER 12

FLIGHT LINE, OCCUPIED RAF OUSTON

0418, 26 September, 1942

Weber walks out on the line with Major Gunter, "So, deliver this to Oberst Ernst Meyer. He's an officer from the future and we work together closely. We next use chaff, but not to avoid a specific missile, but to cover the whole force. The designs should be ready. With it, you may escort the transports to us. Questions?"

"May I lead the mission, Herr General?"

"Of course, you are a good and faithful officer."

USS MISSISSIPPI BB-41, FLAGSHIP OF BATDIV-5, 180 MILES WEST OF GALWAY, IRELAND

0535, 26 September, 1942

Commodore Lewis James reads the message from Commodore Hunt, "Why does she need the makeup of our unit? Does she presume we work for her?"

Captain David Smith says, "Perhaps she does, sir. We are to report to Commander Naval Forces, United Kingdom. Is that her?"

"She calls herself Task Force Yankee."

A petty officer walks in, "A message from CINC, sir."

The Commodore reads it first, then hands it to the captain. He reads it and looks up, "So, we work for her, sir."

"Indeed."

GAWAIN FLIGHT, 30,000 FEET OVER THE RIVER TEES

0740, 26 September, 1942

Thud and Speedy hear, "Gawain, Whiskey Bravo Bravo, raid east. 36 aircraft at 300 knots, angels 25, course 280. Designate Raid 6."

Speedy, "Whiskey Bravo Bravo, Gawain. Roger, we are coming to 085 to engage."

Thud makes a smooth left turn and checks for Trollop and Mouse on his wing.

Speedy, "Okay, Thud, I have them. 150 miles."

Thud accelerates to full military power, "Thirty-six is a lot. What do they look like?"

Speedy, "Fighters escorting bombers or transports. The fighters are a mix of '163s and '262s. I'm picking up search radar. They have us."

Thud, "The '262s, right? The '163 doesn't have radar."

"These do. Do we focus on fighters or bombers?"

"If we chew up the fighters, the Griffins can mop of the others."

"Okay, I have lock. Four are squirting ahead. Engaging those."

Thud volley fires four AIM-1s."

GUNTER'S '262, LEADING THE GERMAN FORMATION

Gunter on radio, "Yellow flight, parallel the group 200 meters higher and drop chaff canisters."

The '163 leader asks, "Once dropped, can we engage the Americans?"

"Negative, it's not the mission."

The four '163s drop the chaff canisters. The canister's parachutes open, releasing chaff as they drift down.

GAWAIN 1

Speedy, "They're dropping chaff and pulling back. I think they're diving to stay behind the chaff."

"Do we still have lock?"

"Trying. Shit, it's a lot of chaff. Dude, it's like seeing through milk. We missed."

"Okay. G's," and pulls back on the stick, climbing, Trollop following. "We just need to climb over it." They invert to see the enemy. Thud, "I see four. AIM-7s and head to head."

Speedy, "We got lock. A little closer. They're breaking off."

"Where?"

"They're heading north to rejoin the group. Dude, the whole group is being shielded with chaff."

"Fuck. Call it in. Let's come around behind them. If we must, we can go to guns."

Speedy, "Yankee control, Gawain 1. The Germans are using a high volume of chaff. Closing to engage."

Swede in Control, "Roger Gawain, continue."

Mouse, "Eight inbound. We have the left."

Speedy, "Roger, Mouse." They close at 1500 mph. Thud fires a quick burst and one of the '163s goes away, dropping out, as they flash by."

Thud pulls vertical, lighting his burners, "G's. Where are they?"

"They're coming up, too."

"Okay, G's." He rolls over the top and sees a '163 a couple of miles away pulling up to meet him. He selects the AIM-7 and fires. It fails to track, but the German reacts by pulling vertical in full afterburner. Thud selects an AIM-9 and gets good tone. He fires and it detonates in the right engine, causing the '163 to lose control and go nose down, spinning into the sea. "Where is Trollop?"

"Ten K below us."

"Okay." Thud inverts and dives to join his wingman. As he does, he sees a SAM launch. On radio, "Trollop, break left, break left, chaff, flares!" A second missile launches and tracks him, "Hold on." He times his maneuver and the missile misses. "Where are we?"

"Near Newcastle. Where did the Germans go?"

"There were six north of us. The others are west, I think. Let's circle to find them."

Thud does a circle and the skies are clear. "Speedy, they had subsonic planes with them. Where did they go?"

"Thud, they're landing at Ouston." On radio, "Whiskey Bravo Bravo, Gawain 1, the Germans are landing at Ouston." To Thud, "SAM! Break!" Thud identifies the missile and breaks east and down.

Mouse, "Speedy, there are a lot of SAMs here."

"Gawain, Yankee actual, return for refuel and rearm."

TARMAC, OCCUPIED RAF OUSTON

General Weber stands with his hands on his hips as sixteen fighters, eight transports, and two tankers taxi into position. The cargo planes disgorge men and equipment. The tanker aircraft start pumping fuel into the German fighters. Major Gunter approaches and salutes, "I will turn around four fighters immediately for air cover. Sir, it went exactly as planned."

"Very good, Herr Major. Keep it a defensive patrol, unless told otherwise. They'll have to come to us."

"Heil Hitler!"

101ST BATTALION, 1ST REGIMENT, 3RD PANZER DIVISION, LEEDS, UK

0810, 26 September, 1942

SS-Obersturmbannfuhrer Ernst Meier stands in the commander's hatch of his Tiger H11 tank, the 125mm gun reaching far out in front of it. His whole battalion is behind him, and behind them straggles the rest of the invasion force. He smiles, "I am at the tip of the spear."

He hears the splat-boom of a rifle round hitting his tank and slews his machine gun toward the sound. He studies the buildings and sees movement behind a curtain. He opens up, and an unarmed old woman falls out of the window. Another round hits the coaming, just inches from his hand. He turns forward and machine guns a butcher shop up the road, "Target the butcher."

The main gun fires, causing the building to collapse. He radios his battalion, "Target all civilians. Target the buildings. There are irregular troops in this town." The tanks open up.

The battalion reaches the bridge over the river Aire. They see a soldier slipping under the bridge and one of the machine gunners fires and he crumples out of sight. "Come right, they're trying to blow the bridge."

His tank swings right and he orders the turret swung around. The other tanks spread out for a clear shot. Then, he sees more men under the bridge and starts firing, "Small arms only. We must save the bridge."

CHURCH STEEPLE, LEEDS, UK

Wingnut is watching the movements of the large tanks with his binoculars. He knows they're firing on the American sappers, "Any Warthog near Leeds, Wingnut."

"Wingnut, Rusty flight 2, go ahead."

"We have troops in contact. Tiger tanks in Leeds attempting a crossing of the Aire."

"Roger, Wingnut. Engaging."

Wingnut puts his binoculars back up and checks the bridge. Most of the sapper unit has been killed. German troops are dismounting. He sees a sergeant under the bridge carefully connecting wires. The unit patch on his shoulder is the red and blue flower with a white center of the 9th Infantry Division. The sergeant stands and his hit. He stays on his feet and pushes down the plunger. The explosives detonate right over the sergeant's head, killing him and dropping the bridge.

Wingnut watches, transfixed. In a Hollywood movie, the hero would walk out of the dust, but this hero is gone. He looks at his watch and starts taking notes, frantically writing, while coordinating with the A-10s. Time, place, unit. "Sergeant, did you see the guy blow the bridge?"

"Yes, sir. He sacrificed himself."

"Take notes: time, date, rank, unit."

"He was 9th Infantry."

The A-10s start their strafing run and one tank goes up. Another starts to smoke and the tanks retreat into the town.

"I agree, and obviously a sapper."

"Why are we documenting it?"

"For a Medal of Honor."

"Yes, sir."

Wingnut, "Sergeant, we need to go. They're going to head west. Let's get ahead of them."

They hear on radio, "Wingnut, Yankee, we need you to the east, in or around York. That's the German's main push."

"Yankee, Wingnut. This unit is heading west."

"Roger, Wingnut. We'll keep an eye on them. Link with the 9th Infantry and coordinate. We're teaching others to be forward observers, but they aren't ready yet."

"Understood, Yankee. Proceeding to York."

Sergeant Johnny Rodriguez, "Roger that, sir. Your chariot awaits." They walk from the church, and a deuce and a half pulls up. The squad scrambles on board and they move out. Wingnut rides in a comfortable chair tied to the bed. He crumples into it and takes a swig of water. The corpsman, Andy Love, asks, "Sir, are you okay?"

"Shoulder hurts like hell, but fuck it. I got it to do."

"Want more pills?"

"No, not yet."

FLIGHT LINE, RAF KINLEY

0840, 26 September, 1942

Swede, Gandhi, Too Tall, Thud, Speedy, Trollop, Mouse, and Spike stand in a circle. Spike, "Okay, we can't get new equipment, short term, so we need new tactics."

Mouse asks, "What is the chaff? I know what we use, and what it does. What is German chaff made of?"

Everyone looks at Thud. He hangs his head and sighs, "All right, the Germans call it Duppel. They normally used strips of aluminum. The strips are of random lengths and widths so they easily disperse in the wind."

Too Tall, "You know, bud, you're an encyclopedia. He's right. It doesn't stop the radar; it massively attenuates it. The signal has to make it through, hit its target, and make it back to the receiver."

Spike, "We need to split up our formations when they use it. Hopefully one bird can get a good lock."

Swede, "The bird with lock fires as the other maneuvers."

Speedy, "We can also fiddle with our frequency to try and peek through. The width of the aluminum strips will cause it to reject a specific wavelength more than others."

Too Tall, "That's only sort of true. If they're using basically aluminum scraps, they might be random enough to stop your entire band. It's worth a shot, though."

Spike, "Another thing. Steer clear of Ouston. They hold it and they're using it. I don't want to attack it."

Gandhi, "Why? Why give them a toehold?"

Spike makes eye contact with each person, "They already have more than a toehold. They have a Corp of five divisions. If we start with Ouston, they'll improve their defense of the place and make it a harder nut to crack."

Swede, "Wouldn't it draw forces from the front?"

"Yeah, maybe, and dig them in where they'd be a bitch to rout out. While they're mobile, they're easier to hit."

Trollop, "So, we let them keep it?"

Spike, "Until we have the forces to take it completely back, we leave it alone. Let them relax and think they're safe. Too Tall, without getting yourself killed, I'd like you to figure out their radar guided missile configuration and start building a plan to wipe out their defenses. No attacks, though, without my permission. Clear?"

Too Tall, "Roger, Spike."

Swede, "Roger, Spike."

RAF ELMDON, BIRMINGHAM, UK

0900, 26 September, 1942

The prototype Lancaster gunship has been pulled out to in front of its hanger and crew and engineers are pouring over it, making final checks. The short barrels of three M61 20mm Vulcan aircraft gun are sticking out of the left side of the fuselage aft of the wing. One of the engineers asks, "How in the hell is the crew going to target this thing?"

LT Oscar Hammond smiles, "By turning."

The engineer spins to face Hammond, "There is no way at all a pilot can shoot out of the side of the plane and accurately hit anything."

Hammond pulls a string out of his pocket and offers the engineer one end, "Humor me."

"You've lost your wits, you know," but he complies. Hammond loops the other end of the string around a model of the Lancaster that is a mock-up of the gunship. The engineer, "Why do you have a model Lancaster?"

Hammond, "Teaching the flight crew. So, the pilot has a sight in the cockpit on his side window. Normally, as he flies the bearing of any specific point on the ground changes." He illustrates by moving the model straight and taking up the slack in the line to keep it taut.

The engineer, "Exactly. Precise aiming is impossible."

Hammond, "But, when the plane is in a coordinated pylon turn, he can point his wing, and thus his guns precisely at a single point on the ground." Hammond moves the model in a turn, lining the stick gun with the string. "Still the job is a challenge because of turbulence, but the guns each fire six thousand rounds a minute. Absolute accuracy is unnecessary."

The engineer is silent and they hear an engine start on the Lancaster. Hammond gathers up his training aid and walks to the boarding hatch, "Are you coming?"

GERMAN HQ, OCCUPIED RAF OUSTON

1015, 26 September, 1942

General Weber looks over a map of England, "She does nothing to attack us here, which surprises me."

His aide asks, "Could she have too few planes to launch an effective attack?"

"She attacked Brest with bombs and landed them close enough to destroy a dry dock. The Scheer is still under repair."

"At that time, she had a larger force."

"True, that may be it. Now, we have a complete missile defense system, and any attack would be futile. Also, after the first attempt, she doesn't even hit our supply formations over the North Sea. It's odd."

"Have we broken her will? Perhaps she cowers in her bed."

"No, not her. She's a shrewd and clever adversary. Know this, Victor, you do well to overestimate your adversary. You court disaster should you ever underestimate their capabilities."

Major Gunter enters and salutes, "Heil Hitler."

Weber, "Heil Hitler. What do you bring me from France, Major?"

"I bring three bottles of brandy and good news. Our long strike missiles are ready."

"Excellent. We must change tactics. Sometimes they shut off their radar."

BLACK BULL, STATION STREET, LOCKERBIE, SCOTLAND

1513, 26 September, 1942

LT Gus 'Cuddles' Grant accepts a draft and takes a long pull. The beer cuts the dryness in his throat, slaking his thirst. He's a sight. His flight suit and the bandages on his head are filthy with blood and dirt. The civilian wool coat hangs over his uniform and he smells of blood, oil, and wet wool.

The bartender, a lean woman in her 50's hands him another

and asks, "You're a Yank, right?"

"I am. Lieutenant Grant, US Navy." He offers a hand.

She takes it with a smile, "Patsy Stewart. I've a room where you can get cleaned up."

"Thank you." Keeping his beer, he lets her lead him into the back.

"Have you any other clothes to wear?"

"Yeah, in my bag, but they're filthy, too."

"I'll clean both sets and get you something dry to wear. What brings you to Lockerbie?"

"The British Army. I've been helping after I was shot down."

"You're a flyer?" She starts filling a tub with steaming hot water.

"A RIO. My pilot is somewhere down south of the German lines. The Germans have stopped and dug in just a few miles away. No one had use of me, so I walked into town. I have money."

"My oldest is in Burma. I've two more in Egypt or there abouts. I'll charge you for food and drink, but the rest is the least I can do."

She takes off his coat and sets it aside. Then, starts helping him peel off his flight suit. He pauses, then goes with it. In a minute, he's sinking into the hot suds. He closes his eyes and lets the heat relax his muscles, and his mind. She carefully washes his head and right arm, removing the bloody dressings. "I'll have someone check on this."

"It's nothing. There's no shortage of soldiers with far worse."

"Well, I've bandages. I'll take care of this. What is the cat tattoo?"

He smiles, "I fly the F-14 Tomcat. The tattoo is the Tomcat logo, 'Anytime Baby.'"

She stands, "I seem to have soiled my dress." She looks him in the eye and disrobes.

A few hours later, he's wearing clean pants and a shirt and his wounds have fresh bandages. He sits with another pint of beer and has a bowl of mutton stew in front of him. By now, the pub is pretty full.

A huge, grey-haired, Highlander, wearing the yellow and black of the clan McCloud, walks into the bar with several older men. They're all carrying Lee Enfield rifles, and in his hand, it looks like a toy. He has a bandolier of ammo across one shoulder. A belt, with a dirk, holds the bandolier in place. His voice booms through the room, "Beer for me and my men."

Cuddles, "God, I hope this isn't the husband."

The Highlander takes a long draft of his beer and turns to the room, "I am Ian McCloud of the clan McCloud. I served our King as a captain of the 1st Battalion, Gordon Highlander in the last war and now, the Highlanders have come to give battle to the Germans who have brought war to our homes. I've over a hundred men, but I'm not too shy to ask for more."

Cuddles stands, "I'm Lieutenant Gus Grant from the Black Knights. I would be honored to fight beside you and call in the air support you will need."

"You're a flyer?"

"Yes, shot down on the beach north of Shield. I supported the Home Guard and then the Leeds Rifles. They've holed up south of here and the Germans have ceased their advance north.?

"They aren't fighting?"

"No, sir, and it make me damn useless. The helicopters are busy with dust off and can't waste time fetching me." He looks at his clothes, "The lady is washing my uniforms."

"It's no problem, laddie. Ye fight with us, you'll wear the uniform of a Highlander."

NORTH OF WIGGINTON, NORTH YORKSHIRE, UK

1604, 26 September, 1942

Tommy 'Wingnut' Urland lies on the slate roof of a barn looking across a large field. The rain is pelting down, causing him to wipe the lenses of his binoculars repeatedly. Sergeant Johnny Rodriguez is lying next to him, the rest of the squad under the eaves below. Wingnut, "This weather is for ducks and Marines. A God loving aviator should never have to get wet."

Johnny chuckles, "There's no way you're an aviator anymore." Ahead of them infantry and tanks are dug in, waiting. They watch the soldiers bailing out their trenches. Beyond, the fields are flooded.

"What do you mean?"

"Well, you're scruffy, dirty, unkept, and oh, you don't have a scarf."

"All logical points."

"Your shoulder holding up?"

"No, but I'll live."

Guardsman Sergeant Tully climbs the ladder, "There's a report that the Germans are advancing in a wedge formation."

Tommy, "Roger," and lays his head down, "Fuck, I'm tired."

Rodriguez, "We stop them here, sir, and we can all get a bath and a long nap."

"We won't. All we have is the Sherman."

"Yeah, we have that, but we have the Warthogs."

"Yeah."

They silently contemplate the distant tree line. A murmur of birds fly down to lite in the trees, then suddenly veer back up. Tommy, "They're here." He turns on his radio, "Any hog pilot,

Wingnut."

Wingnut, "Dog flight 3. Where are you?"

Tommy gives his coordinates and watches the German tanks shaking the trees in the distance. "Bring friends. It's a target rich environment."

FABRIC SHOP, LOCKERBIE, SCOTLAND

Ian McCloud, his voice booming in the small room, "So, you dinna have the red and green of the Grant Tartan? The Grants are a fine clan."

The old woman says, "It tis indeed, but I have none. You do know, sir, that we have a war on?"

Ian turns to Cuddles, "Could you live with this Stewart red?"

Cuddles nods, "Truth, Mr. McCloud, I'm American from 1990. I don't know the difference."

"Well, let me show ye how to put it on and I swear on my father's bones, I'll make a clansman out of ya."

Cuddles walks out of the shop with the red and black of the Stewart tartan across his left shoulder and down his back like a cloak. It's held in place, over his coat, with a stout leather belt. They walk to join the others and Patsy intercepts him, "Darlin' man, you're wearing the tartan of my clan. You need this," and gives him a dirk in its sheath. "It was my Arnold's before he fell to fever. He carried it in the last war, it ought to be used in this one."

"Thank you, Patsy. I'll bring it back, after."

"You do that, darlin' and I'll see to it you never leave again," and lays a passionate kiss on him. He returns it, with vigor.

CHAPTER 13

GYM, RAF KENLEY

0822, 27 September, 1942

Sam, wearing sweat pants and a gray US Navy t-shirt, goes through a kata. She's in her own world, focusing on her body, tightening her muscles in each precise move. She moves slowly, the position of each imaginary foe in her mind, then blindingly fast, she strikes. Moving precisely through the kata, she becomes aware of being watched, but maintains focus and completes the kata. At the end, she turns and looks behind her.

Squadron Leader Maugham is standing there, "I apologize for interrupting."

"So, you're all healed up. Congratulations. What's up?"

"What were you doing?"

"Aikido. It's an ancient Japanese martial art."

"Where did you learn it?"

"A dojo in California when I was in college. Is this why you're here?"

"No, I'm sorry. I was told you wanted to see me. I command your Griffin squadron."

"Oh, the Merry Men. Interesting choice of call signs. You're Robin, correct?"

"I am. Your pilots trained all of mine, and we're acquitting ourselves fairly well, thus far. I'm told you have standing orders?"

"I do, Richard. I want Ouston left alone."

"I heard. To me, your logic is unassailable."

"Next, winning is not the most important thing. We must survive and continue to be a threat. When the Germans spread us out, we focus on the priority missions and pray that, someday, the British people will forgive us for the bombs that get through."

"Yes, ma'am."

Spike smiles and continues, "Our men; their primary job is to fight. Ours is to give them everything we can to make them successful. In saying this, I know a commodore shouldn't fly combat, but in truth, we have so few pilots, I just can't give it up just yet."

"We need you out there."

"Who?"

"Ma'am?"

"Who is the we?"

"Oh, Britain. All of Britain. I doubt you realize it, but you have become a symbol of our resistance. Because you fight up there every day, all the people can believe in victory. We can cast aside our doubts and push on."

"I'm just one pilot."

"No, you're the leader. You lead from the front like the knights of old."

She looks at him, starts to reply, and stops. "I don't really get it, and I suppose, I don't need to. Take care of your people, and they will take care of you. And, yes, don't ask your people to do anything you won't. If there's a problem with a plane or a person, notify my staff immediately. They know when to wake me up. Questions?"

"No, ma'am. Thank you for pulling the families out of Alconbury and Duxford."

"It was the right thing to do. I have a sortie in a bit, and I need to shower."

"Yes, ma'am."

"It's Spike, Richard. Remember? Spike."

"Oh yes, sorry. I forgot. I just thought with you being Commodore..."

"Spike, my friend."

LANCELOT 2 OVER THE BIGHT

0902, 27 September, 1942

The sun is bright in the east and the skies are clear at 30,000 feet. Below them is a lumpy carpet of clouds. LT Lorne 'Jedi' Luke asks his RIO, "You know, I don't recall how you landed your call sign."

LTJG Tyler 'Stinky' Lewis replies, "It was stupid. I guess most are. It was my second hop in the training squadron. The night before, my wife had arrived back home after visiting her folks. The XO said he could smell something fishy in the cockpit. That, and I like things clean. It's stupid stuff that lands you a call sign."

LANCELOT 1

Gunner and NOB hear, "Lancelot, Whiskey Bravo Bravo, raid south east. 20 at Mach 1.8, angels 40, course 340. Designate raid 14."

NOB, "Whiskey Bravo Bravo, Lancelot is in." On intercom, "Damn, that's 14 raids already today, and it's still morning."

Gunner turns his '14 right and comes around, "Let's stay dark."

NOB, "Stinky, lights out."

They hear, "Lancelot, raid 14 has split. Six are turning west." Then, "Lancelot, Little John inbound. We have the west flight."

NOB, "Roger, Little John." On intercom, "So, Gunner, we only have fourteen to kill."

"Just? Let's light them up at sixty."

NOB, "Sixty, aye. Do you think they can keep making more planes?"

Gunner, "I don't know. You'd think they'd run out at some point."

NOB, "Picking up targeting radar." On radio, "Illuminating. Jesus. Break! Break!"

Gunner pulls the stick to his belly, pickling off chaff and flares. They feel a huge kick in the ass and their bird pitches forward into negative G's. Gunner pulls back and lights his afterburners. The engines don't respond, and then, their plane inverts. Gunner counters and regains some control.

They hear, "Little John is hit! Little John is hit!"

NOB on radio, "Lancelot is hit! Lancelot is hit!"

Lancelot, Yankee, which bird?"

"Both birds, Yankee."

ARTHUR'S HANGER, RAF KENLEY

Spike shouts, "Pull chocks and push us out!" To Lizard, "Starting engines. Get clearance."

LANCELOT 1, OVER THE CHANNEL

Gunner lowers the nose to gain speed and works his engine start procedure. "Eyes out NOB. Where's Jedi?"

"Jedi's gone, man. Gone."

"Got it. You gotta focus. Where are the Germans?"

"I see two at nine o'clock."

"Okay, 'Gs'." Gunner pulls his gliding bird around to meet the inbound fighters. He fires his gun and smoke pours from the left engine of the FU-279. It rolls inverted and goes into a tight spin to the sea below. The other passes canopy to canopy. Gunner rolls back into a dive, still trying to restart his engines.

On radio, "Lancelot, Arthur, inbound."

NOB, "They're crossing us."

Gunner, "Left engine, no start. Shifting to right." He pulls, banking back into the German with a diving scissors. The coast is so close. "G's." At 6000 feet he pulls hard and triggers a passing shot at the German. His rounds hit the wing of the '279 and it streams fuel. Gunner stretches the turn toward the coast and the German rolls in on them. He pulls at the last second, and the '279 overshoots, but he loses a lot of airspeed. He inverts and fires another burst, hitting the '279 across the right wing root. The wing swings up like a draw bridge and the German jet falls out of the sky.

Gunner rolls back upright, "Anything else trying to kill us?"

NOB, "Not that I see."

"Okay, jettisoning ordinance."

"Yeah." On radio, "Any unit, Lancelot 1, we're east of London with no engines. We're trying to make it to the coast."

Lizard, "Boss says, as soon as you're feet dry, eject. There's nowhere to land. Don't try the beach."

"Roger." They clear the beach and barely miss a radar mast. Gunner turns the plane back to the sea with the last of his airspeed, and "Eject. Eject."

NOB pulls the handle and the canopy explodes off the plane and NOB is rocketed out of the plane. Next, Gunner's chair ejects him out of the stricken plane. Both men pass out.

ARTHUR 1, ACCELERATING DOWN RUNWAY, RAF KENLEY

The moment the wheels leave the runway, Spike hits the landing gear lever, and cleans up her bird. "Where are they?"

"Just over north London, boss. Two Fox 1s."

Spike pickles off her AIM-7s. "How many?" Climbing out, she follows her missiles.

They hear, "Whiskey is hit. Whiskey is hit." Spike realizes that they're radar plane is going down.

"Twelve, Little John got two." Their closure speed is over 1000 knots and both missiles track and hit. "Ten, now."

Spike can now see them. Some have turned away, but five continue toward her. "Okay, Target the farthest out."

"On it. They're bugging out south and east."

Spike takes a chance and fires her gun at the closing jets. The rounds hit the radome and cockpit of one, causing the German jet to immediately roll into a violent cork screw, shedding parts on its way down. It crashes within the RAF Kenley fence line. The other jets pass by her and she gently turns to help Lizard set up the long-range shot.

"Nose up, Boss." She flattens her turn and rudders up her nose, then looks over her shoulder for the birds she passed. "Good lock. IFF clear. Clear shot."

Spike triggers off their four AIM-1s. She's rock steady and all find targets. Lizard, "Break right! Break right! Missiles inbound!" Spike breaks right and turns into the four inbound missiles. Lizard, "Um, Boss?"

Spike, "Got it." As the missiles close, she starts a gentle negative 'G' dive. Then, "Grunt," and she pulls back hard on the stick, firing chaff and flares. She rolls and pulls back to sight the enemy. The missiles pass harmlessly below them. Then, still inverted, closes on the enemy jets at over 1000 knots, in a shallow dive. She fires her gun to mess up their firing solutions and meets them head to head. Then she rolls into a minimum distance right turn.

Lizard, "They're coming around. Two in a two-circle fight. The others popped."

Spike lights her afterburners to keep her energy up. She times her shot and hits the lead jet, stitching it centerline from the nose to behind the cockpit. It erupts in flames, tumbling forward. As they pass, they see the broken canopy covered in blood.

"He's on us, Boss! One of the jets went high and is coming down on our six!"

"Grunt, Lizard," and pulls back the stick, going high.

"There are two more out there."

Part way through the climb, she snap rolls left, pulling into a violent barrel roll. Tracer rounds pass harmlessly behind. Then she comes off the afterburners and pulls into a '279, manually pushing the wings forward and putting the air brakes out. A half second burst and it's stitched through the cockpit. She's flying close enough to see the shattered canopy turned red with blood. She puts her burners on and the wings fold back.

"Boss, four o'clock high, crossing. He fired!"

"Grunt," and Spike pushes the wings forward again, violently pulling back on the stick. She fires her gun and hits the incoming missile, then meets the two jets head to head. Low on airspeed, she pulls back on the stick and goes inverted, and gets Sidewinder tone. Steadying her bird in inverted flight, she fires the Sidewinder and it tracks a graceful curve right into the left tail pipe of the '279. The missile warhead blows the engine.

Black smoke pours from the engine, but the jet isn't done. The German pilot, on one engine, rolls left and dives for the ground. Spike gets under him, gets a lead, and fires. The rounds stitch the plane from the nose aft, right down the centerline. The plane yaws violently and tumbles out of controlled flight into the ground.

Spike pulls up, looking for the wingman. He's on the deck accelerating away at full burner. She lights her burners, inverts, and gives chase. As she settles on his six, she gets tone for a Sidewinder. She fires at a range of just under a mile. The missile flies directly into a tail pipe and explodes. The '279 pitches up, then down, and the pilot punches out. "Where are they?"

"The last one bugged out for the coast. He's at fifty miles, Boss, out of range."

Spike turns off her afterburners, "Let's find Little John, Gunner, and NOB."

She gently dives and Lizard says, "I found one of the Griffins. He bailed out and landed on the south bank of the Thames. He's okay."

They hear, "Spike, Little John 2. I'm okay. Sorry, I lost the bird."

She keys her mic, "I'm just glad you're down safe."

Lizard, "Valkyrie, we need recovery."

"Arthur, Valkyrie 2, inbound."

"Arthur, Little John 1, I'm hanging from a bloody tree east of Dartford. The locals are coming."

BAWDEY RADAR STATION, UK

Gunner stands up in a field, rolling up his parachute. He sees NOB only a hundred feet away. As he gets his chute under control, he sees a dozen British soldiers running toward him. He drops the chute and lifts his hands.

A sergeant asks, "Are you okay, sir? Can we help you?"

He grins, "Sorry guys, they got me."

"Sir, we saw you shoot two down on your way down. That was legendary."

Gunner hears the sound of a jet and looks up to see Spike flying over at about a thousand feet. NOB walks up with his chute. "You okay, NOB?"

"Yeah."

Gunner says, "Wave at the boss." They both wave and Spike rocks her wings.

NOB, "Jesus Christ, you shot down two without engines."

Gunner, "I had to, buddy." He takes a deep breath fighting tears, "We lost Jedi and Stinky, NOB. Gone."

NOB puts his arm around Gunner's shoulders, and they're silent, surrounded by soldiers respectful in their grief.

A few minutes later, Dim Bulb finds them and comes into a hover to pick them up.

RAF KENLEY

Spike flares and her main gear chirps on the runway. She brings the nose down, rolls out, and makes the turn onto the taxiway. In front of their hanger, "Lizard, I need you to get her refueled, rearmed and checked out. We're going back up."

"Are you okay, Boss?"

They canopy goes up, "I'll never be okay. Just get us ready to fly."

"Roger, Boss."

She waves off Washington and climbs out of the bird. Swede walks up, his face pale and tight. She motions for him to turn around and follow her to the head. He stops and she motions him in. He follows, stiff. She pulls down her flight suit to pee, "Swede, they have accurate long-range missiles. We have to change tactics."

"Are you okay?"

"SWEDE! I don't fucking care how I am. How do we kill the motherfuckers who killed Jedi and Stinky?"

"I don't know."

"Look at me," and makes eye contact. "That isn't good enough, Swede. Our guys need and deserve more."

"Spike, I'm hurting."

"Swede, you're their leader. Hurt later. How do we respond?"

"We could have Too Tall jamming them, when he's available."

"Okay, it's a start. Also, no more flying blind. That, and get Too Tall's folks with Hammond and Fluffy. See if we can rush a jamming pod that our '14s can carry and our RIOs use."

"Okay, I'll get Grumman on it, too. Maybe we can put jammers in the radar birds."

She wipes and stand up, pulling up her panties and flight suit. "Do it. That's a good idea." Her voice softens, "Swede, we think first, and cry later. We're not allowed to feel until it's over. All we can do is keep killing and hope it ends before we lose everyone we love."

Swede smiles tiredly, "Okay. You know, if we keep meeting like this, folks will start talking."

She smiles as she washes her hands, "Maybe it will take some strain off you and Gloria. I had to pee and we needed privacy to talk this out. Out there, we need to have it together."

"How did you know I was a mess?"

"Stephan, you wore it on your face."

They walk out and find Fluffy waiting, his arms crossed, "You two all done?"

Spike says, "Master Chief, we need new gear. Swede will brief you. We also need to plan a funeral. Lord knows when we can find the time."

Fluffy frowns, "You okay, Boss?"

She meets his gaze, "I'm growing weary of that question. Swede, make sure everyone is briefed about the new long-range missiles. The Germans are getting better and we, too, have to get better."

"Roger, Spike."

Fluffy, "Do you have time to talk?"

"No. I have another flight. When I get back, we can talk." She turns her back on them and walks alone back to her jet.

Watching her go, Fluffy says, "Eleven kills in three minutes. Lizard told me."

Swede, "She's pissed. She's so angry, she's draining herself. Find Gandhi for me, I need to get in the air."

GERMAN AIRFIELD, WESTERN FRANCE

0940, 27 September, 1942

The young lieutenant FU-279 pilot stands, shaking before Hermann Goering. "It was the Drachendame. She's like a dragon. Three times I thought I had her and she moved like she could read my mind. Elev...eleven lost... my leader."

"Goering, "But, four planes killed?"

"Yes, my leader, two were the F-14 swing wing type. I am certain. I fired on them as General Weber instructed. They did not have their radar on and hoped to surprise us. The surprise was theirs."

"Did any of your missiles hit?"

"No, it was the others, as I said. I'm sure I hit one of the British jets, though."

"Tell me about it."

"I was in a left turn following my flight leader. I took the lead and fired my gun. I may have hit it, or scared it, but it reversed.

Then I fired a heat seeking missile and it hit the jet near the exhaust and exploded. The engine exploded right after. A left aileron roll and the pilot ejected."

"You have done well, Captain. I am proud of you. You will be assigned to Major Welter's squadron."

"Thank you, Herr General."

ARTHUR 1, 20,000 FEET OVER LONDON, UK

0946, 27 September, 1942

Spike is circling over the port district to the east of London. It's almost completely obscured by smoke. South of her Portsmouth and Plymouth are also nearly destroyed. To the far north, Scapa Flow is also badly damaged. The Germans control an airfield near Newcastle. All this because they have so few planes. It's maddening.

Swede is on her wing. Somewhere near Scapa, Gloria and Thud have just fought some ME-262s. "Is there any Germans out there?"

"No, Boss. It's quiet."

"How are they building so many planes?"

"I don't know. If this continues, our POW camps will have more German pilots than the Luftwaffe does."

"Maybe, I should talk to them. The prisoners. Do you think they know where all the planes are coming from?"

"They should."

GERMAN FRONT, EAST OF YORK, UK

1310, 27 September, 1942

Rommel stands in his Tiger HII's commander's hatch. Ahead of him, the rest of the battalion is in the fields, deployed in chevron formation. A few miles to his right, two brigades are being hammered by artillery and those cursed attack jets. West seemed open, so he chose east. On radio, "The fields ahead are flooded. It's soup."

"Left turn, head due east. Scouts advance ahead. We must find a way south."

BRITISH SABOTAGE UNIT ON THE DERWENT RIVER, SOUTH OF THE GERMAN FORMATIONS

Chris Oliverson stands with binoculars studying the Germans. He's a member of the SIS (Secret Intelligence Service) and is working with the British underground established by Churchill. "They continue east, sergeant."

"Yes, sir." Sgt. Bill Jones, a butcher from Pocklington, watches as the German formation turns to the east. He has a scoped rifle to his eye, counting vehicles. "This is a big force. At least, brigade strength."

Oliverson, "Right, they're going east. Use the tractor to tear the dam apart and tell team three to flood their fields. We'll sow what confusion we can."

GERMAN OCCUPIED, RAF OUSTON

1330, 27 September, 1942

Weber studies the map, "We have eighty aircraft available. Gunter, take your unit to South York. Take out the British and American artillery."

"Yes, sir. We have some iron bombs available. Missiles would be more accurate."

"Bombs. We'll need the missiles later."

"Yes, sir."

"Gunter, are you a member of the party?"

"No, Herr General."

"Good. A soldier should be a soldier and leave the politics for politicians."

"Then you're not a member, General?"

"No. Other than the SS units, have you noticed a shortage of party types here?"

"I hadn't thought of it, sir."

"Nor I. Focus on your mission, but tread carefully"

"Yes, sir. What do you think she'll do?"

"She's already protecting the attack jets. We have yet to provide direct air support. As both are near the lines, we must expect she'll pounce. Be careful. Our foe has proven herself clever."

GUNTER WITH 7 ME-262S, SOUTH OF YORK

Gunter pickles off four bombs in a shallow dive aimed at an American artillery unit. Anti-aircraft guns fire, but the rounds get nowhere near his fast jet. As he pulls out, he sees secondary explosions. "Find your targets. Hit artillery and supplies." Climbing, he studies the cloudy skies. His wingman forms up on him in his slow left turn. "There must be attack jets around here somewhere. Let's find them."

COMMODORE'S OFFICE, RAF KENLEY

1440, 27 September, 1942

Spike sits at her desk, writing. Her pen poised, she stares, then:

Dear Mr. and Mrs. Luke,

I am terribly saddened by your loss. Lieutenant Luke was an outstanding aviator and good friend. We met in training when I was transitioning to fighters and he was learning to be a pilot. He was kind, strong, and very funny. He received his call sign, 'Jedi' from a movie that was extremely popular in 1977. The movie's protagonist was named Luke and he learned to be a Jedi Knight. Kind of a mystical and spiritual warrior, a mix of Samurai and Knights Templar. In no way was Lorne mystical or spiritual. He was the squadron clown. He never said an unkind word, even when prov...

There's a knock on her door. "Radar."

Cooper pops his head in, "I know, Spike, but Patton is on the phone. It's urgent."

She picks up the phone, "Hunt."

"Commodore, the Krauts have changed tactics. They're hitting our artillery and logistics. No way we can hold out at York without supplies."

"Understood. Thank you, General."

"George, please."

"Thank you, George. Sam or Spike, just not ma'am."

He chuckles, "Fair enough."

"I'll direct cover for your supplies."

"Thank you."

TADCASTER ROAD, SOUTH BANK, YORK

1445, 27 September, 1942

PVT Mead drives their M-4 tank down the middle of the road. Most of the refugees have already fled south, so the road is fairly clear. Smoke rises from the rail yard and most of the city. SGT Steve Gains stands in the commander's hatch despite the rain and cold. They're the lead tank in a line of five more M-4s. His captain's tank broke down forty miles ago and his first sergeant's tank broke down outside Cambridge. His second lieutenant is with another platoon somewhere far behind.

A jet swoops over and he sees the cross. "Shit, air raid. Call it out." He swings his M-2, 50 caliber machine gun, but holds fire.

The jet is gone. He searches the sky and sees a bomb right before it lands. It hits two hundred yards ahead of his tank digging a huge crater. Rocks and pavement blocks bounce off his tank and he's covered in dust. "Right track." His voice sounds muted. "Right track!" He cannot hear the reply, but feels the tank turn. "Straight!"

He looks back. The five tanks are hugging the sides of the road where trees give them some concealment. As the jet approaches again, he leads it and fires a long burst. The jet passes too fast, and he misses. "Lead it, dumb shit."

GUNTER'S '262, OVER THE RIVER DERWENT, EAST OF YORK

Gunter rolls his aircraft and looks down. He sees dirt and water shoot up. He makes a large turn and studies the fields. He realizes they are flooded. He switches to ground frequency, "4th Corps, Red 1."

"Red 1, we hear you."

"Nearly all the fields east of York and north of the rivers are flooded. The British are damming the rivers and streams."

"Understood. Thank you, Red 1."

Gunter sees a flight of four American attack jets and turns to close, his wingman on his left.

HEADQUARTERS, GERMAN 4TH CORPS

Rommel studies a map, "If they push me to the coast, I'll be pinned against the Humber and destroyed." He picks up the radio, "All units east of York, reverse. We'll run direct through the city."

FLIGHT 1, VA-11, IRON ANGELS, NOE, OVER THE DERWENT, SOUTH OF GERMAN 4TH CORPS

LCDR William 'Book' Leonard spots the '262s on the deck to

his north and turns toward them. "Rusty flight, Rusty 1, stay on the deck. If they climb, don't follow."

"Book, Mower, who are you talking about. Oh."

Book adjusts and fires his 30mm cannon at the lead plane. It climbs out. He switches to the German's wingman and fires again. His rounds hit and the German plane shreds. His first '262 and sixth kill. "Rusty flight, Rusty 1, we fly a lose right turn if he pounces on one of us. The trailing bird engages."

GUNTER'S '262

In a climbing turn, he watches his wingman auger in. "Fuck. Fucking hell." He rolls over the top and studies the movements of the attack jets. He puts his aircraft into a shallow dive. "They're circling, clever." He pushes his throttles over and makes a pass on the A-10s. He puts rounds in one and climbs out. 30mm rounds fall well behind him. Circling in to try again, he catches a glint above him.

PERCIVAL 1, WEST OF GUNTER

Hot Pants sees the German '262 clearly. The A-10s in camouflage are harder to see, but their movement draws her gaze. "He's diving on them."

GQ, "I got him. Fox 1."

Hotpants pickles off an AIM-7 and watches it streak toward the German jet.

GUNTER

Gunter sees the incoming fire. He breaks north, diving for the ground and laying on all the power he can.

PERCIVAL 1

Hotpants, "We'll let him go. Our mission is to cover the Warthogs and the supply trains."

GQ puts her directions out on the radio as they climb back to 25,000 feet.

Hotpants asks, "How is William? Did he evacuate?"

"Not yet. He's helping move production and assembly gear south. They're going to disperse production so it's harder for the Germans to find."

"But, you two are all right, right?"

"Yeah, he's awesome. We are...we just jive together, you know?"

"I get it. Swede and I are like that. He's an amazing guy. I think most people see a big tough guy, but he thinks deeply about stuff. I was an idiot not to see him before."

"Are you two going to get married?"

"Yeah, when we can. He already asked. Well, I asked and he said yes. Right now, it would fuck up the chain of command."

"You heard about him and the boss in the bathroom?"

"Yes." She laughs and it sounds like water dancing down a brook. "Oh, God. He told me immediately, like I was going to be mad. Those two."

"What was it about?"

"It was right after we lost Jedi and Stinky. My love was a mess and she could see it. She dragged him into the head and chewed his ass."

He chuckles, "She has changed."

"Yeah, a few months ago, she was afraid of command. Now, she wears it with confidence. The kills fuck her up, though."

"Sister, I get that. I have nightmares about it."

"Me, too. Last night, I was in a court room with all the people I killed pointing an accusing finger at me."

"We killed."

"Yes, brother, we killed. Anyway, I couldn't see the judge, but I could hear his voice. It sounded like James Earl Jones. He wasn't happy with me."

GQ, "Last night, I dreamt we were in a night fight. Bullets were flying at us from all directions and I couldn't make sense of it. Parts were falling from our plane. I woke before we augured in."

"What can we do?"

"I don't know. Thirty-four kills. When I was in high school, I would read about World War II pilots. All their kills sounded cool, you know, heroes and shit. Reality is hard."

"It is, damn hard." Hotpants asks, "Do you worry about dying?"

"No. Not really. If we go, we go. I know how good you are, and how good we are as a team. But I also know anything can happen. Hell is going to suck, though."

"You're a good man, Byron."

"I'm a killer and I'm gay. There's no room for my type in heaven."

"Bull shit. Any religion that curses true love is evil. I've heard God loves fools and soldiers. Anyway, we're here to save people, millions of people, and you know it. We are his instruments. We may hate it, but that's what God is counting on; that we hate it, but we do it anyway, because it needs doing. If we loved it, then that's a big problem. Other than that, because God is love, he doesn't care. Okay?"

GQ is silent for a moment, "Wow, you've really figured this thing out."

"Yeah, I had to. It's all that damn Catholic conditioning. I had to understand why we are here. It's to shorten the war so that more may live. Simple. We just can't like it, and that makes sense. He loves you, Byron, never forget it."

"Thanks, sis, I'll think about it.

CHAPTER 14

81ˢᵀ ARMORED RECONNAISSANCE BATTALION, LANCASTER, UK

1544, 27 September, 1942

LT Colonel Charles J. Hoy stands beside the cockpit in the first of eight LCACs as it races toward the low banked shore at nearly fifty miles per hour. He leans his head in, "I see the jetty."

"Yes, sir." The pilot slows the huge hovercraft and they run up the beach, and with a bump, they're onto grass. The long grass is blown away from the hovercraft as it slows to a stop. Hoy, his men, mount their vehicles.

The sailors unchain the armor and the front ramp drops. The lift fans stop causing the LCAC to sit on the ground, making the ramp easier to traverse. Hoy, "Driver, proceed." His tank runs out clear of the LCAC, moves out of the way, and stops. The whole debarkation process takes less than two minutes. In ten minutes, half of his battalion is formed up in the sandy field.

BOOTHAM, NORTH YORK, UK

1620, 27 September, 1942

General George Patton stands tall in his command tank watching the battle unfold in front of him. In trenches dug into the soggy ground and behind stone fences, his men are dug in for the fight. The tank to his right is hit. He shifts his glasses to the front, "Target, tank, eleven o'clock."

The 75mm gun in his Sherman tank fires. He follows the track of the projectile and sees it hit the big German tank and bounce off. "Again."

The German tank fires and another tank to his right goes away.

His tank fires, and hits the German's turret to no effect. "Again."

His crew is well trained and they get off a round before the Germans, but, again, the round has no effect.

His gunner shouts, "Back, right track!" His tank lurches and he feels the German round whip past him.

Patton keys the radio, "Division, Corps, have 67th Regiment fall back. 66th and 41st, hold if you can. I want a pocket."

Major General Ernest N. Harmon, commander of 2nd Armored Division replies, "Sir, we're engaging with artillery. Do you have another plan?"

As they speak, artillery shells fall onto the German lines.

Patton, "Ernest, we need to get a shot at their rear where they're vulnerable."

"Yes, sir."

The artillery rounds continue falling. Patton watches as some hit, but most just explode in the soggy ground. Patton surveys the scene, "The Kraut's will fall back. They have too."

4TH CORPS, GERMAN HEADQUARTERS, NORTH OF PATTON

Rommel surveys the fields from the hatch of his Tiger tank. A junior officer approaches, "Herr Field Marshal, 101st Battalion has broken through west of Leeds."

"Understood." He hears the artillery rounds shrieking in, "Seek cover, Hubert." He keys the mic, "All units, rapid advance. Close the Americans."

His tanks had been dueling, now, they rush forward.

PATTON'S TANK

"You clever, clever bastard." On radio, "They're coming in. Stick with the plan. Get them in the pocket. Hit them on their flanks where they're vulnerable. Send in the reserves."

"Sir, the reserves are already committed."

WIGGINTON ROAD, NORTH YORK

SGT Gains is still at the front of his column. They've been attacked by air again and now have four tanks with extra men hanging onto the operational tanks. He sees a Sherman going in the opposite direction and shouts, "What gives?"

The TC, a second lieutenant, shouts, "They've broken through. We're falling back."

"Did Patton order the retreat, sir?"

The other is silent, "The German tanks, you can't kill them."

"Sir. Turn the fuck around and join us."

The officer's face pales, "No."

SGT Gains, "Sir. If you do not turn around, you will regret it the rest of your life."

"No."

"Then, sir, un-ass your track. I have crew that can use it."

SGT Gains unit finally makes it to the front and he calls on radio, "Any command, we are a tank platoon on Corban Lane."

He hears a British voice, "Yank, you're in our sector. We see you. I've directed a man to guide you in."

He sees the Brit and follows him to the line. Incoming rounds fill the air. At first, he can't see the Germans, then he sees the flash of flame at the tree line. They're close. "Gunner, tank, eleven o'clock."

"Up."

"Away." The round hits the Panzer 4, but it keeps coming. "Again."

PATTON'S TANK

1708, 27 September, 1942

George Patton studies the battle. The pocket never properly formed. Rommel focused his attack on the left flank. The artillery duel continues and attack jets are diving on the Germans, killing them. He sees a lone Lancaster bomber flying over at low altitude.

GULF CHARLEY VICTOR, OVER THE BATTLE OF NORTH YORK

Looking out over one of the miniguns, LT Hammond studies the battle beneath him. He pushes the button on his crew helmet, "Pilot, Hamm. See the troop concentration by the clump of trees next to the ruined green barn?"

Flight Lieutenant David John Pryer Lee says, "Got it." He adjusts his flight path and the gun next to Hammond wakes up. 36,000 bullets rain down on the designated area. What was German infantry, is now a carnage of churned dirt and blood.

Hammond, "Behind the tanks," and the guns speak again. Sparks flash on the tanks. The infantry, not covered by tanks, are pulped by the 20mm cannon.

Hammond sees a missile corkscrew toward them, "Countermeasures. Break left." He hears the rattle of flares and chaff exiting the rear of the plane as it turns violently on its side. The missile explodes behind them, but another is launched.

Flight Lieutenant Lee orients his plane to put the missile on his beam and fires as he rolls. The missile explodes and a moment later, so does the German half-track that was firing it.

RAF KENLEY

0855, 28 September, 1942

Spike enters the landing pattern behind Merlin, their EA-6B. Merlin is making the break when she spots something in the distance. "Bogies twelve o'clock."

Lizard, "Yankee, what do we have to our front?"

"Arthur, Yankee, Navy 122 and 123."

"Roger, Yankee."

Spike, "Two more planes, good." She makes the break and soon their down and taxiing to their hanger.

Lizard, "Admiral Lee?"

"Yeah, Lizard. Two more jets. You suppose he caught hell for flying with us?"

"Probably. But I wouldn't care and I doubt he does. Dixie's a good one."

"Yes, he is."

"I heard he has a girlfriend in DC."

"You heard from whom?"

"Boss, don't a guy get to have some secrets?"

"Okay, Lizard. I hope he's happy. This source of yours, what else are you getting from Washington?"

"The new carrier, Yorktown, has been launched and is being fitted out. It's the one made from a battleship hull."

"That's good. The Midway class couldn't handle Tomcats. Do you suppose this one can?"

"It should. That's what we're building."

"True."

"The Enterprise is launching soon, and the sponsor is the First

Lady."

"I see, and?"

"Puck is in Bethesda."

"I know that."

"Admiral Klindt is getting married next spring."

"Good for him."

"We're finally launching missile destroyers, cruisers, and battleships."

"My friend, Hughes, is serving on one."

"Oh, well, that's about all I know related to the war."

"Okay. If you learn anything relevant and new, please let me know."

"Will do."

Spike climbs down out of the F-14 and stretches her stiff muscles as she walks to the head. When she's finished, she walks back out and toward the new birds. She walks up to 'Dixie' Lee, "Hey, dad. I heard you have a new girlfriend." She grins.

Looking abashed, Lee says, "You're learning to keep your ear to the ground, good. Her name is Ashley Smith. She's beautiful, kind, and smart as a whip. Are you okay with dad having a love life?"

"I'm great with you having a love life. You deserve to be happy."

"You know, darlin, you deserve a love life, too."

She looks away, then turns back and meets his eyes, "Let's go to control. I have a jeep back here."

"I take it Control isn't close?"

"Nope. This base is laid out differently." She waves off her driver and gets behind the wheel.

"They let you drive?"

"I give them no choice."

"Atta girl."

"Dad, we lost Jedi and Stinky."

"Damn. When?"

"Yesterday."

"I'm sorry, Sam."

"The Germans have fielded a new long-range missile. Jedi and Gunner were closing dark and got surprised. Gunner and NOB managed to eject. Jedi and Stinky went up with their bird."

"What happened next, darlin?"

"I got ice cold angry and went on a killing spree."

"How many?"

"Eleven...in about three minutes, Dad. I'm a fucking killer." He sees tears filling her eyes.

"Listen to me, darlin. You're no such thing."

"Dad, I was hitting cockpits. I did it on purpose. I just ended them. I ended them like they ended Jedi and Stinky. I'm a monster." She pulls off on the side of the road near the tower and puts her head on her hands on the steering wheel.

"Darlin, nothing I say, nothing I do, can take your pain away. I want to. Lord knows I want to, but I can't." She turns her head and looks into his eyes. "Darlin, what I can do is tell you, I love you. Unconditional, unlimited, total love, and I can relate to how you feel. That and one more thing."

"What?"

"How you're reacting. How you're hurting. It tells me something profound. It tells me you have not lost your humanity."

"I'm a mess."

"So? You can be a mess with me. Lord knows, I was a mess with you. In that way, we need each other, you and I. Do you recall that night in Rota?"

"Yeah, Dad. You were a mess. It was after you lost your daughter."

"It was after my daughter was murdered and I...I murdered her killer."

"You didn't murder him."

"I did. I took the law into my own hands. He taunted me, admitting he killed her, and he was going to get away with it. He was trying to intimidate me. He was a right bastard."

"You told me that police detective knew you killed him."

"Yeah, the detective knew more than the dude thought. He told me they were considering his killing as gang related, and, that I should wear gloves for a while. The point is, darlin, you have me to lean on and I know I have you."

Sam leans over and hugs Lee. She takes a deep breath and sits up straight, "Thank you, Dad."

CONTROL ROOM, RAF KENLEY

Vice Admiral Lee and Commodore Hunt walk into control and the watch officer says, "Galahad flight is engaged east of Dover over the Channel. Percival is covering the area around York. The Germans have begun hitting the supply chain south of York and the allied artillery positions. Maid Mary and Robin are covering there and battling twelve '262s. The Germans have broken through at Leeds. Patton is falling back from York to prevent being flanked. Gulf Charley Victor is covering the retreat."

Spike, "What is Gulf Charley Victor?"

"It's a Lancaster gunship, Commodore. LT Hammond is on board."

Spike smiles, 'Good. Admiral, York held for a couple of days.

We're slowing them."

"Whose idea was the gunships?"

"Mine. It made sense."

"It does. Good call. Are we making them?"

"Eisenhower asked the Air Corps for them. I put in the specs."

"Do you think the Humber line will hold?"

"For a while. We are exchanging lives and land for time."

Lee nods his head, "Spike, you were right to move your operations here."

"Thank you, sir."

A Marine LT Colonel in dress green enters and salutes, "Admiral, Commodore, Lieutenant Colonel Peter Andrews reporting for duty."

Spike looks him over. His uniform is sharp and tailored. He has a square jaw and an open honest face. "Where do you come from, Colonel?"

"Commandant's staff, ma'am. General Eisenhower sent for me."

"Do you know him?"

"Yes, ma'am, but only in passing."

"So, you're recommended as my chief of staff?"

"It seems so, ma'am."

"Okay, first, stop calling me ma'am. I'm Spike, Commodore, Hunt, Yankee, whatever. Just not ma'am."

"Yes...Commodore."

"Do you know your job?"

"Per the direction I received from Admiral King and Vice Admiral Lee, my job is to run the staff and base so you can focus on war fighting."

She looks at Dixie then back to the colonel, "I see. Well, there are a million details to it. First priority is the fuel, ammunition, and parts our aircraft need to fight. Next is security. This base has to be safe and the aircraft and ordinance protected. Third is crew comfort. I need the guys rested and ready to fight. That includes me. Fourth is ground crew. They need the tools, parts, places and time to keep our birds flyable. They also need to rest. Exhausted people make mistakes. With me so far?"

"Yes, Commodore." He's taken out a notebook and pen and is busily writing.

"Okay, we have four squadrons and three detachments flying for us. Commander Stephan 'Swede' Swedenborg commands the Black Knights and has been my chief of staff. He'll not be a problem, he'll be relieved. Major Floyd 'Sparks' Park commands the Devil Dogs. LCDR William 'Book' Leonard commands the Iron Angels."

Dixie gives her a sharp look.

"What are the Devil Dogs and Iron Angels?"

"A-10 Warthogs. They fly ground attack missions and support our ground forces. Squadron Leader Richard 'Mister' Maugham commands the Merry Men, a British unit under our command."

"The British are letting you command one of their squadrons?"

"Colonel, basically, I command all the air assets in the UK at this point in time. So, now, the Merry Men fly the Griffin jet fighter. We have a helo detachment, commanded by LCDR Sandra 'Cargo Britches' Douglas."

"What's a helo?"

"Helicopter. It's going to take time for you to get up to speed." Cooper joins them, handing Spike and Dixie plates of food. "Thank you, Radar. YN1 Cooper, this is our new chief of staff,

LT Colonel Peter Andrews."

The two men shake hands, and Radar says, "Welcome aboard, sir."

Andrews, "Thanks," and looks back to Spike. "Are there any other units?"

"There is. We have an electronic warfare bird commanded by LCDR Mike 'Too Tall' Mohr and an anti-sub and refueling detachment commanded by LCDR Fred 'Piper' McCrimmon. Finally, a US submarine stationed in Scotland is under my command. It's currently deployed on a special mission."

"Should I know what?"

"No, not yet. Do you feel like you're drowning yet?"

"It will take a bit to sort out, but I'll get it."

"So, YN1 Cooper is my right-hand man. He can get you most of what you need. He knows where all the bodies are buried, and he knows how the system works. I hope you two can work together."

Cooper smiles, "Boss, eat. I'll show him around."

"Okay, Radar. Colonel, set up whatever meetings you need, but schedule them around the flight schedule."

"Yes, Commodore." He salutes and the two men leave.

She turns to Lee, "You didn't mention him."

"What we were talking about was way more important than a chief of staff. He's a Yale graduate with a bachelors in English. His family is New York money, but he knows his business. He did a tour in the Philippines as a JO, so he's not a beltway warrior."

"Okay, if he can run this place without driving the guys nuts, I couldn't care less how rich his folks are. When do you need to leave?"

"In a bit. If possible, I want to attend the memorial for Parley,

Jedi, and Stinky."

"I've no idea when we can break long enough for a service. I fear it will be a service for more than those three."

"Just keep me posted. Next trip, the transport will have new ground crew and additional security Marines. By the way, your friend, Hughes, was in a hell of a battle off Guadalcanal."

"Is he okay?"

"He's not on the list of the dead. A SAG led by the Washington and North Carolina were jumped by a couple of Japanese units. They're calling it the Battle of Savo Island."

"What did we lose?"

"The Minneapolis and a couple of destroyers sunk. The Columbia got hammered. But we hammered the Japanese back pretty good; a battleship and some cruisers. They're calling it a draw. That's all I know."

"Thank you. Any word on the fighting ashore?"

"Yeah, the Marines have mopped up. Oh, and your dad was field commissioned. Did that happen before?"

"He was offered a commission on another island, but turned it down. I'm glad he took it. You know, they were 'mopping up' that island for six months. What changed?"

"Helicopters and the Vinson. They've the Blue Diamonds there now. They don't have field lighting yet for night flying, but that's coming. That reminds me, Cargo Britches should have new SH-60s and H-60s coming soon, by C-130."

Smiling, she asks, "What's going on everywhere else? Like who is CAG on the Vinson?"

"The old air boss, Charley Forrester. Groovy is PCO for the Enterprise and Frosty is PCO for the Yorktown."

"Wow."

"Darlin, we have new air crew in the pipeline, but they're still flying F-1 War Eagles. It's a solid, well behaved, gen 3 fighter. I've got a couple dozen hours in it. It turns like a dream under 15. Up high, it turns like an ocean liner. It can be a little finicky in a stall. It has radar, but it can only swing 15 degrees. Reminds me a bit of the T-45. It's bigger and supersonic, but feels similar." He sees the bemused look on her face, "Oh, sorry. You know me, I get carried away. Anyway, once you have your birds, I'll be helping the school at the Grumman plant in New York. We don't have the luxury of a full training cycle, so how green do you want them?"

"Dad, I'd like them fully trained and ready to fight, but I need them now. Are they learning ACM?"

"In the Eagle, yes. Walker and Klint are their teachers."

"Okay, they're a good choice. So, how are they doing?"

"Getting better. It will be a while before either of them can fly combat again."

"Do you have a F-14 simulator?"

"No."

"How are the RIOs learning their job?"

"The RIOs are learning in the class room on bench simulators. We also put them in the back of a modified Dauntless for ACM familiarization. Rascal's their teacher."

"Jesus, Dad, they won't even know their job. Okay, pick the very best aircrews. I want the first five that can safely and effectively fly the Tomcat. We'll teach them how to fight it."

"Right, will do. If they can compete, I want to send most of the women to you."

"That's fine."

"Darlin, Jackie Cochran is in the class."

"Okay, so?"

"You know who she is?"

"Dad, she's an icon. She opened so many doors for the rest of us. She was the commander of the Women Airforce Service Pilots. She was the first woman to break the sound barrier."

"Not anymore. She's a lieutenant in the US Navy and you are the first woman to break the sound barrier."

"Oh, I see. Is she good?"

"I'm told she's damn good, but she flies with a chip on her shoulder. Do you want her?"

"Yes, Dad, I do. We need the best."

CHAPTER 15

PIER 6, PUGET SOUND NAVAL SHIPYARD

0100, 28 September, 1942 (0900 GMT)

Captain Tenzar watches from his new bridge wing as the hammer head crane lowers Mount 2 into its casement. Because of the modifications Maki designed, the below deck ammunition handling room is now only twelve feet deep.

Tenzar asks, "Captain Warren, where is MM2 Maki?"

"Lieutenant JG Maki is in Detroit right now."

"What the hell is he doing there?"

Warren looks at Tenzar with a slight smile, "Admiral Klindt has him designing a new tank for the Marines."

"A tank? He's a nuke." He stops, thinking, "Well, if I put my nukes to it, they'd design one hell of a tank. Just, they would include room for a keg and an incredible sound system."

Warren laughs, "And, they would include nooks and cranny's everywhere to squirrel away contraband."

Tenzar, now laughing, "And each one would have a custom, incredible, non-regulation paint job."

"Yep, but you know what? It would run like a top and last for years."

Tenzar sighs, "True. I'm not getting him back, am I?"

"I don't know, and that's the honest truth."

PROVING GROUND OUTSIDE OF DETROIT, MICHIGAN

0615, 28 September, 1942 (1215 GMT)

Maki runs his jeep a second lap around the course, then stops, the jeep at a precarious angle on a hill. He pulls out a pad and pen and takes notes. The GM engineer with him asks, "What's wrong?"

"I want this hill to get progressively steeper until the tank rolls. We need a nest of small diameter logs and loose sand so the tank isn't damaged."

"You want to roll it?"

"How else can we honestly say what it can take?"

"We roll test vehicles in a roll rig. It's safer."

"Our Marines won't be static when they roll one. They'll be moving and fully loaded. We got to get it right. Lives depend on it.

TARMAC, RAF KENLEY

1224, 28 September, 1942

Sam takes Lee's hand, "Take care, Dad."

"You too, darlin." They hear the sound of engines and look up. It's the first of four C-130's. "Here are the first of your helo's and crews."

"I'll get Sandra. I need to go."

"Take care, darlin. I love you." He turns and walks to his transport.

SKEDDERGATE BRIDGE, YORK, UK

1244, 28 September, 1942

Patton's tanks race south on Tower Street, the Germans in

pursuit. The turret is rotated facing over the back deck, his gunner looking for targets. He listens on the command net. The 2nd Armored Division is in full retreat. As they approach the tower, a civilian woman runs from a building waving her hands. "Driver, stop."

She looks up at Patton, "Sir, we are ready to blow buildings and bridges. Are you the last?"

"In truth, I'm uncertain." On radio, "Are there any American units in north central York?"

There's no reply, "General Harmon, Patton."

"General Patton, Colonel Grunion, the general's tank was hit a few minutes ago. No survivors."

"Understood. Brigades, report location." His units report in and a German round flies by them, "Target, tank." To the woman, "Blow them and we'll cover your retreat."

"All due respect, sir, but we're staying to bugger up the Germans good." She smiles when Patton salutes, and runs back into the tower.

"Driver, move out."

TARMAC, RAF KENLEY

1335, 28 September, 1942

Two hundred sixty men and women stand in ranks. Behind them are twelve brand new Blackhawk and Seahawk helicopters. Spike's smile is huge as she pins the silver oak leaves of a commander on Sandra Douglas' collar. "Congratulations, Commander. What are you naming your squadron?"

"Helicopter Squadron one, ma'am, the Valkyries."

"That works. You have a lot to do. Now, we can better support the dust-off mission."

HUMBER LINE AT THE OUSE RIVER, NORTH OF SELBY, UK

1644, 28 September, 1942

SGT Gains studies the fields on the other side of the river. His tank is behind a six-foot-high berm that's twenty or more feet thick. The ground is muddy, but the engineers had spread out gravel, making it more manageable. So far, he doesn't see any movement at his front.

A jeep pulls up behind them, "Is this 2nd Platoon, Easy Company, 2nd of the 1st, 2nd AD?"

Gains turns, "Yeah, part of it. Don't know where the LT is."

The Master Sergeant in the jeep asks, "Are you Sergeant Gains?"

Lance swallows, "I am, Master Sergeant."

"Get in. Patton wants to see you."

"Um, roger. Should I get my gear?"

"Nope."

"Roger." He tells his guys and un-asses the tank.

A silent ten-minute drive and he's in Selby, pulling up to a pub name the Unicorn. Gains asks, "Master Sergeant?"

"This is headquarters. Go in."

Gains gets out of the jeep and walks into the low-ceilinged pub. From a corner, General Patton shouts, "Sergeant Gains! Over here," and motions him to an empty seat.

Gains walks up and salutes. Patton smiles around his unlit cigar and returns the salute, "Sit." He pushes a paper across the table and watches as Gains reads it. It's his radio report of the deserters turned into a formal statement.

"You want me to sign this, sir?"

"Is it accurate?"

"Yes, sir."

"Sign it."

Gains does and slides it back. Patton says, "Bring them in."

From a back room, the lieutenant, and the other three crew members from the deserting tank, are brought out. They're wet and disheveled, but unharmed. Patton asks, "Sergeant Gains, are these the deserters?"

Gains looks each in the eye. They appear desperate and defeated. "Yes, sir, they are."

Patton, "Thank you. Provost, I find the lot guilty. Get them out of my sight." The Provost leads them out, their heads down.

Patton turns back to Gains, "I'm told you kept your unit in good order, picked up stragglers, and acquitted yourself well with the British Lancers."

"My lieutenant's track broke down, sir. He told me to continue on and find the fight."

Patton laughs, "And by God, you did. Your lieutenant is well east of your position commanding Delta Company right now, and you need a new platoon officer."

"So, my company is on line?"

"Easy is mostly west of you. The Brit's hold the position between you. I'll have you swap around, but first; we need a new platoon officer. Sergeant, please stand."

Gains stands and Patton swears him in, "Congratulations, Lieutenant. You've much to do. Carry on."

A shocked 2nd Lieutenant Gains salutes, "Thank you, sir."

CONTROL, RAF KENLEY

1702, 28 September, 1942

Spike listens to the radio chatter as she reads reports. An aid whisks away her finished dinner. She initials each report, sometimes putting in a comment. She feels better now that the forward edge of battle is delineated on the board. Now, she can help the A-10s. Right now, the US Army is on the Humber line. Over one hundred thousand refugees are streaming south. A US Army Major walks in and salutes. She returns the salute and motions to the chair next to her. He sits and hands her a message:

FROM: COI

TO: COMTFYAN

REG: Operation Sky Hook

Commander TF Yankee. I've directed Major Robbins to brief you on the above-mentioned operation. Your cooperation is vital to its success.

Donovan

She nods and rises. To the duty officer, "I'll be in my office," and walks out. In the outer room of her new office, Cooper and his assistants are working at their desks. Of the inner offices, one belongs to her chief of staff, one is a conference room, and one is her private domain. "Radar, I have a brief meeting. Is my schedule clear for fifteen minutes?"

Cooper looks up, "Yes, Commodore. Staff meeting in 30, if you can make it. Do you want tea?"

"After, thank you." She motions the major in and follows and closes the door. "You have 15. Start."

"I understand you've met Lieutenant Torrey. We need to extract him from France for another mission."

"That's a low second priority for me. Meaning, we'll get to it when we can."

"Ma'am, it needs to happen soon."

Weary, she sighs, "Explain to me why it is more important than the survival of Britain."

"It's necessary for the survival of Britain."

"The clock is ticking, Major." She sits down and steeples her fingers.

"Russia has a treaty with Germany and isn't fighting. We're training their pilots and sending them back to Russia with new jets, but our intel is telling us they will not be fighting the Germans. It's the ceasefire with Russia that has freed up the German combat units and aircraft to focus on Britain. If Russia re-enters the war, then Germany must pull back."

"Germany can't pull back. Do you think we will just let them leave?"

"They would have to pull back the Luftwaffe. How long would the German Wehrmacht last if your control of the sky was unchallenged?"

"Point taken. Okay, explain your plan."

WATERLOO, UK SW OF LEEDS

1750, 28 September, 1942

Sergeant Johnny Rodriguez motions for the driver to stop their truck. Ahead, an old stone building lays scattered across the road and the towns people are digging through the rubble. An old man approaches and Johnny asks, "Were you bombed, sir?"

"Bombed, eh? No. The bloody Krauts came through with their bloody tanks and shot us up. Destroyed our church. It stood for three hundred years, and now, it's rubble."

"Where are they?"

"I married my Catherine in that church. What, eh?"

"Where are the Germans?"

"They nicked the petrol from the station south of town and buggered off south. Do you all fancy a meal?"

"We have to catch up to the Germans, sir."

"You'll not be giving them a go with a dozen men and a truck. That lot was a full battalion of tanks. All you'll do is get dead."

"We've a wounded American pilot in the back who can call in the attack jets."

"I see, then. Well, it is easier to kill Krauts with a full belly. When did you last have a hot meal?"

"Not since before they landed."

"Then come. I've a pub around the corner. Let's fill your bellies."

Johnny asks, "Sir, how did you know it was a battalion?"

The old man straightens up and salutes, "Sergeant Cox, His Majesties Yorkshire Volunteers. I fought in the last war. Left the service after an injury in '32."

CONTROL CENTER, RAF KENLEY

0500, 29 September, 1942

Spike walks in, "Lancelot and Galahad are up. Galahad is engaged with a flight of six over the Channel east of York. Lancelot is out defending a cruiser group in the North Sea. We directed Robin, Little John, and Maid Mary south of Dover in anticipation. The American, Canadian, and British Armies are getting organized on the Humber Line. The Germans have already hit it at Selby. Dusty 1 and 2 are supporting them there. One of the wounded A-10 pilots, LT Peter 'Loony' Thun is acting as forward air observer. You have a TS message in the box and two letters."

"Thank you." She opens the top secret safe and pulls out the message:

FROM: YANKEE BRAVO

TO: TFYAN

REG: CROSSFIRE

Operation successful. Zero casualties. Commencing egress.

Yankee Bravo

She stares at it, the San Francisco did it. Good. But we could use them out there. She writes:

FROM: TFYAN

TO: YANKEE BRAVO

REG: EGRESS

Remain on station in deep water. Stand by to pick up additional SF via parachute. Op designated 'Hail Mary' in future comms. Maintain current communication schedule.

HUNT

TFYAN

She writes another:

TO: ETOUSA

FROM: TFYAN

REG: AIRBORNE DIVISION

I need the training status of the 82nd and the 101st Airborne

Divisions. Also, it is desirous that they all be qualified and equipped for parachute insertion. The proposed operation is division strength airborne assault on German occupied RAF Ouston. I recognize this will necessitate a significant transport effort. This plan will be called Operation Sunset and is Top Secret.

Thank you,

Hunt

TFYAN

"That will get them moving. What else? Oh."

TO: NAVAIR

FROM: TFYAN

REG: SPECIAL OPERATIONS UNIT

Admiral Lee,

I need a SEAL Team as soon as possible. They need to be equipped and trained for HALO and seaborne ingress and seaborne egress. They must be on station one week before the Russian pilots are released to report. The Russian pilots must travel through England en route to Russia. I have need of the team for a month or more. Operational directive is designated Operation Hail Mary. Top Secret.

Thank you,

Hunt

TFYAN

FISHING WHARF, YOKOSUKA, JAPAN

1513, 29 September, 1942 (0613 29 September GMT)

LT Chris Hisakawa is standing on the wharf sorting and repairing nets. His employer, Haru Satou, comes up, "Ginzo, could you please come?"

"Yes, Captain."

They walk down the wharf, "You have proven yourself a competent mariner and a good fisherman. Seeing that you are unlikely to be making a living with your poetry any time soon, I have thought we would be more effective with another boat." Haru points. The fishing boat is about forty feet long with an aft cabin and a single mast. She's dirty and looks to not have been used for some time. Its black hull paint is peeling and the white cabin is barely there. He looks at Haru with genuine pleasure. "You trust me with your boat?"

"I do."

"Does it have nets?"

"They need repair."

"I will do it. I am honored."

"Good. These are your papers. Make it ready soon."

"May I, then, live aboard immediately?"

"You may wish to clean it first, but yes. Then, when you invite your girlfriend and her grandfather to join you, she will not turn up her nose."

"Thank you, Captain. I though, will bring her now. If she will be fisherman's wife, she will help me."

"Well said. I will leave you to it."

Chris steps aboard. Yes, it's in poor condition, but he immediately sees the potential. Lieutenant Chris 'Chaos' Hisakawa, USN can see the possibilities for escaping Japan.

101 BATTALION, 1ST REGIMENT, 3RD PANZER DIVISION,

HUDDERFIELD, ON THE RIVER COLNE, SW OF LEEDS, UK

0833, 29 September, 1942

SS-Obersturmbannfuhreer Rolf Meier orders his driver to stop. Ahead of him is another obstruction. They've had signs changed, bridges destroyed, and trees felled in attempt to stop their advance. In this village, there are overturned vehicles and collapsed buildings blocking the way. Wood burns in a bonfire in front of the carnage. As he studies the scene before him, he hears the thwack, buzz of a bullet ricocheting off his tank. He swings his machine gun and sprays the buildings to the left of the road. The other tanks follow suit. On radio, "Don't waste ammunition."

BEHIND THE BARRICADE

Jimmy Thatcher is fifteen years old. He and his class mates steal glances over their makeshift barricade. His grandpa says, "Keep your heads down, lads. Be patient."

The lead tank fires. Rocks and dust engulf them. The noise is deafening and the concussion takes their breath. The wood fires, briefly go out. Andy Turner curls into a ball, shaking.

Jimmy puts his hand to his great grandfather's saber. His great grandfather earned the single edged weapon with its cast and engraved bronze hilt and hand guard and leather wrapped wood grip in Egypt. It's his only weapon beside the Molotov cocktail he holds. Only his grandpa and the police woman have a rifle. He hears his grandfather's words in his mind, "Remember Jimmy, should I fall, get the rifle."

He shakes his head, not wanting to think about what that means. Then, he sees the lead tank move forward, "Grandpa, they're moving."

"I see. Everyone, we wait until we can't miss. Then hit 'em."

The huge German tank reaches the barricade. Grandpa Paul rises up and takes two shots. He's cut down with machine gun fire. As ordered, Jimmy grabs the rifle and ammo belt. The police woman shoots, then turns and runs. He can hear the tank crunching up the other side, when he sees a three-inch pipe. "Andy, help me."

Andy pushes himself up beside Jimmy, and the two boys pull the pipe from the rubble. When the tracks of the tank top the barricade, they stuff the pipe into the tracks. The pipe jerks out of their hands as it locks up the tracks and the tank stops moving.

Jimmy and Andy run to a brick garden wall and join the others.

MEIER'S TANK

The tank jerks to a stop, throwing the crew forward. Meier shouts into his head set, "Driver, move!"

"Sir, the right track. It won't move."

"Move!"

"The driver guns it and they hear the sound of breaking metal."

"Damn, damn. Now, your commander will exit the tank to see what you broke." He climbs out of the hatch and feels the burn of a bullet across his cheek. He shouts down the hatch, "Engage, damn you!" And hops off the tanks as another bullet whizzes by.

CHURCH STEEPLE SOUTH OF MEIER'S TANK

Lieutenant Urland reaches the top of the tower out of breath. He gets into position and looks out to the north. He has a clear view down the street and sees the tank stopped at the barricade with the others strung out behind. "Perfect." On radio, "Any Warthog, this is Wingnut."

"Wingnut, Dog flight 3, state location."

Wingnut opens his map and reads off the coordinates, "...and we're in a church west of the rail yard. Approach from the south east, exit west. Tiger tank disabled by local militia."

"Roger, overhead in 6 mikes."

Roger, Dog 3, Wingnut out."

MEIER'S TANK

Meier, his entire crew is out of the tank, except the driver. His driver tries reversing the tank, as the men pull on the pipe. Crew from the next tank in line come over to help. His gunner stands to pull and is hit in the back by a rifle round, "Sorry, sir." He crumples onto the barricade and rolls down. Meier yells at his loader, "Get on the machine gun and silence that rifle."

"Yes, sir." He jumps onto the tank and climbs into the commander's hatch.

100 YARDS SOUTH OF THE TANK

Jimmy's fired seven shots. His last shot hit a soldier and now another is climbing into the tank. He fires and sees his round hit near the machine gun. He forces his breath to slow and aims. He sees the German half out of the tank looking toward him. Jimmy squeezes the trigger, "Please, please, please."

The rifle leaps in his hands, and the bullet flies true. He can see the shock on the man's face, and then he hears, 'Brrrrt.' The tank just explodes. The turret flies off and falls beside the tank hull. On the barricade, the men closest to the tank are dead. The rest start shooting at him, then scramble away. He looks around and realizes he's alone. He slips behind a building and runs, rifle in hand and sword slapping at his side.

GERMAN TANK FORMATION

Meier, covered in dust and blood, staggers down the line. The A-10 is certainly coming back. His men are running their tanks into houses and yards attempting to avoid the Devil's Cross. He runs to a tank tucked between two houses, "Rolf, exit this tank, quickly."

MERLIN, 100 FEET, 45 MILES SOUTHWEST OF OCCUPIED RAF OUSTON

0841, 29 September, 1942

Mike 'Too Tall' Mohr says, "Okay, Sweets, Keg, we know they have at least six radars besides the station radar. Let's see if the station radar crew is talking to the defense operators. Turn us toward Ouston and climb to 800 feet."

His copilot and navigator, LT Tabitha 'Sweets' Younger climbs the EA-6B Prowler, "We've been mapping for three days. When are we going to break these assholes?" The gradual climb pokes the antenna in the vertical stabilizer high enough to pick up radar.

Too Tall, "Spike is right. We hit them when we can destroy them completely."

AC1 Greg 'Keg' Berman, "That would take the army. Um, the targeting radars have lit us up."

Sweets, "Got it," and puts them in a shallow sliding dive. The earth rushes at them and she pulls out at 100 feet, just above the trees.

CHAPTER 16

2ND PLATOON, A COMPANY, 1ST BATTALION, 15TH REGIMENT, 3RD INFANTRY DIVISION, IN THE HILL WEST OF LEEDS

0846, 29 September, 1942

Private Joshua Banner sits on his pack in the trench they've just finished digging. "What a complete waste of time. Ain't any Germans out here." He plucks a bit of grass and winds it around his fingers.

His sergeant says, "Keep a sharp eye out. We're here because they could come here."

PFC Andy McDonald, "Okay, Sergeant Crabtree, but how are we going to stop their tanks if they do come? All we got is 37mm guns."

"Those guns are high velocity. They'll fare better than you think."

Andy moves and turns back to watch the road below and in front of him. Then he sees movement, and a camouflaged Panzer 4 heaves into view, "Sarge?"

"What, Mac?"

"They're here."

As they watch, one of their anti-tank guns opens fire. They can see the 37mm projectile bounce off the front armor. Crabtree, "Hold your fire until we see their infantry." Two more anti-tank guns open up with identical results.

SAINT PATRICK'S CHURCH, HUDDERFIELD, ON THE RIVER COLNE, SOUTHWEST OF LEEDS, UK

0847, 29 September, 1942

Jimmy Thatcher stops running, his side aches and he's gasping for breath. He sees a Yank army truck approaching. PFC Clyde Baker says, "Go away, kid. Yer not safe with us."

Urland comes out of the church, "Time to go, guys. The Germans broke through the Humber line." He sees Jimmy and recognizes the sword, "You okay, son?"

Jimmy looks up at the large man in flight suit and army jacket, spotting the two bars of a captain and salutes. "Jimmy Thatcher, private, Home Guard."

Urland smiles, "If you promise to never salute me in the field again, you can come."

Baker, "Why are we picking up strays, Lieutenant?"

Urland, "This stray disabled a Tiger tank and killed several Germans. They need us east of here. Let's go."

MERLIN, SOUTH OF RAF OUSTON

0851, 29 September, 1942

Too Tall, "Time to pop."

Sweets flies the EA-6B just above the trees. "Popping." She pops the plane up so the tail mounted sensors pick up the German AA radar.

Keg, "Down, got it. 025. Mapping it."

Diving down, Sweets, "Can you take it?"

Too Tall, "Got it." He adjusts his course and says, "Popping."

Keg, "Good music, 028. They're still transmitting."

Sweets has her eyes outside the cockpit and sees a glint to

the north, "Bogey 3 o'clock low." On radio, "Merlin is west of Middlesbrough. We have a bogey to the north. Can we confirm friendly?"

Too Tall rolls left and settles on the deck and takes his throttles wide open. The EA-6B does not have afterburners and cannot exceed the speed of sound. They hear, 'Merlin, Whiskey Tango Foxtrot, contact is a ME-262 out of Ouston. Any allied aircraft, Merlin is in trouble."

MAJOR HEINRICH GUNTER'S ME-262B, DEPARTING OCCUPIED RAF OUSTON

Gunter sees the American jet on his radar. It's the one testing the radars. He slides into a turn on afterburner. The sun catches the gold of the cockpit, "Hmm, what is this thing?"

GALAHAD 1, 36,000 FEET, 45 MILES SOUTH EAST OF MERLIN

LT Kyle 'Gandhi' Jacobs, "Brother Swede, Too Tall is scrambling south with a '262 closing him. Fly 245 to intercept." On radio, "Merlin, Galahad, we have our sword out and we are coming."

On radio, "Gandhi, Sweets, could really use a back rub. We got someone all on us."

Gandhi, "You're doing good, Sweets. In a minute, we'll give you a call to break so we can set up the shot."

"Can't you get missile lock?"

"We are sans missiles, Sweets. We're coming." The F-14's dives at full afterburner, flying at nearly twice the speed of sound.

MERLIN, ON THE DECK, HEADING SOUTH, NEAR THE VILLAGE OF BARNARD CASTLE

Too Tall's going flat out. He clears a hill and pulls a little right trying to screw up the targeting solution of the German. Then he goes left, passing between a church steeple and an old castle ruin. Back on the deck, he sees tracers pass over their canopy and feels the clunk of rounds hitting this vertical stabilizer. "Come on. Come on. Just get us over friendly lines."

Keg, "I'm jamming his radar. Aren't we far enough south?"

"No."

Sweets, "Damn, he's on us again." Then their aircraft shakes as Galahad passes over them at high Mach. They manage to get into some hills and use terrain masking trying to work their way south.

The German gets back on their tail just as they pass out into a broad valley east of Skipton. He gets one more shot on them and hits their right engine just as Gandhi says, "Merlin, break left!"

Too Tall rolls left and Keg says, 'Oh shit, man!"

Too Tall, "Hang on! We gotta be close!" Using his speed, he gains a little altitude and sees a line of German tanks winding out of the hills. The fire warnings sound on the right engine, then the jet yaws to the right. Tool Tall fights for control as his craft starts shaking. Out of altitude and airspeed, he shouts, "Eject! Eject!"

2ND PLATOON, A COMPANY, 1ST BATTALION, 15TH REGIMENT, 3RD ID, VALLEY WEST OF LEEDS

Private Andy McDonald watches the stricken jet, trailing fire and black smoke, streaking across the sky. He sees the crew eject at low altitude and realizes they're going to land between the German position and his own line. He watches the crew come down and two of them immediately cut loose their chutes, and run toward the third whose tangled in his lines.

The Germans start firing and one of the flyers goes down. Andy shouts, "Come on!" He climbs out of his trench and runs forward, not looking back to see if anyone is following.

His sergeant yells, "McDonald! Fuck!"

Andy runs, skidding on the grass, and kneels next to the flyer closest to the Germans. He sees German infantry running alongside the big tanks and opens fire.

Keg, "Thanks man, I'm almost untangled."

"Okay, let me know when you can move." Andy continues firing, picking off soldier after soldier, until they go to ground.

Keg, "Ready." McDonald reloads, stands, and with bullets whipping around him, walks backward.

Andy, "Grab my belt and guide me." He feels the sharp sting of a bullet hitting his leg, but keep firing.

Keg grabs his harness straps and walks them back to Too Tall and Sweets. Too Tall looks up, 'Get down guys. Sweets is hurt."

Keg drops prone and Andy takes a knee. His right leg is aching and he feels blood running down his calf, but he continues firing, "Sir, we have a medic."

Too Tall, "I'm just getting her ready to move. You ready, sweetie?"

Sweets' voice is a whisper, "Yeah, do it."

Too Tall picks her up and runs to the American lines, as the Americans on the line lay down suppressing fire. Andy gets up, walking backward and firing, as Keg guides him back to the trench. The lead Germans tank commander opens his hatch and swings his machine gun toward them, and Andy takes the shot, hitting him in the head. Another round relieves Andy of his helmet and he hits two more Germans just before reaching his trench. Keg, "We're here," and guides Andy back into the trench. As he drops into the trench, his right leg collapses and the world tries to go away.

His sergeant's face swims into view. Sergeant Crabtree says,

"That was the bravest fucking idiotic thing I ever saw, McDonald."

CONTROL, RAF KENLEY

Spike listens to the radio chatter as Swede and Gandhi chase the '262 north and Cargo Britches, in Valkyrie 1, flies north for the pick-up. "Yankee, Galahad, we just dodged a SAM near Ouston. Heading south."

She hears the stress in Gandhi's voice. "Roger, Galahad. The A-10s over York need cover."

"Wilco, Yankee."

"Yankee, Valkyrie 1, we're taking small arms and tank fire. Falling back over the ridge for pick-up."

"Roger, Valkyrie."

LT Colonel Andrews asks quietly, "Commodore, Galahad sounded distraught, but you kept him in the air?"

"If I called them back, it would seem that I don't trust them, and I do. Swede and Gandhi are among our best. They'll shake it off and get mission oriented again. We'll talk it through in debrief."

VALKYRIE 1, SOUTH OF THE 3ᴿᴰ ID LINE

Cargo Britches brings her helo to a hover, one wheel on the ground. She sees the American troops running over the hill with the wounded. In a moment, Too Tall, Sweets, Keg, Private McDonald, and several other wounded are loaded and she lifts, orients, and heads south.

In the back, the medic is working on Sweets as Too Tall holds her, "You're going to be okay."

Sweets, breath labored, "You never were a good liar, Mike." She coughs, and blood appears on her lips.

Mike, "I need you to be okay."

Sweets tries to speak, then coughs and more blood comes out of her mouth. The medic has managed to get in a line and has ringers flowing. The helicopter is so loud, he has to keep his head right next to hers. She tries to smile, "Ever wonder what your last words would be?"

"You have to make it, Sweets. I love you."

"I love you, too, you lug." She stiffens, then her body relaxes, and she's still looking at him, but she's gone. The medic checks her pulse, shakes his head, and shifts to work on another patient.

Mike grabs his arm, pulling him back. The medic looks at him, "She's gone, sir. Let me save the others."

Mike lets go of the medic and wraps Sweets up, rocking her in his arms, his tears washing the blood from her face.

GENERAL MOTORS PLANT, DETROIT, MICHIGAN

0516, 29 September, 1942

LTJG James Maki sits in the loaders seat in a wooden mock-up of a tank turret. Admiral Klindt sits in the gunner's seat. Klindt says, "As I recall, on American tanks the commander sat above the gunner, not behind him."

Maki, "I've seen that, too. But if the tank is hit, the gunner can't get out. This way each crewman has an escape hatch. It also allows the tanks to be lower."

"Okay. Why is the loader's chair sideways?"

"The ammo is stored in a rack at the rear of the turret. Sitting sideways, he can easily grab a round, spin it, and slide it into the gun. Then, he closes the breach and it's ready to fire. If he stands and lifts his seat out of the way, his head and shoulders are out and he can fire his M-1919 machine gun."

"Okay, what is the advantage of a lower tank?"

"The lower the tank, the lower the weight for a given thickness of armor, sir."

"You just have this box thing simulating the gun?"

"Sir, I haven't received the gun from you."

"I'm working on it. The army has an anti-tank gun design that is promising. It's a 105mm rifled gun."

"Yes, sir. Once I know the size, weight, and shape of the gun, I can finalize the turret design. Can I show you the engine and transmission?"

"Sure," and they climb out of the mock up and walk to a metal box on heavy casters.

Maki, "I wanted to keep the fuel to the rear and in a separate compartment from the crew. Putting the fuel tanks on each side of the tank, protects the engine, but it makes maintenance a nightmare. With that in mind, we came up with this." He pulls large slatted double access doors open and the back of the transmission and engine can be seen. "Disconnect power and control cables here. Disconnect the drive lines here and here. Disconnect a quick release for the fuel line up here and remove two bolts here and here. With that done, you can use a ratchet to pull the whole thing out."

Maki demonstrates by hand cranking a speed ratchet and the engine slides out on two beams. The radiator and fan are on top of the engine. The intake and filter box are on top of the transmission. "This makes engine repair and replacement a cinch. Oh, and I've Cadillac working on air conditioning."

Klindt nods, "Maki, this is well thought out, but why air conditioning?"

"Thank you, sir. Well, first, it's for CBR defense. I'm not sure yet how it will work, but I want the crew to be able to work in a CBR environment without using respirators, as long as the tank is buttoned up. Next, it's for crew comfort. On the ship, after a hot watch in the hole, we'd go to an airconditioned space to cool down. These guys have nowhere to go. It seems to me, if they're comfortable, they'll fight better."

"I agree." Klindt looks at the mock-up of the turret. The front and sides slope significantly back. It looks almost like two saucers placed top to top. "How did you pick the slops on the turret?"

"I got a variety a variety of guns and a sheet of hardened steel. We kept changing the angle and firing at it until we found an angle that would ricochet nearly all projectile types. We're building mock up armor to test, as well. I can show you a sample here."

They walk to another stand. The armor has a cross section of a piece of turret. "The trick is to find something light, effective, and easy to build. This one has a ¾ inch hardened steel outer layer, a 2-inch air gap, a 1½ inch layer of mild steel, a 3-inch layer of sand, and a final 2½ layer of hardened steel. We've made sixty of these in various combinations. In a few days, we'll have these at the Dahlgren proving ground for testing. I assume you can get us in there?"

"I'll arrange it. Why sand?"

"Well, it's not just sand. We're trying out other thicknesses and materials, but I thought that the sand might turn into glass, absorbing the energy. I don't know if it'll work."

"Very good. What about the suspension?"

"I was leaning toward a torsion bar, but the Marines you gave me convinced us to use a horizontal volute spring suspension. It bolts to the hull. The torsion bars pass under the tank. Using the springs keeps the underside clean so that the tank can slide over obstacles. Also, it's easier to maintain and replace, and should handle the speeds we want."

Klindt nods, smiling, "Excellent. I'll get you a prototype gun as soon as I can. Build us a prototype to test the layout and undercarriage. Once you have the gun and armored settled, build five fully functional prototypes for testing. You've done well."

"Thank you, sir. Can you get me the length and weight of the gun? I also need the length after the trunnions, which is critical. With that, I can verify function at full rated load."

"Okay, what is a trunnion?"

"I'm learning a lot. It's the point where the gun pivots up and down. The depth it goes into the tank, and height above and below, to allow the gun to elevate and depress are critical to how well it functions. Not something I learned in nuclear power school."

"True. I'll get it for you."

"Thank you, sir."

"You know, Maki. You're becoming too indispensable to send to sea. Are you going to be angry that you missed out?"

Maki is silent, then "Sir, have you read the Horatio Hornblower books?"

Klindt chuckles, "Every one of them."

Make returns the smile, "That fictional British officer is the reason I joined the navy. That said, I want to do my bit, however that should work."

"I understand. Get this going and I'll see what can be done."

"Yes, sir."

GERMAN COMMAND ROOM, OCCUPIED RAF OUSTON

1132, 29 September, 1942

General Weber stands and greets Major Gunter, "Tell me about this aircraft you shot down."

"It was unusual, sir. The wings were swept back about fifteen degrees. It had a single tail with a large square thing on the top. The cockpit was sized for multiple people and it shined like gold. The pilot was good at evasive maneuvering, but could not outrun my beautiful jet. I was jumped by a lone F-14, but succeeded in evading it to return and report."

"The aircraft you destroyed was a radar countermeasure plane. The gold cockpit is a telling feature. You've done very well. The Americans appear to have only one. Your success creates opportunities for all of us."

"Thank you, Herr General."

Weber smiles, "Dismissed. Heil Hitler."

"Heil Hitler."

500 FEET OVER THE RIVER AIRE, NEAR CASTLEFORD

1202, 29 September, 1942

Major 'Sparks' Parker rocks his A-10, studying the ground. The dikes on the Aire and Calder are broken in a hundred different places and the fields are flooded. "2nd Corps, Dog 1, what is your location?"

"Dog 1, 2nd Corps, we are falling back from Selby. The flooding makes the area north of our position impassable."

"Agreed, 2nd Corps. Recommend shifting west."

"Negative, Dog 1. Leeds has fallen. We're racing for the Wash-Bristol line. Please do what you can to delay the Germans."

"Roger, 2nd Corps, Dog 1, out."

CONTROL ROOM, RAF KENLEY

1410, 29 September, 1942

Spike stands, studying the map. The Allied armies are in full retreat. The Luftwaffe is focusing on the A-10s. She's lost two more. The Germans are getting very good at tying up the F-14s, while another group attacks the ground support. Thud walks in, "Spike, I heard about Too Tall."

"I haven't got the injury report yet. Cargo Britches went straight to Guys, but she loaded up with wounded."

"Yeah. Swede has tasked me to help the Brits design a jamming pod."

"Any luck?"

"It can be mounted on the same pylon as the TARPs pod. I checked. All the new birds have the correct wiring."

"I sense a 'but' coming."

"Yeah, the best the Brits can do is a fully manual system. We need it to be at least semi-autonomous so the RIOs can do their regular jobs."

"If it's a broad band jammer, can't it be turned on and left alone?"

"It can't be broad band, that would interfere with our gear, too."

"So, the RIO has to be constantly messing with it?"

"Yeah, not ideal."

"Okay. It does detect radar signals, right?"

"Yeah, it has to. Otherwise, you don't know what to jam."

"Okay, see if you can build a prototype as is, and continue working to improve it."

"Roger that. Um, Spike, when was the last time you slept?"

She takes a deep breath, "Thud, thank you for your concern. I'm managing."

"Okay."

The watch officer says, "Navy 126, 127, and 128 are coming in."

Thud and Spike smile at each other, and Spike says, "Thank you. Well, some good news." They walk out and Spike drives her jeep to the flight line. Standing in the soft English rain, she sees the three brand new Tomcats flare and land.

After they're positioned in front of the hangers, she walks up and finds LCDR Truman 'Johnny' Walker grinning down at her from one of the birds with his infectious smile. Carefully, he climbs down out of his plane. He salutes, then stretches out the stiffness, "Request permission to come aboard."

"Permission granted, you lug. How are you?"

"Still a little sore. Had to bribe a doc to get this flight. Told him it was a 'refamiliarization' flight."

"Right. Are you still training the Russians?"

"Russians, Navy, Army Air Corps, even, shocker, Marines."

"Are we going to let Marines fly our beautiful jets?"

"We are. They even want to paint them green."

"They would." Admiral Lee joins them and they salute.

Lee smiles at Spike, "How are you, darlin?"

"We just lost Merlin. Cargo Britches picked them up under fire and went direct to Guys. The Germans have taken York and Leeds. They also have RAF Ouston and are flying out of it."

Lee frowns, "What's their focus?"

"They're focusing on A-10s. We've lost two more. If the Germans recover one of our A-10 pilots, they kill them on sight."

"I see. Okay, I'll send replacement pilots and aircraft. I've another couple of squadrons finishing up their training. I'll send them over."

"Thanks, Dixie, but what are we going to do with Merlin gone? We don't have a jamming plane."

"Grumman is working on an AE-14. But it isn't ready to fly yet.?"

"Damn. Thud and the Brits are working on a jamming pod, but it's inferior to the Prowler's capabilities."

Lee nods, "Johnny is training a class of aircrew for you and the transport we're flying back is bringing in newly trained ground crew."

"Thank you.

Lee turns to Walker, "Could you excuse us?"

"Yes, sir."

Lee and Spike walk away, and once out of earshot, "What is this I'm hearing about you and Swede?"

Spike laughs, "He was melting down and I needed to pee, so I dragged him into the head. I don't mind the rumors. It distracts folks." She stops.

Lee's eyes narrow, "Who's he with?"

"Way off the record?"

"Of course."

"Swede and Hot Pants are a couple."

"A good pairing, I think. He'll respect her need to fly."

"They got together before he was promoted and given command. Given the situation now, it needs to stay discreet."

"Of course, but how am I ever going to be a Grandpa if you don't get laid?" He laughs at her outrage.

"Dad!"

"A guy can hope, right?"

"You certainly can hope, but right now, that's all it is."

"That's okay, darlin. Hmm, I see they're building hard shelters."

"Yes, enough for eighty planes. They haven't tried a concerted attack on this field yet, but it's coming. We need SAMs, but there hasn't been time."

"They're working on something over in Richland. I'll send you the prototypes."

"Thank you, Dad."

"I got a picture," and he pulls out a black and white photo of a pretty, dark-haired woman with a round face and mischievous eyes. "This is Ashley Smith. Her uncle's on the House Armed Services Committee. I met her at his house during a party."

"She looks like she's waiting for you to sit on a tack."

He nods, smiling, "She can be ornery, but I like that."

"Dad, I'm happy for you. When it comes to it, I would love to stand up with you."

"I can think of no one else. Now, let's talk about you. Are you eating?"

"Cooper says 3,500 calories a day. I just keep burning them off."

"Combat does that. Do you think we can hold against the Germans?"

"We have to, Dad."

CHAPTER 17

ROADHEAD, 14 MILES EAST OF CARLYLE

1522, 29 September, 1942

Ian McCloud leads his two hundred men to the British Army check point south of the village, the Lee Enfield rifle. Behind him walks LT Gus 'Cuddles' Grant, kitted out in a Stewart Tartan over his wool coat and flight suit, and grey wool knit cap.

A sergeant steps from a tent and raises a hand, "What's this?"

"Lad, the Highlanders have come down from the hills and we've our blood up."

"Our orders are to hold here and prevent the Krauts from moving north."

"Aye, lad, that's your orders. It isn't my orders. I told ye, we've come down from the hills and we're spoiling for a fight. There be hundreds of us up and down the line. It be time the Germans learned of Scottish steel. Now, be a good lad, and step aside."

The sergeant looks over the group. Most are over fifty, others are obviously still in school, and there are a few women, but they are all armed. Most of the older men have the look of veterans. He shakes his head, "Look, I can't authorize it. You know you all are marching to your death?"

"Aye, lad, but we'll be bringing more than few with us, and lad, we ain't asking permission." He turns, "Highland volunteers, at the ready! Harch."

A bag pipe begins to play and they move out, mostly in step, each person wearing their own tartan. The sergeant comes to attention and salutes. Cuddles returns the salute, smiling.

ARTHUR FLIGHT, 35,000 FEET OVER THE BIGHT

1423, 29 September, 1942

"All units, Whiskey Tango 7, new raid. 4 fast movers on the deck over Lockerbie. They are west bound."

Spike, "Too far away, Lizard."

Then, "Whiskey Tango 7, Texas, we're out of position."

"Arthur flight, Fighter Control, you're the furthest north. Come to 275 at full military. Hit them on the return."

Spike, "Got it," and on radio, "Fighter Control, Arthur concurs. Yankee, launch alert 5 to replace us." She brings her plane to full military and smoothly turns to 275.

Lizard, "Dixie's still on our wing."

"Okay, Lizard. We know they have countermeasures, so when we're at about 50 miles, volley both of our Long Bows."

"Roger, Boss."

USS JAMES HOLTZ, RADAR PICKET OUTSIDE OF BELFAST

Commander John Dallas walks into Combat. "What do we have?"

The TAO says, "We were warned by a radar plane that a four-jet strike is inbound at 120."

Dallas, "Come to 005. Ahead 1/3rd. Load and prepare for sustained volley."

On radio, "Naval units in Belfast, Arthur 1. The raid is ten minutes out."

Dallas picks up the mic, "Arthur 1, Holtz acknowledges."

He's been frantically training his green crew and finishing the fitting out of the Holtz as they crossed the Atlantic. They're still fixing issues, but the missile systems are ready.

Six seconds after the jets are sighted, the first missile leaves the rail. It hits and a jet tumbles out of the sky. The second missile gets spoofed by chaff, and the remaining jets drop early and pull out south.

ARTHUR FLIGHT, 25,000 FEET OVER THE IRISH SEA

Spike lights her afterburners, "How far?"

"Sixty, and they're south bound."

"Let's hit them before they enter Irish air space."

Lizard, "Volley Fox 3." She fires all four of the AIM-1s."

Packs, "Volley Fox 3," and Dixie fires all four of his AIM-1s.

Eight AIM-1s streak after the three jets. They all fire off chaff, but they are so low, the chaff is of little help. One plane ducks behind a hill, but the other two are hit. The pilots eject.

Spike, "Dixie, take lead."

Packs, "Roger, lead."

The remaining jet turns away, trying to find cover in the low hills, but the Tomcats are closing at Mach 2. It's only a matter of time. Spike, "Lizard, where's the border."

"I don't know."

Spike, on radio, "The border is close."

Packs, "Fox 1, Fox 1." The missiles fly straight and hit the enemy jet. Parts shed into the slip stream, the jet tumbles once, then hits, tail first in a field north east of Castleblayney in the Republic of Ireland.

Lizard, "Break right. Come to 080."

GRUMMAN FACTORY, BETHPAGE, NEW YORK

0944, 29 September, 1942 (1444 GMT)

LCDR Cassidy waits for the C-47 to roll to a stop in front of a hanger. Twenty-four officers get off the plane with their gear. First is Major Greg 'Pappy' Boyington. The last is Lieutenant Phil 'Rascal' Tyler, still nursing his injured leg. Cassidy says, "Please fall in right here," and nods to Rascal as he joins him. Cassidy looks over the student pilots and shakes his head, "Each of you graduated top in your class. Now you must qualify on the F/A-14B. We'll be pairing you up into flight teams. The best of you will be reporting to England as soon as you demonstrate competence in the Tomcat. I don't think I need to explain what is going on over there." He motions and the hanger door rumbles open. "That said, allow me to introduce you to the new love of your life: The F/A-14B Tomcat strike fighter."

They turn to look at a large plane painted in Black Knight colors. Rascal says, "This plane will belong to two of you. I want to be clear, all of you are good at your jobs. If you weren't, you wouldn't be here. What we need from you now is cooperation, not competition. Five aircrews will replace aircrew of the Black Knights. Seven will replace pilots with the Tomcatters. Later students will replace those lost from the Redcocks, Knightriders, and stand up new squadrons. As fighter pilots, all of you are competitive. That is good. Here, you are competing against yourself and building a team. Questions?"

Boyington asks, "Why haven't we been assigned RIOs yet?"

Rascal smiles, "The pilot-RIO relationship is critical. The pilots will fly with a number of RIOs and you'll pair up after that. Permanent assignment will be at your new squadron."

Boyington, puzzled, "As the first Marine jet pilot, won't I be assigned to a new squadron?"

Rascal's smile gets bigger, "Actually, you are not the first Marine jet pilot. Major Mossberg serves with the Black Knights right now. We want you to gain some experience with an existing squadron first."

"I see."

"Any other questions?"

Cochran asks, "When can we start flying?"

"Once you've completed ground school, which starts in a moment. Anything else? Okay, let's get started."

HETHERSGILL, 8 MILES NORHEAST OF CARLYLE, UK

1603, 29 September, 1942

Ian McCloud silently gathers his men behind a stone wall. Using the brambles for concealment, he peeks again at the German garrison. It seems company strength and though there are pickets, the men are amusing themselves and ignoring their perimeter to the north. An old man is standing nude in front of a group of soldiers. They are throwing bits of food at him and laughing.

Ian comes down, "Lieutenant Grant, they're infantry. We shan't bother the attack planes. Now remember lads, pick your targets carefully. Joseph, Connor, you get the radio. After the first volley, the pipes start. Are we clear?" His men nod.

"Let's be at it then." Ian sights on the fellow that seems to be in charge and squeezes the trigger. He fought in the last war and he knows his business. The round hits the man in the head. A ragged volley follows and the pipes start playing 'Blue Bonnets Over the Border.'

The Germans scramble for their weapons, but man after man is brought down. Every man trying to get to the radio dies. A few men high tail it south. "First platoon!" and Grant stands with a line of thirty men and goes over the wall. When a German attempts to fire his weapon, he's hit by fire from the wall. A Scotsman falls. The Scots keep marching in, firing as they go.

The few Germans that are left, break and run, and the volunteers have the field. Ian, "Third platoon, form a defensive line.

Second platoon tend the wounded and police this place." He walks up to the old man, "Where are your clothes, sir?"

He points to a tent, then, "You...your men, they saved me for certain. They were hunting the lasses, but I hid them away."

"Get dressed, sir. It would be best if you and the women head north. There's an army post at Roadhead or Carwinley. They'll tend to you."

One of his men runs up, "Sir, they've a lorry in the barn."

Ian smiles, "Good, we needn't carry our own food, then. Let's clean up and head south."

INFIRMARY, RAF KENLEY

1636, 29 September, 1942

Sam walks in and an orderly stands, "This way, Commodore."

The orderly knocks at a door, "Commodore Hunt," and opens it.

LCDR Michael 'Too Tall' Mohr sits on the end of a bed, stripped to the waist and is being treated for a grazing gunshot wound across his left ribs and another at the base of his neck. He's covered in blood. The nurse is focusing on cleaning off the blood and looking for any other wounds.

Sam says, "That's a lot of blood, Mike."

He replies, his voice flat, "It's Sweet's blood." He looks up at her, the anguish in his eyes a physical thing, "She's dead."

Sam puts a hand on his shoulder, "God, I'm sorry."

He breaks eye contact, "It's my fault. I killed her."

"The Germans killed her."

"It was my decisions."

Sam takes a deep breath, "Right now, I'm going to let you wallow in your guilt. But, Commander, when you leave this room, you will put it behind you and do your duty."

"I...I don't think I can."

Softly, "Commander Mohr, you must. The future of Task Force Yankee depends on you. That means the future of Britain depends on you. Finally, that means the success of the entire war depends on you. It depends on me and all of our people, but you are the only person here that can wild weasel. We need you."

He looks up again and nods. "Yeah, I'll get it together. It's just..., yes, Spike."

"When you need to fall apart, come find me. I'll make the time."

"Thank you, Spike."

"I got to go." He nods and she walks out of the room. Alone in the hall, she struggles with her own tears and forces her body to stop shaking. "Fuck, this is hard."

CONTROL TOWER, RAF ALCONBURY

1650, 29 September, 1942

LTJG Hammond scans the airbase with his binoculars. A detonator is next to him and a fast car is at the foot of the tower. Slowly he scans the perimeter of the base. Then, he sees the bulk of a German tank heave into view. The tank stops, the man in a hatch studying the field carefully. Hamm says, "Come on, man. Take the bait."

The tank finally rolls forward and more follow. An entire battalion is soon arrayed before him; twenty-eight tanks, with infantry carriers and air defense half-tracks pulling AA guns on four-wheeled carriages. He sees exposed missiles. "Damn." He picks up the tower radio, "Any Alpha one zero, it's Hamm."

"Hamm, Dusty flight 2, go."

"Dusty 2, Hamm. Location is Alconbury. One battalion of German tanks. Be advised, they have air defenses." As he watches, the air defenses are set up and the infantry start running into the hard shelters.

"Acknowledge, Hamm. Are you under fire?"

"Negative, Dusty 2. I'm waiting to detonate."

"Roger. We're fully engaged at the moment and would just as soon stay clear of prepared AA."

"Understood, Dusty 2. Any chance you can cover me as I skedaddle?"

"We will do what we can. Note, there are friendlies helping with the evacuation of Cambridge."

"Thank you, Dusty 2." A lot of infantry are in the hard shelters and a truck is heading for the tower. Dusty 2, Hamm. Time to blow and go." He pushes the detonator down and all the hangers, barracks, buildings, and the hard shelters explode, showering concrete and debris all over the base.

He runs down the tower stairs and jumps into his Riley Racing Special and accelerates away. About 200 yards down the road, he stops, jumps out, and pushes down a final detonator. The tower goes away in a cloud of fire and smoke, collapsing onto the truck at its base.

SS COMMAND TANK, 101ST BATTALION, RAF ALCONBURY

SS-Obersturmbannfuhrer Rolf Meier turns crimson. He slaps his tank and screams. "Regroup. Regroup. We must make them pay. His tanks and armored vehicles survive, but a good number of his infantry are gone. "We're near Cambridge. Let's start there. Every English from here to London will die."

COMMAND CENTER, RAF KENLEY

Spike, Swede, Thud, Maugham, Parks, and Leonard study the status map. Spike, "Flooded fields and mixed up traffic signs might help, but we need to slow them further."

Parks, "The German tankers are getting clever at hiding their tracks. I hit one today that was using canvas to look like a truck."

Spike, "Yeah, and their pilots are getting better, too. Thud, if you were a German jet commander, what would you do?"

"Hit Kenley. That and focus on the radar planes again. We really need them."

Swede, "They mostly focus on the A-10s. You Hog drivers have been hammering them."

Spike, "Let's use that against them. We have to stop reacting."

Maugham, "I've an idea. Have my jets fly like we're A-10s, and you guys cover us like you do the A-10s."

Spike, "I like it."

The watch officer, "Commodore, we've just gotten word, Lieutenant Hammond has blown Alconbury. Apparently, he did a lot of damage to a tank and infantry battalion in the process. LT Hammond is safe and returning to base."

Spike smiles, "Thank you. God, the hero gene." She nods, "Okay, let's do this."

NAS ANACOSTA, SOUTH OF WASHINGTON, DC

1136, 29 September, 1942 (1836 GMT)

A C-56 comes to a stop on the tarmac and the engines spin down. Vice Admiral Lee thanks the air crew, picks up his flight bag, and walks down the stairs to a waiting sedan. The wind is bitter and is blowing rain sideways. He hands his bag to an aid and climbs into the car.

Waiting for him is Admiral King, "How was your flight?"

"Good, sir," The car pulls out.

"Any kills?"

Lee meets the CNO's eyes, "Two, sir."

"Your last two."

"Yes, sir."

"How is she?"

"She needs new crews. She needs everything we can send. As soon as I can, I'm releasing VMA-326 and VA-16."

"The aircrew training at Grumman will ferry the remaining aircraft."

"Yes, sir. Sir, the Vinson is on its way to San Diego. Can I ship the Tomcatters and Redcocks to England?"

"The President ordered a full-on effort. Approved. Give me an ETA when you have one. Now, how is she holding up in command?"

"Very well, considering."

"Considering what?"

"Sir, think back to when you were a commander. If we had unceremoniously dumped a battleship squadron and three destroyer squadrons on you to lead all at once, in combat with several of the units from other services and other nations, how would you have held up? Add to that, the consequences of failure? She's getting it done. She's meeting all her commitments, keeping he people alive and combat effective. It isn't easy on any of them."

"Do you think she can hold?"

"Sir, I've never bull shit you from day one and I never will. The entire effort hinges on her success. More than that, it hinges on our ability to give her every chance to succeed. Should England fall, we would have to take it back before we could take Europe. If Russia recommences hostilities with Germany, it could be Russians we meet in France, not Germans.

"I know, we told you about the Cold War. This is why I asked for the Tomcatters and the Redcocks. It's why I'm planning to send every combat capable squadron we can. If she fails, it's because we failed her."

"When England is secure, I want that entire unit to get a prolonged break."

"Yes, sir. We also need to give them one hell of an award."

"We've talked about that, Rick. I don't believe American serviceman fight for medals."

"I agree, sir. They fight for each other. It's been proven. The medals tell them every murder they committed was in the line of duty. It tells them, us REMFs appreciate and honor what they've done."

King nods, then, "What, pray tell, is a REMF?

Lee grins, "A rear echelon mother fucker, sir."

King looks startled, then smiles, "This REMF appreciates what they're doing. Have your staff write it up."

"Yes, sir."

COMMAND CENTER, OCCUPIED RAF OUSTON

1910, 29 September, 1942

General Weber sits at the head of a table listening to a brief. Major Gunter, "They seem to be building new F-14 Tomcats, sir, but they're running out of qualified pilots."

"How can you exploit this knowledge, Major?"

"I'm not sure, sir."

"A dead pilot, is a dead pilot. We draw them north and south, then attack their home field."

"I thought the Fuhrer forbids it. We're only allowed to attack the docks."

"I've submitted the plan. If we destroy their base, we destroy their resistance."

"Isn't it better to kill pilots in the air?"

"Ah, chivalrous knights of the sky. You need to read Clausewitz. There is no honor or nobility in war. You kill the enemy when you, how you can. You keep killing them until they give up, or they are eliminated entire. Save the noble stories for when you have grandchildren on your knee."

"Yes, sir."

"You've done well, Major."

Gunter, "Thank you, sir. A thought, as the allies flee, we can strike their armor in the same way the Devil's Cross does."

"That will draw them out. How do we take advantage of it.?"

"We use focused attacks, sir. Why don't we split into many two or four aircraft elements? They can't be everywhere."

2nd TROOP, 'A' SABRE SQUADRON, 1ST BATTALION WELSH GUARDS, 32ND GUARDS BRIGADE, NORTHWEST CAMBRIDGE, UK

1922, 29 September, 1942

Sergeant Andrew Seymour stands in the commander's hatch of his Churchill tank. He's currently parked in a field next to a barn, his tank shut down. His beret is sopping, and water runs under his coat and down his back. His new troop commander, 2nd LT Barker walks up. Seymour's last lieutenant is still in what's left of his tank outside of York.

The lieutenant, totally unperturbed by the rain, says, "Sergeant, the Hun was recently at Alconbury. The Division is scattered, but we're ordered to hold Cambridge as it's evacuated."

"Sir, do you suppose they might have started leaving a bit earlier?"

"It was hoped we would hold north of here. Now, we have it to do."

"Yes, sir. Do you know what kind of tanks the Hun are using?"

"No, but I'm told they're a bloody bastard to kill. Make your shots count. A few shots and we fall back. We've torn up the road, so they have to deploy in front of us."

"Yes, sir. Sir, how long have you been in?"

"I graduated from Dartmouth in June."

"Okay, might I off some advice?"

"Certainly."

"We've faced the Hun three times now. If we face the Panzer 4, we need to wait until they are less than 800 meters to fire. If it's the Tiger, we should let them pass and hit them in the rear. It's the only way."

"Thank you, Sergeant."

"One more thing, if you survive this, then you're old enough to curse."

"I'll keep that in mind. Do take care, Sergeant."

CHAPTER 18

1950, 29 September, 1942

Sam stares at a blank sheet of paper. Finally, she writes:

Dear Mr. and Mrs. Younger,

It is with great regret I must inform you of the combat death of your granddaughter, Lieutenant Tabitha Younger. She was a dear friend...

She stops, "Too much. Too much." She crumples the piece of paper, throwing into the basket, and starts over.

Cooper walks in holding a tray with sandwiches and a cup of tea. "Let me write them, Boss."

"Radar, they deserve a personal letter."

"And, they'll get one. You need a break." He moves the paper and puts the plate and the tea in front of her, "Now, eat."

"Thank you." She picks up a sandwich, "Chicken salad, good. Any cookies?"

He grins, "I'll get them. Oh, and we got another message from Hamm. He says the unit at Alconbury had embedded air defenses. They're getting harder to kill."

"Okay, I need to talk to Mohr. Is he done at the clinic?"

"I'll fetch him. I know the doc's pulled him from flight status until his wounds heal." He starts to walk out, then turns, "Spike, I'll write the letters, okay?"

She gives him a wan smile over her cup of tea, "Thank you."

GRUMMAN, BETHPAGE, NEW YORK

1510, 29 September, 1942 (2010 GMT)

ENS Von Nix taxies his F/A-14B to the runway. It's his third hop of the day with a different RIO, "I'm still not used to someone else using the radio."

ENS Heather Kohlman, "You know, we're more than communications, right?"

"Yeah. You ready to attack Providence?"

"I think so. It's going to get bouncy, right?"

"Yep, Pappy wants us on the deck."

They get Boyington's signal in the lead jet, and the two planes accelerate down the runway, gently lifting off, and cleaning up their birds. They fly out to sea, slowly climbing to 4,000 feet. Pappy wiggles his wings and turns north, descending. Rather than fly up Narragansett Bay, they go feet dry east of New London. Kohlman says, "Scope and threats clear. This isn't too bad."

"It's really flat here. 'Gs'" He pops over a transmission line. "Still looking for the valley."

Kohlman, "About 8 minutes."

"Okay," They climb over small hills.

Kohlman, "2 minutes."

The two-plane element drops into a north to south valley with a river and a highway. Kohlman, "Turn in 3."

"Roger."

In three minutes, a small town appears ahead of them and they turn out of the valley, heading east. Kohlman, "Faint radar south of us."

"They got us?"

"I don't think so, 5 minutes."

Nix, "Gonna get bumpy."

"Thanks, 4 minutes." Then, "2 minutes. Radar is stronger."

"Okay, bumpy." They're crossing ridge lines and staying low.

The outskirts of Providence pass under them. Pappy pops up to bombing altitude and his RIO, ENS Robert Carnegie says, "Drop. Drop. Drop." On radio they hear, "Tally ho, north." One of the defenders has spotted them. Carnegie, "Illuminate."

Kohlman turns on her radar, "2 bandits, 15 miles at 12 o'clock and angels 10."

Nix, "AIM-7 selected."

"They're closing," On radio, "Fox 1, fox 1."

Then Carnegie, "Fox 1, fox 1."

Jackie Cochran, in the defending flight, violently turns, dropping chaff.

Nix, "Gs," turning to get on her six."

Cochran reverses and they pass head to head about 100 yards apart.

Nix "Gs. Damn, she got close," and pulls into a minimum distance turn.

Kohlman, "Pappy's on the wingman."

Cochran mirrors Nix's maneuver and they are in two-circle fight. Because of the offset, Nix gets his nose nearly on her, and she goes vertical.

Kohlman, "Pappy is three miles right."

Nix lights his afterburners and follows Cochran. He glances towards Pappy. Kohlman on radio, "Pappy, swap targets."

Nix rolls off Cochran and sees a clear rear quarter shot on ENS Mical DeGraaff's bird, "Fox 2."

Kohlman, "Fox 2, fox 2."

Carnegie, "Fox 2, fox 2."

Rascal in the observation plane, "Knock it off. Knock it off. Good kills. All units return to base."

COMMANDER'S OFFICE, RAF KENLEY

2035, 29 September, 1942

Cooper knocks on the door and ushers LCDR Mohr into her office. "Thank you, Radar. Tea?" Cooper looks at Mohr, who nods.

"Roger, Spike."

Mohr is wearing a clean flight suit with his arm in a sling. Spike, "Mike, how are you doing?"

"Doc won't let me fly."

"I know. How are you doing?"

He studies a spot on the wall, "Tabby made it down fine. The fucking Germans killed her. Shot her in the back." He looks at Sam, "She died in my arms." He looks down, tears starting.

Cooper walks in with tea and cookies. He sets down the tray and pours. He looks at Sam and nods, walking out silently.

Mike looks up, "She was special."

"I know she was an amazing person and pilot."

"Sam, I loved her. I told her."

"Did she respond?"

"She said me she loved me, too. Then she died." He takes a ragged breath, "I couldn't tell her before. She worked for me. I couldn't."

"I understand."

He looks at her, "I heard what you did after Jedi and Stinky were killed."

"I was too pissed for my own good. It could have cost me my plane and my RIO because I was so damned angry."

"Do you regret it?"

"No."

"I need to kill them. I need to avenge her."

"Is that what she would have wanted?"

"No, but…but, I have too. I feel so damned useless."

"Look, we're building jamming pods. Work on them and let me know when they're ready. I need you to teach our RIOs how to use them."

"I need back in the air."

"Talk to Swede. We can transition you to the '14. I need the pod soonest. They've got too much anti-air."

"Yes, Spike."

LOUIE'S PUB, BETHPAGE, NEW YORK

1830, 29 September, 1942

The student RIOs are already in the pub when the pilots arrive. Major Greg 'Pappy' Boyington leads, followed by LT Jackie Cochran. Boyington heads straight for the bar, "Beer."

The bartender slides one down, "Ten cents." Boyington slides back a dime. Cochran stands, studying the RIOs. She's flown with Alcott, Kohlman, and Uhle and none of them worked for her.

ENS Julian Everling watches her bemused, "Lieutenant, I have a camera if you want a picture."

She turns and looks at the short ensign. He's considered to be one of the top RIO students. "I'm deciding which RIO I want."

Everling laughs, "You're assuming any of us would put up with you."

Cochran sits down at Everling's table and motions for a beer. "I'm a lieutenant, and you're an ensign. You have no choice."

He stares at her, "Didn't you listen to what Walker said? We have to be a team. If I'm going to put up with you, you better fucking listen to me and not pull rank bullshit. Otherwise, you'll be a dead lieutenant, and I'll be a stupid, dead ensign."

"I like your spunk."

"I like how you fly, but can we be a team?"

Ensign Mical DeGraaff, a beautiful dark-haired woman, acquires two beers, and sits at Ensign Steve Uhle's table. "You and me, what do you think?"

Uhle nods and takes a long drink of the offered beer, "We did well together on that first flight. Yeah, works for me."

Boyington finishes his first beer and gets another. He looks over the groups that are developing. He sees a pretty, auburn haired ensign laughing with another woman. He grabs his beer and sits down across from them. ENS Margaret Alcott says, "Major, have you met ENS Heather Kohlman?"

"She was Nix's RIO on the last flight."

Kohlman, short, pretty, and dark-haired, says, "Good evening, shipmate," and gives him the straight hand.

Nix, at another table, starts laughing. Boyington shakes his head, "ENS Kohlman, could you excuse us?" He turns to Alcott, "Do you want to fly behind me?"

"I'm not a Marine."

"I'm the only Marine here. I need someone."

"Is there room in the cockpit for me and your ego?"

Pappy smiles, "I think I could shoe horn you in."

Nix motions Kohlman over, "Join me. I'll buy you a beer."

"I don't drink."

"Oh, okay, they probably have coffee."

"I've got a coke. I'm fine."

"Right. Look, I liked flying with you today. Do you have a pilot yet?"

"Nope, do you?"

"You know I'm a pilot."

"Really?" She looks around, "Does everyone else know?"

"I sure hope so. Would you like to fly with me?"

"Sounds like you're asking me out on a date. I don't date co-workers."

"God, you're tough. I promise to never get romantically entangled if we fly together."

"Okay, then. I can work with that," and she gives him a dazzling smile.

CONTROL CENTER, RAF KENLEY

0530, 30 September, 1942

Spike sits reading the night action reports. An aid comes in with a tray of food and sits it on her desk. There are at least five scrambled eggs, six slices of bacon, three sausage patties, a pound of hash browns, and four slices of toast. She shakes her head, "Thank you," and keeps reading.

Behind her, Cooper clears his throat. "Yes, Mom." She sets the papers down and starts eating.

He sits down next to her, "Andrews was an inspired choice."

"Good."

"He and I are playing good cop, bad cop."

She swallows some eggs, "What's not getting done?"

"That's the thing, everything is getting done. When there is, say, friction, if he gets involved, they all know he's one step from you. He's the bad cop. They come to me hoping to do an end run around him. I 'solve' the problem by getting exactly what he wants done. It keeps folks happy, because they all think they have a work around, and everything gets done. It's cutting weeks off the requisition process. Although, it doesn't hurt that we are Priority 1 for all war materials."

She finishes a bite of sausage and takes a sip of tea, "So, I don't need to do anything?"

"No, Boss. We're a smooth functioning machine. We have nine barracks under construction and we're nearly done with the hard shelters."

"It's only been a week."

"I know, and it took two days for the concrete to dry. Andrew's a whiz. He really is."

"Good."

Lizard walks in, "Boss, we need to re-engine our bird."

"Already?"

"Boss, we've been running the shit out of it."

"Okay," she sighs and dips her toast in her tea, taking a bite.

Lizard, "I have one of the new birds set aside for our use until ours is fixed."

"Okay, but I have a fondness for 210."

"I know, Boss. They'll have it back on line in about six hours."

CHURCH TOWER, NORTHWEST CAMBRIDGE, UK

0919, 30 September, 1942

"Dusty flight 2, Wingnut, approach from the east up the river. Keep low, the Germans have AA."

"Wilco, Wingnut. Can you mark friendlies?"

"I have it confirmed, we have no armor in Cambridge."

"Good enough, Wingnut, Dusty flight 2, out."

PFC Jimmy Thatcher walks into the tower, "Lieutenant, sir? A Home Guard officer wants to speak with you." The roar of the two A-10s is punctuated by the 'Brrrrt' of their cannon.

"Just a sec." On radio, "Dusty 2, Wingnut. Good kills. Keep it coming." He turns back, "Okay, kid."

A 2nd lieutenant who looks like he should be in high school walks up and salutes. "Lieutenant Ashland, reporting with a message, sir."

Wingnut silently looks him over, "If you salute me in the presence of the enemy again, I will spank you in front of your men. What do you want?"

The lieutenant pales, "My apologies, sir. Major Davis is asking that we delay the Germans outside Cambridge so we can effect evacuations."

"I'm not planting smart soldiers because stupid students failed to leave."

"My pardon, sir. It's not people. It's art and books. Some are truly priceless."

Wingnut nods, "No guarantees, but we'll do what we can."

"Thank you, sir."

"Carry on, and no salute."

"Yes, sir." Again, they hear the A-10s cannon.

101ST BATTALION, 1ST BRIGADE, 3RD SS PANZER DIVISION, SOUTHWEST OF CAMBRIDGE

SS-Obersturmbannfuhrer Rolf Meier, "Gentlemen, our forces attack from the north and west. We circle to the south and gut them. I want you to kill anything that moves, unless it's worth fucking or has intelligence value."

The tanks roll through empty streets. He studies the buildings and sees no one. Something falls in an alley, and one of the tank commanders stitches the wall of a building. He hears the distinctive roar of an A-10. On radio, "Stay close to the buildings." He hears one of his tanks explode and cusses. An old man exits a door five hundred feet ahead and he guns him down.

He sees a glint from the bell tower of a church and sprays the area with his machine gun, 'You God damned pig fucking British cowards. I'll kill you all. I'll end your race, entire."

CHURCH STEEPLE, CAMBRIDGE, UK

From the cover of the stone parapet, Wingnut looks back at the direction the rounds came from and spots a Tiger. "Any Hog, Wingnut, we are taking effective fire from the south west. Say again, south west."

"Wingnut, Rusty 3, on it. Approaching from the south west to acquire."

More bullets embed themselves in the stone and ring the bells, deafening them. He sees a main gun turning, "We gotta go." He leaps for the stairs, taking them three at a time, Jimmy following. They hear the distinctive paper tearing sound of a near miss. They run out of the church, Wingnut shouting, "Go! Go! Go!"

His squad throw themselves into the truck and it starts with a jerk, heading southeast. Wingnut collapses in his chair shaking with pain. Jimmy hands him a canteen and three pills. Wingnut takes it, "Thanks, Jimmy. You're doing all right. Tell Rodriguez to find a place toward downtown. There are some tall buildings there."

COMBAT, USS COLUMBIA CLG-56, 180 MILES EAST OF THE MARSHALL ISLANDS

2224, 30 September, 1942 (1024 GMT)

CDR Shawn Hughes sits in the TAO chair reading reports. Captain Heard walks in and a petty officer announces, "Captain in Combat."

Heard sits next to Hughes, "Still worried about the Marshalls?"

"Yes, sir. I'm glad we have the Yorktown with us. The thing is, if I were the Japanese, I would be expanding airfields and acting as aggressively as I could. Time isn't in their favor, and they know it."

Heard, "It comes down to resources. We have them, and they don't."

"Yes, sir, and we know they're designing new aircraft and new ways to use what they have."

"Wouldn't they focus on preparing home island defense?"

"I don't think so. They need the whole co-prosperity sphere to stand against us in resources. In their mind, it all must be defended."

"Well, hopefully we'll pass unnoticed. The Japanese wouldn't risk their jets out here."

A watch stander, "Yorktown reports airborne contact at 0312, sir."

Hughes, "Plot it, altitude, speed and course."

"Altitude is 40,000 feet, speed is 520 knots, course is 085."

Hughes looks at his captain, "General Quarters. Air action."

Heard nods, "Do you think it's an attack plane?"

"Search plane. The profile is that of a jet and it's too high and too fast for anything else."

"Agreed."

"Admiral Fletcher is ordering us to 0275 to launch aircraft. Requests Columbia take the vanguard."

Heard hands Hughes a helmet, "Very well. Relay to the bridge."

"Aye, Captain."

Heard, "go to your GQ station, Commander. I have the watch."

"Yes, sir."

JAPANESE AIR FIELD, KWAJALEIN ATOL

Captain Hata barely lays his head on the pillow when the siren blares him awake. He stands and throws on his gear, his bombardier gearing up beside him. His squadron of Washi bombers landed two hours ago. Here, because command had word an American task force could be near. He looks down at the sleeping mat, "Oh well, couldn't sleep anyway, too quiet."

The two men run for their plane, admiring its beautiful smooth lines reflected in the moon light. They mount their bird and begin the preflight checks. In a moment, they're rolling down the taxiway. He looks down the line of jets and proudly realizes that his is first out. "Well done, Asahi." Warrant Officer Asahi Tanaka smiles. They receive the order and gun their aircraft into the sky. Fifteen Washi bombers follow and Zero fighters scramble to defend the base.

VF-42, 50 MILES WEST OF THE FLEET

LT Donald Atwood is flying blindly into the night at 25,000 feet in his F4F-3 Wildcat. Night operations are new to him. He looks at the radar screen above the compass. He sees a dot, then several dots. He turns right and left to confirm the contacts. On radio, "Yorktown, Big Bird 121, raid warning. A dozen aircraft at 028."

"Roger, Big Bird. Weapons free."

He descends and loses them. When he climbs, the signals strengthen. "Yorktown, Big Bird 121. They're higher than me. Climbing to intercept."

"Roger, Big Bird 121, Yorktown. All fighters, vector on raid 1."

On radio, "Big Bird, Columbia. Raid is at 32000 feet and 600 knots. Climb to engage."

Atwood has his engine firewalled in a steep climb. At 31,000 feet he starts to level off and pick up some speed. The incoming Japanese jets are specks occluding the stars. He picks one and climbs again, his Pratt & Whitney R-1830-76 double-row radial engine screaming for all it's worth in the thin air. He takes a long lead and fires all four 50 caliber machine guns in a long burst. His tracers arc through the darkness and hit one of the jets. It catches on fire, blinding him for a moment, but he turns and seeks another target. In a moment, the sky is dark again as the Japanese jet spirals to the ocean. "Yorktown, Big Bird 121, splash one."

"Big Bird, Yorktown. Roger."

"Big Bird, Columbia. Dive to clear range."

"Columbia, Big Bird diving."

COMBAT, USS COLUMBIA

Captain Heard, "Missile Mount 2, commence firing."

"Open fire, aye, sir." The fire circuit is depressed and two SM-1ER missiles streak off their rails. "Missiles away."

The missile crews in the Mount 2, Mark-10 launcher place two more missiles and launch, then cycle up two more. The second volley is fired before the first one hits. Two Japanese bombers are blotted from the sky, then two more.

WASHI BOMBER FORMATION APPROACHING FLEET

Captain Hata, "Asahi, do you have good lock?"

"Affirm, Captain."

"The warheads are tracking?" He sees two more jets explode.

"Affirm, Captain."

"Five miles, releasing ordinance." The bomber lurches up as

the four 1000-pound guided bombs are released. "Coming about."

Asahi, "Missile warning!"

"Calm, Asahi." Hata pickles off chaff and makes a violent turn and dive. The missile explodes in the chaff.

USS YORKTOWN

Captain Elliott Buckmaster, on the bridge, looks out to the bow as aircraft continue to take off. All his fighters are airborne and the rest of his aircraft are launching as quickly as possible. He looks to the north where he can see the Columbia's missiles firing in rapidly ascending tongues of flame. Above him he sees the explosions as most of the missiles hit.

CDR Dixie Kiefer, his XO, joins him, "Shouldn't you be in combat, sir?"

"The boys know what to do, and we've done all we can."

Then they hear, "The attacking force is turning back. Vampire! Vampire! Missiles inbound."

All the ships of the battlegroup, even those damaged at Savo Island, fire a wall of flak. Buckmaster picks up the 1MC, "All hands, brace, brace, brace!" He grabs the bridge coaming, bends his knees, and opens his mouth.

The Japanese guided bombs cannot be seen. Six Japanese bombers survived and were able to drop twenty-four bombs. Most were directed at the Yorktown. Eight fail to track, tumbling out of the sky. Five were hit by the Columbia and one by the combined fire of the other ships. Four hit the Yorktown and two hit the already damaged North Carolina. The rest fall into the sea.

Buckmaster gets up, his ears ringing, goes out onto the bridge wing and looks over his flight deck. It's an inferno, burning from the island forward. He picks up the 1MC, "Damage control parties out." The system is dead. He sees his XO struggling to his feet, his right shoulder dislocated. "You need to get to medical!"

"I'm fine, sir."

Buckmaster looks back over the deck. "Turn us around. Steam north backwards, so we can keep the flames on the bow."

"Yes, sir." The XO leaves the bridge wing, and staggers as the ship shakes with secondary explosions.

Then, Buckmaster sees the number two turret on the North Carolina explode. The shock wave hits him in the chest, "My God."

Admiral Fletcher walks out, "How are we, Captain?"

"We're fighting, sir. We'll steam astern to keep the flames forward."

"Very good. Our aircraft?"

"Our stern is clear, sir. When we need to land them, we can."

Fletcher picks up a radio, "Columbia, Task Force 17, what is the status of your missiles?"

Captain heard replies, "Sir, twenty standard left."

"Columbia, we'll send the Roanoke to unrep standard."

"Roger, sir. Standing by. Sir, are our aircraft loaded with ordinance?"

"Affirmative."

"Recommend we hit the bombers as they land."

"Roger, Columbia."

CHAPTER 19

ME-262 DEPARTING OCCUPIED RAF OUSTON

1048, 30 September, 1942

Major Gunter barely clears the trees at the end of the field. He keeps his speed down so his squadron can catch up to him. Each of the ten '262s carries two bombs and two missiles. Before long, they go feet wet continuing east until they can't see the English coast. Gunter smiles as his formation turns south.

IN MARSHAL, USS YORKTOWN

2253, 30 September, 1942 (1153, 30 September GMT)

LT Donald Atwood flies his F4F-3 Wildcat down the port side of the Yorktown at 1000 feet. The ship's stern is up wind, smoke and fire rising hundreds of feet into the sky. Three destroyers are with the sinking North Carolina. Then, on the Yorktown, the bow explodes with a visible shockwave. Atwood turns his plane to take the shockwave on his nose. He still loses lift on the left side, but brings it his aircraft back under control. Then, he looks down. The Yorktown has slowed and the flames are spreading. A gust of wind clears the smoke and he sees fire in the forward hangar. He makes the turn and flies up the stricken ship's starboard side. He can see that it's settling deeper in the water. He hears on his radio, "All units, be advised. Yorktown is foundering. Ditch near the destroyers for pick-up."

ST. JOHN'S COLLEGE, CAMBRIDGE, UK

1344, 30 September, 1942

Sergeant Johnny Rodriguez runs at the front of his little unit. He had twelve men, but after an ambush, he's down to eight, and the Germans are everywhere. They run through ancient buildings with amazing stone architecture, then over the Bridge of Sighs. They make a corner and see a German carrying a painting. Johnny butt strokes him and keeps running. Jimmy grabs the painting, finds a closet, and tosses it in.

Johnny looks out a window, "Oh fuck." Under the trees, about a hundred yards away to the east sit three Tiger tanks and two half-tracks, and one of the half-tracks has a missile launcher. Beside him, holding his shoulder and heaving for breath, Wingnut looks over the situation, "No time to call. Keep going."

"They make it to the northwest corner and look out. It's clear, so they slowly exit, looking for cover. They run for a small brook with brush on its banks and work their way south. At times they're forced to lay down and squirm along in the west grass.

Wingnut gets under a large bush and turns on his radio, "Any Hog, Wingnut." Static. "Any A-10, Wingnut." Static. "Wingnut transmitting in the blind. We have multiple German armor blocking our retreat east of St. John's College in Cambridge," and gives the map coordinates.

He hears something unintelligible in the static and turns off the radio, putting it away. They make it about fifty feet when they hear the panicked sobs of a woman. Peeking between branches, Tommy sees two Germans dragging a young woman by her hair. One German says something and the SS walk straight toward him.

Johnny and Wingnut exchange a long look. They draw their knives. Jimmy Thatcher draws his saber and Tommy motions for him to put it away. The Germans push through the branches right into their knives.

Wingnut thrusts his knife up under the man's ribs and into his heart. The German gurgles and collapses. Johnny slits the other man's throat with a backhand slash, cutting the jugular and carotid, showering himself in blood. Jimmy grabs the girl, covering her mouth with his hand. As she sees her captors die, she starts to shake.

Silently, they ease their way south along the brook. Johnny bends and rinses his hands and knife in the cold water.

ELECTRONICS PRODUCTION PLANT 6, NORTH OF KENNE-WICK, WASHINGTON

0612, 30 September, 1942 (1412 GMT)

Captain Scott Richardson studies the control screen on a new fabrication unit. He now has more than two thousand fabrication units in the six plants. This one is a new design by Raytheon. The tolerances are supposed to be tighter, but as they set up the machine, it's obvious they're not in spec. Richardson pull out a note pad and starts writing calculations. "Try adjusting the laser six ten thousandths inward. Call me if it doesn't get better."

The Raytheon engineer, "Sir, I'm terribly sorry for this."

Scott wearily smiles, "Don't be. This is new technology. It will take time to perfect." Beyond the engineer he sees a lieutenant junior grade waiting. "Can I help you, Lieutenant?"

"Lieutenant Maki, sir," and hands Scott a letter. It's addressed to him from Admiral Klindt.

Captain Richardson,

LTJG Maki is designing a tank for me. He's seeking electronics for the tank. Tank electronics is a tier 2 priority.

Admiral Klindt

Scott shakes his head and looks up, "What is your background, Lieutenant?"

"Four months ago, I was an MM2 nuke on the Long Beach. I solved a problem with the 6-inch triple mounts they're installing on the Long Beach and Admiral Klindt assigned this tank job to me. I'm massively in over my head and doing the best I can."

"Your honest, good. Ten months ago, I was a senior chief. What do you need?"

"I need a laser range finder and I want an integrated ballistic computer. Computer based engine monitoring would be nice, too."

"Your first request is easy. I'm building something similar for block 2 of the A-10 and the F/A-14B. The A-10 ballistic computer may work as well, with some software and input modifications."

"Thank you, sir."

"Tell me, why is the army letting a sailor design tanks?"

"They aren't. I'm designing for the Marines."

"And what have the Marines said?"

Maki grins, "Yes, sir, admiral, sir. You've met Admiral Klindt, right?"

Scott laughs, "I used to work for him on the Vinson and he's here a lot." He pulls the page of calculations out of his notebook and hands it to the Raytheon engineer, "Let me know if the adjustments work. Take your time and be meticulous. Remember, slow is smooth, and smooth is fast." He motions for Maki to follow him, "So, tell me about this tank."

"The Marines insist on gasoline, so the engine will be the

Rolls Royce Merlin. Packard has a license to build them. The admiral scared up a 105mm gun with fixed ammunition. The suspension will be a horizontal volute suspension because they're tough and reliable, and don't get hung up in terrain."

"Not torsion bars?"

"The most critical component of a torsion suspension is the hardest to build. If a torsion bar fails, you're done until it can be dragged back to the shop. If the volute spring fails, you jack the wheels down and keep running, just slower."

"What are the most critical parts of this volute suspension?"

"The pins and arms and they're easy to make and over engineer."

"I think I've heard of the Merlin. It's an aircraft engine, right?"

"Yeah, the torque and horse power ratings are way better than any tank engine made today, and with all the jets we're building, aircraft don't need them."

"You have thought this through, so what has you worried?"

"It has to be made so a fourth-grader can fix it while he's being shot at."

"A fourth-grader?"

"Sorry, a smart Marine."

ST. JOHN'S COLLEGE, CAMBRIDGE, UK

At a hundred yards from the bodies, Johnny's unit is moving carefully and fast. Then they hear shouting from behind them. Tommy stops and peeks through the branches and sees a German running toward the armor. There are Germans everywhere and they're at the end of their cover. There's ten yards of road to cross in the open. A German soldier shouts, and Johnny turns and shoots his BAR from the hip. He gets a few rounds off, and they all run across the road.

A tank fires behind them, the round falling far forward. A machine gun opens up, shredding the bushes behind them and the trees and houses in front of them. Then they hear it, the brrrrt of an A-10. Wingnut yells, "Yes!" They burst through a line of trees and find two German trucks parked, one driver smoking and the other pissing on a tire.

Johnny fires two rounds and Jimmy takes a shot, hitting the smoker. They run for the trucks. One is a fuel tanker under a fabric cover and the other holds supplies. They board the supply truck and gun it east, then turn south at the cross street. Wingnut puts a bag of flour against the front wall to support his back and eases down. He looks over his team, "Jimmy, you can let go of her hand, now."

101ST, SS BATTALION, QUEENS COLLEGE, CAMBRIDGE, UK

1751, 30 September, 1942

Meier climbs out of his third tank. Four German soldiers are walking with a prisoner. In German, he asks, "Who do you have?"

The sergeant salutes, "I don't know, Herr Major. What do we do with him, sir?"

"We will see." He studies the man. The prisoner is wearing a British flight suit. In English, he says, "Cooperate and you will not be harmed."

"You're SS?"

"What unit do you fly for?"

"My name is Guiles Montgomery. I'm a member of the Royal Air Force."

"What aircraft do you fly?"

"A dirigible."

Meier pull his Luger and puts a round in the center of Montgomery's forehead. "What you do with prisoners is, you kill them."

GERMAN 4TH CORPS HEADQUARTERS, CAMBRIDGE, UK

2016, 30 September, 1942

Rommel is livid, "General, Colonel, get control of your men. This ancient city is meaningless to our mission."

The SS General, "Herr Field Marshal, the men have fought hard. Some recreation for an hour or two is nothing."

"It is you who do not understand, General. Your hour or two may be all the British need to counterattack. It may be the difference between success and failure. Your target is London. We must get to London. Anything less is meaningless."

ME-262 DEPARTING OCCUPIED RAF OUSTON

0415, 1 October, 1942

Major Gunter barely clears the trees at the end of the field. He keeps his speed down so his squadron can catch up to him. Each of the ten '262s carries two bombs and two missiles. Before long, they go feet wet continuing east until they can't see the English coast. Gunter smiles as his formation turns south.

BARTON, UK, SOUTHWEST OF CAMBRIDGE

0545, 1 October, 1942

Meier's SS soldiers run from house to house, rounding up civilians at gunpoint. They push people out into the street; old men and women, young girls and boys, and women with small children. Retired Sergeant Mason, too old for regular service, stands at the end of the line. When Meier approaches, Cox asks, in bad German, "What is this? These people are not soldiers!"

Sensing the fear, a six-month-old baby starts crying. Her mother holding her close, shushes her.

The German colonel smiles and orders his men to form a line. Then, he speaks, "All of you. Turn around." The SS soldiers herding them into place, step away.

Sergeant Mason, "Go to hell."

His twelve-year-old grandson, Peter, standing with his mother, steps in front of his little sister, and says, "Yeah. Bugger off."

Meier reddens, "We will teach your countrymen not to resist us. READY!"

Mason begins singing, "God save our gracious King. Long live our noble King..." First one, then another voice, joins in.

"AIM!"

Mason, Peter, and Reggie, the school bully, charge the Germans, as the villagers sing, "God save our King. Send him victories..."

"FIRE!"

Mason reaches Meier and grabs his throat as the soldiers fire. A SS soldier butt strokes him down. One hundred and twenty-four civilians lay dead, the baby still held tightly in her mother's arms.

GABLE END OF A NEARBY HOUSE, BARTON, UK

Chris Oliverson, MI-5, on reconnaissance, reaches the end of his roll of film. He lowers himself to the floor of the unfinished attic and sobs, clutching his camera to his chest. He takes a deep breath and watches as the Germans leave, heading south. He reloads his camera, and when there are no more Germans in sight, he makes his way to the killing field. He checks each one. They are all dead.

Struggling to see through tears, he feels a white-hot rage building inside him. He takes a picture of each face and checks for ID. When he's finished with his grisly job, he runs for his hidden motorcycle. He was there to record the passage of the Germans for his commander. This was not supposed to happen. No one had envisioned this on English soil. He kicks his bike to life, "London needs to see this."

CONTROL, RAF KENLEY

0607, 1 October, 1942

Spike signs requisitions without really looking at them, listening to the radio chatter. Andrews, her chief of staff, "Commodore, you aren't even reading them."

She looks up, making eye contact, "Colonel, I trust your judgement. Trust is binary. Either you are trusted fully, or not at all. How are the SAM defenses coming?"

"Master Chief Bond is setting them up. The Air Corps is manning them and we have Brits learning at their side. When there's enough in place, the coverage will be expanded to include all of London and Portsmouth."

"Good. I understand someone in the army wanted a separate women's club?"

"Yes, I squashed it. It didn't pass the smell test and I believed you'd oppose it."

"I would. In my unit, men and women have equal responsibilities and equal treatment."

A radio talker, "Raid warning south. Designate raid 6. 16 fast movers out of France."

Spike, "Direct Galahad and Percival to the raid. Direct Little John north and Tuck to orbit over Dover. Launch Gawain and Robin."

"Raid warning north. Designate raid 7. 12 fast movers climbing out of Ouston."

Spike, "Direct Little John and Tuck to intercept. Keep them clear of the SAM sites. Prepare my bird. When airborne, direct

Gawain to the north."

She looks at Andrews, "All recreation facilities will be open to men and women, with separate locker rooms. The clubs should memorialize our fallen."

"Yes, Commodore."

She rises and runs out.

GUNTER'S '262, EAST OF THE THAMES RIVER MOUTH

Gunter's ten aircraft formation turns west and flies up the Thames. They dodge fishing boats and small craft on the approach to London. He goes over the map in his head, again. He feels the plink of occasional small arms fire. A British destroyer sits at anchor in the estuary. Several of its machine guns open up and one of his aircraft goes away.

Gunter, "Men, ignore the fire. Time to turn." He climbs his bird to clear the chimneys of London and turns south to RAF Kenley. He loses another aircraft to a barrage balloon.

ARTHUR 1, TAKING OFF FROM RAF KENLEY

Spike cleans up her bird and climbs. At 500 feet, she turns east, "Got 'em." She brings up her nose and rudders over a bit, then fires her 20mm cannon. She hits a jet and it goes down, crashing into a house. "Jesus Christ. Damn, but no way to prevent it." She fires on another and it goes down in a backyard.

On radio, "Birds away." She puts her F-14 on the deck, clearing the space for the SAMs. Then, "Splash two. They're breaking south."

Spike passes over the Tower of London at 300 feet, pulls up to intercept the fleeing jets. "Where are they, Lizard?"

Lizard, "They're scattered and on the deck."

She goes to full military, still climbing, "We'll hit them over the channel."

"Arthur, Yankee, raid warning east. Designate raid 9."

She keeps climbing and orients toward the new threat.

Lizard, "Yankee, Arthur 1, climbing to engage." To Spike, "Boss, they're six aircraft at 2000 feet and six hundred knots."

"Are they transmitting?"

"No."

"Thanks."

As they close, Lizard says, "Jesus, Boss, these things are small."

V-1 FLIGHT OVER THE CHANNEL EAST OF LONDON

Oberlieutenant Munster is flying a modified ME-262B behind five Fi-106 Cherrystone (V-1) rockets. Sitting behind him is a major who is controlling the flying bombs. Unlike the original design, these V-1s have improved engine and control systems. Munster studies the sky in front of his flock as they fly straight on, "Major, I see missile launches ahead."

"We should fall back a little. I'll spread the formation."

Munster throttles back, and watches as three of the V-1s are hit.

The major, "I have set the others, we may go."

Munster inverts and dives away from the fight.

ARTHUR 1, CLOSING THE V-1'S

Spike, 'What the hell are those?"

One is bugging out. The others, I don't know. Lock."

Spike, "Fox 1, Fox 1," and pickles off two AIM-7s. One of the missiles immediately loses lock and tumbles. The other tracks in and another V-1 explodes. The remaining missiles fly by and she gets a good look. "It's a doodlebug, a V-1. Grunt." She puts her bird in a steep bank and turns after the missiles.

"I didn't think they got those made until '44?"

"Well, they've got them now. Call it in." She lines up a gun shot and hits the last missile and it tumbles and falls into a farm, exploding and creating a huge crater. She goes after the rest, picking them off one by one.

GERMAN OCCUPIED RAF OUSTON

0644, 1 October, 1942

General Weber studies the map. An aid come in, "Report from Major Gunter. The raid on Kenley was successful. Six aircraft lost."

"Werner, we can't afford more victories like that. We've lost nearly a hundred planes in a few days."

"Sir?"

"Very well, send him to me when he returns."

Lieutenant Werner, "Heil Hitler!"

RAF KENLEY

0712, 1 October, 1942

Spike flies over the airfield. The shorter runway's been holed, twice. Two bombs hit near the cross where the runways meet. One of the new barracks is on fire, and a hanger. Percival flight ahead of her makes the cut and lands first. Spike is next. She taxies her jet to her hanger and shuts down. A C-56 lands next and comes to a stop nearby.

Spike climbs down, "Lizard, we'll do the post brief in a minute." She walks over to where sailors in dungarees and pea coats are coming off the big transport. Gandhi stands waiting, he shouts, "New personnel to me. Black Knights form here, the other squadrons, form there. Support staff, over here." He walks up and down the line, shepherding the men and women into position.

The last are ten men in black BDUs carrying enormous

amounts of gear. Spike recognizes some of them and calls out, "SEALs to me."

LT Russel 'Triage' Jeremy salutes, "Platoon B, SEAL Team 1, reporting." He gives her a huge grin, "Good to see you, Spike."

Spike returns the salute, smiling, "Good to see you, too, Triage. Please introduce me to your team."

"Yes, ma'am. Senior Chief Pickering is our equipment specialist. MR1 Sebring is his assistant. You've met Broke Dick, Wizzee, and Mac. Meat 1 through 3 are BM3 Doug Adams, BM3 Jacob Warner, and BM3 Paul Peterson. And this is my assistant team leader, Ensign Jeremiah Buford."

Buford, salutes and puts out his hand, "Please to meet you, Commodore." She takes it, meeting his gaze, "You too, Ensign." She turns and goes down the line greeting each person in the platoon.

Cooper runs up, "Sorry, Spike."

"Gentlemen, this is my yeoman, Radar, he'll get you settled in. I need you in my conference room in thirty minutes."

Triage salutes, "Yes, ma'am."

As she walks away, two '14s take off. Swede meets her in the hanger. "What are we doing with SEALs?"

"We're briefing in thirty. I think you should be there."

"Will do. We have new pilots coming in. I'm going to sort them out. Thanks for approving our curriculum."

Spike nods, "It was well thought out. You and Thud did well. We want to keep these guys out of combat until they've mastered the '14, if we can."

"Agreed."

"How are you doing, Swede?"

"It seems there's a new, hard lesson every day. At least I have Gloria, who do you have?"

"It's different with women in command, Swede."

"Yeah. For men it's: Ensigns cannot marry, JGs should not marry, Lieutenants may marry, Lieutenant Commanders should marry, and Commanders and above must marry. For women, being married to the service is supposed to be enough. It's bullshit and you know it."

"Yes, but it's real bullshit."

"Bullshit is bullshit. You don't step in it and move along. Besides, during the war, they waved a lot of that shit."

"Swede, what are you and Gloria going to do?"

"We're getting married as soon as it's okay. I'll do everything I can to support her dreams while chasing my own."

"Are you staying in?"

"Probably. Lord knows, I'm a terrible lumberjack. What about you?"

Spike stops, "I don't know. I joined the navy to be an astronaut. Now, it doesn't matter. Truth, Swede, I have trouble imagining a life after the war."

"You need a dream. Don't you dream of horses?"

She shakes her head, smiling, "That's my families dream."

They watch as new '14s start landing at Kenley. The first of the new planes land and roll out, Spike, "Shaky one wire."

Swede, "Agreed. What do you dream of?"

The next one down, she says, "Okay, two wire."

The third comes down, "Agreed. This one is slow." The plane's nose is too high, dancing on the edge of a stall.

Spike, "We need to talk to that pilot. He's too close to the edge." The fourth plane makes a near perfect approach and landing, "Wow, they have it together."

The fifth makes a good approach, but floats the flare and

touches down too late. They can hear the brakes and tires screeching as they pilot tries to avoid an over run. Swede, "That one needs to be talked to, as well. If it works for you, I'll do the ass chewing."

"It's your squadron." They watch as all five planes taxi to their designated spots and stop.

SEAL BARRACKS, RAF KENLEY

0835, 1 October, 1942

Triage and Buford share a room. As they unload their gear, Jeremiah asks, "Is she married?"

"Who?"

"The Commodore."

"Dude, none of us are married. I had a girl back in San Dog. She won't be born until 1967, and I ain't a fucking pedophile. By the time she's old enough to date, I'll be a sixty-nine-year old codger."

"I'm sorry, sir. I had no idea. I didn't mean to upset you."

"In this job, you need to think. Why do you want to know about the Commodore?"

Buford smiles, "Just curious. Do you know her?"

"I've met her. She started the war on the Vinson as a lieutenant and now she's a flag officer."

"Wow. How did you meet?"

Triage looks at him, "God, you're full of questions. First time I saw her, she was SAR swimming, rescuing sailors from the Stoddard. The boss was chewing her ass."

"Why?"

"Dude, we have an op to plan. Let's go."

COMMODORE'S CONFERENCE ROOM

0900, 1 October, 1942

Spike concludes, "I need the photo's back. I don't have any idea how he will be dressed and he's supposed to be alone. Questions?"

BM1 Steve 'Mac' Cook, "What is so damn important about this guy that we need to fish him of occupied France. It was hard enough getting him in before?"

Spike, "Succinctly, it's none of your fucking business, Mac. Any other questions?"

Mac, "Why?"

She sighs, "Mac, because at this juncture, the less you know the better. If you fail, and please don't fail, you can't reveal what you don't know. Just know it's important."

Buford, "It's important, ma'am, so we won't fuck, ah, foul it up."

She meets his gaze, "You can plan for everything but the enemy." She looks away and turns to Triage, "I trust your judgement out there. Know this, if it blows up, we'll do everything we can to get you out."

Swede, "I'll have two birds in the air as your cover."

Triage, "Hell, guys, if it was easy, the Army would do it. If it was hard and stupid, they'd send in the Marines."

She catches Triage's gaze and grins, "We're a long way from the south Pacific."

He returns her smile, "Yes, ma'am, and this time, you can leave the swimming to us."

Swede sees Ensign Buford watching them, his lips pinched together, eyes narrowed, and brow set. Then, his face flushes, and his eyes widen, and he stares at Sam, swaying toward her. Swede watches, bemused, as Buford's eyes shutter and he shakes his head, looking away. Swede knows that look.

Spike motions to Swede to follow her, and walks to her office. Swede, "At least, it isn't the bathroom, this time."

She laughs, "Yeah, Swede. Look, is this going to work?"

"You covered all the bases. Anything you could plan for, is planned for. Are you okay?"

"I'm tired of that question, Swede."

"Sam, if I can't ask it, then who can?"

"I'm tired. I'm tired of sending good people out to die."

He nods, "Speaking of good people, Gandhi is doing the initial orientation of the new pilots. Shall we check in?"

"Sure."

They go to the ready room and ENS Von Nix shouts, "Attention on deck!" Everyone stands.

Spike looks behind her, then wryly smiles, "Carry on." They all sit back down.

Gandhi, "Commander Swedenborg, Commodore Hunt, may I present our new air crews. The pilots are Major Greg 'Pappy' Boyington, Lieutenant Jacqueline Cochran, Ensign Mical De-Graaff, Ensign Michael Landes, and Ensign Von Nix. The RIOs are Ensign Margaret Alcott, Ensign Julian Everling, Ensign Steve Ulhe, Ensign Robert Carnegie, and Ensign Heather Kohlman."

Swede, "Boyington, how many hours of ACM training do you have in the Tomcat?"

Boyington, "About six hours each. We all have about 300 hours of ACM in the War Eagle, and I have over a thousand hours of actual combat in the P-40."

Swede nods, "What's your impression of the Tomcat?"

"I'm in love, sir."

Swede smiles, "Cochran, what's your impression?"

"It's an amazing aircraft, sir. Its agility, for its size, is incredible."

"Ensign DeGraaff?"

"It's amazing, but it doesn't like to land, sir."

"True. We'll get to that. Ensign Landes?"

"As they said, sir."

"Ensign Nix?"

"It kicks ass, sir. It's fast, agile, and fun as shit, but it's a demanding mistress."

Swede grins, "What do you mean, Nix?"

"Sir, if you don't give it your absolute best, it will make you pay."

Swede, "Agreed. Commodore, do you want to speak to them?"

She looks at the new faces. "I want you to recognize that the German Luftwaffe is getting better each day. To keep up, all of you have to get better each day. If you don't learn, you'll die." She turns to Gandhi, "Are they sorted into teams?"

Gandhi, "They flew in as pairs, but Walker left it to us, Spike."

Spike, "For now, let them choose. Ground school today. Four to six training hops a day with a flight leader. They don't fly combat until you clear them."

Swede, "Roger that." Then, "Who was flying 129 and 131?"

DeGraaff raises her hand, "I was flying 129. I came in too slow."

"If you stalled it would have killed you both. Some of us are going to die. Don't die a stupid, useless death. Know that every landing is graded, and we're grading your judgement as much as your skills. 131?"

Nix raises his hand, "I floated my landing and should have aborted."

Swede, "Yes, you should have. The ground crews are inspecting your brakes right now. You just got here and your bird is broken. The most important thing in aviation is good judgement. Good skills can only make up for so much stupidity. You are all new in type. Normally, you would receive 400 hours of training before we even assign you to a squadron. The war has forced our leadership to send you out with minimal training. That is not your fault. The only way any of you are going to survive the war is to learn your job as quickly as you can, and to make good sound judgements. Sort yourselves out into teams."

The raid siren sounds, "Carry on." They newbies watch Swede, Gandhi, and Spike run out of the room.

Von Nix asks, "What do we do?"

Boyington stands, "We look after our planes, without our birds, we might as well be infantry. Then we get squared away."

CHAPTER 20

GERMAN OCCUPIED RAF OUSTON

1123, 1 October, 1942

Major Gunter taxis his '262 to its hanger and stops. The three other survivors stop alongside him. They had just escorted in sixteen more '262s, ten more '163s, and six transport planes. When he opens his canopy, he's greeted by a light rain. His plane captain gives him a hand and he jumps to the ground. He looks at the new cargo planes. He's never seen such a large aircraft. He's shocked to see the rear of the plane open two huge clam shell doors. He watches the ground crew pull out an odd-looking aircraft. When they open its rotors, he realizes it's an auto-gyro type aircraft.

A staff sergeant salutes, "Major, the general wishes to see you."

A captured American jeep takes him to the headquarters building. He walks into the office and salutes, "Heil Hitler!"

Weber, "How did the operation go?"

"Four aircraft made it over the field and dropped their ordinance. I could see buildings burning and one of the runways was hit at least once. One thing, sir, I couldn't find the fuel tanks. They have to be there, but they were too well disguised."

"It's all right. You did well. We launched five experimental missiles at London as you left the area. It was the counter I promised to help you escape. Radio intercepts indicate you faced the Drachendame. It seems you have tangled with her more times than any living pilot."

"I have been fortunate, sir."

"You have also been skilled. It's my thought that we ought to trap her using her confidence against her. First, we now have helicopters. They can be used to ferry troops around the battlefield. Their primary use will be to evacuate the wounded, but they have other purposes as well. They fly slowly, so it's critical they be protected."

"Yes, sir."

BOEING PLANT, SEATTLE, WASHINGTON

1334, 1 October, 1942 (2134 GMT)

Admiral Lee walks through the door of a huge hanger wearing his flight suit. The lights illuminate the lines of a large delta winged aircraft with four turbojets under the wing root next to the fuselage and a large single vertical stabilizer. A US Army Air Corps major, in his flight suit, comes up and salutes, "Good afternoon, Admiral. It's a glorious day to fly."

Lee absently returns the salute, his attention riveted on the aircraft in front of him. "Good afternoon. Major Connery, please give me the tour."

"Yes, sir. We're designating it B-46. Its theoretic top speed is Mach 2.1 at 40,000 feet. Its payload is rated at twenty tons." They walk around the one hundred twenty-five-foot plane. Its fuselage flows over the engine's nacelles and blend with the wing to fit the four engines. Two internal bomb bays are located forward and aft at the center of gravity. The wings sweep back at sixty degrees. There are two underwing pylons on each side for missiles.

Lee finally turns to Connery, "Have you flown it?"

"Yes, sir."

"Supersonic?"

"Twice."

"Okay, then. I've gone over the flight manual. Let's mount up."

Thirty minutes later, Lee levels the B-46. They're flying at 300 knots when he slows her down, "First test, stall behavior."

Major Connery grins, "Yes, sir."

They continue to slow and at 220 knots, the plane shudders and the nose drops violently. The wings, however, stay level and he's able to recover smoothly. Lee nods, "A bit violent, but controllable." He then accelerates, "Asymmetric thrust." They pass 600 knots and he idles back engines four and three. "Applying rudder and aileron." The plane crabs, but is controllable. "Have you tried this at high Mach?"

"No, sir. We waited for you to test the Mach envelope."

"Okay," He accelerates to Mach 1.5 and repeats the asymmetric thrust maneuver. The aircraft shudders and rolls right, "Okay," and he quickly applies rudder and ailerons. They drop at 1,000 feet per minute as the plane slows. He gets it back under control and climbs her to test altitude. "Let's try this wide open."

"You think that's a good idea, sir?"

Lee looks at the major, "It's necessary. We have to test its flight envelope. What we learn will determine if it's even viable. We don't do this, we're killing aircrew."

"Yes, sir."

He idles engines 3 and 4 at Mach 2, and the aircraft yaws and flips on its back. He idles the other two engines and using his rudder and variable engine power he manages to avoid a flat spin. "Okay, it didn't like that. Let's try again, but we take 1 and 2 off afterburner at the same time."

He repeats the test with the new variable and the plane is more controllable. "We need an interlock for the afterburners. Right now, if two idle back, the other two go to full military."

"Yes, sir."

"Okay, high Mach turns."

VALKYRIE 1 OVER THE ENGLISH CHANNEL NEAR THE HAGUE

0113, 2 October, 1942

Cargo Britches hovers for the twelfth time as she lowers the sonar probe, searching for submarines. This time, the SEALs jump out into the cold water with their inflatable electric boats. As soon as they clear, she pulls up and away. In the dark, she sees a bright line of tracers rise up from the north. The shooter is aiming at the sound of her chopper, so she descends and accelerates.

Keg, in the back, "Commander, we need to do something about that patrol boat."

"They might have moved on by the time we need to be back."

Keg, "What if they're sitting on our LZ?"

"Then, we'll sink it. For now, don't borrow trouble."

The SEALs silently work their way onto the beach. Once clear of the water, they take turns putting on NOGs. That done, they move out, using cover. They see pill boxes on either side of them and a patrol stopped up the beach north of them. Silently, they ghost into the dunes and bury their boats.

They study the dunes and Triage sees foot prints going over the dune, but none taking the easy way between them. Using touch signals, they carefully go over the top of the dunes and Mac, at the end, brushes out their tracks.

A few minutes later, they're tucked against the wall of a house. Triage checks his map and they move, using the buildings of the town as cover. They arrive at their target and Buford takes two minutes to pick the lock and they slip in. Just as the last man gets inside, a German truck passes.

They move into the house, slowly and carefully. In the kitchen two people are waiting, their hands flat on the table. Mac says in German, "The sausage is done."

Spooky, still motionless, replies in German, "Did you remember the ketchup?"

Mac, in English, "Good, Boss."

Triage, "One person."

Spooky, "She comes or I stay. A patrol will be along in a quarter of an hour. After that we move."

Triage shrugs his shoulder. "We only brought one wet suit. If you're important enough for us to come and get you, you're wearing it."

Lisa Anderson says, "MI-6. I can handle the cold. I've been cold before."

Triage, "You're Brit?"

"Yes. I'll not be a problem."

BOEING FIELD, SEATTLE, WASHINGTON

1906, 1 October, 1942 (0306 2 October GMT)

Lee allows his co-pilot/bombardier to land the jet after their second flight. He likes the side by side seating. It makes communication easier. The wheels chirp and the nose comes down, then the parachute deploys, helping to slow them down. When they slow to taxiing speed, they release the chute. Lee shakes his head, "The chute is going to be a pain in the ass in England." He jots down another note.

BEACH NEAR THE HAGUE

0316, 2 October, 1942

The SEALs and their cargo lay waiting on a dune as a German patrol walks by. They've already recovered their boats, but haven't inflated them yet. Two miles out in the water they watch a patrol boat idle by.

When the foot patrol is clear, they silently and swiftly move down onto the beach, watching the patrol carefully. In the water, Buford grabs Anderson and wraps her up for a rescue swim. She doesn't resist and despite the cold is still and silent.

Clear of the surf line, they inflate the boats and turn on the battery powered motors. They all lay down in the boats, minimizing their profile. The patrol boat idling along is smack in their way. Triage stops the boats and touches Mac and Buford. They roll over the side and disappear.

COMMODORE'S OFFICE, RAF KENLEY

0320, 2 October, 1942

Spike, in her flight suit, sits writing letters. Cooper comes in, "Spike, you're killing me. Why aren't you in bed?"

"We have boys down range, Radar. I can't sleep."

"Then, why aren't you in Control?"

"I don't want them to know I'm worried."

"If you went to bed, then they would know you weren't worried."

"If you went to bed, I wouldn't know if they're alright." She stops and looks at her yeoman, "Wait a minute, Radar, why are you up?"

"If you must know, I'm sneaking back to bed after visiting my girlfriend and I saw your light on."

"Who?"

He turns red, "Sergeant Valentine at the control center."

"She's cute, but I thought she was married."

"She was, and she wears her ring. Her husband never made it off Dunkirk."

"I'm just asking. Could he be a POW?"

"No. His sergeant reported him dead. Gunshot. Am I an ass for dating her?"

"No, Radar. She's no doubt as lonely as you are. I'm happy for you."

SEALS, TWO MILES OFF THE HAGUE

0330, 2 October, 1942

Buford and Mac slither back into the boat with Triage. Buford, "How are we for time?"

Triage, "We're okay. How long?"

"Twelve seconds."

A search light from the patrol boat passes over them. They are a black blob on a black ocean.

VALKYRIE 1, 50 FEET, 15 MILES NW OF THE HAGUE

Cargo Britches, "Damn, the patrol boat is back."

Keg, "Cargo, if we strike it, we could hurt the SEALs in the water with the concussion."

"I know. We also have to worry if they're on board." Then the horizon lights up as the boat explodes. "Well, we know they're not onboard now."

Keg, "Got them. Ready for pick up. God, I love SEALs."

Britches chuckles, "Yep, me too." She brings the helo into a hover right above the waves. The first boat comes in wide open and she times the waves. They leap off a crest right into the helicopter. She climbs a bit so they can sort out the back and lowers for the second go.

This one hits the helicopter a little high and it comes down hard on the floor of the helo. The coxswain waits too long to secure the engine and the prop digs into the aluminum of the door.

Cargo Britches, "Are we all aboard?"

Keg, 'Head count plus one."

"Shut the doors."

Keg, "Right door won't secure."

"Damn. See what you can do. Anyone hurt?"

Triage, "My pride, Commander. We came in a little hot."

"It happens. Thanks for blowing the patrol boat." She swings the helo around and accelerates out of the area at high speed.

Triage, "Thanks for coming back."

Cargo Britches grins, "Always, frogman. Always."

COMMODORE'S OFFICE, RAF KENLEY

0414, 2 October, 1942

Cooper is pouring tea when they hear the sound of a helicopter. They look at each other and Spike grabs her jacket and runs out the door. When she gets to it, the rotors are spinning down and the SEALs are getting themselves and their gear off. She counts them, "Who's the extra?"

Spooky walks up to her, "Good to see you, Spike. Call her Sally. She's MI-6."

"Spooky, are you all right?"

He looks starved and his eyes are sunk in a bit, but they are clear. "Fine, ma'am. Thank you."

"Go get some sleep. Sally, Cooper can arrange transport to wherever you need to go. Spooky, guys, I'll brief you at twelve hundred. Get some sleep."

Sally asks, "Ma'am, do you have a pilot called Shotgun?"

Spike does a double take, "I do."

"May I speak with him?"

"Of course. He's flying right now, but Cooper can arrange it after he's had some sleep."

35,000 FEET OVER THE IRISH SEA

1013, 2 October, 1942

Thud and Speedy are orbiting, watching a dog fight between Boyington and a Griffin. The British pilot is experienced in jet fighters. Pappy gets in trouble in a horizontal fight, but goes vertical before his opponent can take advantage. Pappy has more energy and gets on the Griffin's six. Alcott, Pappy's RIO, says, "Guns. Guns."

The British pilot in Phoenix 16 says, "Good kill."

Speedy, "Knock it off. Knock it off. Orbit north of the training area at point Lima. Squire 131 and Phoenix 17 meet at 600 knots in the merge at angels 28. Call go for fight."

ENS Kohlman says, "Gawain 1, Squire 131, go fight."

"Gawain 1, Phoenix 17, go fight."

Speedy, "Fights on."

MAJOR MOSSBERG'S QUARTERS, RAF KENLEY

1025, 2 October, 1942

Shotgun sits on his bed and gives the one chair to Lisa Anderson. "What do you want to know?"

"I was told that during the time travel event you were in Germany at Brendenmeyer Airfield as part of an organization called NATO."

Shotgun rocks back. "Who told you this?"

"US Army Sergeant First Class Henry Holmes and US Airforce Master Sergeant Kelly O'Brien. Is what they told me accurate?"

"Where are they? Are they still alive?"

"Major, your answering my questions with more questions. Yes, they should be alive. An answer, please.

Shotgun, "As I shared with your people, I ditched somewhere off Sweden. I told Holmes to get the others out. We were under attack by Germans. Thank God, they're alive. Where are they? We need to get them out."

"You see, that's the problem. They're in Andorra."

"What the fuck is Andorra? A town?"

"It's an independent principality. It's in the Pyrenees on the border of France and Spain. The Pope brokered a deal to keep the Germans out of there. If we barge in, that will disrupt the whole thing and endanger thousands."

"The Commodore needs to know where they are."

"So, they really are American servicemen and they are important?"

"Yes, they are American service men, and yes, they are important. Can your people get them out?"

"It would be extremely difficult. Why are they important?"

Mossberg stops, "This again. What did they say?"

"They told me to talk to you. Why are they important?"

"I can't tell you."

"You can't say because you don't know, or you can't say because it's classified. We're supposed to work closely together, as allies." She leans toward him, smiling, and lets her blouse open, exposing her cleavage.

He sits back and smirks. "You're acting like I could get laid for that information. No deal. I wouldn't tell your intelligence people when they had me, and I won't tell you now. If you would excuse me, I need to talk to the Commodore." He gets up and opens the door, "Ma'am?"

TARMAC, RAF KENLEY

1102, 2 October, 1942

Spike walks with Swede, "With the Griffins patrolling over the channel, we're short for protecting the Warthogs. They've been stretching us out with two and four element flights hitting us where we are weak. We need the initiative."

Swede, grim, "Any ideas?"

"One, but it is too all or nothing for my liking."

"If I think of something, I'll let you know when I get back."

"I'm glad you have Gloria, Swede."

"Thank you. By the way, do you know who GQ is dating?"

"No one, I know of. Why?"

"Because Gloria is evasive about only that one thing. It's like she's protecting him."

"Maybe she is. No doubt, you and Gandhi have your secrets. GQ gets it done. That's all we need to know."

Swede brightens up, "Okay. You're absolutely right. He does."

"Get up there and kick some ass, Swede." She turns and walks back to the hanger. Fluffy steps out of the shadows, "Spike, can we talk?"

"Sure, Fluffy. I have a few minutes. What's up?"

They walk through the hanger to her jeep. "Spike, we have enough people now to let a few at a time get some time off, even with our op tempo."

"Clear it with the individual skippers, but it's okay with me. What's our manning level now?"

"The Black Knights and the legacy detachments are at 150 to 200 percent manning."

"You think they're using us for training?"

"It makes sense."

"Okay. Give them liberty, but keep them close, the ground crews. We don't have the new aircrew up to speed yet."

Fluffy, "You ever read about Pappy Boyington?"

"Of course, he's a gambler, a drunk, and a womanizer, but he's also one hell of a pilot and leader."

"Then why did you give him a female RIO?"

"They pick their own. Ah, I see. I'm too high up the chain. Have Mouse, Trollop, or Hot Pants talk to her."

"Will do."

Spike, "We have two more squadrons of A-10s coming in soon. We need to accommodate them."

"Already done. All the bomb damage to the field is repaired and we're building new barracks. We're hiding them now. I pointed out that destroying a barracks is an easy way to disable our unit. Beirut, 1983."

"Yeah. Thank you, Fluffy."

"Oh, by the way, the O-club is done."

"Already?"

"Yeah, we had some help from a local pub. You should check it out."

"I will."

SQUIRE 132, 20,000 FEET OVER THE IRISH SEA

1114, 2 October, 1942

LT Cochran says, "What do you know about how Thud fights?"

ENS Julian Everling, "I asked LT Standley. All he said was, we're going to lose and we need to learn from the experience."

"Bull shit. Any pilot can be beat. So, he's over confident?"

"Cochran, he has 87 kills. How many of them thought he was overconfident?"

On radio, they hear Speedy, "Good morning, ladies and gentlemen. Today the hard deck is angels ten. Guns only. We will merge at angels 20. Report ready."

Julian, "Gawain 1, Squire 132, angels 20, ready."

Cochran, "On the merge, we're going to climb and cross."

Julian, "Okay. He's at 350."

"I see him."

Speedy, "Merging. Fight's on."

Julian, "Fights on."

The two jets merge at a combined speed of 1300 knots. Cochran has her jet cocked right, then immediately after the merge, she rolls left and climbs at an angle. Julian, "He's staying in the horizontal, turning left."

Cochran cranks on the 'Gs' going over the top. Julian, unprepared, passes out. The jets merge again.

Julian comes too, "Fuck man, warn me!"

Cochran, "Where is he?" She pulls up again and spins the jet looking for Thud.

GAWAIN 1

Thud manually pushes the wings forward and deploys his air brake as he pulls over the top. Reoriented, he rolls on zone 5 and closes the now vertical jet. He sees them spinning, "Gs," and cranks his jet onto Cochran's six.

SQUIRE 132

Cochran stays in the climb and spins, searching for Gawain 1.

Julian, "He's on our six."

Cochran, "Fuck." She pours on the 'Gs', trying to shake him.

Julian, "Fucking warn me!"

"Sorry, 'Gs.'" She rolls right into a horizontal turn.

Then, they hear Speedy, "Guns. Guns. Knock it off."

On radio, "Gawain 1, Yankee. We have multiple raid warnings. Come to new course 085. Squire RTB.

Speedy, "Yankee, Gawain 1, wilco. Squire, return to base."

Julian, "Gawain 1, Squire 132, wilco."

Cochran, "Fuck. Just fuck. We're armed. We're ready. I want to fight."

Everling, "Yeah, me too. But, if we disobey, we're done. The base is at 105."

CHAPTER 21

EISENHOWER'S HQ, BUSHY PARK, LONDON, UK

0700, 3 October, 1942

Spike sits in a conference with Lieutenant General Dwight Eisenhower, Air Chief Marshal Hugh Dowding, Field Marshal Alan Brooke, Lieutenant General Kenneth Anderson, Lieutenant General James Doolittle, and General Guy Simonds, commander of I Canadian Corps. Eisenhower says, "George tells me your attack planes are indispensable."

"Yes, sir. We just received two more squadrons."

Brooke, "Very good. Tell me, Commodore, what sort of armored vehicles did your army have in 1990."

"It isn't my area of expertise. But, if I recall, they had composite, top secret armor and the gun was a 120mm."

Brooke turns to Eisenhower, "Tell me we're building these future tanks today?"

Eisenhower, "Not that I know of."

Brooke continues, "I am authorized to purchase up to 5000, if you have a tank that can stand against the new German tank."

"Our Shermans and Grants are faring no better. Only artillery or A-10s seem to work. I will make inquiries."

Spike, "I also have some connections. If you like, I will ask, too."

Brooke looks at her, "Could your navy be building tanks?"

Spike smiles, "Yes, for the Marine Corps. Admiral Klindt is Vice

CNO for special projects. If anyone knows, he does."

Eisenhower, "Please do, Commodore. Something else we need to consider; a squadron of Russian fighters is coming to Kenley tomorrow for refueling. They plant to continue to Saint Petersburg. We don't want to have any friendly fire."

Dowding, "I shall brief my crews."

Spike, "As will I. I understand they'll be flying the War Eagle." She thinks for a moment, "Sir, if the Germans engage the Russian planes, that could bring Russia back into the war."

Dowding, "May we direct them to land at Ouston?"

Eisenhower laughs, "No, but if they tangle, they tangle. I don't want to lose a single plane defending a non-combatant country."

Spike, "Are they staying for crew rest, or continuing on?"

"I don't know. Russians are notional."

"If they stay for crew rest, I'll be setting watches to keep them away from our gear."

Eisenhower laughs again, "A good point."

GERMAN OCCUPIED RAF OUSTON

0750, 3 October, 1942

A helicopter flares and lands and Field Marshal Rommel steps out holding his hat. General Weber salutes, "Heil Hitler."

Rommel returns the salute, "Heil. Your office, General." They walk silently into a building just off the tarmac. They walk through the outer office filled with Weber's operations staff, who all stand and salute.

In Weber's office, he pours coffee for them both, "I trust all is well with the advance?"

Rommel sips his coffee, "We advance. In fact, we're nearly on schedule. That, and our 3rd Division friends are a little ahead of schedule."

Weber looks up, "Word of atrocities have reached me."

Rommel waves a hand, "The SS do as they do. Two things, the American fighters have most decidedly not been destroyed, and the cursed Devil's Cross is wreaking havoc on my tank units. We have lost substantially more vehicles than we planned. I do not know if we'll have enough to make our push on London."

Weber, "Victories against the US Navy planes come hard. We recently killed two on the same sortie. Their numbers indicate they're getting new aircraft. We've detected what looks like training flights over the Irish Sea. She's only deploying her veteran crews. The new pilots must be terribly trained."

"Agree. Will you hit the students, then?"

"We will, and prepare an ambush for those who rush to their aid. They also keep trying to fly radar planes. Right now, those planes must fly over the Irish Sea to avoid our fighters. If we can, I want to hit the radar planes as well."

Rommel, "Do we know their base?"

"Yes, it's in Cornwall."

"Hit it as well."

"Yes, Herr Field Marshal."

Rommel puts his empty cup down, "Tell me, old friend, can we do it?"

Weber, "It all hinges on this: as long as Air Marshal Goering continues to replace my losses, I can maintain at least parity. As long as the Drachendrame lives, the battle is in doubt. I have laid several ambushes already, but she either fails to materialize, or she defeats those arrayed against her. The good news is they are leaving us alone here, for now. It's a concession to our success, no?"

Rommel, "Maybe. Now that we have helicopters, I will look

into sending a team to Kenley to capture or kill her."

"That is bold, my friend. Isn't assassination a bit out of character for you?"

"It's a time for boldness. I do not see a choice. If we win here, the Americans will regroup. It buys us time to build our forces. When England falls, Russia will sue for peace. In time, our government will moderate and Germany will be strong."

"Do you think Hitler will allow moderation?"

"I think Hitler will not live forever. Who do you suppose should replace him?"

"A war hero, surely."

"Perhaps. It's my hope, that whoever it is, their policies will be more moderate. Still, he has united us as no moderate ever could."

"If we fail?"

"If we fail, Germany will, almost inevitably, lose out to the production and resources of America. It will all be for naught."

HARD SHELTER, RAF KENLEY

0830, 3 October, 1942

ADC(AW/SW) Robert 'Bobby' Geller helps AD3(AW) Lori 'Sass' Givens and AD3(SW) Greg 'Duck' Newburg replace the left engine and right wing on Spike's Tomcat. They're working to jazz on the radio.

Sass, "She's going to need a new bird soon. This poor thing has been hammered."

Geller, "Look at it, Sass. She's shot down about a hundred planes with this bird. It's always brought her home. Have you ever played sports?"

"Yeah, basketball."

"Did you have a favorite pair of shoes or shorts or something?"

"Yeah, I had a favorite ball. I always shot well with it."

"Well, with pilots, they're trusting their life to a machine. They get damned superstitious about it."

The music changes to a Louis Armstrong tune, then in mid song, the music stops. They turn and look at the radio, then at each other. They hear, "A message from the Prime Minister.

"Yesterday afternoon, in the German occupied village of Waterloo, forces of Nazi Germany lined up one hundred twenty-four men, woman, and children. With absolute cruelty, the Nazis gunned down elderly men and women. They gunned down mothers with their children. They murdered children. We have some names: Ned Mason, 68 years old, and a survivor of the Great War; Ned's grandson, 12-year-old Peter; Mrs. Rose Whitmore and her 6-month-old daughter, Elizabeth.

"Mr. Mason, his grandson, Peter, and another boy, Reggie, charged the German guns as the villagers sang our anthem. They charged their attackers, not to prevent the attack, but to bring focus on themselves in hopes of sparing those innocents behind them.

"The German army did this to cow us; to drive us into submission. They do not understand the character of the British peoples. We will never submit. Never.

"Never in the history of all humanity has there been a conflict that more clearly defined the difference between barbarism and decency. In this great conflict, all that makes us British is being tested.

"The bonds of brotherhood that connect us will endure. The bonds that connect us to our commonwealth will endure. The bonds that connect us to the American peoples will endure.

"Know this for certain, no dastardly, cowardly, cruel, or inhuman act by the evil Reich we fight will ever turn us from our path. As we stand, today, with all freedom loving people on this earth, our great mission will not fail. Our soldiers, sailors, and airmen will not fail. Humanity will prevail and the light of justice will burn out the evil in its very lair. Rise up, Britain. Rise up, world. This is a fight we must win. We must win, and we shall win."

Bobby looks at the others and sees the same rage and sorrow he feels, "Continue. Let's get this bird in the air. I need to talk to the boss."

GALAHAD 1, 25,000 FEET OVER THE IRISH SEA

1015, 3 October, 1942

Swede and Gandhi are flying at 20,000 feet in clear skies above heavy overcast. Squire 128 is on their left wing. Swede, "What do you think of Boyington?"

Gandhi, "To tell the truth, I'm underwhelmed. He flies with a chip on his shoulder."

Swede snorts, "He lives with a chip on his shoulder. Hopefully, we can turn him into a leader and a team player."

"Okay, Boss. We're where we need to be. Whiskey Tango Lima is 80 miles south." On radio, "Squire 128, Galahad 1, hard deck is angels 10. We split and merge. Fight is on at the merge."

Alcott, Boyington's RIO, "Galahad 1, Squire 128, Wilco."

Swede slides into a graceful turn and circles back. "He's used to fighting in the horizontal. We're going vertical. Let's see how he reacts."

Gandhi, "Got it, brother." The two jets meet at 1200 knots closure.

Swede, "Gs."

Gandhi, "He went vertical."

Swede idles back his engines and pushes his wings forward, air brake out, and rolls over the top. He goes back to military power and spins upright, easing back on the stick. Gandhi, "He's inverted, crossing, 800 up."

Swede climbs to meet him and notices the control surface deflection that warns him Pappy is going over the top rather than rolling to keep climbing. Swede lets him start drifting down, then inverts and pulls onto his six. Gandhi, "Guns. Guns."

Then, on radio, "Galahad, Whiskey Tango Lima, raid warning north. 10 bandits. Designate raid 12. 65 miles north, on the deck. Missiles fired."

Gandhi, "Acknowledged Whiskey Tango Lima. Squire, knock it off. Turn to meet them. Turning north."

Alcott, "Galahad 1, Squire 128, wilco."

Gandhi to Swede, "Okay, I got 8 missiles inbound. It's their long-range ones."

Swede on radio, "Pappy, at my call, break, full burner and pickle countermeasures, both chaff and flares."

Alcott, "Galahad 1, Squire 128, wilco."

SQUIRE 128

Pappy, "Okay, our first go. I just don't wanna fuck up."

Alcott, "Amen, Pappy. I have the missiles on radar."

Then, Swede on radio, "Break! Break!"

Pappy, "Gs." He pulls back his stick and takes his bird into a 9 'G' climb, pickling off countermeasures. He spins to acquire the missiles.

Alcott, "We broke lock."

Pappy, "Gs," and turns onto the German aircraft, staying inverted.

Alcott, "Bandits are on the deck. Galahad is 3 miles left in a dive. They fired."

"Who fired?"

"Galahad. Shit, the Germans have too."

"Okay, stand by." Pappy rolls his plane left, "Gs." He goes vertical, again, pickling off countermeasures. "We fucking need missiles." The two missiles pass behind them, detonating in the chaff. He reverses back to the Germans, again, inverting.

Gandhi, "Splash 2. Yankee, we need help."

Alcott, "6,000. 5,000. 4,000. Swede is pulling in."

Pappy, "Gs," and puts his bird into a reverse Immelmann.

As they pull out, Alcott, "Swede is ahead and to the left."

On radio, "Galahad, Arthur, on our way."

Swede fires and a '262 explodes. "Splash 1." Then, Swede goes after another.

Pappy sees another '262 break right. His wings waggle, then, "Fuck. Stay on my wingman."

MAJOR GUNTER'S ME-262 APPROACHING THE RADAR PLANE BASE

Gunter hears the battle behind him, "They're fucking destroying my squadron, again. Where are the '279s?" He pops over a hill and crosses the airfield dropping his bombs. A SAM is fired. "Fuck, come on, Gunter, this is less than optimal." Squeezing between two hills, he evades the missile and is free over the Atlantic.

"I'm so weary of losing men."

GALAHAD FLIGHT OVER NORTHERN WALES

Gandhi, "Splash 1," and another '262 falls to their gun. They're flying toward the cliffs of northern Wales at 550 knots and 50 feet.

Swede pops up and Pappy follows, "Gs."

Gandhi, "2, 1, crossing."

Pappy, "Gs," climbing to miss Swede, then turns to follow. Swede rolls left and pulls onto a '262 flying over the fields below them.

Alcott, "Bandit, 4 o'clock high."

Pappy, "Gs," and pulls up and to the right to face the '262, and fires on it. Not leading enough, his rounds pass behind it. "Gs." He rolls left in a yoyo and pulls onto the German fighter.

They hear Gandhi, "Splash 1."

Pappy's '262 is closing on Swede and Pappy gets on it it's six and squeezes off another burst. His rounds stitch the fighter up the center of the fuselage, hitting the cockpit. The German noses down into a hill, exploding.

Alcott, "Splash 1." On intercom, "Swede is climbing."

Then, they hear Lizard, "Splash 2. Gandhi, where are you?"

Gandhi, "North Wales, climbing."

Lizard, "Galahad flight, we are climbing out north of you. Form on us. Report fuel."

Gandhi, "4.2. Found you."

Alcott, "4.0." Then to Pappy, "She called us Galahad flight. Is that a call sign change?"

Pappy, "God, I hope so. I got a, um, we got a kill."

Alcott, "Yeah, my first."

"My seventh." They settle in on Swede's wing as they approach Arthur 1.

OVER THE BRISTOL CHANNEL

Over the radio, "RAF Angle has been attacked. The German is heading south."

Lizard, "The boss says let him go. The damage is done."

Gandhi, "Roger."

As the two planes of Galahad flight form up on Arthur 1, Pappy asks, "Are you okay?"

Alcott, "I am. God, my mom would be fucking pissed."

He laughs, "It's crazy. One moment, you act like a lady, the next you're out cussing a longshoreman."

She laughs, "My family is Massachusetts proper. I never lived up to my mother's expectations."

"You did good back there. Thank you."

"We're a team. We kick ass together."

"I'm a lucky guy. I fly and fight with prettiest dame in the world."

"Major, if you think you're getting into my bed, you're wrong. I'd rather fuck a goat."

"Why?"

"I let you between my legs, you would lose all respect for me and some German motherfucker would kill us both. Get your quim somewhere else."

"Quim?"

"Vagina, Major. Not a polite word."

They hear Lizard, "Okay, Galahad flight. The boss wants you to RTB, refuel, rearm, and sweep north. We'll handle the sweep now."

Gandhi, "Arthur 1, Galahad 1, wilco."

Alcott, "Arthur 1, Galahad 2, wilco." To Pappy, "We aren't squires anymore."

NEWPORT NEWS SHIPYARD, NORFOLK, VIRGINIA

0600, 3 October, 1942 (1100 GMT)

Mrs. Rayburn, wife of the Speaker of the House, swings a bottle of champagne against the stem of a new aircraft carrier and announces, "I christen thee Yorktown. May God Bless her and all who sail on her."

The Yorktown is built on the hull of an Iowa class battleship and is nine hundred ten feet long and one hundred sixty-five feet wide, with a nine-degree angled deck. Unlike the Essex class, the flight deck is armored. The huge ship is sitting in one of the largest dry docks in the world. The flooding valves open and begin to fill the dock.

Admiral Lee admires the Yorktown and next to it, another carrier under construction in the same class. Captain Todd 'Groovy' Miller asks, "Admiral, a year ago, could you have even dreamed all this?"

Lee smiles, "It would have been a nightmare, not a dream. You've climbed fast. Are you comfortable handling her?"

"If I said yes, I would be an idiot. I'm concerned, sir, but I learned from the best."

"You were an apt student."

"Dixie, how's she doing?"

"She's in three digits now. I think a hundred and one."

Groovy, "Damn. That's way more than any pilot ever got in World War II."

"Yeah. They would send the pilot back to train, so big kill numbers were rare."

"When the Army Air Corps takes over in England, is she going to stay a Commodore?"

Lee, "I don't know. They want to give her a hero's welcome selling war bonds."

"Have you approved that? That could destroy her. She's a warrior, not a cheerleader."

"I have no choice right now and she does need a break."

RAF KENLEY

1110, 3 October, 1942

The two '14s of Galahad flight land side by side. They taxi to refuel and rearm. Alcott, "Major, I need to piss."

Pappy opens the canopy, "Sure. I ought to stretch my legs as well." He climbs down after Alcott and walks over to Swede, "How many?"

Swede looks at him, 'Five. You got one and Spike, two. Do not ever ask her about her kills."

"Why?"

"Because it pisses her off. Don't do it. Also, tonight, you're going to enjoy a wetting down. She won't be there. Don't get too full of yourself because you're the first of the new crew to get a kill. The least of us have over twenty."

"How about you? What's your total?"

"Sixty-five. The kill today gives you three, right?"

Pappy, "Seven."

Swede shakes his head, "I've read your history. We don't count kills on the ground. The kill has to be airborne and manned to count. Do not inflate your kills. No one here will respect you for it."

"Yes, sir."

They hear the sound of jet aircraft overhead. They almost sound like Griffins. Swede studies the sky until the jets come into view. They have swept wings like the F-86 Saber, but the central bottom scoop intake is the same as an F-16s. Painted on each plane is the red star of Russia. Swede drops his head, "Damn, the Russians are here. I got shit to do."

COMMODORE'S OFFICE, RAF KENLEY

1340, 3 October, 1942

Sam walks in after her shower and sits down. Her inbox is full. She opens a drawer and pulls out paper:

TO: NAVAIR

FROM: TFYAN

REG: TANK INQUIRY

Dear sir,

I received a request from the commander of the British army regarding US Army and Marine armor designs, plans, or projects. He indicated that if we had a tank that could stand up to the German tanks, he was authorized to purchase five thousand of them. I told him I would look into it. Do you have any knowledge of such a project? If so, could you arrange to have a project officer brief the British?"

V/R

HUNT

She puts the message into her outbox for Cooper. And picks up the pile of after-action reports. She reads for a few minutes, then stops. She pulls out a map, studies it, then grabs a fresh sheet and writes:

FROM: TFYAN

TO: BATDIV-5

REG: DEPLOYMENT

Commodore,

Move your unit to within sixty miles of the mouth of the Thames. At no time approach closer than twenty-five miles to occupied France. Be prepared to provide naval gun fire support.

HUNT

Cooper knocks on her door and walks in. Sam hands him the messages. "Please, send these out immediately. Inform the watch officer of the movement."

Cooper, "Yes, Spike. Group Captain Holmes to see you. Also, the Russians have arrived. Are you going to meet with their leader?"

She gives him a quizzical look, "Send the group captain in. We'll need tea, and I'll get back to you on the Russians."

Cooper smiles and ushers Group Captain Howard Holmes of the Royal Australian Airforce into her office. He salutes, "Commodore, it's a pleasure to see you again."

She stands, returns the salute, and smiles, "Good to see you, as well. How is Australia?" She shakes his hand and offers him a seat.

"Still plucking along."

"How is Abigail?"

He breaks eye contact, looking down, "Well, unfortunately she is, in part, the reason I stopped by. I'm quite afraid that we are no longer together. We are divorcing."

"I'm sorry to hear that."

"It was all that talk of flying. I understand that you have done quite well, but an officer's wife...It's so unseemly."

"As you might expect, I disagree, sir." She pauses, observing him, "Could you explain how this has led you to me?"

An aid comes in with tea, and they wait as it is served.

"Well, it's the matter of that young flyer who came with you to our home. A Lieutenant Jackson, I believe."

Sam goes still, schooling her face, "Lieutenant Commander Jackson."

"Well, I've the notion that she may contact him. He did make quite an impression. I would like you to prohibit him from replying to any possible letter from her."

"I see." She takes a sip of tea, "I will need her current name and address. Also, her phone number, if she has one."

"Really?"

"With that information, I can notify the censures and prevent any letter from reaching him."

"Oh yes! Quite clever." He quickly writes the information down on the proffered paper and gives it to Sam. "She chose to revert to her maiden name, Case."

"I see."

"Thank you for your discretion in this matter."

"Your welcome."

"The tea is quite good."

"My yeoman is a gem."

"Might I inquire after that red-headed young lady?"

"She's doing well. She's flying a CAP right now. She's quite taken. You know the way of it, all the British flyers around."

"Yes, quite."

BRIEFING ROOM, RAF KENLEY

1430, 3 October, 1942

Thud has just finished his lesson on air combat maneuvering for a group of British and American flyers. As they file out, he gathers up his notes and sees Sam walk into the room, grinning. "Hey, Boss. Class went well."

Her smile gets bigger and there's joy in her voice, "Good. I've got something for you."

Thud tilts his head, "What, Spike?"

"Here's the address and phone number of Abigail Holmes. But her last name is Case, now. They're getting a divorce."

He looks at her, stunned, "Really?"

"Really. Thud, call her. I think you need to talk."

"Thank you. Um…How did you…?"

"A girl has to have some secrets, Frank."

GERMAN OCCUPIED RAF OUSTON

1622, 3 October, 1942

General Weber, face red, sets down the mic, and turns to his aid, "Send the following message to Colonel Stegman, 'You failed to arrive in ambush as directed. Your failure cost eight aircraft and crew. Do not fail me again.' Clean it up and send it."

CHAPTER 22

1700, 3 October, 1942

Lt. Colonel Andrews ushers Majors Nadezhda Popova and Alexander Pokryshkin in and introduces them to Spike. She stands and shakes their hands, "Welcome to RAF Kenley. I hope your flight was uneventful. Would you like coffee or tea?"

Pokryshkin, in accented English, "You are taller than I thought." He takes her hand, "Tea, I think."

Spike smiles, "You're not the first to say that." She nods to the steward, who serves tea and cookies.

Popova, a female pilot, sips her tea and looks up surprised, "This is good. In America, the tea is horrible."

Spike laughs, "You're right. I love English tea."

Popova, "So, why was it important for us to travel through England on our trip home?"

Spike, "I wanted to take the measure of you, and discuss co-ordination and deconfliction procedures should your nation reenter the conflict."

Pokryshkin, "So, I saw your jet. So many kills. What is it you do, that others do not?"

"You've been trained by Lt. Walker, yes?"

"We have."

"He was my wingman. Any insight I have, he has no doubt

shared."

"Yes, but he does not have near as many kills."

She sits silent, then, "The most important thing is to understand your opponent and the capabilities of your aircraft. Deny the enemy his fight and stick with tactics that give you the advantage."

Popova, "You are the most effective flyer America has. Why is it you do not receive the recognition that is your due?"

"I have been recognized."

"Yes, but no more than many lesser pilots. I've heard American flyers discuss it. In Russia, you would be showered with recognition, appreciation, and love."

Spike looks at Popova, "As you train more pilots, is it your intent to teach them all English so they may communicate with our forces?"

Pokryshkin, "It is our intent. Popova is correct, in Russia, you would be praised and elevated."

Spike smiles at them, "Would you please excuse me for a moment?" She walks out, breathing deeply, and walk into Swede's office, "Swede, could you give me a hand with the Russians? They're getting a little difficult. I need them on task."

"Why don't you just have me handle it?"

"Do not go in there alone, that was my mistake."

They walk to Thud's office. Swede, "Hey, Thud."

Thud is on the phone. He looks up startled, "My love, I need to go." He hangs up, "What's up?"

"We need to interview the Russians and we need our poker faces on."

Thud sees Spike face and nods, "Right."

Swede, "Who were you talking to?"

Thud turns red and shakes his head, "Later."

Swede, "Roger that. We got it, Boss."

Spike, "Thanks, guys."

TROLLOP AND MOUSE'S QUARTERS, RAF KENLEY

1910, 3 October, 1942

Lt. Pauline 'Trollop' Cash is sitting on her bunk when ENS Julie 'Mouse' Mulligan leads ENS Margaret Alcott into their room. They've decorated it with posters of the Go-Go's, Marilyn Monroe, Chuck Yeager, and a Tomcat in flight. The top bunk has a rose patterned comforter with a handful of stuffed animals. The bottom bunk has a blue hand-made quilt with matching pillow cases and an extra pillow. Alcott is drawn to the posters, "Who's he?"

Trollop, "Chuck Yeager. He's the first man to break the sound barrier in our time. He's a fighter pilot for the Army Air Corps now."

Alcott stops in front of the poster of Marilyn Monroe, "And her?"

Mouse, "Norma Jean Mortenson. Her film name was Marilyn Monroe. She had an amazing, but tragic life. She's like fifteen or sixteen now. She died of a supposed drug overdose in 1962."

Why do you have her picture up?"

"Because, she was beautiful and tragic. Elton John wrote an amazing song memorializing her."

Alcott, "She's captivating."

Mouse, "Yeah."

Alcott points at the Go-Go's, "Is that how people dressed?"

Trollop laughs, "No, that's their stage outfits. That's a rock band called the Go-Go's."

Alcott turns to her, "Is that why you invited me up?"

Mouse, "It's about Boyington. He's a guy with a history. A good pilot and a good leader, but also a drunk, a gambler, and a womanizer."

Margaret nods, "We had that conversation. I told him I would rather fuck a goat."

Their eyes open wide, and they look at her silently, then they both bust out laughing. Mouse looks at her pilot, "Generally, relations between air crew are a very bad thing. It can screw up the respect dynamic."

Alcott, "That's exactly how I feel."

Trollop, "Where are you from?"

"Boston. My family pursues property, ship building, and social status. I'm such a failure in their eyes. You two?"

Trollop, "I'm from a Podunk town in Arkansas. My dad worked as a truck mechanic and my mom, well, she's a historian of sorts."

"What got you into flying?"

"I went flying with one of my uncle's friends when I was fourteen. It was a Stearman 75, but I was hooked. At seventeen I had my pilot's license, and I had four hundred hours by the time I graduated college."

"I learned on one of those. They're so fun. College?"

"Scholarship to Tennessee, architecture. You?"

"Radcliffe, math." Alcott turns to Mouse, "You?"

"I'm from a tiny town east of Portland, Oregon. I started out enlisted. I have an associates in electronics, which made me an AE. That landed me the RIO gig and a commission. I've only been flying a couple of months. I do love it, and would love to learn to fly. Radcliffe? Wow!"

Trollop, "So, you're okay behind the Major?"

"Yeah, he wants to get kills more than he wants to get laid. We actually work pretty well together."

NEW YORK NAVAL YARD, BROOKLYN, NEW YORK

1500, 3 October, 1942 (2000 GMT)

Vice Admiral Klindt sits on the dais on the pier next to a new battleship. He listens to the chaplain open the ceremony. Clyde L. Herring, the junior senator from Iowa speaks, then George A. Wilson, the governor of Iowa makes his remarks. Finally, Klindt stands and walks to the podium, "Ladies and Gentlemen, crew of the battleship Iowa. Today is an auspicious day. This is the birthday of a new class of battleship, the state of the art in naval technology.

"I have extreme confidence in her and, in you. We need you in the fleet because never before have we faced threats such as we do today. The Battle of Whitley Bay show us the truth of it. Because we did not have missile defenses, we lost the cruisers Omaha, Tuscaloosa, and Brooklyn. We also lost seven destroyers. Our allies lost much of their home fleet. These ships were crewed by brave and able men, but a brave heart does not stop a missile attack. Never again can we be so unprepared for such an attack.

"The Iowa is our answer to that disaster in the cold waters of the North Sea. This is singularly the finest battleship ever made, with the finest crew we could assemble. When you put to sea, our enemies will tremble. Thank you."

The Iowa's new captain, Captain John L. McCrea speaks to his crew and Admiral Klindt gives him his orders. Captain McCrea orders the commissioning pennant raised and says, "Crew, man your ship." The one thousand eight hundred and eighty-five sailors run on board. Captain McCrea turns to the commissioning party, "May I invite you on board, sirs?"

USS CARL VINSON, 300 MILES SOUTH WEST OF HAWAII

1315, 3 October, 1942 (2315 GMT)

CDR Norman 'Oyster' Osterman, CO of the Tomcatters, VF-31, climbs in behind LT Christine 'Lipstick' Collins of the Red-cocks. They get strapped in and hooked up, then go through the checklist, and Oyster says, "Okay, Lipstick, this is your first launch and recovery in the Tomcat. I'm going to just relax and enjoy the ride."

Lipstick, "You're going to handle the radio, right?"

"Yep. I'll be your RIO. I expect you to handle the bird without my help. If you do need me, I'll be here."

"Yes, sir. They're signaling engines."

NORTH OF HALTWHISTLE, NORTHUMBERLAND, UK

0600, 4 October, 1942

LT Gus Grant stands next to Ian McCloud concealed in a copse of trees and studying Haltwhistle, "I see a Panzer in a hole north of town by that stone farm house with the red roof."

McCloud, "I see it. There are half-tracks on each side of town with just their machine guns showing."

"Yep. We can use the burn and the stone fences to get close."

McCloud, "How many tanks do you count?"

"Three; this one, one east of town and one west. They're all Panzer 4s. Maybe four half-tracks. I haven't seen any air defense. An armored platoon with about a company of troops. I can call in a strike on the tanks."

McCloud grins, "I have another idea."

PANZER 4, NORTH SIDE OF HALTWHISTLE, UK

Sergeant Weller rocks back and forth in the command hatch. He's been listening to the guys talk about the sex they're getting. "Fuck, it's cold and wet. Why do you suppose we want this place?"

His gunner grins, "Because the women are warm."

"We shouldn't rape them. When we rule here it will make it harder."

His gunner laughs, "Let me fetch you some vestments, Father Weller."

HALTWHISTLE BURN

Cuddles squats on the bank of the burn twenty feet from a Panzer 4. Thirty Highlanders, crouch around him. For the Germans, the town is too large and their force too small to build and defend trenches, so instead, they spread out and fortified strong points.

Peter McDougal whispers, "Lieutenant, stay here."

Cuddles shakes his head no, and points at himself, then the tank. Peter nods, and Cuddles draws his dirk. Cuddles works his way closer to the tank. They used a tractor to build a defensive berm around it. He sees a tanker standing in a raised hatch with a mounted machine gun.

Cuddles sets his feet and sprints up the berm, jumping onto the tank. Leading with his knife, he sinks it into the German's chest. His feet muddy, Cuddles slips with the force of the blow. The German tries to remove the knife, coughing up blood and gurgling. Cuddles pulls the bleeding man out of the hatch and jumps into it.

The tanks gunner pulls a Luger and fires a hasty shot. The bullet burns Cuddles across the ribs and deafens him. He grabs the gun out of the man's hand and turns it on the loader, who's struggling with his own weapon. He shoots the loader in the throat, then turns and points it back at the gunner. The others have shot or captured the driver and hull gunner. The tank is covered in blood, but they hold it

Cuddles, "Get the bodies out and let's get this thing started." He pulls his dirk out of the German, cleans it on his Tartan, and sheaths it. To himself, "Thank you, Patsy, dear."

The tank reeks of blood and urine, but they have it. He's getting the machine gun into position, when an enemy machine guns opens up. The Scots on his side of the berm fire back, and Cuddles gets his gun turned around and fires a long burst as rounds bounce off the turret.

The incoming fire ceases and the tank engine starts up. The one highlander with tank experience gets into the gunner's seat. His granddaughter, her brown hair braided and wrapped around her head, gets into the loader's spot and the gunner gives her instructions. The gunner tugs at Cuddles shirt and passes up a crew communication head set.

Peter climbs up on the tank and hangs the Scot's flag, the St. Andrew's Cross, off the aerial. "We got the half-track, sir. West then east?"

"Yes, instead of following me, take the road further north and support McCloud. We'll handle the tanks." They can hear the bagpipes sounding. They'll rush soon. Peter jumps off and heads to the half-track.

Cuddles directs his tank down Comb Hill Road, shooting any German he sees. Several run out of houses struggling with their pants. They have their rifles, so Cuddles mows them down. When they see the western tank, it's out of its revetment and turning toward them. His gunner, "We're ready."

Cuddles, "Driver, stop," and they lurch to stop. "Aim and fire."

Their round hits the Panzer 4 in the hull right at the turret. The 75mm high velocity gun penetrates and pops the turret from the tank in a fireball. Cuddles, "Spin around." The reversing tracks tear up the road, and they turn toward the eastern tank.

As they get moving, another machine gun opens up on them,

"Gunner, machine gun, 10 o'clock."

"Where?"

"To the left." Cuddles fires tracer rounds to mark the area."

"Got it." The gunner fires the main gun and the machine gun and the building it's in comes down.

Cuddles, "Do you have a machine gun?"

"Sorry, sir. It's on the loader's side of the tank."

"Okay."

They turn onto the east road out of town and a tank round shrieks by them. The third tank is about a half mile away. Cuddles, "Turn left. Gun it." They crash through brush and small trees, fighting up a hillside. Then, they break into a yard with an alley ahead. "Stop. Spin around."

The gunner asks, "What are we doing?"

"They saw what did, where we're going, so he's going to move to get in front of us. Let's get behind him." The driver floors it and they crash back down onto the street and head east. They turn north on Lany's Lonnen and run up a hill. Cuddles yells, "Stop. I can see the road crossing sign. Sight on it."

The enemy tank comes into view and crosses in front of the sign. They gunner fires and hits the side of the turret. The turret rips off, the tank commander is blown out, and flames shoot out of the hatches.

BRAMPTON, 11 MILES WEST OF HALTWHISTLE

Major Kanther, in command of 1st Battalion, 8th Brigade, 8th Regiment of the 8th Panzer division, stands in the window of the third floor of an old stone major house. An aid approaches, "The Highlanders are attacking Haltwhistle, sir."

"We've only a reinforced company there."

"Yes, sir."

"Pass the word to move out east. They're mocking us."

CHURCH STEEPLE IN A VILLAGE AT THE PERIMETER OF KENLEY

0800, 4 October, 1942

Sergeant Ulrich studies the base with his scope, slowly passing right to left. The line of Russian aircraft draws his attention. He can see they're getting ready to depart. He sees a large American jet. Two Tomcats take off in a roar. He mumbles, "This would be a perfect observation post. I could stay here for days, reporting every takeoff and landing. Oh, well."

He hears his partner approaching, "Fresh water, sergeant."

TARMAC, RAF KENLEY

The SEAL team walk out to the waiting C-56, Commodore Hunt with them, "Remember, if you can't make contact, stay with the aircraft."

Triage, "We got it, Commodore."

ENS Buford studies the surroundings, especially the perimeter; a hunter's habit. He spots a flash of light and grabs Spike, taking them both to the ground, his back to the threat. "Sniper! Church steeple, 4 o'clock!" He feels a solid thump on his back, then hears the report.

Aircrew are scrambling. The SEALs get their weapons out, and Whizee unlimbers his sniper rifle, dropping onto the wet tarmac. "I have him."

A second shot tugs at Buford's sleeve."

They hear the report of Whizee's modified Winchester Model 70 sniper rifle. Meat 1, Whizee's spotter, says, "Good kill. I saw grey." Whizee fires again, and a body drops out of the steeple.

Spike, "Thanks, Ensign. Are you okay?"

Buford, "Yeah, are you?"

"I'm fine, thank you. Um, are we clear to get up?"

Whizzee, "Yes, ma'am, base security is clearing the church."

Buford, "I guess it's alright." He gracefully stands and offers her a hand. She smiles and takes it, pulling herself up.

Mac says, "Holy shit, Buford. Your pack is fucked up." Mac inspects Buford's pack, sliding his hand under it. "No penetration. You okay, sir?"

Buford shakes his head, "I...I think so."

Triage, "What the fuck, superman. Do you think you can stop a speeding bullet?"

Spike delicately removes her hand from Buford's, "Mission abort. Triage, make sure Superman is good to go. If he's good in less than an hour, it's a go."

Base security and ground crew run to Spike. She shakes them off, "I'm fine. Carry on," and after meeting Buford's gaze one more time, she walks off.

She walks into the hanger and Lt. Oscar Hammond runs to her. He aborts his salute, and places himself between Spike and the church. "Are you okay, Commodore?"

"I am."

"With your permission, I would like to arm up all the ground crew and select some for patrol. I'd also like to step up our weapons training."

Spike smiles, "Tell Col. Andrews you have my permission, make it so."

Hammond smiles back, "Thank you, Spike," and takes off, running.

Then Fluffy finds her on her way out of the hanger. He's wearing a battle helmet, flack vest, and carrying a Garand rifle, a toy in his huge hands. "Commodore, are you okay? Do you need to go to medical?"

Spike suppresses a grin, "Fluffy, I'm fine. No medical. Hammond is beefing up the patrols and heightening security."

"Okay," walking beside her, his rifle at port arms. At the door out of the hanger, he kicks it open and rushes out first, "Clear."

"Fluffy, what are you doing?"

"I've appointed myself your bodyguard."

"Don't you have more important things to do?"

He shakes his head, once, "No, Spike. There's nothing else even close."

"Okay, but you can't sleep at the foot of my bed."

He smiles and relaxes a bit, "No, but I will be in the outer room."

They get to her jeep, "How's Donna?"

"Still in DC. She's consulting with, um... radio people."

"Got it. Fluffy, I'm fine. Let's not overreact."

"No. A sniper just tried to kill you. You are not fine. We need to get you a better car."

"Why?"

"You're too exposed."

"Okay, I concede."

"Do you know who that SEAL is?"

"Why?"

"Spike, are you sure you're okay? You're normally not that dense. He took a bullet for you."

"I know he did."

"Commodore Hunt, that's Medal of Honor shit."

"Aren't you overreacting?"

"No."

They pull up to the tower, "His name is ENS Jeremiah Buford, and I don't think he was hunting for medals."

"If he was, I wouldn't be saying this."

"Did you see it?"

"I did."

"Write it up."

They walk into control and Fluffy grabs a chair and sits by the door with his rifle across his lap.

The watch officer looks at him for a long moment, then turns to Spike, "Gawain and Percival are up. Gawain is covering A-10s. Percival is sweeping south up the channel. Tuck is orbiting over York. Rusty 1 and Dusty 1 are working the forward edge of battle, which is now running from Oxford to Colchester. We have four Army Air Corps cargo birds inbound and two A-10 squadrons took off late from Reykjavik due to fog. They're due in two hours."

"Do we have squadron number, name, and call sign?"

"Yes, Commodore, VMA-211, Dragons, call sign Golden Gator, and VMA-213, Hell Hawks, call sign Bad Bird."

"Route them south over Cornwall, then into Kenley."

"Yes, Commodore. Also, there's a massive battle between German infantry and the Highland volunteers near Haydon Bridge. Word is, the Highlanders were blooded bad, but they hold the field. We tasked Dog 3. Cuddles is still with them."

"Thank you." She studies the map. "Hopefully, the Highlanders will force Rommel to reinforce the north. The Germans are closing on London. If it's completely circled, it's only a matter of time."

Lt. Colonel Andrews walks in, "Mail, Spike."

"Thank you." She takes her mail. Three letters are replies from grieving families she's written. One is from Tennessee, and she opens it:

Dear Granddaughter,

The news from England is frightful. We do hope you are well. We heard from John, your father. He's still on Guadalcanal and has been promoted to second lieutenant. We are proud of him, but we so worry about the losses that must have led to his promotion.

He said he received your letter. He also said he was healthy. I suspect that last is somewhat overstated. He sent the photos you sent him home for safekeeping, all except one with you in uniform. We've put up your picture from the newspaper and now, we'll put these up with it. I must say, clothing styles change a lot after the war. If you have an opportunity to send us a picture of you in uniform, we would much appreciate it. We know you're busy, though, so please don't bother if it's too much trouble.

All is well at the Hunt farm. We have two blue stars hanging from our porch. The weather has been mild. We have three horses in foal to tend with very limited resources. Our whole community is aware now, that you are from here. The reaction is very positive. You will receive a warm welcome when you come home. We are delighted those awful reporters are gone. Your grandfather has not had to shoot at any for some time.

Do take care, darling.

Your Grandmother Margaret

Sam laughs and closes her eyes, trying to remember that barn. When she was little it had been her playground. She couldn't recall any damage to the roof. "Oh, what change we have wrought."

Andrews smiles quizzically, "Commodore?"

She turns to him, still smiling, "A letter from my grandmother. It seems grandfather hasn't had to use his shotgun to run off any reporters lately. In a previous letter, she said he had to patch the roof of the barn because he'd put some holes in it with his shotgun. I was trying to remember if I saw any patches when I was little. They weren't any."

"The roof could have been replaced."

"I suppose, but he and dad replaced it when I was twelve. I remember helping them."

"Did your dad have any brothers or sisters?"

"Yeah, a brother, but he died in the war. Wait. He's still in high school. He joined the Army and died on Omaha beach."

"Nebraska?"

She laughs, "No. When we invaded France, the beaches were code named Juno, Gold, Sword, Utah, and Omaha."

"Where was the invasion?"

"Normandy, but this time, they're no doubt going to do it differently."

"So, your uncle could survive?"

"I suppose so." She turns to the next letter. It's posted from Maryland and is from Lt. Eric 'Puck' Hawke, her former RIO.

Dear Samantha,

I'm currently in Bethesda. Doc Osborne and his staff are looking out for me and my prognosis for a full recovery is good. When I asked if I would be able to fly again, he just said, "One thing at a time." He's an admiral now and commands Navy medicine. He's turned Bethesda into a teaching hospital.

When I first arrived, Dixie was here to meet me. He's a good one. Since, I've seen Groovy and Ren. Ren is the vice CNO for operations and is on the presidential staff. Groovy has his captaincy and was attending command college. He's PCO of the USS Yorktown. They're building big carriers as fast as they can. Hopefully, the last is vague enough to pass the censures.

As I am a captive audience, I've had several aeronautical engineers from various companies seek me out for design advice. It's weird. Lee clarified the rules and they moved me to a private room so I can work. I would love to share more specific design information with you, but I know it's way too classified. Suffice it to say, the aviation companies have been busy.

When he was informed, I was back in the States my great-grandfather took a train to Washington. He's exactly as I remember, only a little younger. He's right here with me as I write this. Here he is:

Hello, Commodore Samantha Hunt,

I once saw a strange thing. I saw a Sparrow attack a Hawk. I found it quite odd that this Sparrow thought it was a Hawk, and the Hawk thought it was a Sparrow. So odd.

John Hawk

Me again. I do not know what it means. It's the way of great-grandfather. He's a spiritual leader in our tribe and much respected. If what he writes makes any sense to you, let me know.

I very much hope you are well. I know you have figured it out, but I think Lizard would be a good replacement. I miss you and the guys. Mostly you.

Yours,

Puck

She re-reads it. Andrews asks, "Someone close?"

"My RIO, Eric Hawke. He was wounded the night all this started. At least he's alright."

"I heard about him, he's an Indian, but his name is English."

"Well, he's Lakota Sioux. Many of them took English and Irish and German names. The children were taken from the families and raised in boarding schools in an attempt to eradicate their culture. It was barbaric and wrong."

She reads the letter again and straightens up, "Oh! I see." She turns to Andrews, "Send for the 82nd Airborne immediately. It's time to implement Sunset."

"Roger, Spike."

From the watch table, "Commodore, six bandits taking off from Ouston. Center is scrambling Texas."

Spike, "Direct Percival to engage and Gawain to orbit at point Echo south of Portsmouth. Advance Lancelot to ready 5. Make my plane ready."

Fluffy stands up, "Boss, stay on the ground."

"What?"

"They're trying to kill you. They're going to try in the air, too."

She meets her master chief's gaze, "Chief, I have a job to do. I'm replaceable."

All eyes in the room are fixed on Spike and Fluffy, fascinated. "Due respect, ma'am, but, no, you are not. Our whole country is rooting for you. You're a symbol now."

"God damn it, Fluffy! I am not going to hide while the Germans kill our people. I'll fucking tolerate your security measures on the ground, but when I am needed in the air, I WILL FLY!"

He backs up, "Um, roger that, Spike."

The mostly female control center personnel break into applause, and Spike and Fluffy turn and stare.

FARM HOUSE NORTH OF HAYDON BRIDGE, UK

0913, 4 October, 1942

LT Gus 'Cuddles' Grant watches their two nurses work on Ian McCloud. Ian, "Lassies, stop fussing over me. It's not the first bullet I've carried."

The senior nurse, Molly, says, "Stop whinging Ian McCloud. You're the last of those we might save."

"The bullet went deep."

"It did, but it looks to have missed the artery."

Cuddles, "I've another dust off inbound, Captain. You'll be on it."

Ian makes eye contact with the younger man, "Lad, what of my company?"

"We've nineteen dead, twenty-two wounded, including you, and twenty-five new volunteers just walked in."

McCloud smiles, "Will you do it for me, then?"

"If that's your order, sir."

"It 'tis. I'll tell you, Lieutenant, you've got starch in you, and a good mind. You can handle them."

"You've taught me a lot, sir. When we've chased the Hun off, then I'll be back for the next lesson."

A British lieutenant walks in, back straight, chin raised, and moustache twitching, "Who commands this rabble?"

Ian smiles and nods at Cuddles. Grant straightens and, in a facing movement, turns to the lieutenant. Noting the uniform, he says, "I command the Highland volunteers, Lieutenant. Now salute and state your business."

The lieutenant looks at him with ill-concealed contempt, "And, who pray, are you?"

"I am Lieutenant Grant, US Navy. Now, all the British lieutenants I've met so far start with a salute, Lieutenant. Is there something amiss with your arm?"

The lieutenant pops to and salutes, "No, sir. I have a message for you, sir," and hands it over.

TO: Highland Volunteers

FROM: Commander, 51st Leeds Rifles

The 51st will be advancing south very soon. As your unit has proven its combat effectiveness, higher has suggested we coordinate operations. Please coordinate through Lieutenant Jones and make your advance south, rather than east.

Brigadier James Noel Tetley

Grant, "You have a radio, correct?"

"I do, sir. Why does your unit look in such disrepair?"

"We just met three companies of German infantry supported by Panzer 4s. We sent them packing, but it cost us dearly. Tell the Brigadier that we will move out as soon as we've completed the dust off of our wounded."

"Yes, sir."

CHAPTER 23

ARTHUR FLIGHT, 35,000 FEET OVER LONDON

0922, 4 October, 1942

Spike is in a wide left turn so their radar can identify threats. Thud and Trollop are engaging '262s over York, covering A-10s working over a German supply convoy. Tuck and Robin are engaging V-1s over the English Channel. Hot Pants and De-Graaff are escorting the Russians out over the North Sea. A convoy and amphibious group are off Plymouth.

Lizard, "Boss, six aircraft coming north out of France on the deck at 600 knots."

"Call it. We engage. Launch Lancelot."

Lizard relays and their flight turns south, breaking the speed of sound in the dive at full military. Spike, "Launch at 40 miles and we follow them in."

ARTHUR 2

ENS Nix focuses on staying on Spike's wing. ENS Heather Kohlman says, "Okay, six. We've the right three. Eighty miles. Oh God, we're doing this."

Nix, "Just give me a lock, okay?"

"I have lock. Sixty miles. They have us."

"Okay, AIM-1 selected, master arm enabled."

Kohlman, "Fox 3. Fox 3. Fox 3."

Nix pickles off three AIM-1s and the launch is good. One

misses the beam and flies off, but the other two track. Kohlman, "They've launched and they're turning back."

GERMAN FIGHTER GROUP

Major Kurt Welter looks over his left shoulder at the decoy rocket flying away. He shuts off his radar and continues straight at the Americans. "I very much hope this works."

In the mirror, he sees explosions behind him and smiles, "They've hit the wrong targets." He turns his radar back on.

ARTHUR 2

Kohlman, 'Something's not right."

Nix, "What?"

Kohlman on radio, "The missiles are the jets. We hit robots."

They hear Lizard, "Roger. Close and engage."

"Okay, I have visual. These are '279s. Good lock, select sevens."

Nix, "Good lock, firing."

Kohlman, "Fox 1. Fox 1." Then, "Damn, they're breaking upward. Lock lost."

Nix, "On it." He pulls out of the dive and fires a quick burst, but his rounds fall behind. "Fuck. Gs." He rolls left and climbs, going after the Germans. He adjusts and fires, his rounds sparking off the fuselage at an angle, and the German jet flashes by, rocking them in his wake. "Where's Spike?"

Kohlman, "2000 feet above and behind."

"Gs." Nix levels his wings and pulls up into an Immelmann. Tracer passes below them and another German passes them. "Shit! Where did he go?"

"Where'd who go? Spike is 500 feet above and left."

Nix sees a '279 tumble, shedding parts, and the pilot ejects. "I see her. Gs." He rolls left and climbs. Spike hits a second with a Sidewinder and pulls to climb, a '279 on her six. Spike pickles off chaff and flares causing the missile to miss her and Nix gets a lead and fires his gun. The rounds stitch through an engine and into the fuel tank. The '279 goes up like a roman candle.

Kohlman, "Splash 1. We've got one on our six."

Lizard, "Break right."

Nix puts his '14 on its side and slides down and to the right. A '279 going after Spike cuts across in front of them. Nix rolls left after the jet and they end up canopy to canopy only 60 feet apart. They climb in a spiral. Then, Lizard, "2, break! 2, break!"

Nix spins his plane to exit the roll instead of pushing forward into negative Gs. His left wing hits the German plane just behind the cockpit. Fuel sprays from the '279 and the canopy is shattered. Nix uses his right aileron and gets out of the spin. "Shit! Sorry, Heather. That was a no, no."

Lizard, "You okay, 2?"

Kohlman, "We got the roll sorted out."

Lizard, "The second was a good kill. He ejected at 500 feet. Boss says you're not supposed to slap them out of the sky."

Nix on radio, "Sorry, Spike. I did a no, no."

Spike, "That's okay, No-No. We all make mistakes."

Kohlman, "Wow, Nix. You just got your call sign and it was from the Commodore."

"I guess I did."

Lizard, "Damage check."

PADDOCK NEAR EASTBOURNE, UK

Welter drifts down in his chute, landing in a horse paddock. He gathers up his parachute and looks around. A farmer strolls toward him, his shotgun in the crook of his arm. The farmer smiles, "Well, come on, now. I've sent for the police, but we can get some soup and a cuppa in you before they arrive. It'll probably be your last for a bit."

ARTHUR 2, ON APPROACH TO RAF KENLEY

Nix, "Okay, a one engine landing. Speed is same, but…"

Spike, "No-No, Spike. Normal approach, but increase landing speed by ten knots. Don't flare. Get on the ground and get on the brakes. I'd rather you smoke them, then over run and foul the field."

No-No, "Roger, Spike." Then to Kohlman, "The fire department is out. We won't need it."

She laughs, "Yes, but remember, every landing is graded."

"Thanks."

Kohlman, "100. 80. 50. 20. 10." Their bird lands hard but the nose wheels stays straight and Nix practically stands on the brakes.

Spike roars by, "Good landing, No-No and Robot."

As they taxi to their hanger, Nix laughs, "You got yours, too."

C-56 OVER THE BALTIC SEA

1232, 4 October, 1942 (1132 GMT)

The aircraft depressurizes and the side door opens. Over the roar of the wind, Triage shouts into his radio, "Yankee Bravo, Sierra Bravo 2." He repeats.

Then, finally, "Sierra Bravo 2, Yankee Bravo. We're at point Alpha."

"Roger, Yankee Bravo. 5 mikes to Lima."

He turns to his team, "Op's a go."

Spooky, "This is crazy."

Mac laughs, "Not as crazy as Korea."

They jump out of the plane in a group.

NORTH COAST ROAD, GUADALCANAL

0150, 5 October, 1942 (1450, 4 October GMT)

LT John Hunt grimly hangs on as his sergeant, Steven Lewis, drives the deuce and a half truck at thirty miles an hour, in the dark, without lights, down a roughly graveled road not suitable for speeds over ten. They hear a large explosion in the hill ahead. Lewis, "Jesus Christ, Mother Mary. What was that?"

Hunt, "They're clearing a spot for the artillery. Focus on your driving."

"How soon?"

"We got two miles and the Japs have boats in the water. They've grounded a destroyer and the navy is coming. We'll be first."

"How many?"

"I don't know. At least a few hundred. Probably over a thousand."

"Is that all?"

"Yeah."

"Well then, no problem. The coast watch should have this mopped up before we get there."

They see the flicker of machine gun fire over the water and see tracer rounds passing ahead of them. Out over the water, Hunt can see the shadow of another Jap plane. The plane catches fire and they hear the roar of an F/A-18 passing over. The '18 curves and drops a bomb on a Japanese ship. It explodes, the light from the flames show five more transports with four destroyers. A missile launches from a destroyer and the '18 drops chaff and evades.

Hunt, "Five transports, at about 500 each. We're looking at 2500, or so."

They roll into a village. Lewis, "Is that all?"

Hunt, "We're here. Yep, just 2500 Jap Marines. We got this."

Theirs is the first of ten trucks, each with 14 Marines. Hunt unasses his truck and shouts, "Second Platoon to me!" His unit, 2nd Platoon, Bravo Company, 1st of the 7th, is down to twenty-seven men. They gather around him as the other platoons form up. "Okay, defend the machine gun squads. Remember to hold fire until they're well within effective range."

His men, calm, shout, "Hoo-ah."

SGT Lewis, "This is gravelly sand, so dig out, as you dig in."

They can hear helicopters moving the guns.

Captain Morris, his company commander, walks up, "Good spot, Hunt. We're going to be spread over a 400-hundred-yard front, so there will be gaps. When the enemy gets established on the beach, make an orderly withdrawal to that hill," he points. "Once the guns are in place, the helo's are going to lift Charley company up there. Our resupply is there as well."

"Yes, sir. Do we have a signal for withdrawal?" As Hunt speaks, the Japanese naval guns start the barrage.

"You'll have to use your best judgement."

"Yes, sir." Then, they hear the machine guns open up.

A few minutes later, LT Hunt is in a slit trench looking out over the Japanese landing boats. They're smaller than a Higgins, and they have a front ramp. He directs the machine gun crew to fire on the ramps. There haven't been any ricochets. The first boat lands on the beach and drops its ramp. A pile of bodies falls into the water. Behind them, the rest of the Japanese troops climb over their fallen.

His guys are getting the job done, so, he puts his rifle to his shoulder and shoots the boat coxswain. He goes for another on a boat closing the beach and the boat swings and capsizes, spilling its human cargo. The enemy soldiers struggle out of the water and into withering fire. Hunt, "Lewis, check our ammo and send someone back for more."

"Yes, sir," and he scrambles out, keeping low, going from position to position.

Hunt tells his runner, "Have Ernst target the boat drivers."

"Yes, sir," and he sprints off.

Hunt stands, exposed to the waist and looks over the battle. Two more transports have been hit by the '18s, and the artillery is taking out some of the landing craft. Dead Japanese marines are piling up on the beach. He senses someone sliding into his trench and looks over. Standing next to him is LT Colonel Lewis Puller.

"Um, sir?"

"How are we doing, Marine?"

"We're giving them hell, sir." A machine gun round creases Hunt's helmet, twisting it over his eyes. He takes it off and looks at it, and tosses it aside. "They're giving it to us, sir, but my boys are finding the fight digestible."

"Good. You're Hunt, right? Your daughter's the fighter ace?"

"Yes, sir." Hunt sees a dozen Japanese leap to up from behind a pile of bodies and charge. Hunt calmly positions his rifle and shoots, dropping four. His guys get the rest. One manages to get to his trench and jump in and Chesty Puller shoots him twice with his pistol.

Sergeant Lewis joins them, "We're down to sixty percent and more ammo is coming. I reminded the gunners to swap barrels. Douglas is gone and Ernst is wounded. Doc is sending him back." He picks up the dead Japanese and shoves his body out in front of their trench.

Hunt, "Thank you, Sergeant Lewis." He grins, "Meet Colonel

Puller."

Lewis resists the urge to salute, "We're giving them hell, sir."

"I see that. Lieutenant, can you hold this beach?"

Hunt looks out over the beach; many of the Japanese boats are drifting or sinking. He sees one of the destroyers going down. He nods, "Sir, I can hold as long as you need us to. Just keep the ammo coming."

"Okay, Hunt. Just don't get your balls shot off. We need more pilots like her." He grins as he gets out of the trench and leaves.

"Yes, sir."

PERCIVAL FLIGHT, ORBITING OVER DOVER

1604, 4 October, 1942

Hot Pants and GQ hear, "All units, Whiskey Tango Foxtrot, raid warning north. 10 bandits climbing out of Ouston. Designate raid 26."

GQ, "Whiskey Tango Foxtrot, Percival flight, roger."

"Percival flight, "Yankee, come to 350. Close and engage. We're scrambling the Merry Men."

GQ, "Yankee, Percival flight, wilco."

Hot Pants waggles her wings and accelerates north. LT Cochran and Ensign Everling stay on her left wing.

"All units, Whiskey Tango Foxtrot, be advised. Raid 26 is NOE."

GQ, "Whiskey Tango Foxtrot, Percival flight, acknowledge."

PERCIVAL 2

LT Jackie Cochran hums into her mic. ENS Julian Everling, "Will you stop, Lieutenant?"

"What, Ensign?"

"Quit humming. It's annoying."

"We're about to get our first kills and you're worried about that?"

"Fuck, yeah. We have to survive to kill anything. Get your head back in the cockpit."

"We're way better than anything we will face."

"Are we? How the fuck do you know?"

"Trust me, Everling, I got it."

Then, GQ, "Percival 2, 1. Two AIM-1s at 40. Follow them and climb out."

Everling, "Percival 1, 2. Roger."

At 40 miles and at 18000 feet, they pickle off two AIM-1 missiles. Cochran keeps the nose on target as Everling guides them in. On hits, but one target turns at the last moment, and the missile misses. Everling, "Splash 1."

GQ, "Splash 2. Pull."

They climb out and turn for another dive. GQ, "Fox 3. Fox 3."

Cochran pickles off two more, "Come on, Everling, two kills this time."

Everling, "Working it. They're scattering. Slow down and a little right." Cochran eases back on the throttle and adjusts their course. "Good. Come on, come on. Yes," On radio, "Splash 2."

GQ, "Splash 2. Percival 2, 1. We're going in. Stay on top."

Everling, "Wilco, 1."

The lead F/A-14 inverts and dives. Cochran rolls left and starts a turn. "Can you see them?"

Everling, "Yeah. We got two climbing. We need to meet them."

Cochran inverts, "Gs." Pulling her nose around, she sees two delta winged fighter bombers in a loose deuce climbing towards them. A missile drops from the right plane. Cochran,

"Gs." She pulls away, dropping countermeasures. One of the '262s rolls on its back and dives, and the other continues toward them. She goes to zone 5 and goes after the diving jet. The German comes out horizontal, then rolls into a left turn. She goes with, trying to get a lead on it.

GQ, "2, break! 2, break!"

Everling, "The other jets on our six. Break!"

"I almost have it."

GQ, "Break, damn it!"

Everling, "He's on us!"

They feel rounds hit their plane just as Cochran squeezes the trigger. Her rounds hit the tail of the '262, shredding it. In their cockpit the warning lights are lit up: fire in both engines; master warning; hydraulic failure in two systems. Everling looks over his shoulder and sees black smoke and flames.

Cochran, "Pulling the extinguishers. Hydraulics are mushy."

Everling, "We need to eject, damn it!"

"I've got this. I've got this. One more minute." Then, the '14 tries to invert and there's an explosion behind them.

"Everling, "Eject! Eject!" He pulls the ejection handles and is blasted into the slipstream of the falling jet. He comes to in his chute and sees the ground rushing up.

PERCIVAL 1, IN THE FIGHT

GQ, "2 is hit! Percival 2 is hit! We're south west of York, about ten miles. Two chutes."

"Percival 1, Valkyrie 1, airborne in 2 mikes. Can you orbit?"

Hot Pants, "Hang on!" She cranks the '14 over in a violent left turn, applying dissimilar thrust and rudder to avoid cannon fire from a '262." They're pushed back into their seats as she applies full burner in pursuit. She slews her aircraft right, skids, and fires, "Got you, fucker." The '262 tumbles, trailing flames and black smoke.

GQ, "Roger, Valkyrie 1. We're clearing the skies for you."

Hot Pants, "You see them?"

GQ, "Yeah. Fuck! Break right and dive!"

She twists the '14 into another spinning roll to orient toward the parachutes and sees a '262 circling the helpless pilots. "I got it." In a screaming dive, she fires a burst at the German vulture, and hits, tracing a line across the fuselage at the wing root. The left wing folds and the low flying fighter spins into the ground.

GQ, "Truck, 10 o'clock." A German army truck is speeding toward the hill where Cochran and Everling are coming down. On radio, "Any Hog, Percival, emergency tasking."

Gloria, "We've got 75 rounds left." She circles back, strafing the truck. Her rounds hit the fuel tank, and the truck goes up, spilling out soldiers.

HILLS SOUTH WEST OF YORK, UK

Everling lands as he was taught, rolling to absorb the impact. He stands and gathers his chute into a pile. Percival 1 roars by, then it goes quiet. The silence is deafening. He sees Cochran land two hundred yards away. He grabs up his chute and walks to her. They're completely exposed on the bare hillside.

When he's about a hundred feet from his pilot, hears gunfire. Cochran is up and gathering her chute in. She looks up at the sound. German soldiers are running at them, firing their rifles.

"Come on, Jackie! We got to go!"

"Yeah." She looks at her parachute, then dumps it on the ground and starts running up the hill. The Germans keep shooting. Julian shakes out his chute, letting it catch air and snags the harness on a bush, and follows Jackie up the hill. She looks back as he joins her, "Good idea."

"Thanks. Keep moving."

Bullets are ricocheting off the rocks around them as they crest the hill. Everling pulls his pistol and looks back just as Percival 1 roars over their heads. The Germans are spreading out, still firing. He sees a German fire just as he pulls the trigger. Everything slows down, and he clearly sees the flash as the bullet hits him high in the left chest, barely missing his shoulder. He spins from the impact, and the next round hits him in the right shoulder and he falls in a heap.

Jackie tries to get his hand and pull him up. Then, Valkyrie 1 rises above the hill. The helicopter turns and unmasks its minigun. The door gunner opens up, spitting a constant stream of bullets. Julian feels hands pulling him into the chopper and he passes out.

MILTON KEYNES, UK

1618, 4 October, 1942

Chris Oliverson stands in a stolen SS Major's uniform at an intersection next to a stolen black Mercedes. He sees a line of German trucks coming toward him and waves it over. Stepping onto the running board of the first, he says in perfect German, "Go down this road. Stay on it. You'll receive additional directions." He steps off and waves them on.

"Yes, Herr Major." The driver turns his truck towards Wales and drives on. Four trucks follow with supplies and troops.

CONTROL ROOM, RAF KENLEY

1620, 4 October, 1942

Spike walks into the control room, "Thud, what happened?"

LCDR Frank 'Thud' Jackson is focused on the new radar repeater. It's designed so the women in the pit can add grease pencil labels on the tracks. It has a permanent outline of the British Isles. Thud looks up at her, his jaw tight, "I lost them. They were heading north to hit a fighter group out of Ouston. Cochran and Everling went down."

Spike, "I see. Status."

The watch officer, "Um, ma'am, Lieutenant Cochran and Ensign Everling went down…"

"I know. The war goes on. What else is happening?"

"Shotgun is on ready 5, call sign Camelot. Little John's covering Rusty flight as they attack the German columns heading south. Dog flight 2 is attacking near Carlyle in support of the Scottish volunteers and Leeds Rifles. The Germans attacked Scapa, again. Most of the fleet is at sea or in Belfast. Miami is covering the coast from missile attacks. Percival 1 is returning and Lancelot is leaving on a sweep…"

"Stop." She picks up a mic, "Lancelot flight, Yankee, fly direct to Charley and orbit."

NOB, Gunner Hardin's RIO, "Wilco, Yankee. What's up?"

"Lancelot, Yankee, we're getting too predictable." She looks down at the sergeant, "Continue."

"Sixteen new German fighters flew into Ouston escorting transports. We've lost another radar plane over the Irish Sea. Battleship Division 5 reports on station. What's left of the British Mobile Division, Canadian 1st Armored Brigade, the US 1st and 2nd Armored Division, 3rd and 9th Infantry Division, are all fighting a rear-guard retreat to London. 1st Armored Recon Battalion is attacking east from Manchester. We have indications the Germans are pulling units from the main attack to respond. Patton ordered them to run through the countryside 'shooting and scooting,' ma'am. His words. We have reports of Germans in Birmingham. Our A-10s have reported the destruction of more than one thousand tanks."

"Do we have an estimate of what they have left?"

"Not at this time, Commodore."

Andrews walks in, "I heard."

She nods, "Warthogs report one thousand kills. Could you find out how many tanks the Germans have left?"

"I'll share that info with Eisenhower's staff and ask. Here's your mail."

"Thank you. Later."

A radio talker, "Valkyrie 1 is lifting from Guys enroute to Kenley."

Spike, "Roger." She picks up a phone.

A tired voice answers, "Swede."

"Sorry to wake you. You've lost Percival 2. One of the crew is at Guys. The other is inbound on Valkyrie 1. Percival 1 is on final. You should meet them."

"On it."

She turns to Thud, "You alright?"

"No. Damn it, Spike. I will be."

"You know, we've come a long way, you and I. It won't be long before you get your own squadron."

"Yeah, it sure is a steep learning curve."

"It is, Thud. Do you know why the WWII generation was called the greatest generation?"

He gives her a wry smile, "Because they had a hero complex?"

Spike smiles back, "Nope, it's because they faced struggles that allowed their hero complex to shine. Every generation has heroes, Thud, but not every generation has villains who polish the hero and let him shine."

"Right now, who is your villain?"

"The faceless German officer dictating their air war. It's a chess game, except each of us get new pieces. The side with the most resources has the advantage. At the beginning, that was Germany, but increasingly, it is us. Do you want to meet Percival 2 when Valkyrie 1 lands?"

"Yeah."

"Go, Thud. I got it here."

Thud walks out and she sits and picks up her mail. The first letter is from Dixie:

Hello, Darlin,

I'm not ashamed to say I'm afraid for you and your people. I admit, I'm also jealous. Ashley and I are sending a care package. The letter will no doubt get there first.

I hit my knee and made us official. Wished you could have been there for it, but I just couldn't wait. You will stand up for me when we do the deed. Before I met you, I was broken. You put the pieces back together and helped me find functionality. Ashley has healed me. We're looking out for Audrey and Donna. I'm campaigning to get the war brides here as soon as possible. It's an up-hill battle.

So, I was interviewed by Stars and Stripes. They couldn't care less about this salty admiral. They wanted to know about you. I know you value your privacy, but please understand, you've reached a level of celebrity that is difficult to fathom. I think, if you met Elvis at his prime, he would ask for your autograph. I read a piece in a newspaper that said how you're from a family of fighters because your grandfather shot at him with a shotgun. I've no doubt it happened. The weird thing is that the reporter wrote that more in awe than in anger.

So, I told them a bit. I said you were always a gifted pilot. Admitted I knew you before the deployment that brought us back. I told them about you kicking my ass in training. I hope you don't mind. Roosevelt was telling the truth when he said the people need heroes right now. They're starving for good news. Each time you manage to pull off a victory, it lifts morale.

Another thing I think you should know about, every now and again your pa gets invited into some very high-level meetings. I managed to successfully argue for the release of interned Japanese-Americans. The whole thing was a racist stain on our national identity. I'm pretty sure I pissed off some folks, but it was the right thing to do. It's exactly what we're fighting against out there.

Ashley and I had dinner with Klindt and his fiancée, Evelyn. She's a good fit for him. Laid back intensity, I think I'll call it. Klindt has his fourth star now. Ashley and Evelyn get along pretty well, but they're very different people. Evelyn is from one of those industrialist families in up-state New York. As far from good ole boy as you can get.

I very much hope this letter finds you and all your people well. If you have need of anything, please let me know. As I learn relevant Washington gossip, I'll share it."

Love you,

Your Pa

In the fold of the letter is a picture of Lee and Ashley on the Mall. She smiles. They look so happy. "Yeah, I love you too, Dad."

CHAPTER 24

HELICOPTER PAD, RAF KENLEY

Swede and Thud hang onto their hats as Valkyrie 1 lands. The door slides open and LT Cochran gets out. Swede says, 'Welcome back, Cochran. Have you been checked out?"

"No, sir."

"Right. Look, after each ejection a pilot has to be cleared medically before they can fly again."

"I'm not grounded, sir?"

Swede, "Do you want to be?"

"No, sir."

They turn and walk towards Swede's jeep, "What happened?"

"I didn't break when I was told to."

"Did you get your target?"

She stops and tilts her head, "My target?"

Thud, "You were target fixated. Did you get your target?"

"Yes, sir, I think so."

Swede, "Cochran, it happens. Learn from your mistake and move forward."

"Yes, sir."

"Commander Jackson will take you to medical. When you're cleared, and when you've had some rest, you'll be back on the roster. We'll get you a new RIO."

"Yes, sir."

Swede gets into his jeep and heads for the flight line.

CONTROL ROOM, RAF KENLEY

The next letter is from Mrs. Roosevelt:

Dear Samantha,

I hope this letter finds you well. I admit to listening to the news with fear in my heart. Franklin assures me that we, over here, are doing everything possible to aid you in your efforts. I have no doubt the military is solving every problem it can in the effort to support you. Please, be aware that our nation is praying for your success. What I do not yet know is whether you have any need, personal or professional. Please, tell me if there is anything you need and I will do my best to get it for you.

With that in mind, I wish to give you some measure of good news. The Naval Equality Act of 1942 has passed and been signed into law. It opens all rates to all races based only on ability. It also integrates the naval air and surface fleets, but allows time for the integration to happen. All new vessels, cruiser sized and larger, must be built and manned with integrated crews. All existing ships, cruiser and larger, must be integrated as they go through overhauls. All smaller surface ships will start integration after two years in a like manner as the larger ships. Submarines, being uniquely limited, will stay all male.

Also, the Wartime Resource Act has provided protections for women and minorities in the workplace, including precluding discrimination on hiring based on race or sex. On the surface this act seems to be a wartime exigency, but it does not have an expiration clause.

These things are a beginning. The activities of you and your people were used as the argument for much we have achieved. If there is anything you are in need, whether personal or professional, please let me know so I can be of aid.

Your friend,

Eleanor

Sam takes a deep breath and closes her eyes. The gratitude she feels threatens to overwhelm her and she feels tears forming.

Andrews, "Are you okay?"

She puts the letter down, "Colonel, it has been a hard day and I just got some good news."

"I'm glad, then. May I ask?"

"Congress just passed a law saying that I and my female crews have a right to exist. It offers additional protections as well."

"That is good news. I have some more good news. We received a message saying we're getting twelve more F/A-14s, with crews."

"Really?"

"Yes, Spike. They're transitioning to the Tomcat right now."

"A new squadron?"

"It said they're for the Black Knights."

"Hmm, that's odd. Can you get me Fluffy?"

"Roger, Commodore." He gets up, then stops and looks back, "May I ask why he is called that?"

Sam smiles, "I know. There isn't anything fluffy about him. It's one of those reverse names; the heavy guy called Slim; the bald guy called Harry."

"Got it. He's outside the door." He turns and heads out.

HANGER 17, RAF KENLEY

1731, 4 October, 1942

Gloria and Byron climb out of their jet as the ground crew get to work checking out their bird. Swede walks in, "How are you two?"

Gloria looks into her fiance's eyes and smiles. Byron asks, "Any word on Cochran and Everling?"

Swede, his gaze on Gloria, says, "Cochran's in medical getting her post-ejection physical. Everling's in Guys."

Byron, "Everling was fucking brilliant on the ground. He inflated his chute and tangled it in the foliage to act as concealment, and he was shooting back."

Swede, "Okay, write it up," and he and Gloria start walking away.

Byron, "It'll be on your desk in a couple of hours. Guys, will you two just kiss."

Swede stops, startled, and turns, "Not in public."

"It's the worst kept secret of the war. We're happy for you, now snog so we can finish the post brief."

Swede turns back to Gloria. With a big smile lighting her up, she steps up to him and puts her arms around his neck, pulling his head down, and kissing him. Byron and the crew watch, fascinated. Then, Swede pulls back and takes a deep breath, looking down at Gloria. They look up, startled, when they hear the crew and Byron applauding them. Swede blushes and Gloria takes a bow.

Byron smiles and continues, "Cochran refused to break. She got target fixated."

Swede, "She said as much. Do you think she's capable of learning from her mistake?"

The three continue out of the hanger. Gloria says, "She's smart and a good pilot. The problem is, she wants to be an ace so bad it impairs her judgement." Gloria laughs, "That's it. We hang it around her neck like an albatross. Her call sign should be 'Ace.'"

Swede and GQ chuckle, "Yeah. Make it so. What do we lay on Everling?"

GQ, "He was the shit down there. Make him 'Deuce.'"

Swede nods, "So it is." He looks around. They're alone and no one is in earshot. "Can I ask you something, GQ?"

GQ goes still, "You just did."

Swede, "We're so close, I see no need for secrets between us. Gloria and I are transparent with each other about everything but you. So, who were you with in that hotel room?"

GQ takes a breath and looks at Gloria. "I'm sorry, Byron. I haven't said anything." He turns back to Swede, "Are you asking as my commanding officer?"

"No, Byron, never. I'm asking as your friend."

"I was with my boyfriend. I can't share his name." GQ is looking Swede straight in the eyes.

Swede, "I thought so. It's cool with me. If there's anything we can do to protect you two, just ask, okay?" Swede pulls GQ into a hug, then reaches for Gloria. For a moment, they're still, then GQ pulls back, "Thank you, Stephan, that means a lot."

FOREST EAST OF BIALYSTOK, POLAND

2131, 4 October, 1942 (2031 GMT)

LT Francis 'Spooky' Torrey is still, listening in the dark of the forest. A Russian infantry unit is only two hundred yards to his north. The Germans are six hundred yards to his south. He opens his pack and quickly spreads out some papers. He walks a few feet east, careful to avoid making tracks. He puts a Russian pattern cover on his boots and lays down a few tracks, then opens fire with a Russian PPSh-41 submachine gun. He swings up on a branch and jumps to a fallen tree. There, he removes the covers from his boots and stows them. He jumps back to the papers and moves out carefully and fast, spilling drops of blood from a bag.

GERMAN OCCUPIED RAF OUSTON

2100, 4 October, 1942

LT Kegan stands in front of his commander, "I'm sorry, I lost my aircraft."

Major Gunter, "You killed one. It's enough. If we could exchange one for one, they would be gone in a day. Are you fit to fly?"

"Yes, Major."

"Good, but we first must address an issue with your uniform."

"Sir?"

"Gunter smiles, "You need to start wearing the pip of an Oberlieutenant." He hands Kegan his promotion insignia.

The new Oberlieutenant salutes, "Thank you, sir. Heil Hitler."

HEADQUARTERS, COMMANDER, EUROPEAN THEATER OF OPERATIONS

2130, 4 October, 1942

Spike, in dress greens, is escorted into Eisenhower's office. She salutes and he returns it, standing to offer his hand. "Coffee, please, Kay." His secretary nods and leaves. "How are you, Commodore?"

She smiles, "Managing. Can we hold at the line?"

Eisenhower motions for her to take a seat, settles into his chair, and steeples his hands. "We haven't done so well in the holding department, have we?"

"It isn't a criticism, sir, it's a question. I'm running our A-10s ragged and it's getting harder to find German tanks. I'm hoping we're making your soldier's job a little easier."

"You are. We've lost the equivalent of two divisions of armor trying to stop Rommel. Materials and troops are starting to come in from Canada and the US, but these are all green troops and they'll be facing Hitler's elite."

Eisenhower's secretary, Kay Summersby serves coffee and leaves. Spike smiles, remembering her history. Eisenhower, "Thank you, Kay."

Spike, "We trained the A-10 pilots on night vision devices and they're getting really good. But, General, how are we preparing our defense of London?"

"Trenches and fortifications and artillery spots are prepared. It'll be an integrated, layered defense, the best I've ever seen."

"A thought, sir, we've been transporting troops over by ship with all their gear. Around London, it seems to me, that we need bodies as much as gear. Could we fly troops straight in and unite them with their heavy equipment later?"

"Fantastic idea. I'll implement that immediately. The 82nd is preparing to lift. I could use them as well."

"Sir, I have them tasked for taking back Ouston. We've a plan to destroy their air defenses, then static drop the division."

"Operation Sunset, right. That will clear the skies of some of them, but they'll still be flying in from France."

"We have more aircraft and crews coming in. Once we retake Ouston, we'll hit the German airfields and hammer their positions in France and Germany. Thus far, I've been a hawk acting like a sparrow. It's time to go on the offensive."

"Agreed. You were tasked with defense, but you're right, it's time."

"Another thing, I placed BATDIV-5 off the Thames. When the Germans close within range, I'll have them drive up the Thames for artillery support."

Eisenhower looks stunned, "Excellent. I got word they were moved, but not your intention. They should move on the next high tide. Notify the Admiralty and order them as far up the river into London as they can go and still safely fire their guns. What is their range?"

"Yes, sir. About seven miles. Are the Germans that close?"

"No, not yet, but they will be soon. At seven miles, they could cover much of London."

"That was my thought, sir."

Eisenhower takes a sip of coffee, "I heard about the sniper. I passed the news to our British friends and they're searching diligently for any others."

"It was a gambit that failed. They'll try something else next."

"You're not worried?"

"Sir, failure worries me. If I die, I die."

"The SEAL team that was in Kenley, can you tell me what their mission was?"

"You don't know?"

"I do. What do you know?"

"They were extracting, then re-inserting an OSS agent. The agent was to plant information meant to restart the eastern front. The President hopes it will take some of the pressure off England."

"Do you know the exact plan?"

"No, sir. I didn't need to know, so I didn't ask."

"Commodore, you're smart. Smart and wise." He looks at her quizzically, "You know my future. What are you willing to share?"

"Sir, please understand, none of what I know is inevitable. Our coming back changes everything."

"I understand, still it may help me to know."

"Yes, sir. Most relevant now, in Operation Overlord you plan and execute the invasion of France. This happens in 1944 because of the African and Italian campaigns. It's Churchill who pushed for both of those. He rightly recognized that the allies needed war fighting experience before tackling fortress Europe. I think the British Theater has given us a great deal of experience."

"You know the name of the invasion?"

"It's historical record. We created an elaborate ruse to convince Hitler that we are landing at Calais and, instead, land at Normandy. The ruse was so powerful, so good, Hitler refused to reinforce at Normandy."

"Hitler would know all of this now?"

"In the public consciousness, it's known as D-Day. It's celebrated each year. Also, we landed special forces at Point Du Hoc. This time it will have to be totally different."

"What would you recommend?"

"Sir, invasion planning is way out of my wheel house."

"You've done well so far. We'll develop a plane. I'd just like your gut opinion."

"Okay, it's still going to take time. We need new, better equipment, and we need to train everyone on how to use it. You know the armor we have isn't up to the task."

"I do."

"Armor is just the start. We need armored personnel carriers so infantry can keep up with the armor."

"What's wrong with a truck?"

"Tanks can go places trucks can't, and trucks are terribly vulnerable. Trucks deliver supplies to the front, armor fights the battle, and Europe will be an armor battle. I've gotten word that Admiral Klindt is designing a tank. I sent him a message asking him to send someone out to brief your staff and the Brits on it. It gives the designers a chance to see what we need, too."

"Thank you. Where would you land?"

"Why land in one place? By then, we'll control the sea. Why not land one place, give a day or two for the Germans to orient, then land somewhere else? As they scramble to face two threats, give them three or four. If we land, or feint a landing, up near Bremerhaven, they have to respond. It draws forces away from the Atlantic wall."

"That would be a vast enterprise to manage."

"It would, but it would also have a high probability of success."

"I'll have my staff look at your ideas. Is there any other advice you have?"

"I know that even now, you're contemplating the presidency. You're not the only officer who is."

"Nimitz?"

"No, sir. He retires to a quiet and private life in Texas. Mac-Arthur has ambitions. None of the naval leaders enter politics, as I recall. Some may serve a stint in congress, but that's about it."

"I heard that I win the presidency."

Spike smiles, "You did. You were after Truman, who replaced Roosevelt when he died. But I've no idea what will happen this go-around. Roosevelt did a good job as president and continuity is critical right now, but normally four terms are too long. A whole generation grows up with one guy in charge. It gives too much power to the presidency. In the fifties, they passed an amendment limiting presidents to two terms."

"Do you have political ambitions?"

"Right now, sir, I have survival ambitions. I'm not thinking about my future in a post war world."

"I understand Hitler is acting very differently than he did in your history."

She smiles, "Yes. The problem with the little corporal is that he shot himself in the foot before. Now, he's still shooting himself in the foot, but with different ammunition."

Eisenhower laughs, "If you were in his shoes, what would you do?"

Spike is silent, thinking, "I would sue for peace and gather all I could in resources as I pulled back. I would try to incorporate as much of the gains I'd made as I could, particularly in Poland and the Balkans. Then, I would build up my people and industry and try to dominate the world peacefully through commerce. There is no way whatsoever that Germany can win now that America is in the war."

"Even if England falls?"

"Yes, sir. The fall of England would be a disaster, but we would still win. They do not have the resources to defend all they control. In another six months to a year, the US Navy will be larger than the rest of the world's navies combined. The Atlantic will be an American pond. The German subs are a problem, but we have subs, too, and better technology than they do. That wasn't true in my WWII, not yet anyway."

"You're overconfident in the political will of America. If we stood alone, I think we would be far too tempted to cut our losses and settle for the new way of things."

"Sir, yours is called the greatest generation. They will fight. They must fight. All our futures depend on it. When we win, we will shape a world of peace and prosperity. If we lose, the future will be shaped by Kryukov, Tojo, and Hitler. Millions will die for the egos of evil men."

HIGH STREET, LLANDOVERY, WALES

2226, 4 October, 1942

Four German trucks stop in the center of town. Sergeant Bergen steps out of his truck and looks around. He followed the major's instructions, but now must admit he's lost. His men clamber out of the trucks and several go into a pub. He follows them in, looking for someone to question.

OFFICER'S CLUB, RAF KENLEY

2226, 4 October, 1942

This is the first time Sam has been to the club. It's built in an unused WWI ammunition bunker. From the outside it looks like a hill. She and Gloria walk in through a zig-zag concrete passage and Gloria opens a large iron door. "Welcome to the Bunker." The first thing she sees is the left vertical stabilizer of a German MiG-29. The iron cross is large on it, but there are also fifty-two vertical bars. Above each bar is a roundel, five American, thirty-two British, and fifteen Soviet red stars.

Spike asks, "Who belongs to this?"

Swede hands her a beer, "The plane belonged to a fella named Colonel Getz. They found it on the beach near South Shield. The investigators had to scramble, but they got this."

She looks around. There are pictures on the wall of all those in the squadron they have lost, each with a piece of their aircraft, if recoverable. Under Papa's picture is the section of his fuselage with his kill flags. Above their heads is the wing of a F-14 that has many holes in it. Swede sees her realization, "Yeah, it's your old wing."

"Wow, the Italian lace wing," and takes a sip of her beer. The bar is classic British pub oak with mirrors and lots of booze oriented on the back wall. Behind the bar are the bathrooms. Most of the airmen are in quiet conversation. Her gaze is drawn to Major Boyington who's drinking alone, his elbows and arms on the table, surrounding his drink.

Gloria shakes her head, "Hey, guys, do you really think 'Deuce' Everling would want this place to be a morgue?"

Every eye turns to her and Pappy says, "What do you know of it?"

Sam steps between them, "Enough."

Boyington abruptly stands, his chair toppling over, "What do you know of it, Commodore? Do you even feel pain? Do you know hurt, Ice Queen?"

Sam says, "Major, go sleep it off. We still have work to do."

Boyington swings a haymaker at her jaw. She easily sidesteps the punch. He swings two more times without connecting and then bull rushes her. Sam grabs his wrist, stepping aside and swings his hand down. Boyington flips forward, landing hard on his back.

Sam, "Enough!" But, Boyington is now enraged, and puts his head down, rushing her again. Once again, he finds himself on his back. He staggers back to his feet, this time moving in slowly, trying to pin her against the bar. She reaches for his hand, locks his wrist, and spinning, plants his chest against the bar. She starts to speak, but Swede waves a hand, and throws a pitcher of water in the major's face.

After a moment, Swede lowers his face right to Greg's, "Are you done yet? She could kick my ass with one hand, Major. You don't stand a chance. Now go to bed."

Pappy mumbles, "Why?"

"Do you think you're the only one hurting, dumb ass? Go to bed. That's an order."

"If I don't?"

"I'll knock you the fuck out, and carry you to bed. And Major, you'll never fly again."

Pappy deflates, "Yes, sir."

THE KING'S HEAD INN, LLANDOVERY, WALES

2240, October, 1942

Sixteen men of the underground wait as their commander discusses what to do about the Germans in town. Lisa Anderson walks in with the lookout, who says, "She's cleared."

Captain Daniel Evans asks, "Who are you?"

She hands him ID, "I'm military intelligence."

One of the guys laughs, "Isn't military intelligence a contradiction in terms?" Several of the men guffaw. She turns, stone-faced, and looks at him. The mouthy guy says, "I'm sorry, ma'am."

"Yes," and turns to Captain Evans, "What are you planning?"

"We passed more beer in the back. We're letting them get drunk first. We're sorting out how to handle the sentries."

"I've an idea for that."

WAR OFFICE, WASHINGTON, DC

1800, 4 October, 1942 (2300 GMT)

LT General Ridgeway walks into General Marshal's office. Marshal looks up, "Good morning, General, how may I help you?"

"Sir, these orders from the Navy? Does Commodore Hunt know 'airborne' is an infantry designation and not aviation?"

"I just left a meeting with King and Lee about this. It seems your unit survives the cutbacks after the war and becomes quite famous. I'm told Commodore Hunt knows exactly what your unit is and exactly how to use it. Your orders are to report to RAF Kenley with everything you need to do a division strength drop."

"Where, sir?"

"I don't know. They're rightly keeping that close. Assume it will be in the British Isles somewhere. Also assume this mission is critical to the overall defense of England. If she wanted security guards, she would have asked for them."

"Yes, sir. What is she like, sir?"

"Never met her, but I know she has nearly one hundred kills. Lee thinks the world of her. She's a southerner for what that is worth."

"Why would a woman do what she does?"

"Why do you, General?"

"It's my duty, sir. Also, I really enjoy it, building a group of men into a fighting force."

"I would assume her motivations are much the same. After all, women belong to the same species as men."

"Yes, sir."

"Should you get any insight on her, please share it with me. Her success is reshaping warfare."

"Yes, sir."

RED DRAGON PUB, LLANDOVERY, WALES

2313, 4 October, 1942

The beer has flowed freely, and Private Munster stands on watch, missing out. A pretty red-haired woman walks up to him with two mugs of beer. He smiles and sets his rifle down, taking the proffered mug. She salutes him with her mug and a flirtatious smile. Then he feels a gun barrel pressing against his back. Lisa Anderson, in perfect German, "Finish your beer. It will be your last for some time."

All thirty-six Germans are rolled up and taken to a POW camp without incident.

FIELD MARSHAL KRYUKOV'S OFFICE, KREMLIN, RUSSIA

0600, 5 October, 1942 (0300 GMT)

General Davydov, his intelligence officer, is escorted in by an aid bearing a tea tray. When the aid leaves Davydov opens his briefcase and removes some blood-stained papers. "These, Field Marshal, were found between our lines and that of the Germans. A soldier left his compound to shit and stumbled on a German junior officer and took him under fire. The latch of a case must have opened. And, what he was doing so close to our lines, I don't understand. Regardless, these were recovered. I recommend the soldier for the star."

Kryukov studies translations of the papers. They are mission orders to front line troops for recommencing hostilities. Each is prefaced with the information that England is teetering and will soon fall, freeing the Luftwaffe for the eastern front. "These are authentic?"

"I saw the scene myself. Blood everywhere."

"But, no body."

"No body, Field Marshal. There was a trail of blood drops leaving the scene toward the German lines. The boot prints were German and of high quality. A lost junior officer, I think."

"The American jets and training are up to specifications. We have three more squadrons being trained as we speak. It isn't my wish to strike now, but this leaves me little choice." He pushes a button on his desk, "Irina, please gather the general staff." He looks to Davydov, "Thank you, General. I will see you in the meeting in a few minutes. There you can share this with the staff."

BLACK KNIGHT READY ROOM, RAF KENLEY, UK

0600, 5 October, 1942

Major Boyington walks in with Ensign Alcott. Major Mossberg stands and walks straight up to Boyington, "A word, Major." Mossberg leads him outside.

"What do you want, Major? I've no issue with blacks."

When they're out of site and alone, Mossberg grabs Boyington by both lapels and lifts him off the ground, gives him a shake, and pushes him away. "Fucking listen to me. You're a good pilot, but you have a chip on your shoulder that you had best resolve right fucking now."

"What?"

"If you ever lay so much as a finger on her again, I will personally kill you and dump your body in a hole."

"She kicked my ass."

"She shouldn't have had to. I had a talk with your ground crew. They were grumbling about fucking with your plane. We fucking love her."

"I'm sorry. It was the drink."

"Then you best not touch another drop. I know who you are. I know you better than you know you. Change your ways, or I will end you. Do we have an understanding?"

"Yes, sir."

CHAPTER 25

WOLF'S LAIR, AUSTRIA

0707, 5 October, 1942 (0607 GMT)

Hitler pounds the table, "Why has London not fallen? Why?"

His generals and admirals sit silently around the table, then Field Marshal Keitel says, "We have central England, Mein Fuhrer. Rommel races to London now. Our fighters fly from English soil. The issue now, as ever, is air superiority."

Hitler, calming, "Yes. Goering, how many American planes have we bought with our scores of fighters lost?"

"Six, Mein Fuhrer."

"And how many did they have at the onset?"

"Four, Mein Fuhrer."

"How many do they now have?"

"We estimate twelve, Mein Fuhrer."

"So, General Weber has lost and that bitch has won?"

"Mein Fuhrer, General Weber has used superb tactics to suppress and destroy the enemy. We set his primary mission as support of our armor. He does this. Many of their tank destroying aircraft have been lost. And more each day. When London falls, they are lost."

"I want that bitch. I want her dead or captured. They rally to her. She is the symbol of their resistance. Destroy her and they will fail. Make that clear to Weber."

"I have, Mein Fuhrer. He has a bold strategy to make it so."

"And just what is this strategy?"

"We firestorm London with our V-1s, combined with a concentrated air attack at night. The airfield will burn. With no airfield, there are no Americans."

"Why not attack the field directly?"

"Our V-1s are not so accurate. Fire will destroy everything."

"Very well, everything south of the Thames. Save Buckingham Palace for my summer home."

COMMODORE'S OFFICE, RAF KENLEY

0630, 5 October, 1942

Spike finishes her enormous breakfast, sets the tray aside, and starts reviewing reports. An aid comes in and removes the tray. Cooper knocks and pops his head in, "Lieutenant Cochran to see you."

"Send her in."

Cooper, "Tea?"

"No, after. Thanks, Radar."

LT Jackie Cochran walks in and comes to attention. Spike, "Yes?"

"I would like to discuss the loss of my plane, ma'am. You haven't spoken to me at all. May I ask why?"

"Lieutenant, you work for Commander Swedenborg. It's not my habit to step on my unit commanders."

"I'm sorry about the aircraft."

Spike's voice is calm and flat, "You're sorry? Have you apologized to your RIO for nearly killing him yesterday? Did you apologize to Lieutenant Houlihan for disobeying her order? Lieutenant, your ego is writing checks your ass can't cash. If you pull another stunt like that. If you disobey your flight lead. If you exercise poor judgement again, you will go back to ferrying aircraft and never see combat again. I don't give a shit about your legacy or your legend. Were it not for dumb luck, I would be writing your parents right now. Dismissed."

Cochran starts to speak, shuts her mouth, performs a crisp about face and walks out.

Cooper comes in with tea and pours for both of them. "Boss, I've never heard you cuss someone out before. Remind me to stay on your good side."

"Cooper, you haven't killed anyone, have you?"

"Not that I know of. Why? She's an icon. Is she going to make it in this war?"

"The problem is that she knows she's an icon, and I'm stealing the fame she wants for herself. She's a talented flyer. If she can just get her head straight, she'll do fine."

"If she can't?"

"She'll go back to ferrying planes. Radar, I don't bluff."

"Roger, that."

THAMES RIVER NEAR RATCLIFF

0652, 5 October, 1942

USS Mississippi BB-41 leads the USS New York and USS Texas into the Royal Docks. Small boats await to tie them to the quays. The buildings and infrastructure around the docks have all been destroyed. The caissons holding out the tide have only recently been repaired. The pilot says, "This dock will keep you afloat at low tide. Otherwise, your keel would be in the mud."

Captain David Smith, "So, this is as far up the river as we can go?"

"Afraid so, sir. On a good tide, I could get you to Tower Bridge, but when it turned, you'd be in the mud."

The heaving lines are thrown out and the boatswain announces, "Moored, shift colors."

Captain Smith sighs, "Thank you, sir." They shake hands and the pilot departs.

A messenger enters the bridge, "A message from Commodore Hunt, sir. She's sending a helicopter for you and the other captains and the commodore."

Smith says to the OOD, "Have the XO meet me on the fantail."

"Yes, sir."

Smith goes to his stateroom, packs an overnight bag, and walks to the fantail. He arrives just as a helicopter arrives. His XO salutes. "Commander, keep the boys at gunnery stations and keep everyone aboard. You can secure half the boilers in each plant. We won't be maneuvering."

"Yes, sir."

Commodore James joins him and the two men get on the helicopter. The chopper rotates, lands on the other two ships in turn, picking up their captains, then climbs for altitude for the short flight to Kenley. The four men look out the window. James says, "Wow. I can see battle damage, but London isn't as bad as I thought it would be."

A few minutes later, they touch down at Kenley. Spike is waiting for them in her flight suit. They climb out and salute. She returns the salute, "If you would join me in my car."

The five get into her armored car and James asks, "An armored car, ma'am?"

"We had a sniper incident the other day, and now my guys insist."

Smith asks, "How long is this drive?"

"About ten minutes, why?"

"I would like to know, you being an aviator, if you understand the precarious position you have placed our ships in?"

She schools her face, "Go on."

Smith looks nervously at Commodore James, "Our ships are effectively trapped in a wash basin. We cannot maneuver if attacked."

Spike, "So, you feel your vessels are too important to be hazarded in battle?"

James, "They're warships. Of course, they can be hazarded in battle. It just seems a stupid risk."

Spike looks at the other men, "And do the rest of you doubt my judgement in this?"

They avoid eye contact.

James, "This is not insubordination, ma'am. It's a question."

Spike, "Thank you, Captain Smith for having the balls to ask the question. You other two, if you have the same doubts and remain silent, shame on you. Now to address the concern you have. I'm operating under the assumption that the invasion is common knowledge in the states. Has status of the invasion reached the other side of the pond?"

James, "It has."

"And the four of you are concerned that I'm taking stupid risks with your ships?"

They all nod and Smith says, "They're capital ships."

"Yes, they are twenty-five plus year old capital ships that are too old and too slow to operate with the carrier battlegroups in the Pacific. Still, they're a valuable national asset. I do not risk them foolishly. Gentlemen, this is London. The capital of the British Empire and Kingdoms of England, Scotland, Wales, and Northern Ireland. Should London fall, England falls.

Should England fall, Great Britain will fall. Should Britain fall, her empire may well fall with it. There is historical precedence for such things.

"Loss of this island would, at best, set back the war effort for two years. We would have to liberate Britain before liberating France. Russia would likely stay out of the war, so we would be alone. This would place the entire effort in question. We could lose the war and have a fascist, German owned, Canada on our border.

"In essence, the war will be decided in the next day or two. Weighted against what is at stake, I will hazard your vessels. I will hazard my whole command. We are all in this together. London must not fall."

They are silent for a moment, then, Commodore James says, "Yes, ma'am."

Spike smiles, "I'm glad we discussed this in private. Here we are." She pulls up to the Control Center. "Now, please, join me in the command center so we can go over the maps."

GESTAPO HEADQUARTERS, BERLIN

0900, 5 October, 1942 (0800 GMT)

Two men drag LT Peter 'Moses' Moskowitz from his prison cell. They take him to an interrogation room, handcuff him to a chair, and walk out. He hears the door behind him open and a woman's voice speaks in German, "Remove his restraints. He will not harm me."

As the handcuffs are removed, the woman walks into view, and, in English, says, "Hello, Lieutenant."

He studies her for a moment, taking in her fine clothes, her perfect makeup, and well styled hair. She's smiling, almost flirtatiously, but there's an edge, a hardness in her eyes. He nods, "Hello."

"I have the permission of the Gestapo to see the prisoners. I bring sausage," and offers him a steaming bratwurst on a warm piece of cloth.

He salivates and leans forward to take a small bite. It's been a long time since he's eaten food this rich, so he must be careful.

She smiles, "Come now. Please, eat it up quickly. They haven't given me much time."

He stops chewing, "So, it's drugged. Should have known. What's your game?"

Exasperated, "It is not."

He studies her eyes, "Well then, you're thin. We should share it."

"I'm quite fine, thank you. I wish to help you."

"If you wished to help me, the Gestapo would never have let you in. Still, you're a pleasant change of pace. What's your name?"

"I am Lina. What's yours?"

"My name is Peter."

"They do hope to learn something, so, what is your rank?"

"Lieutenant."

"Do you like it?"

"What?"

"Flying."

"It's exhilarating and sometimes terrifying."

"When is it terrifying?"

"Landing. The night landings at sea, in high seas and storms, that's terrifying."

"You fly the plane?"

"I operate the equipment behind the pilot."

"What kind of equipment?"

"What's in the wurst?"

She chuckles, "A mild sedative and hallucinogenic. It will not cause permanent harm. I'm told some even enjoy it."

"There's radar, pretty long range. I operate the radio."

"Do you know Commodore Hunt well?"

"Commodore now. Wow."

"Yes."

"What happened to Papa, Um, Commodore Holtz?"

"I'm told he was shot down and killed. The Luftwaffe has shot down many of your squadron friends."

"But, not Spike."

"No, not her. Why is she called Spike?"

"She's quiet and strong and tough. There's a cartoon with two dogs, a yippy dog named Chester, who won't shut up, and a strong, quiet dog named Spike. Her first RIO in training was Chester and wouldn't shut up. His mouth was always running. We could see it irritated her, and one day, she had enough and told him to shut up. That's how she got her call sign."

"I see. She seems the perfect pilot."

"She doesn't make mistakes in the air."

"Do you love her?"

"In a sense, we all do. She's that kind of leader."

"I mean romantically."

"What? Me? No. I don't have a clue what her type is, but it isn't me."

"Is it because you are a Jew?"

"That isn't it, no."

"You are aware the meat you just ate is pork, no?"

Moses chuckles, "I could not care less. I can't tell you the last time I went to synagogue."

"So, your faith is unimportant to you."

"Millenia old dietary restrictions are unimportant to me."

"You're from the future, yes?"

"I am."

"Then you know the fate of your people."

"I do. Your people murder my people and then pretend to be good Christians. I lost family in the camps."

"If you refuse to give me something useful, you will soon join them."

He just looks at her, calm, serene, and smiles.

"So. Very well." She takes the sausage and walks out.

Outside, she tells the waiting colonel, "He'll not break. I recommend you send him to the camps."

EAST END OF LUTON FIELD, 27 MILES NORTH OF LONDON

1034, 5 October, 1942

LT Gains walks from tank to tank, checking in with his men. They have two replacement tanks. He steps up on one, "Okay, Sergeant, how new are you?"

"We got off the boat in Portsmouth the day before yesterday. They broke up our brigade to fill in holes."

"Right. Do you figure you're extra brave?"

"What do you mean, Lieutenant?"

"Extra brave makes you extra dead. We have to work together if we're going to get it done and not get ourselves dead."

"Yes, sir."

"When I call formations, say advance or fall back, we do it together. You can't damage a Tiger from the front. A hull shot on the side or rear will take one out. If we run into Tigers, we call for artillery or A-10s to hit them."

"Yes, sir."

"Where are you from?"

"New York City."

"I'm from Jackson Hole, Wyoming. The thing is, Sergeant, we have something in common. We both want to go back those places. Brave is good. Smart is better. As long as you can, keep yourself up out of the hatch. Just button up for artillery or snipers. If you can't see the enemy, you can't hit the enemy."

"Yes, sir."

Gains walks to the next new tank and has the same conversation. As he's walking back to his track, he sees movement at their front. He sprints to his tank and bounds up into the commander's hatch. "What's that down there?"

Nicholson, his gunner, "They're Panzer 4s. Three of them. They're heading south in line crossing our front."

"See anything else?"

"No, sir."

Gains, "Sparky, call company. They're trying to flank us. Request air support."

Then four trucks come into view behind the tanks. He checks his radio is tuned to the platoon net, "Fire them up."

Sparky, "Company says advance and engage."

"Right, send the 'yes, sir.'" Back on the platoon net, "Four and three, turn north, stay in the trees and get behind them. Take out the rear two tanks, then the trucks. One and two, advance on line. They're side on to us. They're about 1200 yards off, so use the trees. Fire at 600 yards. Take the lead tank. Advance."

Tanks three and four move north, turn and come at the German line from the west. Tanks one and two roll forward over the crest of the hill. They make it about 200 yards when the Germans see them. The lead German tank swings his gun toward them. Gains, "1, 2, evasive." The German fires and misses and the Americans keep coming, zig-zagging on 20-degree angles. The Germans stop. Gains, "Nic, fire on the first tank."

His gunner fires, but they're still 800 yards away and moving. Then the German fires and almost hits tank 2. The Sherman rolls through the debris and keeps going.

Then, to their right, Gains hears the sound of tanks three and four firing. The last Panzer in line is hit with two rounds at its side and its turret pops off, flying into the air, ammo blowing up. Then the three trucks go away, one at a time, as they attempt to drive off the road and into the trees.

Tanks one and two are still rolling forward. The last two Panzers are stopped and laying down continuous fire. Just as the Sherman's reach 600 yards, a round hits the track of tank two, and it skids, tearing up the ground. Gains, "Stop, Fire! 2, un-ass your track. Get clear now! Driver! Back track. Go. Go."

The men scramble out of 2 and one gets clear when 2 is hit in the turret and the ammo cooks off. Gains, "Nic, target left, AP."

"Up."

"Away." The round flies true and hits the first Panzer at the base of the turret.

Then Gains sees the second Panzer in line hit by a round in the back of its turret. The turret blows off and the ammo explodes. Tanks three and four roll toward them out of the trees. The three remaining Sherman's fire on the last Panzer.

The Panzer's turret tips off and its ammo cooks off, flames shooting out of every hatch and opening.

It goes silent. Then they hear rounds plinking off their tanks and realize there are German infantry out there from the trucks. Gains and the other two tank commanders unlimber their machine guns and open up. Soon, it is silent again.

Gains looks around. He's lost one tank, "Driver, takes us to track 2. We need to check for survivors."

On radio, "Check for survivors."

They all head for tank two.

101ST SS PANZER BATTALION, FARM HOUSE, WEST OF OXFORD, UK

1100, 5 October, 1942

Meier lays in the farmer's bed trying to sleep. The noise of his men raping the farmer's wife in the kitchen wakes him again. He gets up and walks down the stairs. When he gets into the kitchen and the men see him, the room falls silent, except for the crying of the woman. He pulls out his knife, walks up to her, and slits her throat. "Now, go to sleep. We move out tonight."

They hear an American attack jet fly over. Their vehicles are in the barn or hidden in the trees. There's nothing to see, and the plane continues on.

NORTH OF LUTON, UK

1219, 5 October, 1942

Patton stands in his tank in the rain. His artillery is exchanging fire with the Germans to the north. There are at least two regiments of German armor reinforced infantry a few miles ahead of him. He gets on the radio, "Where is Rommel's armor? I don't think this is the main thrust."

His operations officer, "We had a platoon engage east of the air field. Our boys destroyed them."

"Have the Canadians to our east heard anything? Have the A-10s take a look."

They hear, "4th Corps, Wingnut. The A-10s are having problems with this low ceiling. I'll ask."

"Thank you, Wingnut."

EAST RIDING OF YORKSHIRE YEOMANRY, NORTH OF AYLESBURY, NORTHWEST OF LONDON

1408, 5 October, 1942

Sergeant David Preacher sits in the command hatch of his Covenanter tank. His company is arrayed to his left; the five remaining tanks from two platoons. To his right is the beginning of the Canadian line, their Ram tanks only moderately superior to his. His gunner says, "Sergeant, as I see it, we've two options. Either you can shut the fucking hatch or we can break out the soap. It's fucking pissing."

"It'll get warm soon enough when the Krauts arrive."

"I heard they're rolling through Luton east of us."

They hear the shriek-boom of a Canadian tank getting hit. Preacher, "Hold fire. They're coming, but I can't see them." The rain is coming down so hard, he can only see maybe a mile. One of their own tanks to the left brews up. Then another. He listens to the chatter on the radio, waiting. Then he sees the German tanks materialize out of the mist like grey ghosts. "Okay, boys. We face the Tiger."

"Bloody hell, Sergeant, should we just paint a bull's eye on us?"

The German Tigers are a third of a mile away when word comes down to charge. On the company net, their commander says, "Their turrets are slow. If we charge, some of us will get behind and hit them in the arse. At the ready! Charge!"

Preacher orders his tank forward. Once in the clear he looks to either side. About a third of the battalion has not moved. On the net, he hears calls of mechanical problems. "Fucking cowards." His driver is taking it slow down the slippery berm. A tank to his left brews up. "Floor it, Clyde. Fucking, floor it!" His tank picks up speed, slipping and churning down the slope.

British tanks are getting hit all up and down the line. Then the Germans start reversing. Preacher's tank is faster and they pass a Tiger so close he could chat up its commander. Preacher, "Right turret. Right turret. Fire!" Their 40mm auto-cannon round hits the engine deck. The engine explodes and the tank catches on fire. "Right track, elevate, and fire!" Their second round hits the rear turret and its ammo cooks off. The battle is on, with tank rounds and machine gun fire every-where.

Preacher, "Bloody hell, it's working. I thought the duffer was daft. Go! Go! Go! Track left. Turret left, target tank."

"Away," and they hit another Tiger in the rear and it goes up.

Now, the Krauts are backing up. Preacher sees a few other Cov-enanters and Rams with him. "Left track. Left track. Go. Turret right. Tank."

"Away," and they hit another engine, disabling the Tiger.

"Reload. Reload. Target." A round hits his tank in the rear and throws him forward. Flame leaps up in the rear of his track and he shouts, "Out!" He swipes off his head phones and pushes himself out, falling and burning his hands and arms. He man-ages to get to his feet and run with his driver. They can hear his men's screams as they struggle to get out of the burning tank, then, the ammo cooks off. They're thrown forward by the shock wave, hitting the dirt.

The driver and hull gunner of the last Tiger they hit walk out into the clear. The only sound is the crackle of the flames as the tanks burn. The four men look at each other. They're all wearing pistols. Preacher wearily smiles, reaches into his pocket, and pulls out a pack of cigarettes. He shakes one out and offers it to the nearest German. The German moves for-ward and accepts it. The four men are standing amid the carnage, enjoying a smoke, when the British army catches up to them.

CHAPTER 26

'A' SABRE SQUADRON, 1ˢᵀ BATTALION WELSH GUARDS, PUCKERIDGE, UK, 25 MILES NORTH OF LONDON

1555, 5 October, 1942

SGT Andrew Seymour looks over his shoulder. The better part of a Panzer Division is chasing them. "Driver, stay on the road. If we get stuck, we're fucked."

"Roger, Sergeant. The rain is splashing on my face and my goggles are all fogged up."

"Take them off, Richie. We got to go." A Tiger fires and the round hits a tank behind them. He hears on the platoon net, "Men, we need to find a place to stop and fight."

Another voice on the net, "Sir, there's nothing for miles. We need to get to the London and make our stand there."

"We must blunt this advance so our allies aren't trapped."

"Roger, sir. Looking for big trees."

TOKYO BAY NEAR YOKOSUKA, JAPAN

0500, 6 October, 1942 (2000, 5 October GMT)

LT Chris Hisakawa raises the one large sail as Grandpa Asahi Koizumi manages the tiller. Chris ties off the halyard and walks aft. In Japanese, Chris asks, "Is the tiller heavy?"

Asahi, a professor of sociology at the Seisa Dohto University before the time travel event says, "I'm no fisherman, Genzo. Please. You check."

Chris takes the tiller, "Not so bad. There's some growth on the hull, but once it's off, we'll be a little faster. Still, thank you so much for your help." The fishing boat is now clean and tidy. There are curtains in the cabin, a small kitchen and sitting area where grandfather sleeps. Behind a curtain is another bed for Chris and Fukue.

Asahi, "Thank you, son, for bringing us here."

Chris smiles at the old man, "You are so very welcome."

Fukue joins them with tea, "Here my grandfather." She smiles at Chris, "My beloved."

Chris happily accepts the tea with his free hand. He says, "My love. My honored grandfather. At this point, I have another secret to share. As I said before, I came from 1990. I, however, did not go through the storm at Chitose. I went through the storm over a thousand miles away in the Pacific."

Asahi nods, "And your major was not theater. I know you are much more educated than the fisherman persona you wear."

"I am. My major was mechanical engineering at Annapolis."

Fukue, sitting in the cockpit, looks up at Chris, "You...you are a U.S. Naval officer. Genzo, how old are you?"

"I'm twenty-six. I am a U.S. Naval officer. My rank is Lieutenant Junior Grade and I was shot down near here when we attacked Tokyo. I've been hiding as Genzo."

Asahi says, "This is a huge secret you trust us with. Why now?"

"Because, I hope to escape and wish to take both of you with me."

Asahi asks, "But, how will we be treated in America?"

Chris grins, "You're the family of a naval officer. There I can provide a decent home and a future. In time, you will acquire another teaching position if you wish, or return to Japan after the war."

Fukue asks, "Your real name isn't Genzo?"

"My grandfather in Kobe called me Genzo. He owned a small fishing boat and I would go out with him when we'd come to visit. My father was an engineer with Apple. I grew up in San Francisco. We had a sail boat at Oyster Point and I'd practically live on it during the summer.

Fukue asks, "What did your mother do?"

Chris face becomes solemn, "She raised me and my two sisters. She took care of her home like the Japanese culture expects. She should have taught interior design. It was her passion. Fukue, things are going to change. I love you and I want you as my wife, but I want you to chase your dreams, too. I will support you."

COMMODORE'S BEDROOM, RAF KENLEY

0230, 6 October, 1942

Sam starts awake. She hears her phone ring again and answers it, "Hunt." She looks at the clock, 0230. "Commodore, a major attack from multiple directions."

"Make my plane ready." She hangs up and dresses in her flight suit and gear. She hears the roar of ready 5 launching. As she walks into her office, she hears two A-10s launch, followed by two more F-14s. She climbs into the Beaverette armored car and tells the driver, "My plane."

MAJOR GUNTER'S SQUADRON, IRISH SEA

Finally, they are properly attacking the Americans. He pulls back on his stick and sees the flash of a missile launch in the distance. He turns on the jamming pod mounted on one of his missile pylons and looks at his radar trying to find the British radar plane. He sees several blips closing his aircraft and one turning south. He focuses his reticule on the plane flying away south and fires two missiles. Then, he switches his focus to the

British fighters. One of them goes away, hit by another German missile. He dives, firing his gun on another fighter, smiling when his rounds hit. In the distance, he sees his missiles hit the radar plane. He blasts past the falling Griffin and turns toward Wales.

FU-279, 3000 FEET OVER NORMANDY

Oberst Albrecht Meyer flies his FU-279 immediately behind two V-1 missiles. With him are forty-eight Focke-Wulf fighters. They are nearly all of the advanced fighters Germany has left. They're following a total of ninety V-1s, all at the same altitude. A Junkers JU-88 equipped with radar is watching for the enemy.

The V-1s are following a radar beam, when they cross another beam from Brittany, they will fall on their targets. In the distance he sees the flames of missile launches. By now, they're over the English Channel, and they're under attack from British fighters. Several of the V-1s are hit and fall into the sea.

On radio he says, "Now!" The '279s pull above the V-1s and fire a barrage of anti-aircraft missiles. Seven British fighters are blotted out of the sky. As they pass over the chalk cliffs of Dover, they're fired upon by ack-ack and anti-air missiles. They lose planes, but continue on, dodging the curtain of anti-air fire.

Then, the '279s peel off on their bomb runs. Meyer on radio, "Remember, only south of the Thames. Focus on bombing first. Afterburners on." They all light up their 'burners and scream toward London.

The V-1s drop. Some have high explosive warheads, but most contain napalm.

ARTHUR 1, TAKING OFF FROM RAF KENLEY

Spike cleans up her '14, climbing for altitude. Explosions light up the sky, "Give me targets, Lizard."

"It's a mess, Boss. Okay, right."

She turns her bird. The radio chatter is edged with panic. Spotting a FU-279 between her and the fire, she turns after it, "Grunt."

She watches it drop it ordinance just as she fires a Sidewinder. The heat seeking missile tracks toward the German, but veers off and explodes in a fire on the ground. She switches to guns and gets the line as the German starts climbing out. She puts her rounds behind the cockpit and straight through it, and the bomber rolls left and spins into the inferno below.

She pulls up, going for altitude, "Grunt." She keys the radio, "Calm, people. Use the fire below to silhouette your targets."

ARTHUR 2, TAKING OFF FROM KENLEY

No-No pours on full burners, feeling the thrust at his back. Down runway a napalm bomb detonates, spreading burning liquid everywhere. "Hang on." He rotates early and the big fighter claws its way into the sky, blasting and scattering napalm. As he cleans up the aircraft, he sees tracer fired coming at them. He steepens the climb, then stands the '14 on its tail, but with a full missile load and full tanks, his plane slows. The German plane shoots by him and Von pushes the stick forward, "Come on, baby. Come on."

Robot, "400 feet. 300 feet. 200 feet."

Gradually, No-No gets her under control and they pick up airspeed. A stream of tracers passes in front of them, missing by feet. Finally, the big plane picks up speed and Von goes after the German. He fires a sidewinder and it goes into a burning building. He follows the '279 in its climb and when he's reflected in the fire below, fires another Sidewinder. It flies true, right into the German's right engine.

ARTHUR 1

Spike spots another '279 and fires a Sidewinder, taking it right up it's right engine. They pull up, grabbing for more altitude and tracer rounds pass beneath them. "Where is he?"

"High, right, crossing."

"Roger." She climbs higher, spins, and levels out, right onto the German's six. He pulls up in a right yo-yo and she follows, bleeding energy. The German dives out of the yo-yo, attempting to speed away. She turns into the dive, putting her plane on its right wing, lowers the nose and fires her gun. Her rounds hit the plane's engines and they detonate, pitching the plane forward and down into the conflagration below.

GAWAIN 2, 3000 FEET, IN THE FIGHT OVER LONDON

ENS Mical Degraaff and ENS Steve Ulhe look for their wingman, "Where's Thud?"

Ulhe, "I can't see. It's a mess."

She turns and sees a '279. She adjusts and goes into a shallow dive, firing her gun. Her rounds just graze the enemy's nose and he pulls up. "Gs." She climbs after him and hears the growl of the AIM-9 and pickle it off. It drives right up the '279s engine and explodes. The '279 goes into a spin, then flips, as a wing breaks off. The pilot ejects.

Uhle, "We got one on us." DeGraaff pushes on the throttles and lowers her nose, pulling right to miss a church steeple. "He's still on us, Mic. Break right."

Mic breaks, turning steeply right, them climbs into a yo-yo. "He's still on us. Missile incoming."

She pickles off countermeasures and pulls up violently, "Gs, man." They're hit on the top rear of their fuselage and they go inverted. Mike rolls upright, and the '279 passes right in front of her. She fires her gun barely hitting hits vertical stabilizer.

Their plane is losing altitude rapidly, her throttles wide open, but there's no power. "Steve, we're going down!"

Uhle, "Gawain 2 is hit. Eject. Eject." He pulls the eject rings and blacks out as they shoot out of the aircraft into the night sky.

GAWAIN 1, 1000 FEET IN THE FIGHT

Thud, "Where are they?"

Speedy, "Behind us somewhere. Another '279 on our six."

Thud, "Grunt." He pulls the stick back, hard, leaving controlled flight, his nose going up, then back. Inverted, he hits the German plane with a burst from his gun, rolls level, and climbs out on afterburners, gaining airspeed and controlled flight, leveling off at 200 feet. Below them is hell. South of the Thames, London is burning. Thud climbs for altitude, "Find me something to kill."

"Looking. They're bugging out east."

Thud goes to afterburners, again, racing east.

ALLIED HEADQUARTERS, BUSHY PARK

Eisenhower walks out of his headquarters building carrying files in a box. The building is on fire from a napalm hit. He pauses on the steps. The entire horizon is on fire. The acrid smell of napalm and burning buildings is nearly overwhelming. He walks down the steps and gets into his car and puts the box next to him. His driver, Kay Summersby, asks, "Where?"

"First, Kenley."

She slides their car into the line of trucks and cars streaming south.

GAWAIN 2

ENS Steve Uhle lands in the Thames upstream of the Tower Bridge. He struggles with his chute and manages to get clear. Their jet landed downstream. It missed the Tower Bridge by mere feet. He sees his pilot swinging from a tree on the south bank. The entire sky behind her on fire. He swims to shore and runs down the embankment to the tree. Fire tops a nearby roof as the building collapses. The heat flays his face and raises steam off his wet clothes. He starts climbing the tree.

Mical shouts, "I got it."

There's an explosion close by and flaming debris falls around them. The top of their tree catches fires. She's stopped cutting the shrouds and is slapping at her burning clothes. He gets to her and grabs her around the waist, "Keep cutting! I got you!"

She cuts the last shroud and slumps into his arms. His hands are sticky with blood. She grabs the tree, "Let go. I can get down."

When they are down, they look at each other and turn to jump into the river, swimming for the Tower of London.

GALAHAD FLIGHT

Swede and Pappy race south down the English Channel. Swede, "Brother, what do you see?"

Gandhi, "It's a fur ball over London. There isn't a clean shot."

"Okay, can we hit them exiting?"

"Maybe." On radio, "Arthur, Galahad. We're south bound at high mach. Please advise."

"Galahad, Arthur, welcome to the fight. I hope your knife is sharp."

Gandhi, "Roger, Arthur. Three mikes out."

Then they hear GQ, "Galahad, some are bugging out east."

PERCIVAL 1, IN THE FIGHT

Hot Pants, "Hold on!" She rolls into a tight turn and fires her gun, hitting a '279 as it flashes by. The German's engine explodes. They feel the shudder of rounds hitting their bird. "Fuck no!" and pulls hard for altitude. "Gs." She spins and rolls over the top at 400 feet. "Come on, motherfucker." She rolls upright and fires, hitting her adversary. It inverts and augers in.

GQ, "We're low, sister."

"I know. Shit, I know." She levels off above the rooftops of west London, flying at only 200 knots. She lights her afterburners and tries for altitude and her plane starts pulling to the left. "We have some issues, GQ." She keeps her plane in a slow climb.

PERCIVAL 2, 200 FEET, WEST OF LONDON

LT Pauline 'Trollop' Cash asks, "Mouse, where's Hot Pants?"

ENS Julie 'Mouse' Mulligan, "I don't know. Fuck. Climb. Select AIM-1s." On radio, "All units, Percival 2. Raid warning west. Nine bandits."

"Percival 2, Arthur, engage. We'll come as soon as we can."

Mouse, "Arthur, Percival 2. Roger." On intercom, "I've good lock. Four."

Trollop, "Volley Fox 3," and fires all four of their long-range missiles.

Mouse, "They're firing. On the deck."

Trollop inverts and fires countermeasures. They level out at 100 feet and the German missiles lose lock in the ground clutter. Trollop, "Shit! Gs!" She pulls up violently, barely missing the tower of Windsor Castle.

Mouse, "Two hits. Seven left. They're boring in."

"Okay, we're going to pop under them. Altitude?"

"They're at 4K, 20 miles."

"Great. Hang on." She lights her burners and climbs nearly vertical, then levels off to acquire.

Mouse, "Double Fox 1."

Trollop pickles off two AIM-7s and both missiles hit their targets.

Mouse, "Guns. Break left! Break left!"

Trollop, firing blind, hits a '262 that explodes in front of them. She misses the German by a few feet, the bottom of their plane peppered by shrapnel as they skin by.

MAJOR GUNTER'S '262, WEST OF LONDON

Gunter, "Red flight, time to go home. Report."

His three remaining '262s join with him and they fly north at high speed.

PERCIVAL 1 OVER WEST LONDON

Hot Pants, "It looks ugly down there."

GQ, "I'm looking for a place to land."

"I got good engines. I think the slats are gone on our left wing, but we're flying okay. We're bleeding hydraulic fluid from system 2. One is holding. And, we're bleeding fuel."

"GQ, "So, overall, a good day."

"Yep. Shit. Fire warning. Pulling 2."

GQ looks over his shoulder, "Um, hate to give bad news, but we're on fire."

"Pulling 1."

"Gloria, it's time to leave."

"You're right." She levels the wings and points her bird at a dark patch of ground, "Okay."

GQ, "Percival 1 is punching out over west London." He pulls the ejection handles and they separate from their bird.

FIRE BOAT, THAMES RIVER NEAR WESTMINSTER

Three fire monitors spray water from the Thames onto the buildings on the south bank. The buildings are silhouetted by the flames behind, some of the windows are bright orange eyes glaring out over the city. They are deafened by the roar of the fires; the very air being sucked from the lungs by the heat.

The captain shouts, "Up river!" A pool of burning napalm is floating on the river. The forward fire monitors spray down the floating pool of flame, which scatters it, but does not put it out. They redirect their hoses and spray at the front of the pool, pushing it toward the south bank and away from Westminster.

GALAHAD FLIGHT, 25,000 FEET, NORTH EAST OF DOVER

Gandhi, "Okay, brother Swede. I have good lock and good ID." On radio, "Pappy, volley Fox 3."

The two F/A-14s fire six AIM-1 Long Bow missiles at the retreating FU-279 fighters. Four German planes are blotted out of the air.

Gandhi, "Three are turning toward us."

Swede, "Well, let's thank them for their efforts."

Gandhi, "Lock."

Swede, "Fox 1, Fox 1." The two missiles track towards their target. One is lost in countermeasures and the other flies true, destroying its target.

Both of Pappy's missiles miss and the four jets merge at a combined speed of 2000 mile per hour.

Swede, "Gs," pulling up and taking his engines off afterburner.

Gandhi, "I can't see shit. Hang on." They invert as they slow and Gandhi says, "Pappy broke left. The Germans are bugging out. He might get a shot."

GALAHAD 2

Alcott, "Turn right a little more. Okay, eleven o'clock and closing. 5 miles."

Pappy, "I can't see him." The AIM-9 growls in his ear, "Fox 2." Pappy's Sidewinder flies true, hitting the German jet in its right engine and it detonates. The plane goes into a flat spin and the pilot ejects.

They hear, "Galahad 2, Galahad 1, time to head home. Good shot."

PERCIVAL 2, 2000 FEET, WEST OF LONDON

Mouse, "Damn, he got us." Their Tomcat is shaking violently.

Trollop shuts down the left engine. It grinds to a stop with a loud shriek. "I got alarms on number 2. Where the fuck are we?"

Mouse, "Turn south. Just turn south."

"Okay, but we need a place to land."

Mouse, "I know. Looking." On radio, "RAF Hartford Bridge, Percival 2. Please turn on your lights for emergency landing."

"Percival 2, Hartford. Lights coming on." Then, to their left, they see runway lights turn on.

Mouse, "Thank you. We have visual. Request clearance for emergency landing."

"Percival 2, the field is yours. Winds at 210 and 10 knots. Rolling the fire brigade."

Mouse, "Roger. Thank you." On intercom, "Can we make it?"

Trollop, "I don't know. Stretching it out." When she puts down the flaps, the plane buffets, but their sink rate slows. She lowers the gear and they hear banging and grinding.

Mouse, "This is going to be fun."

Trollop, "Hang on." She flares and touches down. When the main gear hits, the left tire explodes and they veer left. She counters with rudder and cuts her right engine. The plane skids down the runway, then lurches left onto the grass. The right main gear collapses and the right wing digs in, spinning them right. The left gear fails and the tail hits the ground. They stop, nose up, facing back the way they had come in.

Mouse, "Good landing."

TOWER, RAF KENLEY

LT Hammond walks around the top of the tower. Kenley is burning. A fire engine is spraying burning napalm off the runway. Firefighters are battling the burning A-10 hangers and the engulfed barracks. The fires are too close to the JP-5 tank farm. LT Colonel Andrews joins him, "Can we land planes?"

"In a bit. We need to clear the runway."

"The Commodore is overhead."

"Oh." He picks up a mic, "Arthur, Hamm, in Yankee tower. Request status?"

Lizard, "Good to hear you, Hamm. Is the field clear?"

"Negative, but should be in about 15 minutes. Napalm on the runway."

"The boss wants to know if you have a head count."

"Negative. We will have losses."

"Roger."

An ammo bunker goes high order. In the light from the fires, they can see the shock wave coming at them as a cloud of debris shoots hundreds of feet into the air. The shock wave hits, shattering the tower windows and hitting them in the chest like a sledge hammer. Fiery debris rains down onto the runways.

Hammond gets up and gropes for a mic, "Arthur, Hamm, make that 40 minutes on the runway. Did you see that?"

Lizard, "Yeah, we saw. Roger, 40 minutes." Then, "All units, Kenley is closed. Alternate field, Hartford, is open."

Hammond, "My apologies."

Lizard, "Boss is asking if we can get an away team to Hartford?"

Hammond, "We'll make it happen."

ARTHUR 1 OVER RAF KENLEY

Spike, "Okay, we need a fuel check." After the fuel check, she gets on the radio, "All open airfields in southern UK, this is Arthur. If you are open for landing, please turn on your lights."

"Yankee, Hartford, lights on."

"Yankee, Biggin Hill, lights on."

"Yankee, Tangmere, lights on."

"Yankee, Middle Wallop, lights on."

"Yankee, Dover, lights on."

"Yankee, Heathrow, we are closed."

Spike, "If you are closed, standby. Are there any other open fields?"

The radio is silent. "Very well. All squadron leaders, Yankee, sort out your birds to keep a quarter in the air at all times. They should have gun ammo and fuel at the outlying fields."

All remaining squadrons check in, "Roger, Yankee."

Major Floyd B. Parks, USMC, commander VFMA-324, Devil Dogs, "Arthur, Dog 1, be advised, I'm down to 5 usable aircraft."

Spike, "Understood, Dog 1. How are Rusty and Dusty?"

LCDR William N. Leonard, USN, commander of VA-11, Iron Angels, "Arthur, Rusty 1, I have 6. Three of them made emergency landings."

"Understood, Rusty. How are Golden Gator and Bad Bird?"

"VA-211, Dragons have lost two, and VA-213, Hell Hawks, have lost one."

"Keep me posted. Status on Percival flight and Gawain 2?"

Mouse, "Arthur, Percival 2. We're safely down at RAF Hartford. Bird needs significant repair."

Spike, "Injuries?"

Trollop, "None, but my pride."

Spike continues, "Percival 1? Gawain 2? Percival 1? Gawain 2? Anyone know where they are?"

Speedy, "We lost them over London."

Mouse, "Sorry, Arthur, we haven't heard from them."

Then, "Arthur 1, Valkyrie 1, we're recovering downed pilots as fast as we can. All birds are out."

Spike, "Valkyrie, Arthur, roger." On intercom, "Fuck. Fuck. Fuck." She turns on her running lights, and on radio, "No-No, get on my wing. We're going hunting." She turns her plane east.

Robot, "On our way, Spike."

Speedy, "On our way, Spike."

NOB, "On your wing in a bit."

Spike, "Galahad, take the rest and refuel and rearm."

Gandhi, "Roger, Arthur."

Then, they hear Air Chief Marshal Hugh Dowding, "Spike, Stuffy, what are your intentions?"

"Stuffy, Spike. Fighter sweep up the channel. They need to know we still have fight."

"Spike, Stuffy. God speed. God speed."

CHAPTER 27

WESTMINSTER, LONDON

0339, 6 October, 1942

Churchill stands at a window looking out across the Thames. South London is burning. People are fleeing across the bridges. Fire fighters are desperately trying to save all they can north of the river, battling scattered fires. Air Marshal Arthur Tedder says, "Sir, Yankee has lost three Tomcats and nine Warthogs. No status on two of the crews."

"Thank you, Arthur." They stand, mesmerized by the magnitude of the fire. A fire boat gallantly attempts to put down flames on the south bank.

"Sir, is it as bad as it looks?"

Churchill sighs, "Worse."

"Sir, please? Is the King safe?"

"He is. His heir, though. We've lost contact."

"Where was she?"

"Somewhere between Buckingham and Windsor. Heathrow was hit by V-1s and bombs, and it's so near Windsor."

"Why was she moved in the middle of the night?"

"My fault. When I realized the target was London, I asked him to split them up, so at least one would survive."

"But she was at Windsor."

"She was. When I realized the Germans were leaving north of

the Thames alone, I ordered them back."

"Heathrow is still manned. I'll put out the word."

"Do so, but don't make a fuss. His Majesty would not approve."

ARTHUR 1, 35,000 FEET OVER DOVER

Spike on radio, "Lights on. Stack it up. Close formation." The big planes move very close together, wings overlapping.

Lizard, "Boss, what are we doing?"

"We're presenting one radar return." Again, on radio, "Once we break, the lights go off. To avoid collisions, any one of us can call lights. If we hear the call, we turn on our lights for one second then shut them off. We use vertical separation. I have the top, angels 20 and up. No-No, you have 15 to 20. Gunner, you have 10 to 15. Thud, you have 10 to the deck. If you have to leave your zone, call the name of the pilot your swapping with and say up or down for the direction they need to go. Clear?"

The three RIO's answer in the affirmative.

GERMAN AIRFIELD, NORMANDY

0503, 6 October, 1942 (0403 GMT)

Oberstleutnant Albrecht Meyer climbs out of his fighter shouting, "Refuel! Schnell! Schnell! Rearm!"

A sedan pulls up next to his plane and Reichsmarschall Hermann Goering climbs out. Meyer salutes, "Heil Hitler!"

"Heil Hitler. Tell me Oberstleutnant, how did the battle go?"

"Herr Reichsmarschall, General major Weber's plan went very well. We've destroyed at least four of their fighters and south London burns. I over flew their airbase at Kenley and it was in flames and an ordinance bunker went up. Those that survive are scattered to other fields. Some may have run out of fuel. We must strike again, immediately."

PERCIVAL 1, EAST OF RAF HEATHROW

0406, 6 October, 1942

Gloria looks around, her parachute bundled in her arms. She's standing in a small field and a stone barn is silhouetted against the flames in the east. South of her trees are burning, the flames crowning and jumping from tree to tree. West of her, there is less fire. She sees the fire from her own aircraft. Spinning again, she sees movement and walks toward it, finding GQ struggling to his feet.

He looks up at her, "Am I glad to see you. Please, a hand. I hurt my knee."

"Yeah," and she pulls him up. "We need to go." They hobble to a nearby farm house, but the door is locked and there's no one home. "Damn, I left my lock picks in my other pants." She hears a noise and looks out. She sees the beam of a flashlight illuminating the fender of a car.

She helps GQ to sit on the stoop, "Stay here. Hopefully that light is a ride."

She walks rapidly toward the light and sees a large car on a road. 'Hello? Is your car running?"

The person holding the light spins and shines it in her eyes, "If it were, we'd be on our way, wouldn't we?"

Gloria grins, "Yeah. Light down please? Lieutenant Houlihan. We were shot down."

The man bent over the engine straightens up, "Do you know anything about vehicles?"

"I do. What's the problem?"

"Well, we seem to have sprung a radiator leak courtesy of all this debris."

There's a long thick branch sticking out of the radiator. She checks and the engine is extremely hot. She stops and thinks,

"Look, I think there's a chicken coop back there. So, I'll go get some eggs. Do you have any tools?"

"There's a small kit in the boot."

"Right. You get the tools, I need pliers. I'll get the eggs and find some water."

"You can get us on the road with eggs?"

She chuckles, "Oh, yes. Then, can you give my RIO and myself a ride to Kenley?"

"You're one of the Yank flyers. Of course, we can."

GERMAN AIRFIELD, NORMANDY

0521, 6 October, 1942 (0421 GMT)

Oberstleutnant Meyer cleans up his aircraft and makes a climbing left turn as his twenty-four FU-279s can join him. When he reaches altitude, his radar warning goes off, "What is this? They know we're coming. Should I abort? This is the main chance. If we wait, they will reorganize. We go."

ARTHUR FLIGHT, SOUTH ENGLISH CHANNEL

Robot, on radio, "Raid warning. Ten plus climbing through angels 6 bearing 035. 60 miles out."

Lizard, "Roger, Robot. Break on my mark. We volley at 25 miles."

"Roger." On intercom, "No-No, we found them first."

"Good work, sis. Shit, this is hard." No-No focuses on Spike ahead and above; Thud above and right; and Gunner above and left. They're so close their wings overlap, presenting one radar return.

Spike, "I'm transmitting in the clear."

Lizard, "What are we doing?"

"Baiting the hook." In the clear, "Hey Hans. Aren't all you ass-holes called Hans? The Dragon Lady is flying. Let's dance."

MEYER'S FU-279

His men are all talking at once, and there she is, clear in his scope. "Attack group, shut up. We shoot on the numbers and God damn it, don't run into each other."

To himself, "Okay Drachendame, what's your game? You don't give up so easy."

He sees explosions in the sea below, "Damn you all. Don't drop your ordinance. Jamming pods on." He flips the switch.

ARTHUR FLIGHT

On radio Spike, "Knights, break, break."

Nix gently dives to clear Spike's plane, "Do we have a radar picture?"

Robot on intercom, "Roger. 24 inbound. They're jamming. I think they've fired."

Nix on intercom, "I see it. Fox 3. Fox 3. G's" He inverts and dives, firing off countermeasures.

Speedy, "Bust some moves, Thud."

Thud, "Nope, it's one missile. Keep radar lock on."

Speedy, "What?"

Thud aligns his plane and fires his gun. The inbound missile explodes and their two missiles find their targets.

MEYER'S FU-279

Meyer sees the one jet become four on his screen, 'Shit! Shit! Shit!" He releases his air to ground ordinance and climbs for altitude, spinning around looking for the Americans. In the dark, he sees nothing.

ARTHUR FLIGHT

Spike, "Walk me onto a target, Lizard."

"We have four climbing. Our guys are diving. Okay, good lock." On radio, "Fox 1."

Spike fires one missile and it corkscrews into its target. The '279's engine explodes and it falls, streaming fire.

Lizard, "Missile, 10 o'clock, low."

Spike, "Got it." She inverts and crosses the missile firing off chaffs and flares. She climbs to engage the enemy, "Where is he?"

"Two, high."

Gunner, "Lights."

Spike flips on their lights, then off. The plane in front of her does not. "Get me lock."

Lizard, "Fox 1." She fires.

Gunner, "Splash one."

Spike's missile tracks right to the '279's engine, detonating, perforating the aft fuel tanks and blowing both engines, creating a comet tail of fire. They see the pilot eject. Lizard, "Break left. Countermeasures."

Spike turns sharply and pulls up, pickling off chaff and flares, and the German missile explodes in the cloud of chaff.

Speedy, "Lights."

Spike flips her lights on and off again.

MEYER'S '279

Meyer turns right, missing her break. He sees the lights turning on and off and sees she's above and to his left. He pulls violently to the left, and on radio, "They're using lights to avoid friendly fire."

Thousands of feet below him he sees a fireball.

It's the third time he's set up his quarry, but she has evaded him. It has to be the Drachendame. In the light of another destroyed plane, he sees a '14 below him and pursues. He can see lights below. He's somewhere over England. On radio, "When they turn on lights, turn yours on."

ARTHUR FLIGHT, 17,000 FEET OVER DOVER

Robot, "He's pulling right. 8 miles."

Nix, "On it."

Robot, "Good tone." On radio, "Lights."

Nix flashes his lights on and off, but the fighter in front of them does not, "Fox 1."

Their AIM-7 flies straight into the enemy plane and detonates. There's a massive secondary explosion and the plane falls out of the sky like a spent firework.

Nix sees the shadow of a plane dive past him. He inverts and pursues. "Gunner, swap up."

Gunner, "Will do, No-No."

Nix tells Robot, "Lights." She makes the call and he fires his gun. As the tracer track meets the jet, he sees the light come on, "SHIT!" The rounds hit, taking out the cockpit.

Robot, "Good kill, No-No." On radio, "Splash 1."

Nix, "The lights?"

Robot, "Wrong configuration."

Spike sees a '14 and a '279 below her, "Gunner, break up. Swap."

Gunner, "Breaking."

She follows the '279 as he flattens out and begins climbing

to pursue Gunner. "Lights." The plane she's chasing turns his lights on a moment after she does. He inverts and dives.

Spike, "Thud, you only, lights." Thud turns on his lights and so does the plane she's chasing. She fires her gun and nails both of his engines.

MEYER'S '279

Meyer feels the rounds hit his jet. The screaming, grinding noise is deafening as his engines detonate. Warning lights show both engines on fire and his aircraft is shaking violently. He pulls the extinguishers and levels out. He looks at his compass and turns north. Mid-turn there's a loud bang and he starts rolling. The nose angles down in a spin.

On radio, 'Gold 1 is hit. Going down. The fucking Drachen-dame got another kill." He pulls the ejection handle.

ARTHUR FLIGHT

Speedy, "They're bugging out. Lights."

The Black Knights turn on lights and Thud fires an AIM-1 at the fleeing Germans. No-No, Gunner, and Spike fire their remaining missiles. Despite evasive maneuvers and countermeasures, three more jets go away. One hit by Gunner and No-No, and one each by Thud and Spike.

On radio, "All units, Whiskey Golf Sierra, raid warning north. 16 climbing out of Ouston. Designate raid 4."

"Texas flight, Center, engage raid 4 with all available aircraft. Arthur, Center, status?"

Spike, "Arthur flight is bingo and skosh."

Gandhi, "Center, Galahad and Camelot flight is up. Kenley is back in business."

Spike, "Galahad, Arthur, roger. Did you get my pre-raid brief?"

"Arthur, Galahad, roger. We will adopt."

"Galahad, Arthur, roger. Good hunting."

CHAPTER 27

BARRACKS, GRUMMAN FACTORY, BETHPAGE, NEW YORK

1144, 5 October, 1942 (0444, 6 October GMT)

CDR Norman 'Oyster' Osterman, commanding officer of the VFA-33, Tomcatters, is in his flight gear and running from door to door, knocking and shouting, "Brief in twenty minutes. We gotta go."

CDR John 'Marshall' Dillon, commanding officer of the VFA-22, Redcocks, steps out in his boxers, "What's up, Oyster?"

"London is burning. They need us there yesterday."

Marshall nods and goes back into his room. A female ensign walks out in her pajamas, "Does this include the pilots for the Knights?"

Oyster, "It includes everyone who's completed '14 certification. Get your people going."

PERCIVAL 1, EAST OF RAF HEATHROW

0512, 6 October, 1942

The car is so hot the thermostatic slats are open. Gloria reaches in and pinches closed all the damaged radiator tubes she can reach. Then, she accesses the radiator through the engine compartment and pinches the tubes inside. GQ has limped his way over and is sitting on the running board. "Gloria, did you notice that this thing is a Bentley?"

"I did."

The driver asks, "Sir, are you okay?"

"My knee is banged up, but I'll live."

The back door opens and a teen-age girl steps out, "Sir, I heard you are injured. May I help you into the car?"

He struggles to stand and the girl helps him. Once on his feet, he looks out at the fires. The smoke is getting heavier and the fires closer. "Gloria, you don't have time to let it cool down."

"I know, Byron. Almost done."

"I'm not rushing you, but the fires are getting closer."

Gloria asks, "Does this car have anything I can mix the eggs in?"

The girl says, "We have a container for ice in the back."

Gloria stands up, "Please, fetch it."

The girl gets the container, then helps GQ into the left front seat. Gloria breaks three eggs into the container and beats them up with her knife. The girl asks, "May I ask how this will work?"

"Where the egg escapes the radiator, it cooks and plugs the leak."

"Amazing."

Gloria looks at the driver, "Start the car and let it idle. Don't rev it."

"Yes, ma'am."

Once the car is running, she adds some water, then the eggs, then fills it up with water. She checks for leaks. At first, it leaks pretty good, then the leaks slow to a drip. She tops off the water and puts on the cap.

They all get in the car and Gloria says, "Kenley, please."

"Um, ma'am, I have another stop first."

The girl says, "Donald, the lieutenant said Kenley."

"Very good. Lieutenant, do you have a radio?"

GQ grins, "I've already called it in."

YANKEE CONTROL, RAF KENLEY

0551, 6 October, 1942

Spike walks in, "Report."

"Texas has hit three fighters. Galahad and Lancelot have accounted for five more. Texas has lost one. Valkyrie 027 is outbound to recover. Four A-10s are supporting the recovery..."

Fluffy and Andrews walk into the control center. Andrews says, "Boss, go to bed."

Spike spins, acquiring her target, "We have fighters engaged and pilots down."

Fluffy shakes his head, "And the duty officer can handle it. We need you sharp and you haven't gotten shit for sleep for two days. Go to bed."

Spike shakes her head, "Not while I have a pilot down."

Fluffy picks up a phone, "Are you going to force me to call the flight surgeon? He's treating burn victims and has more important shit to do. Go. To. Bed."

Cooper walks in with a plate of food. "Fluffy's right, but eat first. I'll brief you on our personnel casualties. That, and I have a message."

She reads the message, hands it back, takes the plate, and sits back down. "Go ahead."

Cooper says, "In the entire detachment, we have 23 fatalities and 51 injured. Most fatalities and wounds are from fire and falling debris. Because of our overmanning, we are still fully functional. Fuel farm was protected. We lost four barracks, two ammo bunkers, and six hangers. Most were for the A-10s. All the hard shelters survived. As you no doubt know, London is burning. Something to note, Old Coulsdon, Whyteleafe, and Warlingham all sent their fire brigades to protect the base, instead of taking care of their own towns. We have to do something for them."

Spike nods, "We will. I need some ideas, so please write it up."

Fluffy, "Any orders for when you are asleep?"

Spike gives him a wan smile, "Fluffy, my notification orders stand." She takes the last bit of a sandwich and looks down. She doesn't remember eating both sandwiches, but they're gone. "You're right, guys. Good night."

EASTERN FRONT, NORTH EASTERN POLAND

0708, 6 October, 1942 (0608 GMT)

The sky is slowly turning grey as Hauptman Schwartz lies on the roof beam of a damaged barn, scanning the Russian positions to his east. All night he's been hearing engines in the distance. Then he sees a tank, then the vague outline of another, then another. They're hidden, but his position allows him to see their movement. He keys his radio, "Battalion, Watch Post 3, the Russian armor have closed the frontier in regimental strength. It's the big gun tanks."

"Are you certain?"

"I see over eighty tanks, but many are hidden. They're moving very carefully."

"Understood."

COMMODORE'S BEDROOM, RAF KENLEY

1146, 6 October, 1942

Sam wakes up. She stretches and rubs her face. Light is streaming in from the window. She hears two F/A-14s land. Climbing out of bed, she sees her flight suit and gear laid out. She hears two more '14s land. She heads for the shower.

Clean, brushed, dressed, and finally awake, she walks into her office. She stops abruptly, sitting with Andrews and drinking coffee are CDRs Osterman and Dillon. They're both in flight gear. "Oyster? Marshal? It's really good to see you, but why? I thought the Vinson was in the Pacific." She hears more aircraft landing and Radar hands her a cup of joe.

Oyster grins, "It is. We flew to Bethpage, picked up new Tomcats, and came out here to lend a hand."

Marshall laughs, "We heard there was a short mustached son-of-a-bitch making a fuss."

Spike smiles in return, "God, it's good to see you guys. How many aircraft?" She hears a turboprop coming in.

Oyster, "We're both fully manned with twelve. I have the Tomcatters and Marshal has the Redcocks."

Marshal, "We also escorted twelve replacement A-10s, twelve more turkeys with new crews that are slated for you and four replacement birds."

Spike takes a deep breath, "Thank you. We're on the raggedy edge. I got the message last night. They want to split the squadron. Radar, if they're on the ground, I need Swede and Thud. Oh, and get me Too Tall."

"Yes, Spike," and walks out.

She looks back to Oyster and Marshal, "Guys, we need everyone sorted out. We lost barracks last night. We were fire-bombed. Master Chief Bond will help you with that. I'll brief you in when you've had a chance to get settled." She stands and they do too, "Oh, and guys, pass it around to your people, I don't need or want the pomp and bullshit that comes with a star. I'm Spike, okay? And guys, thank you so much for coming."

Oyster, "Yes, Spike. We get it. And, you're welcome." As they walk out, Cooper comes in with Swede and Thud. Cooper pours coffee for everyone, "Too Tall is in Portsmouth."

"What's he doing?"

"I'm not sure. AC1 Berman helped him load a bunch of radar equipment onto a truck. Said it had to do with the V-1s."

Spike nods, "Okay," then turns to Swede and Thud. "They want to split the squadron into two. Swede, you'll keep the Black Knights. Thud, you'll command the new squadron. Who do you guys want for XO?'

Thud, "Shouldn't Packs get the top job? He was XO before me?"

Spike, "I've chosen you two. He'll get his own squadron soon."

Swede, "If I ask for Packs, do I get Mossberg, too?"

"Yes."

Swede, "Packs is a great XO and the two of them are a great flight team."

Thud, "I thought you would choose Hot Pants."

Swede looks at him, "I take it you know?"

Thud laughs, "If I know, everybody knows."

Swede, "If I choose her, it's a conflict. With her and GQ in your squadron, we can go public."

Thud turns to Spike, "Do you think Hot Pants is ready for XO?"

"I do."

"I do, too. So, I want Hot Pants and GQ. It feels like we're choosing teams for after church softball."

Spike laughs, "Okay, Boyington and Alcott have been flying with you, Swede, so keep them. You can also keep Gunner and NOB. Thud, I want you to get Trollop and Mouse. I know you've been flying with Degraaff and Ulhe, but Degraaff is in the hospital and GQ is injured. Do you think Ulhe can fly with Gloria?"

Thud, "I'll try it out. I'll also keep GQ and Degraaff on the books. Maybe they can make it back."

Spike, "Okay, of the original crew, that leaves Bug and Joker along with Wingnut and Cuddles."

Swede, "Thud, you have walking wounded, to I'll take Wingnut and Cuddles. They've been trooping around with the green machine, so they might be healed up."

Thud, "Then, I have Bug and Joker."

Spike, "Okay for our old new people, Swede, can you take Cochran and a wounded Everling?"

Swede, "Yeah, but Everling is going home, four broken ribs."

Thud, "I'll take No-No and Robot and you can have Landes and Carnegie. That give me six and you six."

Swede, "Good."

Spike hands them each a paper, "Here are your new aircrew and ground crew to sort out. We need a name for Thud's squadron."

Thud grins, "That's easy, the White Knights. Do we have a number?"

Spike, "No, that didn't give us one, so we'll choose. You'll be VFA-155. Sister squadrons."

Swede, "That leaves call signs."

Spike smiles, "Yeah, the Monty Python names don't stretch to two squadrons. Any ideas?"

Thud, "How about we keep Galahad and Gawain?"

Spike, "The only issue I had with Gawain is it's hard to make out sometimes. Lancelot is clearer." She pauses, "You know, we don't need Monty Python any more. Our encryption is good. So, let's change everything. I'm thinking the Black Knights go back to Knight and the White Knights go with Rook. I'll continue as Arthur, unless I'm in control, then I'm Yankee actual. That way we're not confused about whether I'm in the air or on the ground."

The two CO's look at each other and smile. Thud says, "Perfect."

EMBASSY DISTRICT, STOCKHOLM, SWEDEN

1433, 6 October, 1942 (1333 GMT)

Joachim von Ribbentrop, the German Foreign Minister rides with the German Ambassador to Sweden in the back of an embassy car racing from the airport to the Russian Embassy. Ribbentrop says, "The message I deliver is urgent. The Russians are massing at our border and our intelligence suggests they believe it is us who are preparing to attack."

"Why would they believe such a thing? Surely, they understand that England must fall first?"

"We don't know. What we do know, it must be stopped."

Their car speeds around a corner and plows into a truck pulling out of an alley. A man runs from a doorway and looks into the back of the embassy car. He checks the bodies, the driver and both passengers are dead. He takes Ribbentrop's briefcase and walks away.

The driver of the truck climbs out and waits for the police, not looking at the British man walking away. He smiles. The Brit paid him very well.

CONTROL TOWER, RAF KENLEY

1510, 6 October, 1942

Spike is on the outside walkway of the tower. She can see the entire base. Already, heavy equipment is clearing debris and construction is underway. Thank God, the medical clinic was spared. It's packed and they're using the gym for the overflow. All the medical facilities in London are overwhelmed, so she opened the base clinic for injured civilians. The hard shelters survived, and the fuel storage yard.

She looks out north. London is still burning, a dark, ugly haze rising from the city. Another thing to be thankful for, it's raining.

The flight line is packed. There are forty F/A-14s, thirty A-10s, and cargo plane after cargo plane bringing in people and equipment. They had to park the Merry Men at RAF Biggin Hill about five miles away. She watches two '14s take off in a beautiful roar. They're Tomcatters, "I've no idea who's flying those planes. I need to meet the new people."

Then, another C-130 lands and drops its ramp. Marines come out, hauling their equipment and are met by a line of buses ready to take them to the front. Andrews joins her, "Spike, the commander of the 82nd Airborne, Major General Ridgeway, would like to see you."

She takes one last look and turns to the door. As she's walking down the stairs, Fluffy bounds up, three at a time, "What were you doing?"

"Fluffy, I was looking at the damage."

"A sniper could have shot you."

She sighs, "I'm sorry, Fluffy. It didn't cross my mind."

"Boss, there are times when you terrify me."

"Well, right now, I have to talk to a general, okay?"

"Roger, Spike."

She walks into her office, "General Ridgeway, good morning. Welcome to Kenley," and she offers her hand.

Ridgeway takes it, "You're taller than I imagined."

Spike smiles, "I get that a lot. I'm so glad you came."

Ridgeway, "This is my chief of staff, Colonel Douglas."

Douglas shakes her hand, "A pleasure, ma'am."

Cooper pours coffee for her and Andrews and refills Ridgeway's and Douglas'."

Spike, "Well, let's get to it. How many transports do you have?"

Ridgeway, "Twenty-four. The division is scattered across three airfields. I know you asked for us, specifically, and I've been assured that you know what we can do. But what is it you have in mind?"

She nods, "I need you to make an opposed landing on an airfield. With twenty-four transports, how many battalions can you drop into a hot LZ at once?"

"A hot LZ?"

"Sorry, a landing zone. A hot LZ is an opposed landing."

"What's the enemy troop strength?"

Spike, "According to the Brits, it's about two battalions. These guys are Germany's best."

"Twenty-four isn't enough. I need at least another twenty for the first wave to have a chance."

"How many transports for your whole division?"

"It's never been done. Seventy more transports to drop the whole division. Almost one hundred planes."

Spike nods in satisfaction, "I'll get them. This is the plan, gentlemen..."

SLIPWAY 2, NAVY YARD PUGET SOUND, BREMERTON, WASHINGTON

0838, 6 October, 1942 (1638 GMT)

Admiral King is at a podium near the immense bow of the new supercarrier Enterprise. "I am extremely proud of our ship yard team; the engineers, the craftsmen and women, the thousands of people who worked extremely long hours in incredibly difficult situations to produce this first in class aircraft carrier. I would also like to recognize the hard work and extreme diligence given to this project by the Defense Special Projects office represented by Admiral Klindt, the director, and Commodore Warren, the carrier projects officer. Captain Warren has logged thousands of flight hours between three shipyards and his exceptional attention to detail is now bearing fruit.

"I would like to recognize Captain Winters. Captain Winters came back in time as the commanding officer of the VFA-22, Fighting Redcocks. He was promoted to Captain and given command of Carrier Air Wing 9. Most recently, he commanded the heavy cruiser, San Francisco. I have full confidence in his ability to navigate this vessel into harm's way. Before I invite him up, I would also like to acknowledge the crew. A shipyard builds a warship, making it strong and powerful, but only the sailors who man her can give the vessel it's heart and soul. Although, it will be some time before she is ready for sea, the crew assembled here is working alongside the shipyard. They're learning their ship, by helping to build her. Captain Winters, please address your crew."

Captain Jeremy 'Frosty' Winters walks to the podium. "I would first like to thank Mrs. Roosevelt, The First Lady of the United States, for honoring us with her presence and agreeing to christen this vessel. Thank you, Admiral King, Admiral Klindt, Rear Admiral Freeman, Rear Admiral Taffinder, Commodore Warren. Thank you for coming and thank you for bringing this warship to life. Rear Admiral Taffinder, your engineers, architects, and superb craftsmen have taken an enormous leap forward in what is even possible to be built. Commodore Warren, your encyclopedic knowledge of ship design and modular construction methods have made this day possible. Rear Admiral Freeman, this project required coordination of subcontractors, water access, rail and motor access throughout this region. Naval District 13 moved mountains to make it all work. Admiral Klindt, your steadfast leadership brought all of this together into a complete whole.

Admiral King, thank you for trusting a group of officers not yet born to contribute to the battle we all now face.

"My crew, each of you will contribute to the soul and spirit of this vessel. Fifty years from now, you may have grandchildren serving where you now stand. The war fighting spirit, positive attitude, and gumption, you build into the very grains of her metal will be a guiding light for them. On the eve of battle Admiral Horatio Nelson famously wrote out in signal flags, 'England expects that every man will do his duty.' When the battle then ensued, the combined French and Spanish fleets were destroyed at Trafalgar. America expects we of the USS Enterprise CV-14 to do our duty and steam across war torn waters to deal decisively with the forces of tyranny arrayed before us. Thank you. Madam First Lady, do you wish to say anything before we proceed?"

Eleanor Roosevelt walks to the microphone, "Thank you, Captain Winters. Gentlemen, your words are inspiring. This incredible feat of American industry is amazing. It is also, very, very important. The forces of Imperial Japan, the forces of Nazi Germany, the forces of fascist Italy, must never prevail. My only wish is that the President could have excused himself from his duties and been here to see this. Thank you so much for inviting me to participate in the birth of a new navy."

She steps from the microphone and takes her position just off the stem. There is a banging as the final holding blocks are released. The ship sits motionless. They can hear the hydraulic jacks pushing the huge vessel. She swings the bottle of champagne, and just as it shatters against the stem, the Enterprise begins to move.

The great ship picks up speed and there's an enormous rattle of slowdown chains and the whir of the slow down cables. The stern meets the water, creating an immense wave. The spectators on Bay Street in Port Orchard scramble out of the way of the incoming wave. As the stern lifts in the water, the ship groans and the blocks tumble. Then, she's fully in the waters of Sinclair Inlet and gliding toward Port Orchard. Tug boats pull on their lines and the big ship slows and stops. Never before has so large a ship been launched on ways. Then, the tugs maneuver her to pier 3 where she'll be fitted out.

BRIXTON ROAD, SOUTH LONDON

1640, 6 October, 1942

It's Sergeant Thompson's first ride on a double decker bus. The view is incredible, but the sights are tragic. They're surrounded by burned out and still burning buildings. The stench of smoke, burning fuel, and burned bodies is pervasive. His bile rises and he fights it down. He realizes that these people need him. They need the US Marines.

Lieutenant Maki climbs the stairs and sits down with Thompson, "You know, sir, when the admiral finds out you're here, he's going to be pissed."

Maki grins, "He told me to come. I'm supposed to brief some people tomorrow. I told him today I needed to see what the Germans have."

"He's allowing you on the front lines?"

"That's where the German tanks are."

"When the shooting starts, stay in the rear, and stay down."

"I know how to shoot."

"Yes, sir, but you don't know how to be a Marine. You'd just get in the way."

"Fair enough."

YANKEE CONTROL CENTER, RAF KENLEY

1656, 6 October, 1942

LCDR Michael 'Too Tall' Mohr skids his jeep to a stop and

jumps out. He grabs a rolled-up map and nods to the security guard as he goes into the building. He goes to the Commodore's office, knocks, and walks in. He stops when he sees a general shaking Spike's hand, "I'm sorry, ma'am, um, sir."

Spike, "General Ridgeway, this is Commander Mohr. What he doesn't know about electronic warfare has not been invented. He's the officer I told you would eliminate the German anti-air."

Ridgeway shakes Mohr's hand, "A pleasure, Commander."

"Thank you, sir." He turns to Spike, "I'm sorry to interrupt, but I got it."

Spike sees his suppressed excitement, "I see." She turns to Ridgeway, "I'm sorry, but we have a great deal to prepare. Could you excuse us, please?"

Ridgeway smiles, "Of course. Your plan is good. Hopefully, we can get the pieces together." He and his chief of staff walk out.

As the door closes, she turns to Cooper and hands him a note, "Take this to the tower. Thank you." Turning back to Too Tall, "You figured out what?"

Mike smiles, "How the Germans are targeting the V-1s." He lays out his map. "I identified discrete radar frequencies transmitting here, here, and here. I found them again over London. The three beams are aimed to converge over the southern part of the city. They pass right over Kenley. That gives the V-1s a vector, but not a range. That's when I discovered another radar beam transmitting from Brittany. It intercepts the other three beams over London."

"Huh, well, son-of-a-bitch. It's simple and really smart. What are you going to do with it? You do have a plan, right?"

"I outfitted a British destroyer with a directional beam of the same frequency as the one from Brittany. The beam is adjustable if the Germans change frequency. The Royal Navy is parking it in the channel. When the radar bird picks up a missile attack, the destroyer will illuminate. All the buzz bombs will crash into the channel."

Spike starts laughing, "Oh, my God. I'm glad you're on our side."

"It's a good idea then?"

"Yes, Mike. It's brilliant. It will work. It'll look like the missiles hit a wall. They'll waste time, money, and resources building weapons that no longer work."

"I just wish I could have finished it before the last attack. I'm sorry."

"Mike, you can't dwell on it. It will destroy you. We win every battle we can, and learn from our losses. You figured it out. That's what's important."

"I don't know. Thousands of people died because I was too slow. If I can't save them, how can I be a leader?"

She motions him to a chair and puts her head out the door, "May we have tea and some cookies? Thank you." She sits down. "You know, I asked Dixie that once. He told me that no one is ever ready for leadership. When we look up at the wise leaders above us, we all count on their experience, wisdom, and nobility of purpose. He told me the truth. They're a bunch of terrified old guys hoping and praying they don't screw things up. It's how it has always been. No one is ready. What counts in the end is character, and you have that."

He looks up and meets her gaze, "Thank you, Spike."

"We need to finalize the plans to take back Ouston. We go tomorrow morning."

"I'm on it."

"Thank you, Mike." She smiles as he walks out the door just at the tea tray is being carried in. She nods as the aid pours her a cup and sets two cookies on the saucer. "Thank you." She takes a deep breath and picks up the top paper in her in box.

There's a knock and Squadron Leader George 'Johnny' Johnson, commander of the RAF Griffin, Texas squadron, walks in, "How's it going, Spike?"

She looks up and smiles, "A hell of a night."

"Yes, it was. I have an official question, then a personal question. What order would you prefer?"

"Right now, professional first."

"Righty-o. We have the Merry Men at Biggin Hill. With all the Yanks showing up, do you want us to transfer them back to the RAF?"

"I'm perfectly happy with that. Would you allow me to write up awards for them? They were indispensable."

"American or British awards?"

"American, if I can. I would rather not delve into the arcane magic of the British award system."

"Okay, I'll pass it up the chain, but I don't see a problem. Now to the personal."

"Sure."

"If things settle a bit, are you still willing to honor your promise of a date?"

She's silent, then, "Oh, I remember. Of course, when we can find the time. You're not making a big deal out of this, are you?"

"Of course not. I'm looking forward to it though. An island of normality in a river of chaos."

"Any idea what you would like to do?"

He smiles, "I was thinking of dinner, a walk, and the theater, if there's any left. Now, do you have any idea how we may finish this nasty business?"

"I do, and I'll need your help."

CHAPTER 28

RUSSIAN AIRFIELD, WESTERN BELERUS

1820, 6 October, 1942 (1720 GMT)

Major Nadezhda Popova completes the engine start-up procedure for her War Eagle fighter. It's so familiar, she doesn't need to consult the check list, yet, drilled by habit, she does anyway. Her canopy is closed to block out the bitter cold. Under her wings are four AIM-9 heat seeking missiles and two radar guided missiles of Russian manufacture. She completes the pre-taxi check list and looks down the line of jets in her squadron. On radio, "Tower, Witch 1. Witch squadron ready to taxi."

"Witch 1, Tower, you are cleared to taxi to runway 17 north."

She trips her brakes and leads her five jets to the runway.

ROMMEL'S HEADQUARTERS NORTH OF LONDON

1741, 6 October, 1942

Rommel picks up the radio phone, "Yes, sir?"

Goering says, "Have you taken London?"

"We prepare for the push. It will fall in three to four days."

"You do not have three days. You must take it now. We suffered defeat in the air last night. The Fuhrer will no longer countenance delay."

"Understood."

"Heil Hitler."

"Heil Hitler." Rommel sets the radio phone in its cradle and stares at it. He abruptly about faces and walks out of the farmhouse he's using as a headquarters. He walks down to the river and looks south.

His chief of staff joins him, "Sir, what is the word from Berlin?"

"Twenty-five miles away, beyond the hills and trees, the British, Canadian, and American armies are entrenched. They have at least 14,000 soldiers and over 800 artillery tubes dug in using crossed fires zones and pre-planned artillery fire. We have 145 Tiger tanks, 264 Panzer 4s, and 17,000 troops. We attack tonight. We must." He turns back, taking a deep breath, "We must."

WITCH 1, 10,000 FEET OVER NORTH EASTERN POLAND

1850, 6 October, 1942 (1750 GMT)

Major Nadezhda Popova watches as her Sidewinder zig-zags and hits a German '262. "Splash 1." To herself, "That's four. The American training is good."

Below her, the Second Tank Army streams west over the border. Using her radar, she makes slow sweeps right and left, searching for targets.

'A' SABRE SQUADRON, 1ST BATTALION WELSH GUARDS, 32ND GUARDS BRIGADE, GUARDS DIVISION, NORTH OF LONDON

1930, 6 October, 1942

The German artillery barrage takes on a life of its own. It becomes less a noise, than a pounding physical presence. Sergeant Andrew Seymour is buttoned up in his Churchill tank, well camouflaged in the trees and bushes. It is war scarred and battered, but it's taken him from north of York to here. He peers through the view slits looking for Germans. In the flash of an artillery round, he sees them. Dark, foreboding hulks moving closer, A near miss shakes the Churchill and rattles his view, but it settles again. He sees infantry with the tanks. On radio, "Sabre 1, Dagger 2, Tigers, 800 meters at my front supported by infantry."

"Dagger, Sabre, hold fire. Report when 500."

"Wilco." Off radio, "Bloody hell, right I'll hold fire. Tell the fucking Germans to hold fire and we could mop this up."

A tank to his left opens up at 700 yards and its rounds ricochet upward off the Tiger's hull. Counterfire takes the tank out. Seymour, "Damn it. You can't hurt them that way."

An A-10 swoops down, its gun breathing fire. A German tank explodes and the A-10 pulls up, "Boys, we got a dragon out there breathing fire all over the Hun."

Then, another A-10 comes in. Before he can fire, a German tank explodes. The A-10 pilot corrects and hits another tank.

"Sabre, Dagger, they're in the minefield."

"Roger, Dagger. Hold position." Another Tiger hits a mine. The German line stops.

Seymour, "Sabre, Dagger, they've stopped at 500 yards."

"Roger, Dagger, inform your infantry to take cover."

"Sabre, Dagger, "We're under full German artillery bombardment. If they aren't holed up, they're dead."

"Roger." And artillery falls upon the German line.

Seymour watches, "Give 'em bloody hell. We're dropping the world on them fellas. They'll fall back for certain."

But they don't fall back. They move forward into the minefield, pushing a dead tank to clear the mines. Seymour, "Will, load AP. When I call fire, bloody well fire as fast as you can."

"Can do, Sergeant."

Sergeant Seymour deliberately lets the Tigers come on. Two more British tanks get hit, then the Tigers roll past his position. "Richie, back hard on the left track. Turn us." The tank jerks back. "Left turret. Move out," and they jerk forward and left.

Seymour, "Target tank, 10 o'clock."

The gunner, Corporal Keith Thatcher says, "Away." He fires his gun. The nearly point-blank shot hits the rear of the turret and the turret flies off the Tiger as its ammo goes up.

Seymour, "Good kill. Target tank, 11 o'clock."

"Up."

"Away." He fires, hitting another Tiger in the rear of its turret, and the ammo detonates.

"Good kill. Right track. Target tank, 10 o'clock."

Thatcher fires and a third tank explodes.

Seymour, "Richie, turn right." They turn down a lane, destroying a fence and a tank round shrieks past them. "Target tank, 6 o'clock. Hard right. Hull shot, AP."

The Churchill spins right as Thatcher spins the turret, "Away." The round hits a Tiger on the front glacises. The Tiger's turret keeps tracking them.

"Back, Richie. Hard left." The Tiger misses again.

Willy, "Up."

Thatcher, "Away." The AP round hits near the hull gunner, to no effect.

They back into a ditch, their nose pointing to the sky. Seymour screams, "Out! Out! Get out!" He scrambles out of his hatch. The Tiger's next shot hits the floor pan under the driver. The crew is killed instantly and Seymour's thrown 15 feet into the brush.

WESTMINSTER PALACE (PARLIAMENT)

0614, 7 October, 1942

Churchill looks out at the devastation to the south and east. He's looking for those new Yank landing craft. Field Marshal Alan Brooke and Admiral of the Fleet, Sir Dudley Pound stand beside him. Churchill asks, "Admiral, have you seen these air cushion contraptions?"

"No, Prime Minister."

An aid enters, "Prime Minister, Parliament has approved the funds for rebuilding the infrastructures destroyed."

Churchill looks at the aid, "Thank you. Of course. Many lost their own property. Any word on the fires?"

"No, Prime Minister."

Churchill looks at Brooke, "I would, in normal times, ask the army for aid in fighting these fires, but these...these are not normal times."

They watch as four F/A-14s climb out of Kenley. Churchill nods, "At least, we have the Knights. It's my thought, Admiral, to offer knighthoods to most of the air crew and some of the deserving ground crew. I have write ups from Air Marshal Dowding to that end. Do you suppose the American Navy would oppose?"

"I do not, Prime Minister. If you wish, I could ask."

"Please do. What would you consider appropriate for Commodore Hunt?"

Brooke smiles, "I don't know if she would or could accept it, but I would elevate her to the peerage. No one person has contributed so greatly and directly to the defense of our nation."

Admiral Pound says, "The American Constitution forbids it."

Churchill, "Congress just passed an exception for military awards. I do not believe a peerage would constitute a military award. Still, we must show our appreciation."

They hear a beating roar and look out and downstream. They see several LCACs racing up the river, Sherman tanks in each craft. Clouds of water mist and shoot away from beneath the skirts as the ducted fans move to change the direction of travel. The three men are silent, watching the line of LCACs speed by.

Finally, Pound asks, "How many can we buy?"

Churchill grins, "Lend Lease. How many do you want?"

Pound, "With those, we could race to the beaches of France, at least a thousand."

FRONT GATE, RAF KENLEY

0630, 7 October, 1942

A black Bentley pulls up to the gate and the British guard comes to the front side window. It's rolled down, so he looks in, "Can I help you?"

GQ shows his ID, "They're giving us a ride."

"No problem, sir. We're getting crowded with planes." He motions for the gates to be opened.

As they pull onto the base, Gloria asks, "What did that mean?"

EPSOM, SOUTH WEST OF RAF KENLEY

0656, 7 October, 1942

Wingnut's driver skids their truck to a stop and the squadron climb out, helping Wingnut. They hear the squeak-clink of tanks. Wingnut gets himself up and over a pile of debris and looks west. Smoke rises from the rubble and the only building still standing is the clock tower. He turns on his radio, "Any Hog driver, Wingnut."

"Wingnut, Dusty 1. State location."

Wingnut gives him the map coordinates, "I hear tanks west of us. They sound German."

"Roger, we're engaged north of London. We'll get there as soon as we can."

Then, "Wingnut, Yankee. Confirm. Where are you?"

"I'm in Epsom near the clock tower. I can now see at least four Tigers and over a hundred infantry."

"That's only eight miles from Kenley."

"Affirmative. What do we have between Epsom and Kenley?"

Silence, then, "Wingnut, Spike. We have nothing between Epsom and Kenley. We're scrambling forces. Can you delay them?"

He watches the tanks rolling closer.

"They also have a half-track missile launcher." Wingnut looks back at his small band of men. Eight people with light arms to stop four tanks and all those Germans. He takes a deep breath and nods, "Spike, Wingnut. We'll do what we can." He looks at Thatcher, "Jimmy, give me your sword." Then, "Rodriguez, what do we have for grenades?"

Sergeant Rodriguez looks up at him, "We have some. What do you want to do?"

101ST SS PANZER BATTALION, EPSOM, UK

SS-Obersturmbannfuhrer Rolf Meier is standing in his commander's hatch and scanning the rubble. He started with sixty-eight tanks, fifty-two vehicles, and nine hundred forty-six men. All that's left is six tanks, with two of them under tow. Of his other vehicles, he has twenty-seven. He still has six hundred and ten of his infantry and his objective is nearly at hand. His gunner is swinging the turret from side to side, checking for threats.

The battalion is spread out, picking their way through the ruin of Epsom. A figure slips through the rubble, blending in with the gray morning. The man waits until the turret is facing away from him, and jumps up onto the engine deck and tosses a grenade down the gunner's hatch. He dives off the tank, rolls away into the rubble, and disappears.

Meier hears a muffled explosion behind him and turns to see a man crawling out of a tank. Then he hears another, and another. On radio, "Stop! Report!" Infantry are running toward the tanks, the men shouting. Then, Meier hears a huge explosion toward the north and realizes that one of his ammo trucks has just gone up.

Then, to the south, there's another explosion, then another, and men are running into the town, some of them on fire. One of his remaining working tanks, that has a broken-down tank in tow, is trapped in the rubble. He hears a truck engine revving and see two of his truck running down the perimeter road and heading east. "Stop those trucks!" He waves his men east, but the trucks are gone and out of site before anyone reacts.

Then, silence. Meier looks around at the chaos. "Driver, forward." His tank moves forward, skirting a debris pile. When they reach the town center, a tall blonde man stands waiting. He's wearing a flight suit with an American flag on the shoulder. Meier looks behind the American and sees no one. He shouts, "Hold fire!" as his infantry runs up into position to cover the enemy.

HANGER, RAF KENLEY

Chief 'Bobby' Geller is training some of the new ground crew when they hear Chief 'Fluffy' Bond on the announcing circuit, "All ground crew auxiliary, muster on the flight line immediately with your weapons." Fluffy repeats the order.

Bobby looks at his new crew, "Can any of you shoot?"

A few raise their hands, and one asks, "What's going on?"

"No time, you who can shoot, come with me. The rest of you sit tight and stay under cover." He goes to his locker and gets his BAR and a bag of magazines. He leads his people out.

LT TOMMY 'WINGNUT' URLAND AND SS OBERSTURM-BANNFUHRER ROLF MEIER, EPSOM, UK

Wingnut, waiting, observes the man in front of him; the gray and black uniform with lightning devices on the collar. Relaxed, his hands behind his back, Tommy draws on his high school German, "Sprechen Sie Englisch?"

Meier smiles, "I do. If you surrender, you and your men will not be harmed."

Tommy nods, "I see. You know, we've been chasing you all over the place." He hears F-14s taking off in the distance.

"You have?"

"Yes. You rolled south from South Shield, swung west, and hit Brancepeth. Then, you went through Middleton, Leeds, Waterloo, and Hudderfiled. Ah, was it your tank that was blown up on the debris hill?"

"It was."

"You passed east of Coventry, and ran south, passing through the Bight-Bristol line before it could properly form. It was a good move because it caused the line to collapse. They all thought you were going to flank them. What you wanted, though, was Alconbury. I'm betting that was a surprise."

"It was. You are very well informed."

"I am. Next, you vented your spleen on Cambridge. A beautiful historic college town that didn't deserve it. After Cambridge, you must have realized we'd moved to another field. You received information we were flying out of Kenley, so you took another west hook to get here. That's your mission, right? To hit our airfield? But there is something I don't understand in all of this, why Barton? Why kill those people in Barton? Why?"

"Your airfield is my objective. Barton? Was that its name? The

English needed to be taught a lesson. You seem not to have learned that lesson. Are you going to surrender?"

Tommy smiles and shifts his weight, "You know, I was going to ask you the same thing." A pair of F-14s fly a pass to the north.

"Never."

"It was worth a try, but I thought so. Do you ever wonder what will happen to you when you die?"

Puzzled, Meier answers, "No. Whatever my soul is, I do my duty, so it is pure. Do you?"

"Yeah, I do. Especially, lately. I hope God can forgive me for what I do."

Meier smiles, "And what do you do?"

Tommy slowly brings his left hand up and grasps his pistol, in its shoulder holster, by his index finger and thumb. The Germans watch him remove the pistol, totally focused on his left hand. Tommy wraps his right hand around the hilt of the sword, its sheath taped upside down to his back, and pulls it free. "Now!" He shifts to his left and rushes Meier, bringing the sword up back-handed, and stroking it across Meier's throat.

At his command, Wingnuts men open fire, taking out the front row of infantry. Meier pulls the trigger on his Luger just as the sword touches his skin, and hits Tommy in the right chest. Tommy reverses the sword, and pushes it into Meier's neck, severing his trachea, then his hand lets go and he drops the sword.

Meier, eyes wide in disbelief, fires again and again, hitting Wingnut in the chest and gut, then shooting into the air. Tommy falls and rolls onto his back, trying to get his gun up. He can barely see. His world is contracting and getting dark. Then he sees two F-14s dive in. Tommy smiles, "Yes! It worked. We did it."

ROOK 131, OVER EPSOM

Nix, in a shallow dive, sees Wingnut fall. "Selecting ground." He opens up with his 20mm cannon, hitting a tank, then a truck that explodes spectacularly.

Robot, "SAM launch at our six."

"Got it." Nix triggers off chaff and flares and hugs the ground, then climbs as the missiles crash into the ground behind him.

Arthur is next in to strafe. Lizard, "Spike is in."

Robot, "Watch the SAMs."

Lizard, "SAMs are gone. Spike out."

They circle back, as each '14 takes it turn strafing the German unit. "Thud in. Thud out."

"Swede in. Swede out. We see a tank trying to advance in the rubble."

"Gunner in. Gunner out."

"Pappy in. Pappy out."

"Nix in." He settles on a group of trucks and takes them out, scattering troops as he goes. He hits a tanker truck, and it goes away, sending a shock wave through the trapped unit. "Nix out."

As Nix pulls out, two A-10s join the line. In minutes, all the tanks are smoking hulks, the trucks are all on fire, and the remaining infantry are dead or running like hell, trying to hide in the ruined town.

EPSOM, UK

Sergeant Johnny Rodriguez and the medic run out to Wingnut, grasp him by the shoulders, and drag him back to cover. The corpsman cuts open Tommy's flight suit, "Damn, three, we got three. Sergeant take this compress and get pressure on his upper chest. NOW!"

Rodriguez presses the bandage onto the wound, blood running over his hands. Tommy's eye's flutter open, "Stay with us, Lieutenant. Stay with us."

Tommy smiles, "God, you're an ugly angel. Johnny, get them home."

Johnny fights back tears, "Come on, Boss. Stay with us."

The medic, Franks says, "There, got those, now," and turns to work on the last wound. A shadow covers them, and the medic looks up. The largest black man he's ever seen is looking down at him.

Fluffy asks, "How is he?"

"I think the external bleeding is under control, but he's got three bullets in him and he needs a surgeon."

"Roger, that." He turns to the sailors that came out with him, "Bobby, call it in. Tell them to meet us with an ambulance. Wingnut's critical."

"Aye, Chief. Okay, let's get this done. The sailors sling their weapons and pick Wingnut up. Tommy's squad forms the perimeter and they move fast toward Kenley's perimeter.

AC-130, 5000 FEET OVER EPSOM

Major Albert Maki looks out his side window as they approach their target. "Get ready for action, boys." On radio, "Yankee, Specter 1, I can see the area of engagement south west of Kenley. Are there friendlies on the ground?"

"Specter 1, Yankee actual, affirmative. They're to the east heading back to Kenley out of the debris field."

"Roger, I've acquired them. So, the troops heading after them are the enemy?"

"Specter 1, Yankee actual, affirmative. You are weapons free.

Take them out."

"Weapons free, roger."

Maki turns his Specter C-130 on its left wing, sights out his window, and opens fire.

LEAVING EPSOM

Fluffy and Rodriguez are on drag, walking backward and firing. A bullet takes off Fluffy's ball cap. He stops, reaches down, picks it up, and puts it back on his head. When he looks up, three SS are running over the top of the debris.

Then hell rains down, and the SS disappear in a wall of bullets. Fluffy looks up and sees the Specter, "Oh hell, yes. Run boys. God's taking care of the bastards."

Fluffy sees that the men carrying Wingnut are struggling to hold on to him. He runs in front of them, "Stop." He bends down and they put Tommy on his left shoulder. He straightens up and turns, running to the base and the waiting truck.

CHAPTER 29

1ST BRIGADE, 18TH PANZER DIVISION, COMING UP ON WOOFORD WELLS, NE OF LONDON

0816, 7 October, 1942

The brigade commander is standing in his hatch studying the village in front of them when he hears the loud, paper tearing, sound of incoming artillery fire. He shouts on the radio, "Button up!"

Most of them are already closing their hatches when the rounds start falling on them.

VALKYRIE 1, 100 FEET, SIX MILES EAST OF THE GERMAN 1ST BRIGADE

LCDR Douglas sees the where the shells fall and reports, "Mississippi, Valkyrie 1, good shots. Fire for effect."

All three battle wagons open up. Thirty-four 14-inch guns hammer the German formation. Bodies and tanks and vehicles fly into the air.

Douglas to her new co-pilot, "It's hell, pure and simple. See what we have wrought."

BRICKET WOOD, HERTFORDSHIRE, UK, 14 MILES NW OF LONDON

0820, 7 October, 1942

Sergeant Tommy Thompson and Lieutenant Maki, still in his

khaki uniform, step off the bus. The platoon lieutenant calls his men to muster. Maki wanders into an aid station in a church. The vicar and his people are helping the nurses and one doctor. The place smells of iodine and alcohol. A nurse notices him, "May I help you, Captain?"

"Lieutenant. May I speak with the men?"

"Of course. Are any of them yours?"

"No, ma'am. I just want to help."

Another ambulance pulls up and she walks away.

ROMMEL'S HQ, LUTON, UK, 25 MILES NORTH OF LONDON

0824, 7 October, 1942

Rommel, on radio, "First of the 18th, fall back. Fall back! Those are battleship guns." He turns to his aid, "Get me Weber." He shakes his head, looking at his map.

His aid hands him the radio, "Weber, sir."

"General, they have battleships somewhere in the Thames estuary. They're a secondary priority behind the Devil's Cross, but please, they need to be destroyed."

"Can you avoid them for now?"

"I can, but it forces me west and our enemy knows that."

"Understood, sir."

VALKYRIE 117, FIELD SOUTH OF ALYLESBURY, 36 MILES NW OF LONDON, UK

0850, 7 October, 1942

Lieutenant Jim 'Smooth' Lowandowski hovers his SH-60 as his sensor operator and a corpsman, HM3 Franks, run out for a wounded A-10 pilot. The SENSO slaps the center console when they're back on board and he rolls on the engine power, increases his rotor pitch, and pushes the stick forward. The bird transitions to forward flight and climbs out. Smooth, like his call sign. He turns south for Guys Hospital.

In three minutes, they're crossing the German lines. Out of the corner of his eye, he sees a missile launch. "Hang on!"

He drops the collective and the chopper drops. Applying collective and throttle, he slows as the ground comes up. The missile turns and explodes against the cockpit roof. The engine grenades and Smooth adds more collective and pulls up a bit. The helicopter lands flat and slides into a stone barn. Smooth and his co-pilot are instantly killed.

The corpsman hauls the SENSO and the A-10 pilot out of the burning wreckage. Alders is treating the two men when German soldiers walk up. They do not interfere as he gets the pilot stable and covers the SENSO's burns, then gives them both a shot of morphine. He sits back, they should recover.

Then he looks up and sees a smiling SS officer approaching. Alders stands and puts his hands up. The German's smile broadens, and he opens fire with his machine pistol, killing all three men.

FIELD HOSPITAL, BRICKET WOOD, HERTFORDSHIRE, UK

0856, 7 October, 1942

Lieutenant Maki kneels next to a soldier with burned arms and hands, "How are you?"

The man answers in a British accent, "Better than a lot of my mates, sir."

"What branch are you with?" Maki takes out a notebook and pen.

"Armor, sir. Trooper David Preacher, East Riding of Yorkshire Yeomanry."

"An honor to meet you. I'm Lieutenant Maki, US Navy. May I ask you some questions?"

"Of course, sir."

"I'm with the Navy Design Bureau. We're working on new tanks. Have you faced the German tanks?"

"Bloody hell, I have. Begging your pardon, sir."

"No problem. What can you tell me about them?"

"We're facing two kinds. The smaller is the Panzer 4. A fine tank with a high velocity 75mm gun. My Covenanter, with its two pounder is no match for it, but we gave them hell, anyway."

"And the larger one?"

"It's mobile death, sir. From the size of hole it puts in our armor, it has at least a 120mm high velocity gun. It can shoot accurately from over a mile. Artillery will kill them, and the amazing Dragons. They chew them up. But my rounds, just bounced off their hull."

"Thank you. Obviously, a new tank has to have a big high velocity gun, and respectable armor. I know a tank should be easy to maintain in the field, but what other characteristics do you think it should have?"

The young Brit pushes up onto his elbows, "You're asking me? I've never built a tank?"

"You've fought in them. What couldn't your tank do, that you needed it to do?"

"Um, as low a silhouette as possible."

Maki writes, "That requires the commander's hatch to be separate from the gunner's hatch."

"Yeah, that would be brilliant. When you brew up, the gunner might escape. The tank needs to be powerful and as fast in reverse as it is in forward. When you see a turret tracking to you, you want to back up as fast as possible and get something solid between you."

"That makes sense. How does the driver know where he's going?"

Preacher laughs, "He don't. The commander or loader gives him directions. When the Hun is firing at you, you don't much give a fuck if you hit a farmer's fence."

A nearby nurse frowns at them, "Begging your pardon, ma'am. Speaking of fast, the faster the better."

"I agree. Most tanks have gunner and commander on the right and loader on the left. Does that arrangement work?"

"It kinda has to. There's no way the loader can manage the gun left-handed. Well, not most loaders. You ain't thinking of building lefty tanks, are you?"

"No, the tanks all need to be the same."

Then, a man runs in, "We got to move. The Hun broke through."

CONTROL CENTER, RAF KENLEY

0915, 7 October, 1942

Spike is back in control, listening to the progress of the battle. "BATDIV-5, Valkyrie 1, cease fire. I repeat, cease fire. All enemy is destroyed."

Spike looks at the map, "Good, now they have to go west. Inform the Warthogs that the Germans will be shifting west."

They hear Commodore James, "Valkyrie 1, BATT DIV, what percentage of kills?"

"BATT DIV, Valkyrie 1. One hundred percent destruction. There is nothing left."

Spike shakes her head. She knows it was the right decision, but... Andrews joins her, "Most of the ground crews are back at work. We've lost nine," and he hands her the list of dead and wounded.

"Damn, I saw what Wingnut did down there. He bought us time. Here's a draft for the CMH and one for a Navy Cross for his sergeant. Those men saved a hell of a lot of lives."

"Yes, Spike. One of them would like to see you."

"Okay, send him in."

Andrews motions and Jimmy Thatcher walks in carrying his sword in its sheath. Jimmy salutes Spike, "Private Thatcher, ma'am."

She smiles at the slight boy, "Hello, Private Thatcher. That's a nice sword."

"Yes, ma'am, a saber. My great-grandfather earned it in Egypt in 1890."

"I see."

"My grandfather died at Hudderfield where I met the Lieutenant. His men, the airborne rangers, teased me about carrying it into battle, but it's all I had, until Grandfather died, and I got his rifle. I cleaned the sword up, ma'am. It's for you."

"What do you mean?"

"This is what Lieutenant Urland used to kill the Nazi commander. He had us tape it to his back. He took that Nazi's head clean off. Well, mostly off. The sword should go to Lieutenant Urland, but they won't let me in to see him. So, could you take it and make sure he gets it?"

"What would your father think about you giving the sword away?"

"Ma'am, my father died at Dunkirk. My Grandpa died at Hudderfield. My mum died of the fever years and years ago. It was just me and Grandpa, and now, it's just me."

"I'm sorry. Private, what's your full name, and how old are you?"

"James Thatcher, ma'am. Grandpa called my Jimmy, and I'm sixteen."

General Ridgeway walks into control.

"Thank you, Jimmy. Colonel, keep him with the airborne fire team who was with Lieutenant Urland. They need rest. He's going to need gear. Draw the expense out of my personal account. Private Thatcher, we'll get you sorted. Don't worry."

"Ma'am, me and the Sergeant, and the guys, if there's fighting to do, we'd rather be fighting."

"I'm sorry, Jimmy. I'm not authorized to send someone sixteen years old into battle. That, and if you die, your whole family line dies with you."

"Did I say sixteen? I meant nineteen, ma'am, and begging your pardon, I'm not in the royal line. I'm not even noble. If my family's gone, it's no difference to nobody."

"It makes a difference to me, okay?"

"Can you keep the sword safe until Lieutenant Urland's healed up and you decide what do to do with me?"

"Yes, that I can do." She hands the sword to Andrews, "My office, thank you." Andrews guides Jimmy out and she turns to Ridgeway. "General, do we have enough planes?"

Ridgeway grins, "You grounded every C-130 that landed here until we did. The airborne unit you were talking about, it's led by Sergeant Rodriguez, correct?"

"Yes, I think they need the rest."

"They think they need another combat drop. They've already drawn gear."

Spike takes a deep breath, "Damn. I need statements from them for a CMH investigation."

"I gave the reports to Andrews. Are you putting the kid in for a medal?"

"I'm putting Rodriguez and Franks in for the Navy Cross, the other five for bronze stars, including Private Thatcher."

"Good. I've set H hour for 0630 tomorrow. It'll be full dark on the ground, but we'll have some light at altitude. Once we're down, we'll have daylight to secure the field."

"That works. I'll have my units up and briefed. We'll synch with your schedule."

Ridgeway, "I've studied what we have on their air defenses. Can you take them out?"

"We must. If we fail, then you'll abort."

"Yes, ma'am."

IMPERIAL COLLEGE, WHITE CITY, NORTH LONDON

1310, 7 October, 1942

Lieutenant Maki walks backward carrying another stretcher. He and the soldier on the other end are directed to a classroom. When he's delivered his patient, he goes out front and finds his transportation gone. Going back into the building, he sees a British soldier crawling toward a rifle leaning against the wall.

"Can I give you a hand?"

The young man looks up, "Do you have one to spare?" Maki turns red, the man's left hand is gone. "You could get me my rifle."

"Why?'

"Because I'm fucking useless in bed, and no bloody way the Hun will find me asleep in bed."

"We'll stop them."

"And how do you know that?"

"Truth, I don't. I do know some of the Marines at our front, and they know their business. I know Patton has tanks and he knows his business. And, Commodore Hunt is still flying. I trust her."

Maki gets the rifle and ammo belt and gives them to the soldier, "Can I ask what happened?"

"I'm a sniper. A tank took the building I was in. It fell and crushed me. Now, I'm useless. My rifle can't speak." He looks at Maki, "Why are you here?"

"I'm US Navy. I'm here to learn how to defeat the German tanks."

"Then pick up my rifle and face them."

Maki flushes, "Who are you?'

"Sergeant Murray, Recon platoon, 6th Battalion, Gordon High-landers."

"Lieutenant Maki, Navy Special Projects. If the Admiral finds out I was in combat, he'd be so pissed."

"So, you're neutered?"

"If you'd made it to your rifle, what would you have done?"

"I'm done. I'm useless like this."

"Look, if I take your rifle out there, you'd better be here when I get back."

"Do you know how to shoot, Navy man?"

"I grew up in the woods of Washington State. I killed my first deer at fifteen."

"That ain't killing a man. You want to understand, you pull the trigger and hit the person you're aiming at, then, when you come back, we can talk."

"Yes, Sergeant." Maki picks up the Lee Enfield and its ammo belt and walks out of the college. He looks up at the sun and walks north.

HEADQUARTERS, OCCUPIED RAF OUSTON

1644, 7 October, 1942

Weber sits listening to an after-action report.

"...The Tomcat fighters were everywhere. We closed with two of the Devil's Cross. They broke away and flew NOE. Two Tomcats were on us before we got closer than three miles. I broke hard right. Hans, in 2 plane, broke left. They hit him and he crashed without a chute. I ran north. On the way, I had to dodge four more Tomcats. These had different rudder markings."

"Weber, "What did the markings look like?"

"Like a creature running with a round thing."

"Yes, I've reviewed the intelligence we have on the American squadrons who came back in time. You describe the Tomcatter logo. Continue."

"When the Americans turned south, I did a climbing turn. I still had missiles. I was immediately tangled with a different aircraft. These had a bird and the rudders had black and grey squares."

"The Redcocks. We now face three fighter squadrons."

"Yes, sir."

UXBRIDGE ROAD, EALING, WEST LONDON

1820, 7 October, 1942

General Patton walks in the south door of an old house on the south side of Uxbridge Road. The machine gun and rifle fire are deafening. He walks to the front of the house and hears one of his Sherman's firing from an alley nearby. The front windows are shattered and a dozen men sit or lay in the room, sweat and dirt streaking their faces. The Sherman discharges again. Then, they hear the shriek of a German 75mm tank round. It hits the house next door, making the house they're in shake, plaster showering down. Several of the men get up, and run towards the south door.

Patton, "Where the hell are you going?"

"They're coming!"

"Hell, yeah, they're coming. And, we're going to meet them right here!"

"But...but, we always fall back."

Patton's face turns scarlet, and he reflexively grabs the handle of his pistol. He conversation with Commodore Hunt pops into his mind. "You're right. But, no more. We back up no more. We stand. Get on the windows and give them hell!"

ARTHUR 1, 200 FEET, 10 MILES SOUTH OF GERMAN OCCU-PIED RAF OUSTON

0624, 8 October, 1942

Too Tall, behind Spike, says, "Climb a bit. Okay, left 15."

Spike makes the adjustment.

Too Tall, "When I say, pop up two hundred, fire the Harm, then back down and hard left turn."

Spike, "Got it."

Too Tall, "Pop!" She pulls up two hundred feet. Too Tall, on radio, gives the call for friendly anti-radar missiles, "Magnum." Spike fires a HARM anti-radiation missile, then dives and turns left. A minute later, Too Tall, "Come to 350 and pop 200." Spike repeats the maneuver and fires another HARM. She sees the fire ball from her first target.

They blow one more, then, "Arthur 1, Knight 1, raid warning, designated raid 1. Multiple fast movers out of Ouston. We've kicked the hornet's nest."

Too Tall, "Knight 1, Arthur 1. Roger."

Gandhi, "Volley Fox 3. Spike, keep your head down."

Too Tall, "Wilco."

To their east and north, they see several explosions. Then, Too Tall, "Come to 030 and pop." She complies and fires another

HARM. They continue for one more, then are out of missiles.

Thud, with Keg in the backseat, takes over.

As they circle, Spike's radar warning lights up. She breaks and pickles off countermeasures. "Where are they?"

Too Tall, "5 o'clock low. Two of 'em. Sorry."

"Grunt," Spike does a tight turn and meets the lead '262 head to head. The German fires his machine gun. The rounds hit their left wing. Spike rolls right, "Grunt." She pulls into a tight, nine G, minimum turn.

Too Tall, "He's reversing."

Major Gunter pulls the stick hard into his belly, begging his plane to turn. He engages afterburners and puts out his airbrake. "I know I hit them. Now, I have to finish them. Have to."

Spike sees the afterburners and leads the German. When her Sidewinder growls in her ear, she fires. It corkscrews, latching onto the heat from the German's afterburners.

Major Gunter sees the flash of the missile firing and pickles countermeasures, throttling back his engines. The Sidewinder loses track. He rolls on his burners and lines up for another head to head pass.

Spike sees the Germans burners light and does a tight barrel roll, lining up a gun shot. Her plane is shaking and the master alarm has sounded. She can hear the chatter on the radio; the A-10s are taking out the radar guided and heat seeking missile launchers. They've destroyed the radar sites.

She watches the '262 turning toward her and lines up, going head to head, and takes the shot. Two fifty round bursts fly right up the air intake on the right engine and it grenades.

Gunter finds himself fighting his aircraft, his right engine gone and his left engine surging. He levels and attempts to climb, exchanging speed for altitude. "Fuck! Fuck!" Looking out, he sees he's very close to the field. The jet bucks and the left engine shuts down. Alarms are screaming. He points toward darkness and ejects.

ARTHUR 1

0630, 8 October, 1942

Spike climbs. As her jet slows, the shaking subsides a bit. They hear Parker, "The bird is plucked, send for the special sauce." All the German air defenses have been destroyed. Ridgeway calls, "Hotel minus two."

Spike slows and circles the field. Fires are burning at the defense positions. Six helicopters are using thermal sights to engage the perimeter with their miniguns. Transports fly below her and streams of paratroopers disgorge from the planes. She sees the sparkle of gun fire below and the streams of tracer fire from the choppers. Doing a gauge sweep, she says, "We're losing fuel."

Too Tall, "Twenty minutes most economical to Kenley."

Spike, "Not enough. We land here."

"In a gun battle?"

"I'll keep us in the air as long as I can." On radio, Spike, "Arthur is hit. We are circling. Can someone let the paratroopers know we'll be landing soon?"

Gandhi, "Spike, the brother suggests an alternate."

Spike, "Not enough fuel. It will be here."

Marshal, "We have you on radar, Spike, and can escort you down."

Too Tall, "Thank you, Marshal."

LCDR Douglas, in Valkyrie 1, "Spike, Cargo Britches, we have relayed to the 82nd. They're expecting you."

Too Tall, "Thank you, Cargo Britches." On intercom, "You want to be down there, don't you?"

"I do. I want to meet the guy we've been fighting. I'm pretty sure he's here."

"I'm sorry I wasn't head checking."

"It's okay. It gives me the excuse for this."

WEST END OF THE RUNWAY, OCCUPIED RAF OUSTON

0630, 8 October, 1942

Major Gunter winds up his parachute just off the west end of the runway. "Come on, aircraft are coming. Come on." He can hear the turboprops. Then he sees soldiers landing by parachute all around him. "No way, she shot us all down. No way."

Jimmy Thatcher shouts in English, "Are you the Commodore? Shit, it's a Kraut. Hands up! Hands up!" Jimmy pushes the muzzle of his Garand rifle at Gunter, "I'm gonna kill you!"

Gunter hastily raises his hands, and in German, "What is this?" He hears gun fire in the east and sees the anger in the young man's eyes.

Sergeant Rodriguez lifts Jimmy's gun barrel, "We don't kill prisoners."

"They tried to kill the Lieutenant." Several the soldiers run west toward the perimeter. A machine gun opens up and is silences by a dozen rifles.

Johnny Rodriguez holds his rifle on Gunter and calmly motions for his pistol. Gunter slowly, carefully takes it out and hands it over. "Keep your hands where I can see them." Light finally twinges the eastern sky.

Gunter hears the whine of a jet engine approaching and looks west. In the gloom, the jet slowly materializes, unmistakably an F-14. Gunter watches in amazement as it grows closer. As it flashes by, he sees the stacks of flags on the fuselage, making the pilot's identity clear. It's the Drachendame.

Gunter is silent; head down; eyes closed. He turns to his captor, and in German, "Would you take me to her?"

"What? English."

"Commodore Hunt," and he points down the runway.

Johnny nods, "Come on, Jimmy. You know I'm going to catch hell for letting you jump."

"I go. Surrender to her." Gunter points and raises his hand again.

Sergeant Johnny Rodriquez motions with his rifle and the three walk down the runway.

CHAPTER 30

ARTHUR 1, RAF OUSTON

Spike parks her jet near the tower and shuts it down. Fuel has finally stopped leaking because the tank that was hit was isolated. On radio, "Knight 1, Arthur 1, status?"

Gandhi, "The skies are clear of hostiles. The A-10s are standing by. How are you?"

"We're safe for the moment. I'm going off line to un-ass the bird."

"Roger, Spike. So far, there's no response from France. Keep your survival radio on so we can keep you informed."

"Will do." On intercom, "You know, Too Tall, this poor bird has been through it."

"It has, Spike. Good landing."

Spike sees soldiers to her west leading a prisoner her way. Then, she sees a German emerge from a building, his hands in the air. She opens the canopy, "Time to get out."

She hits the tarmac and her legs try to buckle. She forces herself to stand straight, using the plane for support. The two Germans are making a bee line for her. She waits. The gun fire dies down. There's an occasional shot. The lone German arrives first, "I, to you, surrender this facility. To you."

She looks him over. His uniform is impeccable. His manner is upright. At his neck is the Blue Max. On his left breast, the Iron Cross. "I accept. Your name, sir?"

"General Ludwig Weber," and he carefully draws his Luger and hands it, grip first, to Spike.

Spike, speaking slowly, "You tell them all. Put down," and pantomimes putting the Luger on the ground.

He nods, "It is done."

Next, she sees Jimmy and Rodriguez escorting a German in a flight suit. "Ma'am, this Kraut wanted to surrender to you." The firing has completely died out. Rodriguez hands her Gunter's Luger.

Spike ignores Jimmy. She checks both guns are on safe and sticks them in her jacket pockets. She sees General Ridgeway and a platoon of Paratroopers running toward them.

Gunter, "Ich ubergebe mich dir." He stops, "I give. Aufgeben. Up to you, Drachendame."

"You want to surrender to me."

"Ja."

She smiles, "Name?"

"Major Heinrich Gunter," and straightens.

She nods, "I accept your surrender." She grabs her radio, "All units, Arthur. Ouston is ours. Good job." Ridgeway arrives, and "These two have surrendered. The base is ours."

Ridgeway smiles, "Your plan worked. Are you two okay?"

Spike motions at Gunter, "I think he's the one who got the rounds in our bird, but we're fine."

Gunter, "Drachendame, you shoot me. Three times."

Confused, she says, "But, I only hit you once."

Gunter continues, frustrated with his halting English, "Once in '109 over Cornwall. I limp to France. Next, I get '163. Good jet. Fast. Turn good. You shoot me down over North Sea. I fall on destroyer. Last, today, in '262. It is less than optimal."

Spike smiles, then, "You still live. That is optimal." Turning to General Weber, "Latrine?"

HARROW ROAD, WIMBLEDON, NORTH LONDON

0723, 8 October, 1942

Sergeant Thompson stands at a broken window in an empty store searching for the source of the sporadic firing. His lieutenant peeks around the window next to him and takes a round in the throat. "Corpsman!" He breaks cover and fires his BAR at two Germans skulking in the alley across from his position. "Sniper!" They drop. He sees some of his men moving to a brick wall and lays down cover fire.

His corpsman gets to the lieutenant, checks him out, and looks up, "He's gone, Sergeant."

One of his corporals stands to throw out a grenade and gets hit in the throat. The grenade falls to the floor and Thompson scoops it up and throws it out, ducking back to cover. The grenade detonates, throwing shrapnel in the street.

He hears the bang of a rifle being fired from a floor above. Tom looks out and watches a German sniper fall from an open window in a tall building at the end of the street.

"Shit! Okay! We're clear! Sniper down! Keep shooting! Here they come!" He fires again as six Germans rush their position. The rifle above him fires again, and the lead German's head snaps back and he goes down. His men open up on the now fleeing Germans, who run back into hiding.

Thompson turns to his corpsman, "Get the lieutenant out of here." The corpsman drags the bodies in the room out the back door.

Now, they wait.

VALKYRIE 1, SOUTH BOUND OVER OCCUPIED ENGLAND

0723, 8 October, 1942

Spike sits behind and between the pilot's seats looking out the windscreen of the new SH-60 helicopter. Her helmet is plugged into the crew comms circuit, "Sandra, can you patch me into the radio?"

"Sure, just tell me when to key to the mic."

"I'll touch your shoulder."

"Okay," she touches Cargo Britch's shoulder. "All units, Arthur actual, unit commanders report unit strength."

Swede, "Knight has twelve, four birds in the air."

Thud, "Rook has twelve, six birds in the air."

Marshall, "Beefeater has twelve, six in the air."

Oyster, "Felix has twelve, two in the air."

Major Parks, "Dog has eight usable, six up."

LCDR Leonard, "Rusty and Dusty have six usable, all up."

The other four A-10 units report in at full strength.

Then, "Yankee actual, Yankee, we have two squadrons of Fox-trot 1's on final."

Spike smiles, "Acknowledge, Yankee. Refuel them and stand by. Swede, Thud, how do you have twelve?"

"Spike, Swede. Lizard is behind Cochran and you have Too Tall. The new crews are limited."

"Spike, Thud. I got DeGraaff, and GQ cleared. Still training the new crew."

Spike feels the beginning of relief, "Roger. Stuffy, Spike."

Air Marshal Dowding comes on the radio, "Go for Stuffy."

"Stuffy, Spike, I have a plan..."

BUCKINGHAM PALACE

0824, 8 October, 1942

Churchill is guided to a sitting room. The King stands at a south window looking out. Churchill stops, bows, and approaches, "Your Majesty?"

"Will we hold, Winston?"

"We will. We must."

"She lost several aircraft yesterday."

"They've already been replaced and several more squadrons have flown in from America."

"Is it enough?"

An aid opens the door, "Air Chief Marshal Dowding, Your Majesty."

Dowding steps in, bows, then approaches, "Your Majesty, Mr. Prime Minister."

"Good morning, Air Marshal."

Dowding grins, "Your Majesty, Ouston is ours. The Commodore's plan worked. The 82nd Airborne quickly gained control and the General in charge surrendered."

"The Commodore?"

"A German ace got some rounds into her plane, but she was able to make an emergency landing, at Ouston. She took the surrender. She is quite alright." Dowding eyes are twinkling, "In fact, Your Majesty, Mr. Prime Minister, if I could draw your attention to the south window?"

The three go to the large window. In the distance a great number of small specks appear out of the high cloud cover and into the sunlight.

ARTHUR 1, 3000 FEET, SOUTH OF LONDON

In her new plane, Spike leads a formation of every air capable unit she commands. In chevron formation behind her are the Black Knights, the White Knights, the Tomcatters, and the Redcocks. Then a break and the six squadrons of Griffin fighters. The third formation is all six squadrons of A-10s lead by the Devil Dogs and Iron Angels. Then, come two squadrons of F-1 War Eagles.

Spike, "Yankee formation, Arthur 1, slow descent to angels 1."

BUCKINGHAM PALACE

King George is riveted, fighting his emotions, "Dowding, does that mean what I think it means?"

Dowding, his delighted smile lighting up the room, "Your Majesty, it does. We should hear from Rommel within the hour, if not sooner. He knows what that flight means. We own the skies."

Winston, overcome, gropes for a chair and sits, his head down.

ROMMEL'S HEADQUARTERS UNIT, WEMBLEY, UK

General Erwin Rommel is studying the battle map with his staff when they hear the thunder of jets above them. He and his men look at each other, then rush outside and look up. Rommel sees, at low altitude, an enormous formation of jet fighters, all with US and British insignia. Then, they're gone to the north. He watches the formation split, half peeling off west and half to the east, and come around.

He looks down, nods his head, then turns and re-enters his headquarters. He motions to his aid, 'It's done. They have the skies. Tell our men to lay down arms."

"But, General, we are so close."

"Did you not see? They control the air. We've lost Ouston and Germany has no more planes to send. We have very little armor. They grow stronger as we weaken. It is over. I will lose no more men. Send the message."

The aid looks at his commander for a long minute, "Yes, sir."

ARTHUR 1

Spike, "East flight, circle back and form up on west flight." She leads her command from west to east over London. She sees white flags held by German soldiers in the streets of the outlying suburbs and hamlets. As they clear London and make the turn to fly back over Rommel's position, she hears, "Arthur 1, Yankee, we have word from Eisenhower. Rommel has surrendered."

For a moment, Sam closes her eyes, fighting the relief rising in her chest. To herself, "God, I wish Papa and Puck were here to see this." Then, "Thank you, Yankee. Thank all of you. Rook, fighter sweep the channel. Iron Angels patrol from London north looking for pockets of resistance. All other units, return to base. We still have a war to fight."

HARROW ROAD, WIMBLEDON, NORTH LONDON

0835, 8 October, 1942

There are dozens of dead or dying German soldiers laying in the street in front of Sergeant Tom Thompson's position. He checks his magazines. They need more ammo. When he looks back out of his window, he sees eight German soldiers walking out into the street without rifles and waving a white flag. Corporal Henry, "Is it a trick?"

Then, on radio, they hear their company commander's voice, "Check fire. Check fire. The Germans are surrendering. They're laying down their arms."

He listens as the other platoons check in, then his captain, "Lieutenant Shay?"

Thompson keys his radio, "3rd Platoon acknowledges, check fire. Sir, Lieutenant Shay is dead."

"Is this Thompson?"

"Yes, sir."

"Take charge of your platoon, Lieutenant Thompson and begin policing the area."

"Yes, sir."

Thompson looks at the men in the room, "George, Willy, go accept their surrender. Make sure they're disarmed. I'm going to see who's upstairs." He walks up the stairs to the third floor and into the front room. Standing in front of the open window is Lieutenant Maki, holding a Lee Enfield rifle. There's vomit all down his front and on the floor, but his rifle and hands are clean. "What the fuck were you doing, Lieutenant?"

Maki looks stricken, "I had to. I couldn't just sit in the rear. Please, don't tell the Admiral."

Thompson starts laughing, "Like I hang out with Admirals. God. Oh, and good job. Thanks."

REICHSTAG, BERLIN, GERMANY

1135, 8 October, 1942 (1035 GMT)

Hitler sits in an overstuffed love seat with Eva Braun drinking coffee and talking. An aid walks in and hands him a message. Hitler reads it, and his hands start shaking. He abruptly stands, throwing the message onto the floor. Grimacing, his face red with rage, he stalks across the room, "Get my generals! Get my admirals! Germany has been betrayed. It will not happen again!" Spittle sprays the staff officers face.

"Yes, Mein Fuhrer!" He runs out of the room.

Hitler spins back, and looks at Eva. She's shrunk back into the love seat, trembling. "The Americans will pay. That bitch will pay!"

FARMAN FACTORY, CHATEAUFORT, YVELINES, OCCUPIED FRANCE

1201, 8 October, 1942

Goering slowly walks around the huge Heinkel jet bomber. The six engine pods are attached, but the engines are not yet installed. On each wing, there's an inner pod near the fuselage with two engines. Outboard of that is a single engine pod, with the outboard landing gear. The main gear is installed along fuselage just to the sides of the front and back bomb bay. The tandem cockpit is small. But it's the wings that draw the eye, they're extremely long, at a ninety-degree angle to the fuselage, and tapered their entire length. He asks, "Why does this bomber have glider wings?"

Ernst Heinkel smiles, "So, it may fly extremely high. Even the American missiles cannot reach it."

Goering, "But with the wings so straight, it will be slow, yes?"

"This bomber depends on altitude, rather than speed. The Americans will look up and feel helpless as the bombs fall."

"How many bombs?"

They walk under the fuselage and Heinkel points up to the three open bomb bays. Under the front and rear bomb bays are large fuel tanks on carts. "This is the genius. To reach America, the front and rear bays will have fuel tanks. The center bay can support the design weight for the special ordinance, when it is done. For Moscow and London, the fuel tanks are removed and additional bombs may be carried. It can carry up to forty thousand kilos of ordinance."

Goering smiles, "Good. We gained this design from our American guests, yes?"

"Yes, Reichsmarschall."

"The Horton flying wing is still very early in its development. When will this aircraft be ready?"

Heinkel, "It's progressing. If our engines arrive on schedule, we'll be ready to start testing in a week or two. We'll be able to build enough to deploy in one to four months."

An aid runs up, salutes, and hands Goering a message. He reads it and freezes. He looks up, biting his lip, and crumples the message.

Heinkel, "Reichsmarschall?"

"Sheisse. England is lost."

LAMMAS PARK, EALING, WEST LONDON

1510, 8 October, 1942

Showered and in a clean uniform, Lt. Maki climbs into an undamaged Tiger tank. His guide, a British officer, says, "One of my men found it hiding here in the trees." There are only two rounds left, otherwise, the tank is complete.

"I'll be taking it back to the states."

"I expected so."

Maki, "I need to brief Field Marshal Brooke and General Eisenhower. Can you arrange to get this to RAF Kenley?"

"Of course, but we wish to inspect it as well."

"Not a problem. The tank we're designing is meant to meet the requirements of both armies. God, what a find."

COMMODORE'S OFFICE, RAF KENLEY

1538, 8 October, 1942

Spike walks in and sits down at her desk. Cooper immediately follows with a cup of tea and a plate of sandwiches. She laughs, "Thank you, Radar."

"Is it over? Have we won? Is it real?"

"Yes, Radar, it's real. We may have a few SS units that won't surrender, but, by and large, it's over."

"Thank God."

"There's a knock on the door and Gloria walks in. She spreads her legs and puts her hands on her hips, "What are you doing, young lady?"

Cooper chokes on his tea.

"I've a lot to do, Gloria."

"You have higher priorities. That flight suit will not do. Let's get you into your greens. Hanger 9, Radar. Go!"

Radar jumps to his feet, "Yes, ma'am."

Gloria drags Sam into her bedroom. "Get undressed." She turns on the shower, "Well, hurry up." Sam strips down and gets into the shower. Gloria hauls out her dress greens, "I see Cooper is keeping up your sartorial splendor. Your ribbon bar is up-to-date. Good." She lays out Sam's clothes and shoes.

"What's going on, Gloria?"

"Young lady, over three thousand flight and ground crews want to celebrate and you must be the guest of honor."

"Gloria, I'm tired. Please?"

"Be tired later. We need our leader." She hands Sam a towel, "Sam, we really do."

"Okay. But we haven't talked since I dragged Swede…"

"Darling girlfriend, you gave him what he needed and I love you even more for it." She hands Sam her uniform, piece by piece, then checks her out. "Okay, comb out hair. You need a haircut."

"No time."

"You and your no time. You have time for everything and everyone, but never yourself. Thank God for Cooper, or you'd be dead of starvation and lack of sleep. Get a haircut."

"Yes, ma'am."

"Let's see. Looking good. See, that wasn't so bad. Let's get going." Gloria drags Sam out to her sports car. She drives them, at speed, to one of the few remaining hangers. Sam can hear music as they near.

When they walk through the back door, a huge, ear-numbing cheer breaks out. Gloria leads her to a stage improvised on top of some white gear. As they walk through the crowd, men and women touch her on her shoulders, her arms, her back. It's a sea of faces and she knows so few of them.

When she gets to the stage, the band gets down, except the drummer. He starts a drum roll as she climbs up. She looks out at the expectant joyful faces looking up at her. She steps to the microphone and can see a wet bar in a corner with kegs of beer going. The hanger is packed, the doors open. As she stands there silent, the crowd quiets down, and someone shouts, "We love you!"

Laughter ripples across the hanger and she smiles, "Thank you. I love all of you, too." Her people cheer, then settle. "I... I am struggling for words. To find a voice for how I feel. There are few parallels in history for what we have accomplished. For what each of you have done. We fought a battle we had to win. We had no choice. The consequences for our countries, for the war, for our future were dire.

"If we had failed, the world would have felt the pain for generations. But we didn't fail. A million tiny details that had to be gotten right, were done, and done correctly, every single time. Our sortie rate was unprecedented. You did that."

They applaud, cheering.

"It wasn't without cost. We lost so many. Bright, kind, dream filled, beautiful people, who are now gone. Friends. Colleagues. Each time, I...we lost a piece of our hearts. Their loss could have broken us. But it didn't. We lost them, and we miss them, but in their names, we did this. We won.

"We have tasted war, hell, we have lived on a steady diet of war. I find the taste bitter...but acceptable. I will miss Sweets and her kind soul; Jedi's surf's up act; Stinky and his absolute fetish for cleanliness. I miss Papa. I miss them all, as you do.

"I miss them, but I understand that their loss was the price we had to pay for our freedom and the freedom of our children; our children's children. What we do here, what we have done here, will reverberate through history. People whose grandparents are not yet born will know freedom, because we fought here, and won.

"It isn't over. There's still much fighting to do. Some of us may yet fall. It's the price I chose. It's the price we've all chosen. It's the burden we each lifted when we took our oaths and put on the uniform.

"Today, we rightly celebrate. We celebrate our fallen. We celebrate life. We celebrate our victory. Thank you."

The cheering roars through the hanger, deafening in its intensity. Fluffy, in his booming voice, "To Spike!"

It becomes a chant, "Spike! Spike!"

Lt. Jeb 'Skeeter' McAllister makes his way up onto the stage with two beers and hands her one. She smiles and lifts the glass, and all goes silent, "To victory!"

The shouted response is deafening, "To victory!"

As it quiets, Skeeter says, "I met your dad."

"What?"

"I was winged over Guadalcanal and made an emergency landing. Under fire, he used a bulldozer to clear the field of unexploded munitions so I could land. You have one hell of a pop."

Sam can't help the tears now, "Thank you, Skeeter. Thank you. And, thanks for the beer." She laughs.

She sees Cooper making his way through the crowd, a piece of paper in his hand. She shouts over the noise, "Can't it wait?" He emphatically shakes his head and hands it up to her. She takes it and reads it.

Sensing something, the rowdy crowd quiets.

Wiping away her tears, she looks up, realizing they're waiting to hear. She smiles and nods her head, "From, Commander Naval Air Forces, to Commander Task Force Yankee. Regarding reassignment of VF-154, VF-155, HS-1 and attached units. After completing at least two weeks of turn over training transferring Task Force Yankee to Commodore Earl Carpenter, former Commander Naval Forces, Australia, those squadrons and attached units will report to NAS Patuxent River, Maryland for thirty days leave."

The hanger reverberates to the loud roar. She waits and when they quiet, "Following leave, squadron personnel will complete carrier qualification for reassignment. Signed, Admiral Lee." She looks out at her people, "We're going home."

THE END

COMING SOON

BOOK 2

OF

THE FIGHTING TOMCATS HUNTER/KILLER SERIES

TO HUNT AND PROTECT

AND

BOOK FIVE

OF

THE FIGHTING TOMCATS

ROCKS AND SHOALS

NOTES

When starting a novel of this type it is necessary to decide at the outset how to tackle a number of issues. The Navy uses a great deal of jargon, technical terms, and acronyms that are used in speech. Eliminating this techno-speak from dialogue would remove the character of the whole story. We also recognize that leaving jargon in could be confusing to readers not familiar with the military. It was decided to include a glossary and leave the language as it would be spoken with a few exceptions. When ships communicate over radio each ship has a code name that is used in place of the actual ship's name. As this would be confusing, we opted to use the ship's actual name.

Many complex procedures are simplified to keep the story flowing and reduce confusion. Aircraft numbers are generally based on the bureau (serial) number of the plane, regardless of who the pilot is. The exception is the commanding officer's plane whose number is always one. Though this may be confusing, generally the reader should be able to follow the dialogue without the number cue.

Where events are occurring simultaneously, yet in different time zones, the author chose to adopt Greenwich Mean Time for clarity. In all other sections, local time is used. A number of other technical details were changed to prevent revealing classified information.

A note on naval rank structure. In other services an enlisted person is addressed by rank, "Corporal, Sargent," etc. In the Navy, sailors are addressed with rate and rank. An E-6 is not normally addressed as "Petty Officer First Class." He or she is addressed as "MM1, BT1, BM1," etc. The rate is the job classification of the sailor, be that machinist mate (engine room equipment operator), or mess specialist (cook). A more comprehensive list of rates can be found in the glossary or on line. The ranks of enlisted sailors are in three groups of three ranks. E-1 through E-3 sailors are non-petty officers. These are new sailors who may or may not yet have a rate. E-4 through E-6 sailors are petty officers. These sailors are the technical experts and watch-standers who keep the navy running. E-4's are third class, E-5's are second class, and E-6's are first class petty officers. E-7 through E-9 sailors are middle management. They are Chief, Senior Chief, and Master Chief. Chiefs are systems experts who train, lead, and guide instead of operating equipment. The colloquial for E-7 is "Chief," for E-8 is "Senior," and for E-9 is "Chief." No one calls a Master Chief "Master." Calling a senior of master chief "Chief" is not an insult.

There are essentially two types of officer. Line officers can command vessels and aircraft. Non-line, or limited duty officers are doctors, dentists, chaplains, civil engineer corps, or have other specific duties.

GLOSSARY

16: VHF channel 16 is the international emergency channel. It is also, generally the channel used to communicate in the open, or non-encrypted communications.

1MC: General announcing system. Ship wide loud speaker system.

2nd Lt.: Second Lieutenant. Army and USMC rank. (O-1)

(Number)K: Fuel state. K for thousand pounds.

AA: Navy rank. Airman Apprentice (E-2).

AB: Navy enlisted rate. Aviation Boatswain's Mate. They do many duties on the flight and hanger decks and maintain other aviation equipment. ABAA through ABMC.

AD: Naval aviation rating. Aviation Machinist. ADAA through ADCM. AD's maintain aircraft structural components, flight surfaces, and engines.

ADM: Admiral. Naval Officer rank (O-10). Also used colloquially for Rear Admirals Lower and Upper, and Vice Admirals (O-7 through 9).

AE: Navy rate. Aviation Electrician. They maintain the electrical generation, conversion and distribution systems associated with jet aircraft. AEA through AECM

AGL: Above Ground Level.

Ahead (Bell): The standard bells, or speeds of a ship are ahead 1/3, ahead 2/3, ahead Standard, Ahead full, and Ahead Flank.

The number is the amount of revolutions per minute of the shaft.

Ahead Flank Emergency: Order to come to the fastest ahead speed as fast as possible. See Bell.

Air Boss: The ship's force air department head. The air boss commands all operations on the flight deck and hanger deck.

Air Chief Marshall: Royal Air Force Officer rank. Equivalent to Vice Admiral or Lieutenant General.

Air Commodore: Royal Air Force Officer rank. Equivalent to Captain or Colonel.

Air Marshall: Royal Air Force Officer rank. Equivalent to Rear Admiral or the current Rear Adm Upper Half or Major General.

Air Vice-Marshall: Royal Air Force Officer rank. Equivalent to Commodore or the current Rear Adm Lower Half or Brigadier General.

Amphenol: Multi-prong electronic or electrical connection.

AN: Naval Enlisted non-designated aviation rank. Airman (E-3).

AO: Enlisted rate. Aviation Ordinanceman. AOAA through AOCM. They inspect, care for and handle air delivered ordinance.

Arco: When an aircraft flies as a refueler they are given a special call sign. Usually the name of a gas station chain.

ASROC: Anti-submarine rocket. A torpedo delivered by a rocket.

ASW: Anti-submarine warfare.

AT: Navy rate. Aviation Electronics Technician. They maintain the complex electronic equipment associated with jet aircraft. ATA through ATCM

Auto-gyro: An emergency landing technique that uses the wind blowing through the helicopter rotors to keep them spinning, then uses the collective to slow the bird's descent at the last moment.

(AW): Naval specialist Badge. Air Warfare Specialist. Placed after rate such as AD1(AW).

Back (Bell): Astern bells for a marine engine. Back 1/3, Back 2/3, and Back Full.

Back Full Emergency: Astern bell to be answered as fast as possible.

Bandit: NATO code for enemy aircraft.

Battalion: Army/USMC tactical unit smaller than a brigade or regiment but larger than a company. Smallest unit designed to function independently. Generally commanded by a LT Colonel.

BDU: Battle Dress, Utility. The basic Army and Marine uniform.

Bell: The speed a ship is traveling at: Ahead they are Ahead

1/3, Ahead 2/3, Ahead Standard, Ahead Full, and Ahead Flank. Astern they are Back 1/3, Back 2/3, and Back full. In an emergency the order given is ahead flank emergency, or back full emergency which is a command to go as fast as possible.

Bearing: Compass or relative bearing in degrees from 0 to 360. Compass is true north, not magnetic north. Relative bearing puts 000 as straight in front of the bow of the ship and clocks degrees clockwise around the ship.

Bingo Fuel: Near the minimum to safely return to base.

Binnacle List: List of people sick or injured. Every unit and division maintains the Binnacle List and turns it in daily.

Blow: Submarines use ballast tanks to surface or submerge. By blowing high pressure air into the tanks water can be displaced and the vessel surfaces.

Blue Tails: Nick name for the VAW-122 Griffins. VAW-122 flies the E-2C Hawkeye radar plane.

Blue Water Ops: Carrier operations beyond reach of alternative air fields. You land on the carrier or swim.

Boatswain's Mate of the Watch (BMOW): In charge of all the lookouts, the helm and lee helm. The BMOW pipes (whistles) required ships announcements.

Bogey: An unidentified aircraft.

Boiler: Boilers generate the steam for propulsion, electrical generation, water distillation, and other uses.

Bolter: An aircraft missing the arresting wire.

Bridge: The ship's navigational control center. Where we drive the ship. The Officer of the Deck (OOD) is in charge except when the CO or XO are present. The Conning Officer directs the ship's coarse and speed. The Boatswains Mate of the Watch (BMOW), Quartermaster of the Watch (QMOW), Helm and Lee Helm are stationed here.

Brigade: Army/ Marine Tactical unit smaller than a Division and larger than a Battalion. Sometimes called a Regiment. Generally commanded by a Colonel or Brigadier General. They are usually armor, infantry, or airborne focused for the Army but still contain other units to permit independent operations.

BTOW: Boiler Technician of the watch. Senior watch in a boiler room.

BT: Navy Enlisted rate. Boiler Technician. BTFA through BTCM. Currently the BT rate is merged with the MM rate. Boiler Technicians operate and maintain marine boilers.

CAG: Commander Air Group. The CAG is in charge of all the air squadrons attached to the ship. The CAG is the counterpart to the ship's commanding officer. The carrier CO is always the senior.

Call the Ball: The Landing Signal Officer asks the pilot if they can see the Fresnel lens that shows the correct glide slope for landing.

Control: In a submarine Control is a room and watch station equivalent to both the bridge and combat control center on a surface ship.

Calico: NATO brevity code for an intruder on the radio net.

CAP: Combat Air Patrol. A fighter mission to circle an area ready to defend the fleet.

CAPT: Captain: Army and USMC rank. (O-3)

CAPT: Captain: Naval Officer rank (O-6).

CATCC: Carrier Air Traffic Control Center. This center controls all aircraft within 50 miles of the ship and manages take offs and landings.

CAV or Cavalry: Specialized Army Unit: These are units historically used for reconnaissance for larger units. They can be Armor, Airmobile, or Airborne. By WW2 the CAV distinctions were somewhat less than in wars past. Today the distinction is more historical than practical.

CDR: Naval Officer rank. Commander (O-5).

CHENG: Chief Engineer. Engineering department head.

CMAA: Chief Master at arms. A senior cop on a Navy ship.

COL: Army and USMC rank. (O-6)

Combat: Sometimes Combat control center. Weapon's and communications control center on a naval ship. The CO generally goes to combat during battle stations (General Quarters).

Combat Engineer: Specialized Army or USMC person who is trained to support combat operations by destroying obstacles. Structural engineers build things. Combat engineers blow them up.

Commodore: USN Officer rank. Equivalent to current Rear Admiral Lower half or Brigadier General. This rank was re-authorized in 1942 and discontinued after the war. It has been brought back, changed, and discarded since for the rank Rear Admiral Lower Half. If a unit of ships does not have an Admiral in charge, the senior or assigned Captain can take the title Commodore to designate they are in charge of the group. This does not involve any change of pay or rank.

Company: Army/Marine tactical unit. Generally Commanded by a Captain. They are made up of a number of platoons and are organized into Battalions. Generally, companies are too small to function independently.

CORPS: Army tactical unit. Normally commanded by a Lieutenant General or General. It is a group of divisions and/or other units. Corps are not permanently assigned their divisions but rather receive and lose units based on need.

COTAC: Copilot Tactical Coordinator. Antisubmarine duty on S-3 Viking Aircraft.

Decimal: On radio the word 'Decimal' is used to indicate tenths. Thus, fuel at 9 decimal 2 is 9,200 pounds. Fuel is always given as weight.

Diesel Dyke: Nickname for women in the engineering fields, regardless of their rating. Obviously, it is not a term of respect and isn't tolerated in the modern Navy.

Division (Army/ USMC): Army and Marine Corps organizational unit. Army/USMC Divisions are tactical units commanded by a Brigadier or Lieutenant General that command a number of Brigades and supporting units. They are sometimes armor, infantry, airborne specific but contain all those other units needed to be an independent military unit.

Division (Navy): Naval organizational unit. Naval units are divided into Departments and Divisions. Divisions are functionally oriented units with all the enlisted members typically of one rating.

Eject: Order to initiate the ejection sequence for abandoning a doomed aircraft. Once ordered everyone must eject.

Electric Boat: Submarine Manufacturing firm based in Groton and other New England towns. In 1952 it merged with General Dynamics. Most US submarines are made by Electric Boat.

ELT: Navy Enlisted trade. Some MM's are qualified Engineering Laboratory Technician (Nuclear). They are chemistry and radiation specialists, though they also stand normal mechanical watches.

EM: Navy Enlisted rate. Electrician's Mate. Electricians operate the electrical distribution system on the ship, and also maintain all the electrical equipment. EMFN through EMCM.

EMP: Electro-Magnetic Pulse. A powerful change in the magnetic field. An EMP could damage or destroy electronic and electric gear.

Engine Room: Space where the main engines, electrical generators, and water distilling unit are located. This equipment is operated and maintained by Machinist Mates.

ENS: Ensign: Naval Officer rank (O-1). Junior most officer. Sometimes called a butter bar for their rank insignia which is a single gold bar.

EOOW: Engineering Officer of the Watch. Watch stander in charge of the propulsion plant. Normally a Lt. on a nuclear ship. Sometimes a senior or master chief on conventional powered ships.

ETA: Estimated Time of Arrival.

F-14: The Tomcat. An all-weather interceptor and fleet defense fighter.

Faking hose: Laying out a hose or line in parallel lines so the hose can be safely charged or the line let go without jamming.

Far CAP: Combat Air Patrol. Far CAP is a defensive position away from the fleet.

Fire room: Location of the boilers in a fossil fueled steam ship.

Fire Team: An Army and USMC tactical unit consisting of two to four people and generally commanded by a Corporal. A squad will typically have two to four fire teams.

Flight Lieutenant: Royal Air Force Officer rank. Equivalent to Lieutenant Junior Grade (Navy) or Lieutenant (Army, USMC).

Flight Sergeant: RAF senior enlisted rank. Equivalent to Master Sergeant. May or may not be air crew.

Flying Officer: Royal Air Force Officer rank. Equivalent to Ensign or Second Lieutenant.

FN: Navy Enlisted rank. Fireman (E-3). A non-designated engineering striker. If designated his rate would precede his rank.

FOD Walk Down: Walking the flight deck looking for FOD (Foreign Object Damage) that could damage aircraft.

Fox (number): Part of NATO brevity code. It is a call announcing the firing of a missile. The number designates the type of missile. 1 is short to intermediate range radar guided missile. 2 is a short-range heat seeking missile. 3 is a long-range radar guided missile.

Fuel state: How much fuel you have on board in thousands of pounds. (10 decimal 1 = 10,100lbs.)

'G's: Gravities. One 'G' is equal to normal earth gravity. Two is twice earth gravity etc.

General Quarters: The call to man battle stations and prepare the vessel to fight.

Gertrude: Nick name for a short-range underwater phone.

GMG: Navy Enlisted rate. Gunners Mate Guns. Gunner's Mates operate and maintain the weapons on a ship. The rate is split between Gunner's Mate Guns (GMG) and Gunner's Mate Missiles (GMM). GMGSA through GMGMC.

GMM: Navy Enlisted rate. Gunners Mate Missiles. Gunner's Mates operate and maintain the weapons on a ship. The rate is split between Gunner's Mate Guns (GMG) and Gunner's Mate Missiles (GMM). GMMSA through GMMMC.

Gold Eagle: Official nickname of the Carl Vinson. Every Navy ship is given an official nickname. The crews often give an unofficial nickname. In our novel series we sometimes use these as radio call signs. That would not normally be true ship to ship, but often used in air operations.

Group Captain: Royal Air Force Officer rank. Commander or Lieutenant Colonel.

GySGT: Gunnery Sergeant. USMC enlisted rank. (E-7) Generally an assistant Company commander or assistant to a higher rank officer or enlisted. As an assistant company commander, they are responsible for training the company commander and all servicemen under them. It is a critical and important job.

HT: Navy Enlisted rate. Hull Technician. HT's are Damage control and repair experts. They also operate the sewer system on the ship earning them the undesirable nickname "turd chaser". HTFA through HTMC.

HY-80: Hardened steel used for special applications by the Navy. 3/8" will stop most rifle bullets.

ILS: Instrument Landing system. An aircraft system that helps pilots line up with a runway they cannot see.

Khaki: Navy slang term for chiefs and officers because they wear khaki colored uniforms.

Knight (number): Call sign of fighters flying for VFW-154, the Black Knights.

Landing Signal Officer: A pilot positioned near the rear of the carrier to help guide pilots in. The LSO also grades landings.

Law of Continuity of Suckage: Submarine phrase. Once the hatch is shut suckage can neither be created or destroyed. Meaning when one person gets a good deal another gets screwed. This is what happens when you lock a bunch of nukes in a tube for months on end.

Laze: Use a laser to designate where ordinance is to drop.

LCDR: Naval Officer rank. Lieutenant Commander (O-4).

LPO: Naval enlisted position. Leading Petty Officer is the "Foreman" for a division. Usually an E-6.

Lt: Army and USMC rank. (O-2) Lieutenants are generally platoon officers or assistants to the commander of a larger unit.

Lt.: Naval officer rank. Lieutenant (O-3). Generally, a Division Officer in smaller units a lieutenant might be the XO or even CO.

Lt. COL: Army and USMC rank. (O-5) Generally commands a Battalion sized unit or serves as an assistant to the commander of a larger unit.

Lt. JG: Naval Officer rank. Lieutenant Junior Grade. (O-2.) Generally, a division officer or assistant to a more senior officer.

MA: Navy Enlisted rate. Master at Arms. Similar to Military police MA's enforce uniform and behavior rules. As such they are generally disliked. MA3 through MACM.

Magic (number): Call sign for an EA-6B Prowler, radar jamming aircraft of VAQ-133 Wizards.

MAJ: Major: Army and USMC rank. (O-4) Majors are sometimes company commanders but more often serve as assistants to higher rank officers. In the Pentagon you can't throw a stick without hitting a Major.

Marshall of the RAF: Royal Air Force Officer rank. The senior officer of the service. Equivalent to Chief of Naval Operations or Army Chief of Staff.

Master Chief: Naval Enlisted Rank (E-9).

Mini Boss: The air boss's assistant. They divide the observation duties in PRIFLY.

MM: Navy Enlisted rate. Machinist's Mate. They operate and maintain the machinery associated with ship's propulsion, auxiliary gear, and nuclear power systems. MMFA through MMCM. All nukes leave A school as MM3.

MMOW: Machinist's Mate of the Watch. Senior watch stander in an engine room. Sometimes called the Engine Room Supervisor. It is a watch station and not a rank.

MOS: Military Occupational Specialty. It is what a soldier or marine is trained to do. Be that infantry, armor, special forces, supply, radio operator, combat engineer or a myriad of other jobs. Generally, it is not used in the way one's rate is in the navy. You don't call a sergeant in the infantry an infantry sergeant. There are some positional title changes for those in special units such as cavalry.

NAM: Navy Achievement Medal. A medal for individual meritorious accomplishment. When a V device is added for valor it signifies the award was for combat actions.

NAVSEA 08: Designation for the leader of the U. S. Navy Nuclear Power Program.

Navy Expeditionary Medal: Medal issued for service in a combat zone designated by congress.

NOE: Nap of earth. Order to fly as low as safely possible.

NTDS: Naval Tactical Data System. A system that shares sensor data with other ships.

Nuke: Nickname for anyone in the nuclear power career field. It is sometime used derisively. It is even said "Fuckingnuke" is one word.

Nuclear waste: Nickname for anyone who fails to complete nuclear training or is otherwise removed from the program. It is generally used with respect by nukes.

MW: Megawatt. One million watts. 1,000,000 watts. Most nuclear power plants are measured in MW.

O-2 Plant: The oxygen generation plant which removes atmospheric oxygen and compresses it into liquid oxygen used by medical and as pilot breathing air.

Officer of the Deck (OOD): In charge of the operation and navigation of the ship underway. In port the OOD is in charge of the ship's duty section and all operations during their watch.

Op-tempo: Rate of operations over time.

OPPE: Operational Propulsion Plant Exam. Same as ORSE for conventionally powered vessels.

ORSE: Operational Reactor Safeguards Exam. Scheduled examination of propulsion plant material condition and operational compliance. A poor grade on ORSE causes career ventilation. It can be a negative mark on every nuke on board.

Passageway: Navy speak for a hallway.

Petty Officer: Colloquial phrase for an E-4 through E-6. Generally, it is only used by officers or master at arms who are about to correct the Petty Officer's behavior. Instead a sailor will address the Petty Officer with their rate. MM1 instead of PO1.

PFC: Private First Class. (E-3) Army and USMC rank.

Phoenix: AIM-54 Long range air to air missile. The F-14 was designed to carry and fire this missile. In reality the USN never actually fired one at an enemy aircraft.

Platoon: Army and USMC tactical unit consisting of two to four squads. With armor this is three to four tanks. Platoons are generally commanded by a Lieutenant or Second Lieutenant and have a Staff Sergeant, called a platoon sergeant, to train the officer and men.

PQS: Personal Qualification Standard. PQS is the system used by the Navy to qualify sailors to do their jobs.

Propulsion plant drills: Engineering operator training practicing possible casualties and problems. Continuous training is the reality of most sailors. This is to prepare operators for problems that only occur very rarely but have huge consequences if the watch team does not know what they are doing.

PRYFLY: Primary Flight Control. The highest deck in the island structure where all flight deck operations are managed.

QAO: Quality Assurance Officer. The QAO manages inspection paperwork from repairs and also personally inspects critical repairs. No system, or aircraft can be used as designed until the QAO has approved the work.

Quartermaster of the Watch (QMOW): In charge of providing navigational information to the OOD and Conning Officer. The QMOW is required to keep the ship's position updated on paper and electronic charts.

Rainbow side boys: The traditional side boys for a senior visitor, only wearing the various flight deck colored jerseys.

Reactor Auxiliary Room (RAR): The RAR is the space where the reactor support and monitoring equipment is located. It shares most of the same functions that a fire room in a conventional vessel would have. Generally, the Naval Reactor is in a separate room inside this room.

Rear Admiral Lower Half: Naval Officer rank. One Star Admiral (O-7). See Commodore for WW2 usage.

Rear Admiral Upper Half: Naval Officer rank. Two Star Admiral (O-8). Called Rear Admiral in WW2.

RIM-7: Rail launched intermediate range air to air missile. Sea Sparrow.

RIO: Radar Intercept Officer. The RIO operates the radar and weapons system in the back seat of the F-14. They are a critical half of the in-flight team for fighting the aircraft.

RM: Navy enlisted rate. Radioman. They operate the radio communications gear for the Navy. They are, generally the most secretive because they are forbidden to share anything of what they see and hear.

Roger Ball (Number): Roger ball means the pilot can see the Fresnel lens glide slope indicator. The number is the total weight of the aircraft in thousands of pounds.

RTB: Return to Base.

SAM: Surface to Air Missile.

SAR: Search and Rescue.

SFC: Sergeant First Class. Army rank. (E-7) Generally an assistant company commander or assistant to a higher rank officer or enlisted. As an assistant company commander, they are responsible for training the company commander and all servicemen under them. It is a critical and important job.

SGT: Sergeant. (E-5). Army and USMC Rank. A sergeant generally is in charge of a tank, squad, or fire team. That or they serve as the assistant to more senior enlisted or officers. They are the back bone of any service.

SGT MAJ: Army and USMC enlisted rank. (E-9) Sergeant Major is the senior enlisted rank. They generally serve as senior instructors and advisors to major commands. They may have a staff under them.

SIS: British Secret Intelligence Service. Now called MI6.

SLQ-32: Called the "slick 32" it is a multi-function radar jammer carried on USN ships.

Snap 2: Early supply computer.

SOB: Son of a Bitch. Even cuss words have acronyms.

SSGT: Staff sergeant. (E-6) Army and USMC Rank. A staff sergeant is generally an assistant platoon leader or assistant to a higher ranked person. In the role of platoon sergeant, they are responsible for training the platoon officer in how to be an effective leader while also training all their subordinate servicemen. It is a vital position.

Start the Music: NATO Code phrase for commencing jamming.

Squad: Army and USMC tactical unit. Generally made up of two to four fire teams and commanded by a Sergeant. In Armor this is typically one track or vehicle.

Squadron Leader: Royal Air Force Officer rank. Equivalent to Lieutenant or Captain.

Squawked: Identification, friend or foe (IFF) Code signal.

ST: Navy Enlisted rate. Sonar Technician. Responsible for operating sonar systems on ships and submarines. STSA through STMC.

Switch Gear Room: Space where the electrical distribution system is operated. EM's stand watch in Switch Gear.

TACAN: Radio beacon aircraft use to find the carrier.

TARPS: Tactical Airborne Reconnaissance Pod System. A camera system mounted on a hard point and controlled by the RIO.

TG: Turbine Generator. An electrical Generator powered by steam.

TG/DU: Turbine Generator and Distilling Unit watch. An Engine room watch stood by an MM.

Thwarts ship passageway: A hall way aligned from side to side rather than forward and aft.

TLD: Thermal Luminescent Dosimetry. A radiation measuring device to monitor crew exposure. The nukes sometimes call it "the little dicky."

VHF: Very High Frequency. A line of sight radio.

Vice Admiral: Naval Officer rank. VADM (O-9).

Wave off: Order to abort a landing and go around.

Wing Commander: Royal Air Force Officer rank. Equivalent to Lieutenant Commander or Major.

Yankee Search: Active sonar search.

YN: Naval Enlisted rate. Yeoman. Yeomen are the administrative grease that lubricates the functioning of the Navy machine. When an officer has a good yeoman, they guard him or her jealously. It is an unofficial sport to poach one's yeoman. YNSA through YNMC.

XO: Executive officer. Second in charge of a vessel or unit. Actual rank varies based on the size of the unit. A patrol craft or air squadron XO could be a Lieutenant. On a super carrier the XO is generally a Captain.

X-Ray: Material condition X-Ray. Lowest level of water tight integrity. Only set during a work day in port.

Yoke: Material condition Yoke. Middle level of water tight integrity between X-ray (in port on work day) and Zebra (Battle Stations). At sea yoke is checked at least daily.

Zebra: Material condition Zebra. Highest level of water tight integrity.

THE AUTHORS

MM1 Maki is a retired US Navy nuclear field machinist mate with twenty years of active service, who served on the USS Carl Vinson, CVN-70, and two cruisers. During twelve years of duty at sea, MM1 Maki circumnavigated the earth once, transited the Panama Canal three times, served on the USS Carl Vinson during Enduring Freedom, and earned multiple campaign awards.

Sofia R. Maki has a background in criminal justice and accounting.

Email us at RoseHillPress17@gmail.com

Made in United States
Orlando, FL
21 April 2022

17057199R00296